T0160119

LIGHT SHINING
OUT OF DARKNESS

Light Shining Out of Darkness

AND OTHER STORIES

HUGH HOOD

With a foreword by John Metcalf

BIBLIOASIS
WINDSOR, ONTARIO

Library and Archives Canada Cataloguing in Publication

Hood, Hugh, 1928–2000
[Short stories. Selections]
    Light shining out of darkness / Hugh Hood.

(Biblioasis reset series)
Short stories.
ISBN 978-1-77196-188-2 (softcover)—ISBN 978-1-77196-189-9 (ebook)

    I. Title.

PS8515.O49A6   2018   C813'.54   C2017-906997-7

Readied for the press by Daniel Wells
Copy-edited by Cat London
Cover and text design by Gordon Robertson

Published with the generous assistance of the Canada Council for the Arts,
which last year invested $153 million to bring the arts to Canadians throughout
the country, and the financial support of the Government of Canada. Biblioasis
also acknowledges the support of the Ontario Arts Council (OAC), an agency of
the Government of Ontario, which last year funded 1,709 individual artists and
1,078 organizations in 204 communities across Ontario, for a total of $52.1 million,
and the contribution of the Government of Ontario through the Ontario Book
Publishing Tax Credit and the Ontario Media Development Corporation.

PRINTED AND BOUND IN CANADA

CONTENTS

FOREWORD

by John Metcalf

CLARK BLAISE once told me that when he was in the writing program at Iowa in 1963, Dave Godfrey came into the Quonset hut where some of the students were housed waving a copy of *The Canadian Forum* that contained his review of *Flying a Red Kite* and calling out, "Modernism has arrived in Canada!"

The term "modernism" means that period of turmoil, revolution, and experimentation in the arts that gripped America, England, and Europe from, roughly, 1890–1930, a movement of which Canada was largely oblivious.

I wrote of this somnolence in my book *The Canadian Short Story*:

> Canada, languishing in its time warp through all the furore and ferment, slumbered on. The Ryerson Press, owned by the Methodist Church, published a few titles annually under the authority of The Book Steward. The barrenness and artistic bankruptcy of Canadian writing in the early years of the twentieth century might be suggested by the jacket copy on Paul A. W. Wallace's *The Twist and Other Stories* published by the Ryerson Press in 1923.

"A purely Canadian book of stories is considerable of a novelty [*sic*]. These included in this volume are characteristic, striking tales of romance, adventure and whimsical nonsense written in a most vigorous style and set in such familiar locations as Banff..."

Flying a Red Kite had a bombshell effect in Canada.

W.J. Keith (Professor Emeritus of English at the University of Toronto) in his book *God's Plenty: A Study of Hugh Hood's Short Fiction* wrote of the story "Fallings From Us, Vanishings," "There is a sophisticated confidence and subtlety in the writing here that must have seemed startlingly original to a Canadian literary generation for whom Callaghan and Hugh Garner were considered major practitioners."

Reaction to *Flying a Red Kite* was country-wide.

"...gives Canadian fiction a vitality, an intelligence, and a grace it has never known before." – *Winnipeg Free Press*

"...The first time I read these stories, I thought they were brilliant, and I think so still." – *Tamarack Review*

"Outstanding collection." – *The University of Toronto Quarterly*

"...the most interesting young prose writer to turn up in English-speaking Canada in several years..." – *The Canadian Reader*

"Such talent appears once or twice in a generation..." – *Toronto Telegram*

"...jubilant eloquence almost unique in contemporary Canadian fiction..." – *Evidence* Magazine

In brief, then, in 1962–63 *Red Kite* was an Event.

I must admit that in the past I have proclaimed *Red Kite* the first modernist story collection in Canada. I no longer hold that opinion. I can see why I made that claim. I was seduced, perhaps even eager to *be* seduced, by any Canadian literary writing showing signs of life, of sophistication; most of the stuff acclaimed, most of the stuff receiving the imprimatur, was dead and deadening. What short stories existed prior to *Red Kite* seemed to have emerged from an hermetic Canada which was entirely ignorant of what was being done and *had been done* in the USA and England. I know that this *could not* have been true, yet there was little achieved evidence to the contrary.

When I read statements from writers along the lines of "There were no books in Saskatchewan when I was growing up" or "I hadn't realized it was possible to write about Canada," I wondered why they hadn't been haunting the local library, libraries having been dotted about Canada from coast to coast by the American largesse of Andrew Carnegie. But that is a thought that falls into the Prohibited category.

In 1963, the year following *Red Kite*, the Governor General's Award for Fiction was bestowed upon the threadbare *Best Stories* of Hugh Garner.

Canadian reaction and evaluation tend to be myopic or to suffer from tunnel vision so it is salutary to set *Red Kite's* reception into context and perspective by glancing at some of the titles being published in the USA and UK around the same date.

In the USA:

Christopher Isherwood. *Down There on a Visit* (1962), Bernard Malamud. *Idiots First* (1963), Flannery O'Connor. *A Good Man Is Hard to Find* (1955) and *The Violent Bear It Away* (1960), Thomas Pynchon. *The Crying of Lot 49* (1966), Philip Roth. *Goodbye Columbus* (1959) and *Letting Go* (1962), J.D. Salinger. *For Esme With Love and Squalor* (1953) and *Franny and Zooey* (1961), John Cheever. *The Brigadier and the Golf Widow* (1964), Richard Yates. *Eleven Kinds of Loneliness* (1962).

In the UK:

Samuel Beckett. *Happy Days* (1961), Kingsley Amis. *Lucky Jim* (1954) and *One Fat Englishman* (1963), Philip Larkin. *The Whitsun Weddings* (1964), John McGahern. *The Barracks* (1963), Muriel Spark. *The Prime of Miss Jean Brodie* (1961), V.S.

Pritchett. *When My Girl Comes Home* (1961), Evelyn Waugh. *Sword of Honour Trilogy* (1965).

I will not further belabour the obvious.

It might amuse younger readers interested in learning something of Canadian criticism's lower depths that the citing of the foregoing names and titles would have been derided and dismissed—*was* dismissed—by the Carleton University professor Robin Mathews, nationalist ideologue and Neanderthal author of *Canadian Literature: Surrender or Revolution*— as kowtowing to "the imperial centres," the centres being New York and London which Mathews saw as suppressing CanLit's challenge to their dominion.

Canadian Literature: Surrender or Revolution was published in 1978.

The passage of time has obliterated it.

Time would also reveal that Godfrey's claim that "modernism has arrived in Canada" was shy of the mark by several centuries.

* * *

One afternoon in 1974 or thereabouts, I was in the Monkland Theatre in Montreal watching *Carry On Highwayman*, the twenty-sixth, and what turned out to be the last, *Carry On* film. Such plot as the film had was concerned with attempts to capture the notorious highwayman, Dick Turpin, referred to throughout, nudge nudge, as "Big Dick." The film showcased a galaxy of coarse delights—Sid James, Barbara Windsor, Kenneth Williams, Hattie Jacques, Bernard Bresslaw, and Joan Sims.

I had arrived just as the lights were going down and it took me some moments to realize that there were only six or seven darker shapes occupying seats. By the loudness and particular timbre of one shape's laughter, I realized the shape was Hugh. I waited for him outside and we spent some minutes rejoicing in Sid James's leer, in Kenneth Williams's pinched prissiness, in the comically brazen charms of Barbara's bosom.

Hugh knew every *Carry On* film, their casts, directors, script writers, probably knew every film's Best Boy. He was devoted to the compositions of Franz Joseph Haydn, music I thought etiolated, and relished the schlocky recordings of Bing Crosby and could detail not only Bing's backing orchestras and bands but also the names of obscure sidemen and session musicians. He had something like a photographic or eidetic memory and could and would, unless stopped firmly, quote *pages*.

As we were drifting along that afternoon, he started talking about *Armies of the Night: History as a Novel, the Novel as History,* Norman Mailer's book about the anti–Vietnam War march on the Pentagon in 1967. Hugh's opinion of Mailer extended into a disquisition on the New Journalism in general—Joan Didion, of course, Capote, Tom Wolfe, Gay Talese, Hunter S. Thompson—all the usual suspects—had I read that guy in Toronto? Bruce. Harry Bruce. *The Short Happy Walks of Max McPherson*—riding on the coattails of *Around the Mountain*, of course—my breaking in to say how much I liked the illustrations in Thompson's books by Ralph Steadman, reminiscent of George Grosz in their spiky savagery.

It somehow emerged spontaneously that we were both, unknown to the other, in thrall to a much earlier sort-of-New Journalism forerunner, the *New Yorker* master, Joseph Mitchell, author of *McSorley's Wonderful Saloon* (1943) and *Old Mister Flood* (1948). I had long since elected Mitchell to my pantheon. I had read him again and again, *bathed* in him, as one reads a poem until it becomes a part of the way one sees and apprehends the world.

Here follows the opening page of *Old Mister Flood*:

A tough Scotch-Irishman I know, Mr. Hugh G. Flood, a retired house wrecking contractor, aged 73, often tells people that he is dead set and determined to live until the afternoon of July 27, 1965, when he will be 115 years old. "I don't ask much here below," he says. "I just want to hit 115. That'll hold me." Mr. Flood is small and wizened. His eyes are watchful and icy-blue, and his face is red, bony, and clean-shaven. He is old-fashioned in appearance. As a rule, he wears a high, stiff collar, a candy-striped shirt, a serge suit, and a derby. A silver watch-chain hangs across his vest. He keeps a flower in his lapel. When I am in the Fulton Fish Market neighbourhood, I always drop into the Hartford House, a drowsy waterfront hotel at 309 Pearl Street, where he has a room, to see if he is still alive.

From *McSorley's Wonderful Saloon*, Hugh's favourite pieces, it turned out, were "Professor Sea Gull" and "A Sporting Man," mine, "Hit on the Head with a Cow."

These revelations as we drifted along led on and into Hugh's devotion to *The Thurber Carnival* (1945). I offered "The Black Magic of Barney Hallet" and "What Do You Mean it *Was* Brillig?" Hugh countered with quote after Thurber quotation until I was wet and half-blinded with laughing, begging him to stop.

"Do you know 'Bateman Comes Home'?"

"Hugh! *Please.*"

"The *deep* South," said Hugh. "Old Nate Birge. . ." he declaimed as I was wiping at myself with the back of my hand.

"'Old Nate Birge. . .'"

"Stop!"

"'. . . chewing on a splinter of wood and watching the moon come up lazily out of the old cemetery in which nine of his daughters were lying, only two of whom were dead.'"

* * *

Much of the contemporaneous and early enthusiasm for *Red Kite* tended to focus on "Silver Bugles, Cymbals, Golden Silks" and "Recollections of the Works Department." The point towards which I've been wending my way is that both pieces are, within the entire body of Hood's short fiction, anomalous. In other words, in the 129 stories he published in ten collections over the years, he never wrote like this again yet these two pieces coloured reaction to the entirety of his first book and contributed largely to the misreadings that dogged him for years to come.

Readers and literary critics celebrated *Red Kite* as a "modernist" work because they recognized the two charming, anomalous pieces—so overwhelmingly lucid and original in the context of Canada—as kin to the alluring work in *The New Yorker* and, later, to the vibrant and seductive *Atlantic*. Charmed and dazzled by "Recollections" and "Silver Bugles," critics and readers accepted the book's other stories as more of the same, as "modernist," when patently they were not.

What did *Hood* think he was up to?

In the author's introduction to *Red Kite* (Porcupine's Quill, 1987) he wrote of "Recollections":

> It was written in Hartford [Connecticut] in May, 1960, and was aimed specifically at *The New Yorker*; it was an essay in the genre which Thurber had created and *The New Yorker* made its own, the affectionate memoir of one's early life. I nearly sold it there. The editors held it for a long time, then finally wrote me, saying, "We almost took this one and we find it charming but we really have had a lot of pieces like it..."

(His use of the word "essay" in "an essay in the genre which Thurber had created" is used in the sense of "an attempt" or a "venture.")

Earlier in the Introduction, he writes:

The Thurber Carnival included the complete text of a classic in another genre, *My Life and Hard Times*, unquestionably the masterwork of a literary kind which Thurber may even have invented with the able assistance of Andy White [E.B. White], the loving, fantastic memoir of one's childhood and adolescence told in an exactly voiced idiomatic American English with all the refinements of fictional technique.

(Hood describes Thurber's invention as "the loving, *fantastic* memoir," thereby allowing for a generous salting of invention. I've always sensed in "Silver Bugles" a Catholic colouring in the child's *faith* in the band, in the sense of the band's omnipresence in the child's world, its "set-apartness," it's almost "holy" existence and endurance through changing circumstance—Cardinal Newman's *Quod ubique, Quod semper.* I've always sensed, too, that Catholic colouring in the child's uncritical embrace of hierarchy, his vision of the glorious uniforms, uniforms that seem almost like *vestments...*)

What of the other stories in the book?

W.J. Keith wrote in *God's Plenty* that "Flying a Red Kite" is "the modernist story par excellence."

It may now be but wasn't always.

Here is Hugh Hood talking about the story in the author's introduction:

That July [1961] I wrote "Flying a Red Kite" which is, I suppose, my best-known story. It is firmly based on observation, referring in its second sentence to its narrator's recent arrival in Montreal. But the picture of "the flying red thing" which I meant as a reference to the Pentecostal tongues of fire which descended on the Apostles, pulled the story into a very expressive formal design. It originally had an additional three paragraphs, a solemn coda which moralized the meaning of the narrative, but

Jake Zilber of *Prism International* [the literary magazine of the University of British Columbia] gave me the most effective bit of advice an editor has ever given me. "Drop off that last page," he said, "because the story ends when Fred sees the red stain on Deedee's cheek." He was exactly right; the story was published with its present ending.

Only a clairvoyant could have seen "the flying red thing" as Pentecostal tongues of fire and I'm not sure what tongues of fire pulling the story "into a very expressive formal design" *means*. Bill Keith wryly commented that kites go up and Pentecostal tongues descend.

But what should interest us as readers are the missing three paragraphs. What do they tell us about the story? What *would* they have told us? The present ending ". . . he turned away and saw in the shadow of her cheek and on her lips and chin the dark rich red of the pulp and juice of the crushed raspberries" would have been diluted and essentially ridden over in the moralizing explanation. That the story now ends on, and stands on, the picture, the image, is the work of Jake Zilber rather than that of Hugh Hood; we might say that Zilber sculpted the finished story from Hood's approximate marble, that his editing made the story "modern" by investing "pulp and juice" with an emphasis and significance Hood had not, that he bestowed "modernity" upon it by giving the reader the responsibility of apprehending meaning.

We might also say that Zilber transformed a religiously allegorical story into a secular one.

In a most un-modernist way, Hood seems not to have realized the power of the image; only Hugh could have imagined a kite as Pentecostal tongues. Similarly, I still remember his sheer *astonishment* that I had not *immediately* grasped that the three grocers in "The Fruit Man, The Meat Man, and the Manager" represented the persons of the Holy Trinity.

In the author's introduction to *Red Kite*, he writes:

> "By now I was nearing university enrollment. When I
> went there I was soon introduced by Marshall McLuhan
> to the radical importance and value of the work of Joyce.
> Marshall McLuhan understood Joyce very intimately
> and insisted on the central importance of the stories in
> *Dubliners*. They are the classic case in modern literature
> in English of the merger of the methods of symbolism
> with those of naturalism, producing a literary type which
> dominated new writing in Europe and America until the
> late 1950s.
>
> From university, besides a lot of academic detritus
> and a doctoral degree, I took away a very close knowledge
> of Joyce, [and] a much extended reading of Hemingway...

That he had "moralized the meaning" of "Flying a Red Kite"
suggests that his understanding of *Dubliners* and of Hemingway had not "taken" as profoundly as he claimed.

Related to this matter of imagery, it is instructive to read
Hood's comments over the years on the origins and gestation of stories. In the author's introduction to *A Short Walk
in the Rain* (Porcupine's Quill, 1989) he writes: "... I almost
never write a story that I haven't been thinking over for a
long time, sometimes ['Breaking Off' in this book] as long
as thirty years." He frequently refers to the "idea" of a story. I,
and I would guess perhaps a majority of story writers, come
upon stories, not as "ideas" but, especially in their origin and
gestation, as unanchored feeling, insistent pictures, heard or
invented dialogue, odd wisps of memory.

Alice Munro described this odd experience exactly in
"What Is Real?", an essay she wrote for my anthology *Making
it New* (1982):

> There is no blueprint for a structure. It's not a question
> of "I'll make this kind of house because if I do it right it
> will have this effect." I've got to make, I've got to build up,

a house, a story, to fit around the indescribable "feeling" that is like the soul of the story, and which I must insist upon in a dogged, embarrassed way, as being no more definable than that. And I don't know where it comes from. It seems to be already there, and some unlikely clue, such as a shop window or a bit of conversation, makes me aware of it. Then I start accumulating the material and putting it together. Some of the material I may have lying around already, in memories and observations, and some I invent, and some I have to go diligently looking for (factual details), while some is dumped in my lap (anecdotes, bits of speech). I see how this material might go together to make the shape I need, and I try it. I keep trying and seeing where I went wrong and trying again.

In *The Canadian Short Story* I wrote:

> When someone says to me, "I have a really good idea for a story" I politely turn my mind off because I know I'm going to have to endure a plot. If, on the other hand, someone says to me, "I've found myself lately thinking again and again about an old Player's *Navy Cut* cigarette tin—they used to hold fifty cigarettes, dark blue with a sailor's head on it with a beard, the picture's inside a gold-coloured circle—was it a lifesaver?—my father kept brass screws in it on his work bench"—yes, if they told me that, then they'd capture my immediate attention.

(Anyone particularly interested in how stories arrive and grow in writers' minds should read the chapter "The Precious Particle" in *The Canadian Short Story*.)

Alice Munro says of a story's conception, "There is no blueprint for the structure"; I would suggest for Hugh Hood there usually was. If the other stories in *Red Kite* are not "modernist," what exactly are they? Here is Hood writing about

"Fallings From Us, Vanishings," the first story in *Red Kite*. From the author's introduction to the Porcupine's Quill edition:

> It was the last story I wrote while we were living in Connecticut. I think that the enormous impending change in my life [moving to Montreal]—now only two months off—created a special pressure of self-awareness which allowed me to make a breakthrough into a voice of my own. "Fallings From Us, Vanishings" has always seemed to me to be the first story in which I am writing wholly as myself, not as a version of Faulkner or Styron or Thurber or Joyce. It has the strongly allegorical cast, the echoes of medieval romance, the Wordsworthian aesthetics and psychology and the perhaps somewhat abstract quality of my later work.
>
> It is that rare thing, a purely invented story, generated from a theoretical notion having no relation to observation. I had asked myself this question. Suppose that a man whose life is wholly given up to the recovery and preservation of the past meets and falls in love with a girl who lives totally and unreflectively in the present. How would their relations work out? "Fallings From Us, Vanishings" is the result. I put it at the beginning of *Flying a Red Kite* because it seemed very personally my possession, something from the depths of my imagination."

When he renounces the influence of Faulkner, Styron, Thurber, and Joyce, the renunciation of Thurber is particularly interesting because it is a renunciation of the influence that produced his two anomalous successes and looks forward to "the perhaps somewhat abstract quality of my later work," a comment to which I shall shortly return.

When W.J. Keith wrote that the story "must have seemed startlingly original to a Canadian literary generation for whom

Callaghan and Hugh Garner were considered major practitioners," I agree entirely. When, however, he says, "There is a sophisticated confidence and subtlety in the writing here," I couldn't disagree more.

"Fallings From Us, Vanishings" (this title is a line from Wordsworth's *Ode: Intimations of Immortality from Recollections of Early Childhood*, a poem that somewhat bears, though vaguely, on Arthur Merlin's preoccupations) "Vanishings" is a story about the "romantic" relationship between Arthur Merlin and Gloria. Arthur is eleven years older than Gloria. As an adolescent, Arthur had lusted after Gloria's mother and still treasures memories of her swim-suited glory. Gloria strongly resembles her.

Arthur is the assistant circulation director of *Pulse Magazine*, "historian, builder of archives, ranker of green filing cabinets." Gloria worked in *Pulse Index*, a job procured for her through Arthur's influence.

"He loved Gloria best; but next to her he loved documents on circulation figures broken down by region, and third he loved the files of *Pulse*."

His own pulse somewhat faint, Arthur lives much in the past; Gloria, living determinedly in the present, often finds him exasperating, though if he'd only stop *dithering* and pop the question, she well might. . . On an afternoon at the beach, Arthur really does intend proposing but . . . there is some frothy and flirtatious chit-chat between them during which Arthur quotes at her from Keats' "Bright star, were I as steadfast as thou art," and from St. John (20:24–9) concerning Christ's wounds.

Then. . .

Time now, unfortunately, for some excruciating quotation.

"Do you remember how you used to bounce up and down on my back?"

A crazy notion. "On your back? When?"

"When you were small."

"Oh, for God's sake, Arthur, I'm not small now. Do you take me around because, once upon a time, I was small? I'm a grown woman. Why don't you treat me as one?"

He was gathering up towels and sandals and stuffing them in the basket. He knelt on his knees beside her and his kneecap touched her thigh. It felt cold. Put your arms around me, she thought, there's nobody here to see, give me a kiss and then we'll have something to go on. But he lingered and did nothing, kneeling and looking at her. What could she do, she wasn't a man.

"It isn't right," she said, "to love a girl because of what she was when she was small." But he was gone again, gone back inside, she could tell from his eyes. They glazed and grew opaque as they always did when he was thinking of something else. She wanted to slap him to bring him out of it.

"Look," he said, "I'm not just a hundred and seventy-five pounds of flesh and bone dropped out of nowhere into the twentieth of June. I've a whole life behind me that I love and that I wouldn't want to lose. I'm everything that I've ever been, I'm what's happened to me, not what's happening this instant, not just that."

"If I prick you with a pin, you'll bleed."

"That's not me, that's not me. You think that anything that happened more than a year ago simply doesn't exist."

"Well, it doesn't," she said deliberately.

It made him groan. "You can't live like that," he declared. "Have you no respect for the past? What about your parents?"

Very patiently she began to explain things to him. "I loved them when they were here. But they aren't here anymore. They're dead, Arthur, they're gone. I don't believe in ghosts." It was quite dark on the beach; it was time to go.

"Gloria, Gloria," he moaned.

"Oh, God," she ejaculated, "didn't you bring me here tonight to tell me that you love me and that you want me to love you? Wasn't that what you meant to do?"

He said nothing.

"I know it was," she said. "I'm certain of it, and I'm proud. It means something to a woman, when a man tells her he loves her and wants her. And, don't you see, here I am. I'm all right here! Oh, you poor dear idiot, can't you see how much I'm here? I'm what they call a beautiful girl, a hundred and twenty pounds of flesh and bone dropped from heaven, not from nowhere. I bloom, can't you see? Damn you, Arthur, I'm packed full of sensation, I ache with it, you ... you exorcist! Just come and get me!"

15

Keith wrote rather gently of this story: "The name 'Arthur Merlin,' we can see readily now with the gift of hindsight, flaunts Hood's allegorical interests, yet at the same time strains credulity. . . When we learn a little later that the surname of Gloria, Arthur's girlfriend, is Vere (truth), we cannot but feel that allegory is being *imposed* on the narrative, though it is true that decidedly few noticed this in 1962. The conspicuous allegorical superstructure is in fact pulling against the realistic detail."

More harshly, I would say that the story is simply a dolled-up debate wherein two puppets argue the pros and cons of past and present. The "dialogue" is ridiculous, as ludicrously over-acted as the gestures in silent film.

That only "decidedly few" were aware that this was not a story in the "modernist" tradition ought to be a matter for amazement.

Keith's comment about "conspicuous allegorical superstructure" brings us close to Hood's intentions as a story writer. He was from the start a determined allegorist. He was reinvigorating allegory, and was therefore more or less forced to invent new shapes for his stories, shapes unlike what had become the traditional shapes of "modernism," but his "new shapes" turned out to be very old shapes, refurbished shapes where "realism" was almost beside the point. He often mentioned as conscious influences on his work Dante, Wordsworth, and Spencer: *Divina Commedia: Inferno, Purgatorio, Paradiso*; *The Prelude*; *Imitations of Immortality, Tintern Abbey*; *The Fairie Queen*, and *Shepherds Calendar*.

He talked about his work as being, variously, "super-realism," "documentary fantasy," "allegory," "a secular analogy of sculpture," and "moral realism." In an interview in 1972, he announced, "Everything I write is an allegory, there's no question about that."

Bill Keith, writing of Hood, preferred over "allegory" the term "moral fable" as he felt "allegory" to be too narrowly restrictive. "Moral fable" was the term used by Keith's famous Cambridge teacher, F. R. Leavis.

What, exactly, does allegory mean?

The Harper Handbook to Literature, in an entry by Northrop Frye, defines allegory as "a story that suggests another story. . . An allegory is present in literature whenever it is clear that the author is saying, "By this I also mean that."

This neat definition implies that the "this" is the primary vehicle. Allegory does not work unless the "this" is as clear, or clearer, than the "that." So we ought to ask the question, "How vivid is Hood's capturing of the real, the realistic, the "this"?

He has asserted the importance of the physical "real" in an unambiguous way in an essay he wrote for my anthology *The Narrative Voice* (1972) ponderously entitled "Sober Colouring: The Ontology of Super-Realism."

"Art, after all, like every other human act, implies a philosophical stance: either you think that there is nothing to things that is not delivered in their appearance, or you think that immaterial forms exist in these things conferring identity on them. . . I think with Aristotle that the body and the soul are one; the form of a thing is totally united to its matter. The soul is the body. No ideas but in things. That is where I come out: the spirit is totally *in* the flesh."

Again in "Sober Colouring" he wrote: "My interest in the sounds of sentences, in the use of colour words and of the names of places, in practical stylistics, showed me that prose fiction might have an abstract element, a purely formal element, even though it continued to be strictly, morally, realistic. It might be possible to think of prose fiction the way one thinks of abstract elements in representational painting, or of highly formal music."

. . . it might be possible. . . Such remarks as these disturbed me deeply as I thought that if one wanted to present vividly or capture the "real," one needed every artifice in the box-of-tricks and that "a purely formal element" was the grace that gave prose life.

Much of what he said about his intentions contradicts his practice. He was not a writer who celebrated the sensuous, the real,

> *All things counter, original, spare, strange;*
> *Whatever is fickle, freckled (who knows how?)*
> *With swift, slow; sweet, sour; adazzle, dim;*
> *He fathers-forth whose beauty is past change:*
> *Praise him.*

Hopkins not Hood.

Much of the time, his "that" dominates the "this."

Most critics and readers saw, and continued to see, *Red Kite* and *Around the Mountain* as realistic modernism. One of the first critics to see the *this* and the *that* in the stories was Robert Fulford.

Keith Garebian in his ECW booklet *Hugh Hood and His Works* wrote: ". . . it was Robert Fulford who concocted the famous canard, commenting that almost everything [Hood] wrote in nonfiction had a 'sharp, clear, truthful ring,' whereas almost everything he wrote in fiction was 'dull, flat and spiritless' when it wasn't simply 'embarrassingly pretentious.' Fulford found in Hood 'a superior journalist' being 'slowly strangled by an inferior novelist.'"

Robert Fulford's "canard" was neither famous nor was it a "canard," a word meaning, in essence, "deliberately misleading." It was honest and uncomfortable criticism. The remarks Garebian quotes are from a review of *Around the Mountain*, the book I regard as Hood's finest literary achievement, but I understand perfectly why Fulford felt like that and, in part, agree with his assessment.

Fulford was one of the first critics to comment negatively on Hood's building reputation but his sensible voice was soon forgotten as critics in the academy suddenly, after years of doggedly following the wrong scent, caught wind of Allegory and snuffled off like truffle hounds.

Critical commentary on Hood's writing, exegeses of the sacred texts, is often bizarre if not flatly comic. I'll let Keith Garebian in his *Hugh Hood and His Works* stand as a representative example. Garebian complained that critics of the early work "usually missed Hood's allegory beneath the documentary veneer."

Veneer!

So much for Frye's "this."

Garebian refers to "Fallings From Us, Vanishings" as "the brilliant Grail story."

Huh? Say I.

Grail? What Grail? Where *Grail?*

When last seen, Christ's cup at the Last Supper and subsequently used by Joseph of Arimathea to catch Christ's blood at the Crucifixion. Or more generally thought of as a quest.

Strewth! I whisper to myself.

Of "Red Kite," Garebian writes:

The kite now is, indeed, something holy for it joins heaven to earth via the ball of string and brings a feeling of accomplishment and peace to Fred, whose name, by the way, is etymologically related to "peace" . . . he is regenerated, as it were, through signs of grace: faith, the spirit (the kite is a cross in its wooden ribs), and sacramental water/blood (the red berry juice)."

. . . *joins heaven to earth via the ball of string* . . .
Strewth!
. . . *Fred, whose name, by the way, is etymologically related to "peace"* . . .
Strewth!
Which, by the way, is a mild oath: literally "God's Truth." Other abbreviations, by the way, of "God's" from the 16c – 18c are found in oaths such as 'sblood! 'sbody! and 'swounds! 19

When confronted in an irreligious age with such earnestness as the foregoing, one feels the need for an oath more immediately offensive.

The mess on Deedee's face might once have been "a sign of grace," "sacramental water/blood," but after Jake Zilber's blessed surgery isn't. It's raspberries.

Or consider the words of Professor Frank Davey, poet manqué, who considered Hood "one of the most accomplished of his generation in the art of invisible craftsmanship." When I read such considered drivel, I think of craftsmanship like, oh, this sentence, two friends in a bar.

"'Not true!' said Joe, muddling his Manhattan vortically."

This is not Hood being archly funny.
"Muddling his Manhattan vortically" means "stirring."
This atrocious line occurs in *Red Kite* in the story "Where the Myth Touches Us," a story that brings us, in a necessary

digression, to Morley Callaghan. "Myth" is a story about an older writer, David Wallace, who becomes mentor and friend and eventually almost a father figure to aspiring writer Joe Jacobson. David Wallace's reputation rests on his early work. He has since been enduring a long period of artistic drought. At the beginning of the story, he is working on a novel that he believes will be his "comeback" book. Joe, too, is writing a novel. Purely by chance, both books, by different houses, were set to appear within a day of each other. Wallace, when informed of this, is violently angry—"We're all competing. What's he trying to do to me? There's only so much review space." He accuses Joe of being a Judas and the friendship is ended.

The events of this story are almost completely autobiographical. Wallace is obviously Callaghan. Jacobson obviously Hood. The story is peopled with other real-life characters—the publisher Jack MacCartney is obviously Jack McClelland and the noted reviewer, Bill Faulkner, is obviously William French, books columnist then for the *Globe and Mail*.

Hood sent a copy of "Myth" to Callaghan prior to its publication with a disclaimer and Callaghan ended their relationship in wounded silence. The book "David Wallace" was working on was Callaghan's *A Many Coloured Coat*. So life followed fiction. The relationship between Hood and Callaghan had been very much a father/son relationship so it is reasonable to assume some commonality of purpose.

In Canada, criticism has hailed Callaghan as "The Father of the Canadian Short Story." Professor David Staines, quondam Dean of Arts at the University of Ottawa and General Editor of *The New Canadian Library*, wrote: "When will we realize that Callaghan was a better writer than Hemingway?"

The short answer is—never.

Callaghan's reputation was much shored up by Robert Weaver. Weaver and William Toye wrote of him in *The Oxford Anthology of Canadian Literature* (1973): "Morley Callaghan is Canada's most distinguished novelist and short-story writer. . . Today he is admired by most younger writers of fiction in Canada as their only true predecessor in this country. . ."

Today (2018), "most younger writers of fiction" have probably scarcely *heard* of Callaghan. They should have done and that they haven't is their loss. Writers *need* communion with the past. We all do, of course, but writers more than most.

Years ago, I ended "Winner Take All," an essay on the general awfulness of Callaghan's stories, with this:

"I think it is *wicked* to teach students that stumblebum writing is great writing."

In the essay I drew attention to the nature of Callaghan's writing by quoting his descriptions of characters at the openings of stories.

> "Her husband, Eric, was sitting by the table lamp, reading the paper. A black-haired man with a well-shaped nose, he seemed utterly without energy, slumped down in the chair."

> "The gas flared up, popped, showing fat hips and heavy lines on her face."

> "Mrs. Massey, a stout, kindly woman of sixty, full of energy for her age, and red-faced and healthy except for an occasional pain in her left leg which she watched very carefully, had come from Chicago to see her son who was a doctor."

> "She stood on the corner of Bloor and Yonge, an impressive build of a woman, tall, stout, good-looking for forty-two, and watched the traffic signal."

I went on to say:

> These openings reveal that Callaghan's approach to his material and to his readers is dictatorial. He is always

completely external to the stories he is telling. The reader is not invited to participate in any way; we are not allowed to experience events in a Callaghan story and neither are we allowed to draw our own conclusions. Rather Callaghan relentlessly tells and explains.

His characters are simple puppets, and that is precisely why he describes them so endlessly; such descriptions are hopeless attempts to cover up the wood with heavy paint. His characters are awkwardly invented "little people" who exist simply to perform the plot. Similarly, because Callaghan is not particularly interested in the physical world, the worlds of his stories are perfunctory and nebulous. There is nothing in Callaghan—despite his assertions to the contrary—of "facing the thing freshly and seeing it freshly for what it is in itself." There is never a loving dwelling on texture as there is in, say, Alice Munro, because these people and their worlds have not been lovingly and passionately observed and invented. Callaghan's characters and the worlds they are supposed to inhabit are subordinate to the author's didactic purpose, and for that reason they never come to life.

These beginnings also have a tone in common. It is the tone of "Once upon a time. . ." or "There once lived in a distant country a prince who. . ." To attempt to disguise this fairy-tale tone, Callaghan would have written: "There once lived in a distant country called Neutralia a tall, dark-haired, handsome prince with a well-shaped nose. . ."—but well-shaped nose or not, it's obvious that we are dealing here with something quite different from the modernist short story.

These beginnings also suggest that Callaghan lacked a sense of humour and suffered from a tin ear. The unintentionally funny sentences—"Most of the evening Mary remained in the kitchen, talking with her father, a quick-tempered, devout, hard-working man in the trucking business"—bring to mind the mighty lines of William McGonagall.

And now to look at some endings.

> As she began to think of the few moments she had had with him, his smooth face and his damp curly hair pressed down against her breast, she said softly, "Maybe he didn't know the way it was with me," and part of a world that nobody else could ever touch seemed to belong to her alone. ("Guilty Woman")

> "I feel very contented now, that's all," she said simply. "Tonight everything is so still on the street outside in the dark here. I was so very happy while Joe was with me," she whispered. "It was as though I had never been alive before. It's so sweetly peaceful tonight, waiting, and feeling so much stirring within me, so lovely and still." ("Ellen")

> In the cold, early-morning light, with heavy trucks rumbling on the street, he felt terribly tense and nervous. He could hardly remember anything that had happened. Inside him there was a wide, frightening emptiness. He wanted to reach out desperately and hold that swift, ardent, yielding joy that had been so close to him. For a while he could not think at all. And then he felt that slow unfolding coming in him again, making him quick with wonder. ("One Spring Night" 292)

What do these endings reveal? Wyndham Lewis's oily review of *Now That April's Here* described the stories as "beautifully replete with a message of human tolerance and love" and as "full of a robust benevolence." Professor Victor Hoar, in the Studies in Canadian Literature series, wrote on *Now That April's Here*: "The one theme recited again and again . . . is the promise of growth inherent in human beings. . . Again and again, Callaghan's protagonists are left enriched and excited by the new vision of themselves and of the world around them" (21).

These endings do not offer me "a message of human tolerance and love," nor do they reveal to me a "new vision" or a "promise of growth"; overwhelmingly, they reveal sloppy, gooey sentimentality. Consider the sheer vagueness of the words Callaghan uses to describe this "new vision": "stirred," "longing," "awe," "secret joy," "lovely," "still," "sweetly peaceful," "stirred and wondering," "secret gladness," "faint elation," "yielding joy," "slow unfolding," "quick with wonder."

Where Callaghan is not unintentionally funny, as in "Ellen," with its preposterous dialogue, he is simply embarrassing. One cannot take seriously the work of a writer who produces lines of alleged dialogue such as: "It's so sweetly peaceful tonight, waiting, and feeling so much stirring within me, so lovely and still." Desmond Pacey wrote of a "certain moral flabbiness" in Callaghan's work; I wish he had pressed through into seeing that "moral flabbiness" is exactly the same thing as verbal flabbiness.

Ten years or so ago I wrote an essay called "The Curate's Egg" wherein I suggested that Callaghan was not really in the modernist tradition at all, that his major impulse was moralistic and didactic and that this impulse was constantly at war within his work against what little artistry he possessed. This brief glance at beginnings and endings tends to confirm for me that suggestion. The forced openings, the fairy-tale tone, the puppet characters, and the cloying endings with their "message of human tolerance and love"—surely this smacks more of Sunday school than it does of the great modernist tradition of Anderson, Hemingway, Joyce, and Mansfield?

These short stories of Callaghan's are in the form of *exempla*, illustrative, moralizing tales used for centuries in Catholic teaching, a form that historically must have served the needs of illiterate communicants, a form that would have been familiar to Callaghan since childhood. I have dragged Callaghan in not only because of his strong personal and artistic connection with Hood but because his motivation in writing was much the same.

Bill Keith writes of Hood in *God's Plenty*:

> "From the Old Testament he encountered stories that 'you turned over in your head with no power whatsoever to banish them from the imagination'. Later, as he says, he 'felt under the sway of parable, with the [Benziger Brothers'] *Bible History* and the readings from the New Testament and equally under the sway of elementary theological reasoning in the *Catechism*.'"

I usually have little or no interest in linking the life of a writer to his or her works. I do read biographies and autobiographies as I'm insatiably interested in the *shapes* of lives but usually it's gossip that grips, not the possible autobiographical genesis of stories and novels. Such excavating seems pseudo-illuminating. All that matters is the shining artifact. Yet the pervading influence on Hood of Catholicism does deserve mention.

He lived his entire life inside Catholic institutions. His elementary school in Toronto was Our Lady of Perpetual Help; secondary school was De La Salle College; university was St. Michael's College, the Roman Catholic college of the University of Toronto (alma mater also to Morley Callaghan). He went on to a doctorate concerning "the medieval views of modes of knowing exemplified in St. Thomas Aquinas and Dante." Upon graduation, he secured a teaching position at St. Joseph's College, a Catholic college for women in West Hartford, Connecticut. In 1961, he returned to Canada to spend the rest of his teaching career at the Université de Montréal, another institution Catholic in its founding and initial purpose.

In the Author's Introduction to *Around the Mountain*, Hood wrote of the book—though his remarks apply generally:

> "My religion makes its predictable appearance in the composition of the book. I have always been a religious believer, a Catholic by birth, upbringing, and mature conviction. While I always drew a distinction between religious conviction and ideology I realize that most secular discourse does not. Catholic belief is far from incidental to the production of *Around the Mountain*. Whether faith and dogma have here degenerated into disingenuous propaganda is a question for readers of other ideological persuasions to propose to themselves."

I have established the close links between Callaghan and Hood but remarks of Hood's in the Author's Introduction to *A Short Walk in the Rain* clinch my proposition that both are writing some version of *exempla*. Referring to the story "The Glass of Fashion," he writes of one of the characters: "Porky Valentine bears the first of those emblematic names that a long line of my characters have worn: Arthur Merlin, Rose Leclair, Matthew Goderich. He is treated as an element in a typological exemplum, not as a character in a story."

When Hood brings together the words "emblematic" and "exemplum," it should be clear that we are at the nub of the matter; his avowed intention was to write allegorically and his stories should be seen as *exempla* just as Callaghan's are. The difference is that Hood was a far better writer and was possessed of, and by, a far more powerful and sophisticated intellect. Many years after the breach with Callaghan, Hood said in an interview with John Mills that Callaghan was "a poor writer."

Hood's religious beliefs should not be a barrier to non-Catholic readers. Fiction is a highway into previously unseen or unimagined territory while bigotry treads a narrow rut. His religion is the emotional ground of his being, not a series of debating points he wished to score. His tendency is always to celebrate and question rather than instruct. One does not have to be Catholic to see-saw with the narrator at the end of "Going Out as a Ghost;" one does not have to be a Catholic to understand and share in the joy and celebration that is "Getting to Williamstown."

Resistance, disappointment, or simple bafflement that some feel with Hood's stories arise, I suspect, less from what the stories are than from what they are not. What they are 27 not are stories in the still-dominant mode of the "modernism" of Joyce, Mansfield, Hemingway, or Welty. I suggest that if the word "stories" is a terminological barrier, call them something else.

If "rapeseed oil" causes disquiet, call it Canola.

For years now, I have thought of Hugh Hood's short fiction as meditations. The *Oxford Canadian* defines "meditate" as "exercise the mind in" (esp. religious) contemplation" and "to focus on a subject in this manner."

Meditations.

A persuasive example of this idea is the story "Breaking Off" in this volume.

This is the story of the failed "romantic" relationship between Emmy and Basil who both work, clerically, in the ergonomically designed office headquarters of a large corporation in Toronto, named, significantly, Jupiter Life.

(Jupiter was the Roman equivalent of Zeus and the name of the Life Insurance company plays with the idea of divinity, an earlier era of human history, and, at somewhat of a stretch, though with Hood you never know, the vision of lives not lived in relation to the divine.)

Emmy works in the photocopying department, daily churning out dozens and dozens of pamphlets, booklets, memoranda, financial statements, releases, and reports. These are distributed to all the desks and open-plan cubicles on all floors by The Boy, actually a series of boys, "identical in manner and costume . . . for all practical purposes a single specimen of the type."

Headquarters is caught marvellously in the language Hood uses to describe it. Bill Keith writes of this perceptively in *God's Plenty*:

> ". . . Hood is preoccupied with a specific language . . . and it is seen as disturbingly similar to the language of advertising:
>
>> 'Here's the constant-estimate-adjustment sheet for the third week of the current quarter, and the departmental breakdown, oh, and the extrapolation for the remainder of the quarter, and . . . the in-field operations costing, and this is the divisional operations summary with three-previous-year comparison parameters.'
>
> Hood makes his point by flooding his text with the adjectival use of nouns now so characteristic of the Computer Age (itself an example)...
>
> But he also records it critically, as a degradation of English style."

Emmy and Basil, defined largely through their possessions, and the possessions they desire, are akin to that sad pair Dreamy and A.O. in "God Has Manifested Himself Unto Us as Canadian Tire."

The cluttered, though empty, language of the description of Headquarters also hints at such dystopias as *Nineteen Eighty-Four*, *Fahrenheit 451*, and *Brave New World*. Hood's dystopia is one of meaninglessness.

"Basil had answered a want-ad to get his job. He had one year at Ryerson behind him; classroom education meant nothing to Basil. He thought that work was better than school. Like Emmy, he enjoyed having money to buy things."

Emmy "earned a surprisingly large salary for a young single woman with a high school education, and spent most of it on her clothes. She was still living at home but thinking about her own apartment."

Neither of them had thoughts of buying a house at some time in the future or of getting married. Neither idea was part of their mental or emotional world.

"Two people with no commitments and twice their individual earnings—an extraordinarily large amount—could have an apartment in a brand-new building, with big closets, full-length mirrors, a crystal room-divider between dining and food preparation areas, and a twentieth-storey balcony with a view of the lake, posters from Marci Lipman Gallery, colour TV, twenty-one-day vacation excursions via Sunflight to Greece or St. Lucia, forever and ever, without having to learn or unlearn anything."

Notice how the words "dining-room" and "kitchen" are disappearing under the welter of verbiage, becoming "areas"; notice, too, in the words "forever and ever" the liturgical tinge. Notice Hood's keen observation of advertising, trends, fads, of patterns of transit, of demographics, of prices of consumer goods.

Emmy and Olive run the photocopying department.

"It was very unlikely that they would remain where they were until they were old. Nobody like them had done this; there were no old people in the office. Some strange process of selection and elimination kept the visible range of people around her at Jupiter Life no more than thirty-eight at the outside. Almost none of the women in the office was older than, say, thirty-four or -five. Where were all the oldies?"

Emmy, at twenty, lived in the family home owned by her retired grandfather.

"For his granddaughter, this very comfortably off, digni- fied, neatly dressed old barber didn't exist. She saw him every night but he wasn't real. She couldn't even begin to guess what his life had been like, or was like now. She could barely understand what her parents said to her, although their sporadic remarks made more sense than her grandfather's disconnected, almost demented—as they seemed to her—observations and suggestions."

The room known as "Emmy's Room"—not her bedroom— was a strange room that might in time past have been a large pantry or somesuch; into it washed up all the unwanted old furniture and household junk, old sofas, an ancient TV, a superseded record player, a hat rack, scattered records, a few tattered Reader's Digest Condensed Books. It also stored a couple of pieces of brand new furniture, furniture Emmy intended, vaguely, for a future apartment. Emmy's Room is also home, in a large cage, to Crackers, the parrot.

Hood describes this room, midway in the house, a room containing together past and future, as a "no-man's-land," referring to the unoccupied land between the German and

British trenches. This description of the room as "embattled," as belonging neither to past nor future is an essential idea in "Breaking Off," where opposing forces face each other over a contested ground of mutual incomprehension.

Play is made of Crackers' ability or inability to speak; doubtless embroidery on the theme of failed communications though I suspect Crackers *really* appears *because Hugh liked parrots*; he had two of them and was so besotted that he granted them the freedom of his house—with consequences obvious and horrible.

With Basil, Hood shifts gear into farce. Basil is "one of those fumbling types who don't swing the bat crisply and with attack." The words "crisply" and "attack" should alert readers to the hovering presence of P.G. Wodehouse, another master Hood could, and would, quote at inordinate length. 31 He draws Basil as a young man constantly needing to take a leak. The breakup with Emmy occurs because, being too shy to ask where the lavatory is, Basil pees in the kitchen sink and Emmy wanders in surprising him.

Following this, Basil tries to woo her back but she spurns his advances. Finally, he buys her a clip or pin "in the shape of a slender feminine hard and wrist, with long, stylized, tapering fingers, a minute shard of genuine ruby tipped onto the third finger—to simulate a tiny ring." Emmy guesses that it was "from one of the better lines of junk jewellery." She refuses to accept this present as she "just [doesn't] feel about you in that way."

The odd use of the word "shard" is interesting.

Emmy is deeply embarrassed when Basil subsequently raffles the clip one afternoon at work; it is won by her immediate boss, Olive, who wears it until she quits to get married.

> "The event was exceedingly public, and Emmy, who did not attend, was sure that everybody there was laughing at her. They weren't. They knew nothing about her."

The story ends with this sentence:

> "Severed hands, and other separated members, became permanent properties of Emmy's visions."

"Properties" and "visions" are interesting usages in this story of severing, breaking, splitting up.

We are likely to find Basil and Emmy to be little better than ciphers. We might be tempted to agree with Robert Fulford that "a superior journalist" is being "slowly strangled by an inferior novelist." Yet the brilliant depiction of the headquarters of Jupiter Life is not journalism at all—a reporting of facts—but is, rather, something approaching caustic poetry. The description is Hood pronouncing an extended anathema, an outraged lament. Funny, too, though. Complicated.

To have introduced into this rhetorical world a "real" Emmy, a "real" Basil, would have been working at cross purposes. Emmy and Basil work perfectly if we accept them as typological characters. Hood used this word to describe the character Porky Valentine referred to earlier. The word means "the branch of knowledge that deals with classes with common characteristics," with "human behaviour or characteristic according to type." (*Oxford Canadian Dictionary*).

That Hood so presents them, then, is not evidence of an inability to write "realistically"; it is important to understand that his writing in this manner is entirely deliberate. Emmy and Basil are typological characters because Hood's purpose is to picture them as representative types playing small parts in a vast social change which is still rending our society. Hood had brooded over this story for thirty years before its publication in 1980. Since that date, all the forces he feared have accelerated beyond imagination.

His concerns in "Breaking Off" if offered, say, in *The Economist* or *Time Magazine* as an essay on generational conflict or patterns of community in large cities or employment demographics within large companies, might be *sort of* interesting but quickly forgotten. It has been my experience, however, that Hood's story, approached initially with some suspicion, grew in my mind, blossomed, remains vital. Now, forty years later, he seems to have been prophetic.

Hood wrote of "Breaking Off" in an essay entitled "Floating Southwards" that he contributed to my anthology *Making It New* (1982):

> The story feels novelistic to me. It is the closest I have come to the novella or long story, and is based on a subject I had been mulling over since about 1948, more than thirty years. It is a very heavily charged donnée, too large really for the short story form. As I was writing it, I knew that I must condense, squeeze, truncate, compress, elide. As my novels do, this story signals the significance of extremely complex patterns of group behaviour—and linguistic usage—using individual lives as enactments of social forms; the story has embedded in it an ongoing criticism of various types of communication, such as, for example, the strange speech of parrots. I'm not talking about mere social history—and I'm not primarily concerned with the multiplication of observed detail, although many of my critics have said that I am. I mean the way that membership in an army, a church, a big business, a social class, a language group, circulates like arterial blood (ha, a metaphor, no, a simile, anyway an explicit comparison for a change) into personal conduct in such a way as to make of occasional selected individuals immensely expressive representatives of what is happening in their world. Emmy and Basil are representative people in this specific sense, doing representative things. Not trendy things or symbolic things. Here I'm placing myself in a relation with Emerson, in his essay on "Representative Men," and with Scott Fitzgerald, who considered himself all his life to be a man peculiarly endowed with a power

33

to express in his life/work the immense social forces that were swirling around him.

Emerson was somewhat more ready than Fitzgerald to see the source of these forces in the will of the Almighty. To that will, I would add the Divine Intelligence which is one with that will, and am happy to trace these currents to such a spring. In "Breaking Off" my central imaginative preoccupation—the powerfully apprehended sensory schema which was lodged in my consciousness as I wrote—is that of an enormous chunk of ice, a part of the glacier, separating itself from the Arctic icecap and floating southwards on the current, gradually diminishing somewhat in size until it becomes an iceberg, smaller than at birth but still immense and capable of destroying the greatest human enterprise. This image is not found in the overt text of the story, except in the implications of the title. The social groups, the language systems, the courtship patterns, which Basil and Emmy share, form a mass like that of the southwards-moving iceberg with nine-tenths of its significance below the surface, but deadly. This isolated chunk of human culture—ourselves in the last third of this century—cannot speak to the times which went before us, cannot hear their voices. "Breaking Off."

This essay was written in 1982. It requires slow and careful reading—several times. It not only illuminates "Breaking Off" but also illuminates Hood's method and intentions in general.

Hood's second book of short fiction was *Around the Mountain: Scenes from Montréal Life* (1967). From that volume, this book republishes "Le Grand Démenagement," "Light Shining Out of Darkness," and "The Village Inside." In an essential way, this is doing the stories a disservice because they were written specifically to fit into a sequence of twelve.

With an endearing innocence, Hood hoped the book would be bought as a souvenir of Montreal by visitors to Expo '67.

Ha!

In the Author's Introduction to *Around the Mountain* (Porcupine's Quill, 1994) he wrote: "I made the book partly out of a series of references to the *Purgatrio* and *The Prelude*, works that if not specifically religious poems certainly represent religious experience, and even mystical experience, as an integral element of their narrative. There is some true sense in which the *Commedia*, *Paradise Lost*, and certain other long verse narratives may truthfully be described as religious poems, while *The Prelude* problematizes the notion of the religious poem. Can there be such a thing as a "secular religious narrative poem"? That's more or less what I hoped *Around the Mountain* might turn out to be. . ."

It is difficult to keep a straight face when thinking of returned tourists—*if any*—opening their souvenir.

Hood also derived the book, in part, from Turgenev's *A Sportsman's Sketches* and Dickens' *Sketches by Boz*. It is interesting to listen in this book to the evolution of Hood's very distinctive tone, that informal formality, that heightened vernacular which seems so easy but is so singular.

This sort of voice:

> "In those days I was spending a lot of time out at the Montrose Record Centre on Bélanger, west of Montée Saint-Michel. As you come over from the centre of town, east on Jean-Talon or Bélanger, you'll be struck by the flatness and lack of charm of this neighbourhood. I've forgotten the bounding streets, if in fact I ever knew them. It's *calme plat, terne*, though you might be interested by the Italian neighbourhood between Papineau and D'Iberville, lots of *gelata* parlours and *sartorie*. On Papineau near Bélanger, there are two dozen brand-new multiple dwellings, quadruplexes and octoplexes inhabited by Italians

who have made a few bucks since they got here; they may own a store, or four dump-trucks, or a gardening business—the city is full of Italian gardeners—in which they employ relatives, more recent arrivals."

Around the Mountain: Scenes from Montréal Life is, despite Hood's ponderous explication of his influences and forebears, a charming book; it is also much more. I would strongly suggest that interested readers consult *God's Plenty* by W.J. Keith and "A Secular Liturgy: Hugh Hood's Aesthetics and *Around the Mountain*" by J.R. 'Tim' Struthers, to be found in *Studies in Canadian Literature.* Vol. 10, 1985.

I am convinced that *Around the Mountain*, Hugh Hood's most triumphant volume of short fiction, will secure for itself a lasting position in any evolving canon of Canadian literature.

John Metcalf
Ottawa, 2018

FLYING A RED KITE

THE RIDE HOME began badly. Still almost a stranger to the city, tired, hot and dirty, and inattentive to his surroundings, Fred stood for ten minutes, shifting his parcels from arm to arm and his weight from one leg to the other, in a sweaty bath of shimmering glare from the sidewalk, next to a grimy yellow-and-black bus stop. To his left a line of murmuring would-be passengers lengthened until there were enough to fill any vehicle that might come for them. Finally an obese brown bus waddled up like an indecent old cow and stopped with an expiring moo at the head of the line. Fred was glad to be first in line as there didn't seem to be room for more than a few to embus.

But as he stepped up he noticed a sign in the window which said *Côte des Neiges—Boulevard* and he recoiled as though bitten, trampling the toes of the woman behind him and making her squeal. It was a 66, not the 65 that he wanted. The woman pushed furiously past him while the remainder of the line clamoured in the rear. He stared at the number on the bus stop: 66, not his stop at all. Out of the corner of his eye he saw another coach pulling away from the stop on the northeast corner, the right stop, the 65, and the one he should have been standing under all this time. Giving his characteristic weary put-upon sigh, which he used before breakfast to annoy Naomi, he adjusted his parcels in both arms, feeling sweat run around his neck and down his collar between his shoulders, and crossed Saint-Catherine against the light, drawing a Gallic sneer from a policeman, to stand for several more minutes at the head of a new queue, under the right sign. It was nearly four-thirty and the Saturday shopping crowds wanted to get home, out of the summer dust and heat, out of the jitter of the big July holiday weekend. They would all go home and sit on their balconies. All over the suburbs in duplexes and four-plexes families would be enjoying cold suppers in the open air on their balconies; but the Calverts' apartment had none. Fred and Naomi had been ignorant of the meaning of the custom when they were apartment hunting. They had thought of Montreal as a city of the sub-Arctic and in the summers they would have leisure to repent the misjudgement.

He had been shopping along the length of Saint-Catherine between Peel and Guy, feeling guilty because he had heard for years that this was where all those pretty Montreal women made their promenade; he had wanted to watch without familial encumbrances. There had been girls enough but nothing outrageously special so he had beguiled the scorching afternoon making a great many small idle purchases, of the kind one does when trapped in a Woolworth's. A ball-point pen and a note-pad for Naomi, who was always stealing his and leaving it in the kitchen with long, wildly optimistic grocery lists scribbled in it. Six packages of cigarettes, some legal-size envelopes, two Dinky toys, a long-playing record, two parcels of second-hand books, and the lightest of his burdens and the unhandiest, the kite he had bought for Deedee, two flimsy wooden sticks rolled up in red plastic film, and a ball of cheap thin string—not enough, by the look of it, if he should ever get the thing into the air.

When he'd gone fishing, as a boy, he'd never caught any fish; when playing hockey he had never been able to put the puck in the net. One by one the wholesome outdoor sports and games had defeated him. But he had gone on believing in them, in their curative moral values, and now he hoped that Deedee, though a girl, might some time catch a fish; and though she obviously wouldn't play hockey, she might ski, or toboggan on the mountain. He had noticed that people treated kites and kite-flying as somehow holy. They were a natural symbol, thought Fred, and he felt uneasily sure that he would have trouble getting this one to fly.

The inside of the bus was shaped like a box-car with windows, but the windows were useless. You might have peeled off the bus as you'd peel the paper off a pound of butter, leaving an oblong yellow lump of thick solid heat, with the passengers embedded in it like hopeless breadcrumbs.

He elbowed and wriggled his way along the aisle, feeling a momentary sliver of pleasure as his palm rubbed accidentally along the back of a girl's skirt—once, a philosopher—the sort of thing you couldn't be charged with. But you couldn't get away with it twice and anyway the girl either didn't feel it, or had no idea who had caressed her. There were vacant seats towards the rear, which was odd because the bus was otherwise full, and he struggled towards them, trying not to break the wooden struts which might be persuaded to fly. The bus lurched forward and his feet moved with the floor, causing him to pop suddenly out of the crowd by the exit, into a square well of space next to the heat and stink of the engine. He swayed around and aimed himself at a narrow vacant seat, nearly dropping a parcel of books as he lowered himself precipitately into it.

The bus crossed Sherbrooke Street and began, intolerably slowly, to crawl up Côte-des-Neiges and around the western spur of the mountain. His ears began to pick up the usual *mélange* of French and English and to sort it out; he was proud of his French and pleased that most of the people on the streets spoke a less correct, though more fluent, version than his own. He had found that he could make his customers understand him perfectly—he was a book salesman—but that people on the street were happier when he addressed them in English.

The chatter in the bus grew clearer and more interesting and he began to listen, grasping all at once why he had found a seat back here. He was sitting next to a couple of drunks who emitted an almost overpowering smell of beer. They were cheerfully exchanging indecencies and obscure jokes and in a minute they would speak to him. They always did, drunks and panhandlers, finding some soft fearfulness in his face which exposed him as a shrinking easy mark. Once in a railroad station he had been approached three times in twenty minutes by the same panhandler on his rounds. Each time he had given the man something, despising himself with each new weakness.

The cheerful pair sitting at right angles to him grew louder and more blunt and the women within earshot grew glum. There was no harm in it; there never is. But you avoid your neighbour's eye, afraid of smiling awkwardly, or of looking offended and a prude.

"Now this Pearson," said one of the revellers, "he's just a little short-ass. He's just a little fellow without any brains. Why, some of the speeches he makes. . . I could make them myself. I'm an old Tory myself, an old Tory."

"I'm an old Blue," said the other.

"Is that so, now? That's fine, a fine thing." Fred was sure he didn't know what a Blue was.

"I'm a Balliol man. Whoops!" They began to make monkey-like noises to annoy the passengers and amuse themselves. "Whoops," said the Oxford man again, "hoo, hoo, there's one now, there's one for you." He was talking about a girl on the sidewalk.

"She's a one, now, isn't she? Look at the legs on her, oh, look at them now, isn't that something?" There was a noisy clearing of throats and the same voice said something that sounded like "*Shaoil-na-baig.*"

"Oh, good, good!" said the Balliol man.

"*Shaoil-na-baig,*" said the other loudly, "I've not forgotten my Gaelic, do you see, *shaoil-na-baig,*" he said it loudly, and a woman up the aisle reddened and looked away. It sounded like a dirty phrase to Fred, delivered as though the speaker had forgotten all his Gaelic but the words for sexual intercourse.

"And how is your French, Father?" asked the Balliol man, and the title made Fred start in his seat. He pretended to drop a parcel and craned his head quickly sideways. The older of the two drunks, the one sitting by the window, examining the passing legs and skirts with the same impulse that Fred had felt on Saint Catherine Street, was indeed a priest, and couldn't possibly be an impostor. His clerical suit was too well-worn, egg-stained and blemished with candle-droppings, and fit its wearer too well, for it to be an assumed costume. The face was unmistakably a southern Irishman's. The priest darted a quick peek into Fred's eyes before he could turn them away, giving a monkey-like grimace that might have been a mixture of embarrassment and shame but probably wasn't. 41

He was a little grey-haired bucko of close to sixty, with a triangular sly mottled crimson face and uneven yellow teeth. His hands moved jerkily and expressively in his lap, in counterpoint to the lively intelligent movements of his face.

The other chap, the Balliol man, was a perfect type of English-speaking Montrealer, perhaps a bond salesman or minor functionary in a brokerage house on Saint James Street. He was about fifty with a round domed head, red hair beginning to go slightly white at the neck and ears, pink porcine skin, very neatly barbered and combed. He wore an expensive white shirt with a fine blue stripe and there was some sort of ring around his tie. He had his hands folded fatly on the knob of a stick, round face with deep laugh-lines in the cheeks, and a pair of cheerfully darting little blue-bloodshot eyes. Where could the pair have run into each other?

"I've forgotten my French years ago," said the priest carelessly. "I was down in New Brunswick for many years and I'd no use for it, the work I was doing. I'm Irish, you know."

"I'm an old Blue."

"That's right," said the priest, "John's the boy. Oh, he's a sharp lad is John. He'll let them all get off, do you see, to Manitoba for the summer, and bang, BANG!" All the bus jumped. "He'll call an election on them and then they'll run." Something caught his eye and be turned to gaze out the window. The bus was moving slowly past the cemetery of Nôtre Dame des Neiges and the priest stared, half-sober, at the graves stretched up the mountainside in the sun.

"I'm not in there," he said involuntarily.

"Indeed you're not," said his companion, "lots of life in you yet, eh, Father?"

"Oh," he said, "oh, I don't think I'd know what to do with a girl if I fell over one." He looked out at the cemetery for several moments. "It's all a sham," he said half under his breath, "they're in there for good." He swung around and looked innocently at Fred. "Are you going fishing, lad?"

"It's a kite that I bought for my little girl," said Fred, more cheerfully than he felt.

"She'll enjoy that, she will," said the priest, "for it's grand sport."

"Go fly a kite!" said the Oxford man hilariously. It amused him and he said it again. "Go fly a kite!" He and the priest began to chant together, "Hoo, hoo, whoops," and they laughed and in a moment, clearly, would begin to sing.

The bus turned lumberingly onto Queen Mary Road. Fred stood up confusedly and began to push his way towards the rear door. As he turned away, the priest grinned impudently at him, stammering a jolly goodbye. Fred was too embarrassed to answer but he smiled uncertainly and fled. He heard them take up their chant anew.

"Hoo, there's a one for you, hoo. *Shaoil-na-baig*. Whoops!" Their laughter died out as the bus rolled heavily away.

He had heard about such men, naturally, and knew that they existed; but it was the first time in Fred's life that he had ever seen a priest misbehave himself publicly. There are so many priests in the city, he thought, that the number of bum ones must be in proportion. The explanation satisfied him but the incident left a disagreeable impression in his mind.

Safely home he took his shirt off and poured himself a Coke. Then he allowed Deedee, who was dancing around him with her terrible energy, to open the parcels.

"Give your Mummy the pad and pencil, sweetie," he directed. She crossed obediently to Naomi's chair and handed her the cheap plastic case.

"Let me see you make a note in it," he said, "make a list of something, for God's sake, so you'll remember it's yours. And the one on the desk is mine. Got that?" He spoke without rancour or much interest; it was a rather overworked joke between them.

"What's this?" said Deedee, holding up the kite and allowing the ball of string to roll down the hall. He resisted a compulsive wish to get up and re-wind the string.

"It's for you. Don't you know what it is?"

"It's a red kite," she said. She had wanted one for weeks but spoke now as if she weren't interested. Then all at once she grew very excited and eager. "Can you put it together right now?" she begged.

"I think we'll wait till after supper, sweetheart," he said, feeling mean. You raised their hopes and then dashed them; there was no real reason why they shouldn't put it together now, except his fatigue. He looked pleadingly at Naomi.

"Daddy's tired, Deedee," she said obligingly, "he's had a long hot afternoon."

"But I want to see it," said Deedee, fiddling with the flimsy red film and nearly puncturing it.

Fred was sorry he'd drunk a Coke; it bloated him and upset his stomach and had no true cooling effect.

"We'll have something to eat," he said cajolingly, "and then Mummy can put it together for you." He turned to his wife. "You don't mind, do you? I'd only spoil the thing." Threading a needle or hanging a picture made the normal slight tremor of his hands accentuate itself almost embarrassingly.

"Of course not," she said, smiling wryly. They had long ago worked out their areas of uselessness.

"There's a picture on it, and directions."

"Yes. Well, we'll get it together somehow. Flying it ... that's something else again." She got up, holding the notepad, and went into the kitchen to put the supper on.

It was a good hot-weather supper, tossed greens with the correct proportions of vinegar and oil, croissants and butter, and cold sliced ham. As he ate, his spirits began to percolate a bit, and he gave Naomi a graphic sketch of the incident on the bus. "It depressed me," he told her. This came as no surprise to her; almost anything unusual, which he couldn't do anything to alter or relieve, depressed Fred nowadays. "He must have been sixty. Oh, quite sixty, I should think, and you could tell that everything had come to pieces for him."

"It's a standard story," she said, "and aren't you sentimentalizing it?"

"In what way?"

"The 'spoiled priest' business, the empty man, the man without a calling. They all write about that. Graham Greene made his whole career out of that."

"That isn't what the phrase means," said Fred laboriously. "It doesn't refer to a man who actually *is* a priest, though without a vocation."

"No?" She lifted an eyebrow; she was better educated than he.

"No, it doesn't. It means somebody who never became a priest at all. The point is that you *had* a vocation but ignored it. That's what a spoiled priest is. It's an Irish phrase, and usually refers to somebody who is a failure and who drinks too much." He laughed shortly. "I don't qualify, on the second count."

"You're not a failure."

"No, I'm too young. Give me time!" There was no reason for him to talk like this; he was a very productive salesman.

"You certainly never wanted to be a priest," she said positively, looking down at her breasts and laughing, thinking of some secret. "I'll bet you never considered it, not with your habits." She meant his bedroom habits which were ardent, and in which she ardently acquiesced. She was an adept and enthusiastic partner, her greatest gift as a wife.

"Let's put that kite together," said Deedee, getting up from her little table, with such adult decision that her parents chuckled. "Come on," she said, going to the sofa and bouncing up and down.

Naomi put a tear in the fabric right away, on account of the ambiguity of the directions. There should have been two holes in the kite, through which a lugging-string passed; but the holes hadn't been provided and when she put them there with the point of an icepick they immediately began to grow.

"Scotch tape," she said, like a surgeon asking for sutures.

"There's a picture on the front," said Fred, secretly cross but ostensibly helpful.

"I see it," she said.

"Mummy put holes in the kite," said Deedee with alarm. "Is she going to break it?"

"No," said Fred. The directions were certainly ambiguous.

Naomi tied the struts at right angles, using so much string that Fred was sure the kite would be too heavy. Then she strung the fabric on the notched ends of the struts and the thing began to take shape.

"It doesn't look quite right," she said, puzzled and irritated.

"The surface has to be curved so there's a difference of air pressure." He remembered this, rather unfairly, from high school physics classes.

She bent the cross-piece and tied it in a bowed arc, and the red film pulled taut. "There now," she said.

"You've forgotten the lugging-string on the front," said Fred critically, "that's what you made the holes for, remember?"

"Why is Daddy mad?" said Deedee.

"I'M NOT MAD!"

It had begun to shower, great pear-shaped drops of rain falling with a plop on the sidewalk.

"That's as close as I can come," said Naomi, staring at Fred, "we aren't going to try it tonight, are we?"

"We promised her," he said, "and it's only a light rain."

"Will we all go?"

"I wish you'd take her," he said, "because my stomach feels upset. I should never drink Coca-Cola."

"It always bothers you. You should know that by now."

"I'm not running out on you," he said anxiously, "and if you can't make it work, I'll take her up tomorrow afternoon."

"I know," she said, "come on, Deedee, we're going to take the kite up the hill." They left the house and crossed the street. Fred watched them through the window as they started up the steep path hand in hand. He felt left out, and slightly nauseated.

They were back in half an hour, their spirits not at all dampened, which surprised him.

"No go, eh?"

"Much too wet, and not enough breeze. The rain knocks it flat."

"Okay!" he exclaimed with fervour. "I'll try tomorrow."

"We'll try again tomorrow," said Deedee with equal determination—her parents mustn't forget their obligations.

Sunday afternooon the weather was nearly perfect, hot, clear, a firm steady breeze but not too much of it, and a cloudless sky. At two o'clock Fred took his daughter by the hand and they started up the mountain together, taking the path through the woods that led up to the university parking lots.

"We won't come down until we make it fly," Fred swore. "That's a promise."

"Good," she said, hanging on to his hand and letting him drag her up the steep path, "there are lots of bugs in here, aren't there?"

"Yes," he said briefly—he was being liberally bitten.

When they came to the end of the path, they saw that the campus was deserted and still, and there was all kinds of running room. Fred gave Deedee careful instructions about where to sit, and what to do if a car should come along, and then he paid out a little string and began to run across the parking lot towards the main building of the university. He felt a tug at the string and throwing a glance over his shoulders he saw the kite bobbing in the air, about twenty feet off the ground. He let out more string, trying to keep it filled with air, but he couldn't run quite fast enough, and in a moment it fell back to the ground.

"Nearly had it!" he shouted to Deedee, whom he'd left fifty yards behind.

"Daddy, Daddy, come back," she hollered apprehensively. Rolling up the string as he went, he retraced his steps and prepared to try again. It was important to catch a gust of wind and run into it. On the second try the kite went higher than before but as he ran past the entrance to the university he felt the air pressure lapse and saw the kite waver and fall. He walked slowly back, realizing that the bulk of the main building was cutting off the air currents.

7

"We'll go up higher," he told her, and she seized his hand and climbed obediently up the road beside him, around behind the main building, past ash barrels and trash heaps; they climbed a flight of wooden steps, crossed a parking lot next to the Ecole Polytechnique and a slanting field further up, and at last came to a pebbly dirt road that ran along the top ridge of the mountain beside the cemetery. Fred remembered the priest as he looked across the fence and along the broad stretch of cemetery land rolling away down the slope of the mountain to the west. They were about six hundred feet above the river, he judged. He'd never been up this far before.

"My sturdy little brown legs are tired," Deedee remarked, and he burst out laughing.

"Where did you hear that," he said. "Who has sturdy little brown legs?"

She screwed her face up in a grin. "The gingerbread man," she said, beginning to sing, "I can run away from you, I can, 'cause I'm the little gingerbread man."

The air was dry and clear and without a trace of humidity and the sunshine was dazzling. On either side of the dirt road grew great clumps of wild flowers, yellow and blue, buttercups, daisies and goldenrod, and cornflowers and clover. Deedee disappeared into the flowers—picking bouquets was her favourite game. He could see the shrubs and grasses heave and sway as she moved around. The scent of clover and of dry sweet grass was very keen here, and from the east, over the curved top of the mountain, the wind blew in a steady uneddying stream. Five or six miles off to the southwest he spied the wide intensely grey-white stripe of the river. He heard Deedee cry: "Daddy, Daddy, come and look." He pushed through the coarse grasses and found her.

"Berries," she cried rapturously, "look at all the berries! Can I eat them?" She had found a wild raspberry bush, a thing he hadn't seen since he was six years old. He'd never expected to find one growing in the middle of Montreal.

"Wild raspberries," he said wonderingly, "sure you can pick them, dear; but be careful of the prickles." They were all shades and degrees of ripeness from black to vermilion.

"Ouch," said Deedee, pricking her fingers as she pulled off the berries. She put a handful in her mouth and looked wry.

"Are they bitter?"

"Juicy," she mumbled with her mouth full. A trickle of dark juice ran down her chin.

"Eat some more," he said, "while I try the kite again." She bent absorbedly to the task of hunting them out, and he walked down the road for some distance and then turned to run up towards her. This time he gave the kite plenty of string before he began to move; he ran as hard as he could, panting and handing the string out over his shoulders, burning his fingers as it slid through them. All at once he felt the line pull and pulse as if there were a living thing on the other end and he turned on his heel and watched while the kite danced into the upper air-currents above the treetops and began to soar up and up. He gave it more line and in an instant it pulled high up away from him across the fence, two hundred feet and more above him up over the cemetery where it steadied and hung, bright red in the sunshine. He thought flashingly of the priest saying "it's all a sham," and he knew all at once that the priest was wrong. Deedee came running down to him, laughing with excitement and pleasure and singing joyfully about the gingerbread man, and he knelt in the dusty roadway and put his arms around her, placing her hands on the line between his. They gazed, squinting in the sun, at the flying red thing, and he turned away and saw in the shadow of her cheek and on her lips and chin the dark rich red of the pulp and juice of the crushed raspberries.

FALLINGS FROM US, VANISHINGS

BRANDISHING a cornucopia of daffodils, flowers for Gloria, in his right hand Arthur Merlin crossed the dusky oak-panelled foyer of his apartment building and came into the welcoming sunlit avenue. Grey-green poplars and shining maples leaned encouragingly over him like counselling elder sisters, whispering messages, bough song, bird song, in his responsive ears in an evening of courtship. He sang softly in stop time:

There'll be no one unless that
Someone is you.
I intend to be independently
Blue oo oo oo
Dada da dee dum.

Volkswagens are period pieces, he thought, circa 1954–1958, the sense of period. Thirty years from now Volkswagen *will* look quaint, fixing a colour page or an old movie as exactly in time as an Apperson Jackrabbit does now. If I conserve my Volkswagen and drive it ten more years I'll begin to be a period piece. He slid back the sunroof and rolled away into the sound of cicadas, the little engine grinding like a coffee mill, energetic, valiant.

Up the avenue and around the corner he surprised his favourite antique, a 1929 Oakland Landaulette, all rich brown body and stiff black leather upperworks, owned by a doctor's widow, ghosting home from the drugstore, its timeless driver erect on the mohair cushions. She preserved the car in exquisite running order as a memorial; Arthur had often discussed it with her. Tonight, as every time he saw the car, his fancies and recollections merged in a *Gestalt* that shot him back there when the 1929 Oakland was modish and new. He could be there in imagination in his body, his present age, in 1929, in 1829. My grandmother was born in 1870, he thought, amazed, and could have spoken to men who knew Mozart, it's possible. You can be there. 1929.

My father had a 1929 Essex Challenger, dark blue, with chased imitation silver handles on the inside of the doors, with little window blinds that rolled zipping up and down, with creamy-fringed tassels. It could take Roxborough Road hill in high gear from a standing start. Then he was three dimensionally in the car, his thirty-four-year-old self, the day they started for the cottage at Rouge Hill in the early summer of 1931. The upholstery, a deep-piled dark blue, exhaled puffs of linty smoke when you bounced on it, motes dancing in the shafts of sunlight. If you drew the blinds, a darkness loomed in the back seat. His mother said:

"Stop for gas, Alex!"

His father said to the garage attendant: "Castrol, please, and put the cap on good and tight."

They didn't see him there, thirty-four-year-old ghost from 1961, in the little boy squirming on the back seat. He shrank into the little boy and swelled into himself in his coffee-mill Volkswagen, and there were two of him, four years old and thirty-four.

"Put the cap on good and tight." Alex turned to Margaret. "Did I ever tell you about the man who drank all the liquor?" They nodded their heads and gazed lovingly at each other and (thirty-) four-year-old Arthur looked on, feeling safe and happy.

Five years later they changed the name and called them Essex Terraplanes and then just Terraplanes and at last they stopped making them. They don't even make Hudsons anymore but we were able to keep that car until the war was halfway over. The two of him expanded into three—as multiple as he ever became, even with his sense of period. I was learning to drive our old Essex the day I first saw Mrs. Vere in Westport. It must have been 1942 because I got my driver's licence the next year, in the other car. I might have had the Essex for my own; but it died with sixty thousand miles on the clock the second time around, a bare grey spot that always hurt my eyes on the upholstery in the driver's seat.

We were by the slips when she came along in the Saturday morning sun. The codgers stared behind her and gossiped as she passed, mourning Lieutenant Vere, hero of Pearl Harbor, and commending his widow's fair beauty. Her four-year-old trailed behind her and, Heavens, thought Arthur seeing it, relishing it, the ghost of twenty-three-year-old Gloria was in that toddler, and I couldn't see her. I saw Mrs. Vere, how I saw her in white tennis shorts, mourning behind her, fine gold fuzz on her legs catching the sun. I saw the glint, cowering in my rickety Essex. How she strode, how she put forward her perfect ankles, coming to look at the sunlight on the water. She looked, oh she looked like a girl, like an attainable girl to me at fifteen, and how I loved her as she sauntered along I feel still, all three of us feel, four, fifteen, and thirty-four, comfortably here in my little period piece.

On the other bucket seat the paper cone of flowers moves lazily with the car's motion, wetness from the leaves shining on the leather, tiny rustle of green leaves, flip of the yellow blossoms catching Arthur's eye as he rolls along in June, coming for Gloria, thinking of her marvellous mother at twenty-six. She looked like a co-ed, with that funny authority one's older sister has, that sway compounded of a trifling difference in age and a cloud of otherness, mystery of being a woman. How I adored Mrs. Adam Vere, that golden widow as she said, looking into my Essex: "Where do we swim around here, that's safe for children?" She listened attentively to my knowledgeable counsel.

> Love me or leave me
> And let me be lonely.
> You won't believe me
> But I love you only.

I gaped, I croaked, I blushed:

"At the boating club," I told her, "afternoons I'm on duty as a lifeguard and I'll look after your little girl." I scarcely looked at the toddler out of the corner of my eye, using her as a comic prop, an introduction-arranger, something out of a comic-strip or the opening paragraphs of a *Ladies' Home Journal* story. There are ghosts out of the future, the unborn, as well as the dead from the past. How could I fathom marriageable Gloria, twenty-three, inside a pouting four-year-old? I looked instead at her unmarriageable mother and yearned and Gloria has her revenge.

She turned away and the back of her knees dimpled at me, her thighs like butterscotch, to the edge of her shorts. Fifteen is hell! I shook all the way home and the knob of the gearshift loosened in my hand. And all that summer I bounced baby Gloria through the wavelets at the water's edge, on her stomach, on her back, rolled her yellow red blue white beach ball along the sand and chased it when the wind caught it and she cried, and Mrs. Vere laughed.

"Get it, Arthur, get it!" they commanded together, their voices blending. That ball took off, sailed, spinning along the tops of the ripples, nothing inside to hold it down. I often chased it a quarter of a mile, coming back digging my toes into the beige sand to lie panting beside Mrs. Vere, while Gloria jumped up and down on my sacroiliac.

"Don't jump on Arthur, sweetie, he's winded!" I peeked, pulse racing, through a screen of sand at an expanse of butterscotch flank, and pressed my aching adolescent length flat on the sand's heat.

Pulse, he thought, that's funny. He was assistant circulation director of *Pulse Magazine,* man of a thousand details, and had spent this long June day checking the results of a sample mailing piece which he'd tested in Philadelphia and Boise. They drew a three-percent response in Boise, so he took the figures to the files, digging out the results from a campaign of thirty-second TV spots which he had tried on Cheyenne, the year before. No one in the world knew as much about the circulation of *Pulse* as Arthur Merlin, historian, builder of archives, ranker of green filing cabinets. He loved Gloria best; but next to her he loved documents on circulation figures broken down by region, and third he loved the files of *Pulse.*

Twenty-five years of *Pulse*—it came out first in 1936 with a famous picture of Boulder Dam on the cover, a picture which he had a hundred times affixed to his mailing pieces. His adolescence and young manhood slumbered in the files. Often on a working day, on the excuse that he was seeking promotional material he spent an afternoon at *Pulse Index* where Gloria worked, or with a swash of twenty-six issues from 1938 on his desk, admiring the page layout, studying the changing typefaces, loving the unlined face of Brenda Diana Duff Frazier, the Jimmy Lunceford piece, the "Studebaker Champion $537 F.O.B. Detroit," all the stories in those old issues landmarks of his trip to adulthood, documents as familiar to him as MS. c (Cotton Otho A. 6) to some brother scholar.

He stopped for a red light and hoped that they would arrive at the beach before the sunshine died. He wanted to see Gloria illuminated by the sunset on this, nearly the longest, day of the year. Lately she had been petulant and pouty which made him think of her behaviour at the age of four. The child is mother to the woman, he reflected as he crossed the intersection, I suppose she'll always be a pouty one. When she had come to him looking for work she'd pouted.

"School's out forever," she said dolefully, "nothing will be the same."

"You can't go to school indefinitely, Gloria," he told her. "I'll help you find a nice job, and you can have some fun in New York. Most girls like to live in New York for a while before they get married."

"I'm not 'most girls.'"

"You're certainly not average," he said, laughing beyond hilarity, "No, definitely not average." He had never really seen her before; he had this troublesome treble vision; but he saw her now and she was very good. "How old are you now, Gloria?" he asked, avuncular, disinterested, beginning to tremble.

"I'm twenty-two, I guess."

"I guess?"

"I never think of it. Are you going to give me a job?"

"I don't give jobs but the company certainly will." On his recommendation they put her to work on the *Index* and he saw her all the time. All day she read stories from the files, and examined yellowing pictures, and prepared case histories; the pictures puzzled her.

"You mean *that's* Frank Sinatra? But he looks young."

Arthur stared at her in amusement. "Frank Sinatra *is* young."

"He's a foolish bald old man."

"Whom do you consider young, for goodness' sake?"

"Any girl whose bust hasn't developed."

"How do you tell about boys?"

"There isn't any decent way," she said, laughing.

So he was afraid to ask her how old she thought him. He hadn't had his real life yet, none of it, he told himself. All his college classmates were settled into the beginnings of middle age, with wives and a plethora of children. Of all his generation, he thought, only a few like himself could sometimes feel like children. I'm young, he swore earnestly, I'm a baby. He picked up the picture of Sinatra and studied it, the floppy necktie, the luxuriant curls, the hollow cheeks, the swaying back and forth with the microphone clutched in both hands. It must be from the story on Frank's first date at the Paramount, 1942 perhaps, certainly no earlier than 1941. Gloria would have been three years old, and should remember the excitement.

"He was a swoon-crooner, Gloria," he said kindly, "surely you remember the phrase."

"A swoon-crooner?" He might as well have said a doughboy, a wise-guy, a tough egg, she didn't understand the language. "Your crowd must have the equivalent, Paul Anka perhaps or Fabian," he hazarded.

"I don't have a crowd," she said positively.

He wanted to shake her but said instead: "Come to the beach with me tonight?" He imagined beach balls yellow red blue white rolling along far stretches of beige sand.

"I love the beach," she said simply, and he took it for assent.

As he handed her the daffodil and watched her bury her face in the petals, he checked his watch and guessed that there were almost two hours of sunlight left. It was a dying sunlight though, a seven-thirty slant of the beams which traced the flowers on the beach robe she wore, and the ties on her sandals. At least she's ready to leave, he realized, we may not get into the water but we can stretch out together on the sand for maybe an hour. The daffodil girl, the primavera.

"Where did you get these, so late in the season?"

"I had them refrigerated months ago, just for you," he claimed extravagantly but truthfully. He had said to the florist: "I want an assured supply of daffodils, I don't care what it costs. Keep them in cold storage for me and I'll pay extra." He thought he stood to win or lose on daffodils, her favourite flower. If he kept her like spring, she might never think of the eleven years' difference in their ages. I'm a child, I'm young, young, he reflected, watching her put them carefully in water, afraid to hurry her. Don't make her think of time, he advised himself, and other voices in his mind supported the strategy, never nudge her out of the glorious present. Don't give her time to think about time. So he waited patiently until she pulled her beachrobe modestly around her and started for the door. He opened it quickly, rang for the elevator with sharp precision, started the car with unobtrusive speed, and hastened across the graceful old town towards the Boating Club, zipped into the parking area, plucked a beach-basket from the back seat, and felt an urgent joy. It would not be dark until nine thirty, lots of time, hours, hours.

"Start down the beach and find a place to sit," he commanded, feeling his excitement stir, "I'll get out of my clothes and catch up to you." He trotted towards the clubhouse and paused at the door to watch her make her lovely way along the beach, no longer beige, the sand, but a darker shadowy hue spreading as the light changed and the shadows lengthened. At every second stride she dug her toes in the sand and kicked out like a colt. The onshore breeze took her robe and filled it like a pregnant sail as she shook out her hair, and then it cradled every yellow lock and made them dance. He broke all records for changing into swimming trunks and chased her down the strip of sand.

A dozen yards from where she halted at their favourite spot, he stood still and watched. Her back was to him as she bent and loosened her sandals, kicking them off. Then she straightened and slipped off her flowery robe, stood erect on her bare toes, scrunching them into the sand for balance, stretching her arms above her head, looking for a bizarre instant like a piece of radiator sculpture. Then her form seemed to zoom in on him, taking his sight, and she was so perfectly *there, so present,* that his heart paused and his throat constricted with his press of feelings. Gazing, he recognized her power and her everlasting triumph, and how it was that the aureole, the haze of recollection in which he wrapped her appearance when he imagined her, was not around her now—the glory was in her. She pressed outwards against the air, filling out her lines.

"She's only a pretty girl in a bathing suit," he told himself, to make his head stop spinning. As he came up to her he made a commonplace remark about the sea. "The moving waters at their priest-like task of pure ablution," he said.

"It's a lot of water," she said inhaling.

"Do you know," he said, a little desperately, "that water connects everything? It's the only element that goes everywhere. This same water washes the shores of the Ganges, the floes in Franklin's Land."

"It's Long Island Sound," she said, looking away, "it comes out of the tap in my bathtub."

"Why do you come to the beach at all?"

"To get out into the air. The beach makes me feel good, I like to get my clothes off. I wish they allowed bikinis at the club."

"They don't forbid them."

"They don't allow them. I know what they think."

He pounced on it. "How do you know?" The trivial question suddenly assumed importance in his eyes. How could she know? How could she ever grasp a tradition or a moral convention? How do these people manage to live, he wondered, how do they make their calculations?

"I don't see anybody else wearing one," she said defensively.

"Why let that stop you?"

"Don't quiz me," she said impatiently, "I'll wear one when I see somebody else wear one."

"Give me the ocular proof," he said, "unless I put my hand in the wound, unless I see the nails, I will not believe." He looked at her but she wouldn't look back. "Blessed are they," he said gently, "who have not seen and yet believe."

"Why can't you be content with me as I am?" she complained. "Instead of puzzling yourself with all that stuff. I came with you, didn't I?"

"I'm glad you did," he said, "and thank you." He returned to the charge. "Don't you feel anything about the ocean, about the water? Think of all the fish in the sea, of all the ships, the treasure. There's supposed to be a galleon lying somewhere off Montauk, blown a thousand miles off its course by freakish gales. And over there," he gestured widely, "lies the *Andrea Doria* with millions of dollars' worth of stuff inside, just out of reach, just too far down."

"Hundreds of people in her," she said, "floating at the portholes, knocking at the glass trying to get out, their hair washing behind them. Do you know where my father is?"

He ought to have remembered, he had remembered, and perhaps that was why they were where they were.

"He's still in the *Arizona*," she said in a shaking voice, "he's down there with hundreds of other men who didn't get out. I've been to Pearl Harbor, you know, and I've seen it. The masts are sticking out of the water and the men are still inside; they've been there twenty years. My father was younger than you are when he drowned. To hell with the moving waters at their priest-like task. They've melted my father's flesh—what do you suppose he looks like now?"

"Forget what I said!"

"How did you hear the news about my mother, Arthur, did you hear it the way I heard it? They called me at the dormitory, I was asleep, and told me that I wasn't going to see her again. She was all smashed to pieces, you know. There were bits of the car along the Parkway for half a mile. They didn't open the coffin, and I hadn't seen her for a month before the accident. She just disappeared; there was nothing left for me. I wasn't born without a memory, Arthur, I just don't want to remember."

"Let me tell you something," he said, "we all become orphans in time. My father died late last year but before that my world was just what you make yours now, static. Things went along and never changed from year to year. Everybody was always there when I went home, the same books and pictures, and the litter of papers maybe a little thicker every spring. Then my father died, and I thought it would all change, that the house would be empty and my mother all at once shrivelled and old."

"And it was!" she positively guessed.

"Not in the least," he denied, "not at all. My mother looks younger every day and my father advises me constantly. He's closer to me than ever. I'm not a superstitious man, Gloria." She laughed. "I'm not superstitious but I can hear him talking to me, telling me how to handle things. It isn't like a voice, it's a … I don't know what it is … it's a tendency, a feeling. I know what to do, because that's what he would have done. It's as though his intelligence were in my own, like a habit."

"That's a hangover from childhood."

"No. It's as if there were another mind in mine."

"You're simply highly suggestible."

"Cut it out," he said, "you have these flashes too, admit it."

"I'll never have them," she said, "I only see what's there."

He saw her mother over again. He had seen her closer to death than Gloria had, the weekend she died, and she had looked as though neither time nor death could ever touch her. At thirty-five she looked exactly as she had looked twenty years ago on this same beach, fresh, unlined, immortal. And over a Saturday to Monday she had disintegrated, to be redistributed along the universe like the moving waters. He shivered. Twilight is coming, he thought.

They were sitting with their backs to a ledge of rock four or five feet high, which ran the length of the beach and some days acted as a windbreak. If you lay down near the ledge, the air was completely still, all its currents diverted and passing over you. You could bake under the ledge in unadulterated sunlight on days when it was downright cool in less sheltered spots. Tonight, in the declination of the sun, the ledge threw a shadow towards them which lengthened as they lay there. Already their bodies lay in it to the waist, and in a few minutes it would cover them up. It was cold in the shadow and soon they both shivered.

"It's too cold to go in," said Gloria, musing.

The sun sat on the edge of the world and to the east the moon was an unimportant shred of cotton batting. Way way out on the sound a single sail hovered, almost seemed to disappear, was there again. Underneath them the sand grew black and lost its daylight warmth.

I never had any father, thought Gloria, it's useless to have a father who dies before you're three years old. I can't remember him. I don't know what he looked like. There was, of course, that formal black-and-white photograph which Mother carried around for years, that stranger with an enormous officer's cap. He must have had a huge head, to wear such a cap. Black tie, black shoulders, white shirt, white teeth. The picture was too matte; there were no glosses, no highlights. When you looked at it closely, it stopped being a face and became a flat arrangement of masses in black and white, and that was Father. *Arrangement in black and white.* Like Whistler's mother, and I can see what Whistler meant. Nothing human was in that picture. Mother, with her mind's inventive eye, could see Adam Vere whom she loved, round and fleshed out, in the harmonies of black and white. All I could see were masses and edges. She looked at the water and the sky and observed the same techniques. Nature imitates Matisse, she thought. He was her favourite painter and almost the only one she knew of.

What I see are flat patches of colour. Three dimensions are a binocular trick of the eye, the chance result of having two eyes instead of one or three. If I had a single eye, the world would be a huge Matisse, flat patches of unrelated colour lying next to one another. She began to feel cold and to reassure herself she looked down, pressing her chin down almost against her collarbone, and stared at the length of her body stretched in an unfamiliar perspective in front of her. Her body looked flat but she knew that it wasn't. I'm not flat, she felt happily, I'm round but I can't see it. I see planes and shadows. I *feel* round.

She put her hands on either side of her in the cold sand and rocked gently from side to side in a movement of dazzlingly innocent sensuality. I *feel* that my hips are soft and round, she realized. I've never seen them. If I shake out my hair my scalp feels good, but I've never seen the top of my head. I only feel that it's here along with the rest of me.

She closed the useless eyes and inhaled, feeling herself from the ends of her hair to her toes. She sensed herself being here. She was simply here with a full dark warm heaviness in her middle that grew cooler towards fingers and toes and scalp. She filled her lungs with cool twilight air and felt it grow warm inside her. She could hear Arthur scratching in the sand for pebbles; he picked them up one at a time and launched them towards the water. Some must have fallen in the sand;

they made no sound; others fell with a plopping noise into wet sand and water at the very edge; a few plinked into deep water. Her weight on her hands made the sand beneath grow harder and harder like a soft pillow beneath an insomniac's head. If she leaned on her hands much longer, she would be able to feel each individual resistant speck of sand pressing upwards against her palms.

The sun had gone down while her eyes were shut. The sea breezes began to flag, grew gentler, licked at her toes with weakening tongues and finally were still.

After the sun goes down on the beach, as the earth loses its daytime heat, the water for a little while retaining some warmth, the air currents begin to shift. The onshore breeze flags and stops; in a few moments the offshore breeze begins. But there is always a moment of calm at the point of reversal. The sand stops moving; the water flattens and is silent; nothing and nobody moves the few grasses and weeds that grow in the sand. The soul of the world turns in on itself and is quiet, just before the dark.

In this moment of temporary stillness, in herself, Gloria felt more a woman than she ever had before. I feel what I am, she realized, with an intense joy. I can taste myself being me. I'm this woman. No, that's wrong. I'm me. No. I. I. I. I. There isn't any way to say it. She fell silent in her thoughts, content to exist.

When the offshore breeze began she found herself wondering what it was like to be a man, though she knew she didn't care for the idea. She looked slyly at Arthur, lying disappointedly beside her, and wondered how it felt to be inside his mind, as he said his father was.

I want your love,
I don't want to borrow,
To have it today,
To give back tomorrow.

He had been whistling that song when he came to fetch her, a song that suited him. If there were two people, and possibly a great many more, congregated in his head, how could she possibly single out one of them, the nominal real he, to love? If she were to love him, as he wanted her to, and as she longed to, it would have to be the only genuine Arthur Merlin in captivity whom she loved. She didn't want that crowd of others along for the ride no matter who they were, his father, her mother. She couldn't compete for his attentions with a host of spirits, and least of all with the spirit of her mother.

He stood up and walked to the edge of the water, putting a toe forward to test the temperature. Then he recoiled.

"When the sun goes down," he exclaimed, "it's impossible. Do you want me to take you home?"

"We've only just come!"

"We've been here over an hour," he said, "it's nearly nine-thirty." She wished he weren't so acutely conscious of the passage of time. It hadn't touched him. She scrutinized his legs and arms and waist as he walked awkwardly back across the sand. He might be any age, she thought. Except for an almost invisible accretion of fat over his kidneys, he looked like a boy her own age. He's young, she realized with surprise. He was part of her present; he had always been around but then so had she. She wished that he would stop mumbling and stumbling and tell her that he loved her. She was sure that he did. What else could all the fussing be about? And he was as good a man as she'd ever known, and part of her scene, her life. Of course she would love him, if only he would come out towards her instead of manufacturing these smoke-screens.

"Do you remember how you used to bounce up and down on my back?"

A crazy notion. "On your back? When?"

"When you were small."

"Oh, for God's sake, Arthur, I'm not small now. Do you take me around because, once upon a time, I was small?

I'm a grown woman. Why don't you treat me as one?"

He was gathering up towels and sandals and stuffing them in the basket. He knelt on his knees beside her and his kneecap touched her thigh. It felt cold. Put your arms around me, she thought, there's nobody here to see, give me a kiss and then we'll have something to go on. But he lingered and did nothing, kneeling and looking at her. What could she do, she wasn't a man.

"It isn't right," she said, "to love a girl because of what she was when she was small." But he was gone again, gone back inside, she could tell from his eyes. They glazed and grew opaque as they always did when he was thinking of something else. She wanted to slap him to bring him out of it.

"Look," he said, "I'm not just a hundred and seventy-five pounds of flesh and bone dropped out of nowhere into the twentieth of June. I've a whole life behind me that I love and that I wouldn't want to lose. I'm every thing that I've ever been, I'm what's happened to me, not what's happening this instant, not just that."

"If I prick you with a pin, you'll bleed."

"That's not me, that's not me. You think that anything that happened more than a year ago simply doesn't exist."

"Well, it doesn't," she said deliberately.

It made him groan. "You can't live like that," he declared. "Have you no respect for the past? What about your parents?"

Very patiently she began to explain things to him. "I loved them when they were here. But they aren't here any more. They're dead, Arthur, they're gone. I don't believe in ghosts." It was quite dark on the beach; it was time to go.

"Gloria, Gloria," he moaned.

"Oh, God," she ejaculated, "didn't you bring me here tonight to tell me that you love me and that you want me to love you? Wasn't that what you meant to do?"

He said nothing.

"I know it was," she said. "I'm certain of it, and I'm proud. It means something to a woman, when a man tells her he loves her and wants her. And, don't you see, here I am. I'm all right here! Oh, you poor dear idiot, can't you see how much I'm here? I'm what they call a beautiful girl, a hundred and twenty pounds of flesh and bone dropped from heaven, not from nowhere. I bloom, can't you see? Damn you, Arthur, I'm packed full of sensation, I ache with it, you ... you exorcist! Just come and get me!"

"It's wonderful," he said, stuttering slightly, "it's unbelievable!"

"What's unbelievable?" She had a horrid presentiment of what it might be.

"You're the heiress of every past beauty," he said exultantly. "I've never seen anything like it. You're your mother over again perfectly, to the last detail, but more than that, you're surrounded by the past. The way you cock your head, your gestures, your words, everything that you do is fixed by the tradition, and that's what makes you a beauty. Your inheritance."

"Damn it," she swore, meaning it, "are you in love with me or with my mother?"

"With all of you, with the whole great gang!"

"They're dead," she shouted, "they're underground. You!" She felt a physical revulsion. "You're haunted! You're a ghost-ridden man, you're a horror!" She wanted to run. "I don't know where you get to, when you disappear inside yourself, but you won't come out, oh, you'll never come out." She turned and strode along the beach towards the car.

He watched her go; and as she began to merge with the twilight and the firm outline of her figure wavered, she seemed to him to be one, only one, of a long file of daffodil girls marching out of the past and into the future, girls he'd read about in story books, girls he'd known, girls he hoped still to meet some day. Multitudes forever young, beautiful golden girls long dead and others unborn, the descending heirs of Eve, all going out of the light through the twilight and into the dark. Away up the beach her form quivered in his sight, and then his eyes lost her and he was standing alone in a sandy place. I'd rather be lonely, he thought.

I'd rather be lonely
Than happy with somebody new.

SILVER BUGLES,
CYMBALS,
GOLDEN SILKS

WHEN I was a child of six, in the summer of 1934, my parents sent me to a camp on the south shore of Lake Simcoe, at the upper end of the Trent Canal system, wonderful trolling and cruising waters in those days, and nowadays just about fished out. The camp was run by a religious community of men, teaching Brothers who also conducted several Toronto schools, and I remember seeing their brochure around the house for several days before my agonized and unwilling departure. It quoted Whittier, as I recall:

> *Health that mocks the doctor's rules,*
> *Knowledge never learned in schools.*

There was a certain amount of truth in the second line. There were little line drawings in a green ink, in this brochure, of boys fishing, diving, running races, gashing their knees on rocks, the whole myth, overnight hikes, nature lore. I was still practically an infant. I hadn't gone to nursery school—it wasn't the fashion in those days—or to kindergarten, as the Catholic School System in the city didn't provide them. So I was still an inhabitant of the warm intimate world of post-babyhood, defined by the length of one's block. I was allowed to cross streets, but I wasn't venturesome about it. I suppose that my parents wanted to get me out of the house for a summer, a motive I would have questioned then, with the fierce possessiveness of the young child, but which I can fully appreciate now that I've two of my own.

The camp seemed enormous to me that first season. Last summer I drove past it, and you wouldn't believe how small and shrunken it seemed. In 1934 it seemed limitless and wild, the woods growing right up behind the straggling line of tents inhabited by the older campers—the littlest kids slept in neat wooden cabins and were very grateful for the added touch of civilization; it meant something to graduate into a row of tents.

In front of the Administration Building stood a tall flagpole, where a flag-raising ceremony was enacted each morning, and where two buglers blew Retreat at sundown. I had never heard the *retreat* call before, and I haven't heard it blown for fifteen years, but I can still whistle it note for note.

Two different boys served as duty-buglers each week. I didn't understand how it was, having learned nothing of the great world as yet, that so many of the older boys at the camp could play this beguiling instrument, on which I longed to be able to execute myself. After I had been there two weeks my parents drove up for the weekend to see how I was getting along, and I can see now that they had been as affected by my absence as I had been by theirs. I had missed them unutterably, though in different ways, my slim pretty mother with her comfortable big French-Canadian nose, her "proboscis" she called it, a funny word which always made me gurgle when she said it, and my handsome excitable father whom I adored and whom I longed to understand. He made a lot of remarks which I knew must be very funny because my mother laughed and laughed at them, and I wished I knew what was funny in what he said. I found out later on: he had a desperate streak of defensive irony. He was a man of position but no education, and it strained him dreadfully to hide this.

I asked them about all these buglers. "Why can Paul and Harold Phelan, and all the Juniors and Seniors, play the bugle? Do you think I could play the bugle some time?"

It happened unluckily that the Phelan boys were the sons of a dentist in our parish whom my father particularly despised for his jumped-up ways. He raised an expressive eyebrow at my mother, as one who regrets an ill-considered action.

"Bog-Irish!" he exclaimed. It was a favourite phrase for he was a man of many prejudices, none of them violent but all irritating to him. He also disliked French-Canadians, which made things difficult with his in-laws, who all had names like Esdras, Telesphore, Onesime, Eugenie, and the like. My mother smiled at him shushingly.

"They're all in the Band," she said, and it was the first time I ever heard about the Band, the famous Oakdale Boys' Band, an organization whose structure was to preoccupy me for a dozen years. The Brothers conducted parish schools in Toronto but also, and pre-eminently, a private high school, Oakdale, "in a park in the centre of the city" as their advertisements had it. It was an institution that one paid to attend which in those Depression years meant that it was exclusive, if only in the sense that you had to be employed to send your sons there. The chief ornament of Oakdale was its famous hundred-piece drum and bugle Band which took part in all the major Toronto parades, the Garrison Parade in June, the Armistice Day Parade, the Argonauts' half-time shows, and ever so many more. The Band travelled all over the province making paid appearances at religious and civil functions. I had never heard of it before and at six years had no suspicion that such marvellous institutions even existed.

"Perhaps you'll go to Oakdale and be in the band," said my mother, off the end of her tongue, making my father glance at her in some perturbation. He didn't say it in front of me but he was likely thinking "yes, and perhaps you won't."

But my fate was sealed, and the sealing was confirmed on Dominion Day weekend when, to my intense gratification, the dozen or more boys at camp who were buglers, and another dozen who were drummers, suddenly blossomed forth early in the morning in gorgeous uniforms, a dress of an absolutely inconceivable splendour. They wore navy blue officers' caps with gold metal cap-badges and white naval cap covers, white gloves, navy blue high-necked tunics with brass buttons, and red, white, and green trimmings at the wrist, and gold-trimmed collars, a golden rope-lanyard across the chest and around the left shoulder, navy blue trousers with a rich gold stripe at the seam and, most bewitching of all, long navy blue capes fastened around the neck and depending in soft folds below the waist.

These capes were lined with golden silk, and the most distinctive mark of the Band uniform was the bright glitter of the silk. It was regimental to make three precise folds in the cape, so that two broad bands of gold hung from the shoulders to the waist. I had never been so captivated in my life and at this revelation would willingly have exchanged my home, my cozy family life, my brother and sister, for the chance to live with these marvellous boys and dress like that. We soon heard that the rest of the Band would appear in the early afternoon for the patriotic ceremonies.

A few of the biggest boys wore *medals*.

At one-thirty three fat old buses appeared at the gates with seventy other bandsmen, the two Bandmasters, Mr. James and Mr. Thompson, the bass drums and tenor drums, and wonder of wonders the mascot, a boy smaller than myself though older, named Jimmy Phillips, who marched in front of the bandmasters and swung a small baton. I have never since seen anything to compare with it for glitter.

Jimmy Phillips was the son of a man who owned a house on the lowest corner of the Oakdale property in Toronto. He had in some way been a benefactor of the school and still lived in the house on the grounds with his family, and his boy was the Band mascot until he outgrew the job. I don't know just what Mr. Phillips' connection with the Brothers was, but it was certainly a matter of money and/or property. And because of it, Jimmy Phillips marched in front of the Band and carried a silver baton ... it was my first faint intimation of the uses of influence and wealth.

When he grew out of the job, he was succeeded by Fred Crawley, the son of a wealthy Catholic stockbroker whose benefactions to the school must have been indeed munificent because Fred wore a special white and gold uniform (which the Phillips' boy hadn't) and held the post of mascot long after he had ceased to be as wonderfully small (isn't he *darling*!) as a mascot should be. At last he was succeeded by the Bandmaster's son, little Billy Thompson, who lasted out my tenure with the Band. This time, the Brothers had to pay for the white and gold mascot's uniform.

That first wonderful day I saw the Band, wheeling and counter-marching in intricate patterns in front of the Administration Building, I noticed many things. For example, the two Bandmasters were of slightly unequal rank. Mr. James was Drum-Major, and Mr. Thompson was merely Sergeant-Major, and the former's gold was shinier and less brassy. There didn't seem to be any animosity or competition between them.

I noticed as well that there were some strutting little boys, scarcely bigger than myself, marching in the cymbal section. I call it the cymbal section, but the line of eight included three awfully small boys who played triangles. As far as I could tell, playing the triangle demanded no musical skill beyond the ability to keep time with a striker, loud enough to be heard in the uproar. I decided right then and there that as soon as I should be sent to Oakdale I would try out for the triangle.

It's singular how sharply the child's mind will calculate. I could foretell at six a course of action I would follow exactly over four years later; and in the interval I forgot not one detail of my plan.

At ten years, having completed the sixth grade, I was finally allowed to quit parochial school and begin at Oakdale. This was a considerable step for my parents to take, because it implied seven years of fees for me, and the like for my brother later on. In 1938 Toronto was by no means fully recovered from the Depression. The parish schools and the public high schools were free whereas my father had to pay for me to go to Oakdale. The fee wasn't outrageous but it was something, and as my father's affairs were at this time not uninvolved, it was a damned decent thing for him to do. To tell the truth, he couldn't afford it, then or long after, but he tried his best to manage the thing gracefully.

So I went, and on one of the first of a series of tender sleepy fall days, hardly fall at all, the soft gold end of September, a meeting for Band recruits was announced for after school in the Cafeteria. I was there with bells on, already clutching my triangle in rapt anticipation. The senior NCO in regular school attendance, a full-grown man of nineteen, spoke briefly. That was Sergeant-Drummer Johnny Delancey, killed two years afterwards in a burning Wellington bomber, over the railway yards at Hamburg. He spoke of the Band's traditions and its reputation.

"You won't see any of us with ten medals on our tunics," he said, with a certain heat. He had a posthumous DFC later on, the only medal he ever won. He was making a dig at the Saint Ursula's Boys' Band, also conducted by the Brothers at a parish school way downtown in a slum district. Saint Ursula's school went through the tenth grade, so they were able to maintain a band almost as big as ours, and there was a sharp rivalry between us. Saint Ursula's went each year to the Band Competition at Waterloo, Ontario, and every year they won their class competition, so that everyone in their outfit had a medal for every year he'd been in the competition.

The Oakdale Band disdained the competition as a rather plebeian thing. Only those very senior NCOs who had been awarded an Efficiency Medal at the annual inspection of the Band and Cadet Corps wore anything on their chests. We Oakdale bandsmen gave out that we were above competition, and we regarded the Saint Ursula's medals as an unseemly display, or at least we were tacitly encouraged so to regard them. A medal in our Band meant something. Johnny Delancey never won one.

"You'll find me conducting practices after school," said Johnny Delancey, "but 'Tommy' Thompson runs the Band, and don't ever forget it. He's the best drum-major in Canada, he used to play with a British Army Band, and everybody at the Armouries—even the Queen's Own and the Army Service Corps—wants him. But he's staying right here and we want you to appreciate him."

I pondered this. There had been *two* Bandmasters up at camp. Where was the other one?

"Now we'll take your names and the instruments you mean to learn. We need some tall fellows for the tenor drums. You there, you're big enough." He pointed at a gangling boy near me, named George Rait.

"I was going to try out for the bugles."

"Tenor drums," said Johnny Delancey peremptorily, determining forever the shape of George Rait's Band career. "Corporal McGarry will take that side of the room and I'll take this." They began to move along the lines of recruits. I was way down at the end, and I grew more and more overawed as big Ted McGarry came nearer. A corporal! Finally he looked down at me and smiled.

"What would you like to be, sonny, mascot?"

"No," I said indignantly. After all, I was ten, and going into Junior Fourth (Grade Seven as it is now) and I couldn't quite allow "sonny."

"I want to try out for the triangles," I said, abashed but outspoken, the way I've always been.

Ted McGarry was very decent. "Triangles it is!" he said, writing down my name. "One of the most important sections in the Band." He passed on to the end of the line. Afterwards they announced the hours of the recruit practices, telling us that we would have to learn our instruments, how to march, the meaning of the various commands, and how to care for a uniform, before we were accepted. Those who didn't cooperate with their instructors, and those who couldn't maintain a decent standard of drill, would be rejected and would have to join the Cadet Corps. Then they let us go and I ran all the way home to tell my mother.

Toronto is not a beautifully built city by and large, though you can find good-looking buildings if you know where to look. But the natural situation of the city is attractive, the long gentle slope of the hill rising off the lake. And the light can be superb, especially in the spring and fall, a clear but oddly smoky light softening and enriching the raw green of spring and especially grateful to the mellow browns and yellows of early fall. All through late September and early October of that year the weather held on beautifully, the air soft and clear, and the lovely Toronto light—something nobody in the city ever talks about, as though they hadn't noticed it or took it for granted or were afraid to praise lest it should disappear— the faintly smoky hazy yellow light ran on and on as we little kids drilled and practiced our rhythmic noises on the campus, under the direction of the junior NCOs.

Just before Armistice Day we were told whether or not we would be accepted, so that the successful candidates might march in the big memorial parade to the Cenotaph. One Friday afternoon we were admitted to the Bandroom, a cubbyhole on the ground floor of the Cafeteria, where the sixty-four bugles could be racked up line on line in a glass case, to draw our uniform issue. Brother Willibald was there, the teacher in charge of Band activities, and he presided as chief outfitter as one by one we were herded in and matched to tunics and trousers and, best of all, our capes. None of the uniforms was quite new and the gold on some of the capes was a little greenish when you saw it close to; but if anybody noticed it, nobody said anything, we were all too excited.

They had a little trouble fitting me, I was small for my age and for a moment I was terrified that I might be turned down. But kind Brother Willibald, seeing my desperation, rummaged at the very back of the closet and came out with an old discarded uniform of Jimmy Phillips, the ex-mascot.

"Have your mother adjust the cuffs," he advised, "and be sure you have the whole uniform cleaned and pressed before Armistice Day." I nodded mutely, frozen with excitement. "Are you sure you know how to clean your buttons?" I nodded again, afraid that at the last minute he might change his mind and not give me the uniform. But then he smiled and handed it to me, and told me to pick a triangle and striker off the rack. I did as he said and left the Bandroom as quickly as I could for fear somebody might take it into his head to shout after me, "You're too small!" I was always hearing that.

But no one did, and in common with the other recruits I appeared at band practice the following Wednesday night for our first formal practice with the Band. When the weather was clement we practised outdoors on the lower campus, and the sound of the music could be heard rolling across the city a good three miles and more. After I left the Band years later, when I was living down on Sussex Avenue, over two miles from the school, I used to hear the music of the evening practices as clearly as if it were coming from the next room. God only knows what the apartment dwellers next to the parade ground thought of these practices, for the music was indeed cacophonous; they made constant efforts to have them stopped, or at least muted in some degree, but nothing ever came of it.

As it was now early November and the yellow light had gone blandly grey, the late fall rains setting in, we practised that night upstairs in the Cafeteria, the tables and chairs shoved to the wall, and you can imagine the impression made upon the nerves of the recruits by the noise of thirty-two snare drums, eight tenor drums, two bass drums, sixty-four bugles, and eight cymbals and triangles. It was Homeric in scope, at least as far as volume was concerned; musically it was constricted. We were then using the conventional British Army brass bugle on which an ordinary bugler could produce five notes, or if he were better than average, six. To these bugles could be fitted a "crook" which changed the key of the instrument by lengthening the air column. Another four to six notes could be produced with the crook, in the key of the dominant, and these ten to twelve notes constituted the whole musical range of the Band, the drums and percussion being tuned to no key. And yet we had a repertoire at that time of over sixty marches from the simplest, "Cry Baby," to a pretty jazzy number called "Susan Jane," which Mr. Thompson had just put into the book, and which we supposed him to have composed himself. As a matter of fact he hadn't for he got his new material out of British Army manuals, or by attending other band practices at the Armouries, but we didn't know this and we regarded him as an accomplished musician and composer. He used to teach us new marches by humming them to us, first the open and then the crook parts:

> Dee-dickety-dee, dee-dee, dee-dee
> Dee-dickety-dickety-dee, dee-dee.

If there were any special effects for the drums he would illustrate them until the N.C.O.s caught on; then they taught them to the other drummers in the afternoon. Our repertoire seemed almost illimitable to us, but to the uninstructed listener it must have seemed as though we were always playing the same tune, just as Corelli, Torelli, Boyce, Vivaldi and Handel sound alike to the ignorant.

"Tommy" Thompson—the very senior NCOs called him "Tommy" but to the rest of us he was always "Mr. Thompson"—was a remarkable man in his way, though not a musician. He had formerly been second-in-command with the rank of Sergeant-Major, and people sometimes forgot and referred to him as "Sergeant-Major Thompson." The Brothers sometimes did this, whether accidentally or to keep him in his place I'm not certain. But his former superior, Drum-Major James, had quarrelled with the Brothers of Oakdale in some obscure way, and had left the Oakdale Band and gone over to Saint Ursula's where he now fed the flames of his resentment by attempting to bring the Saint Ursula's Band to the same pitch of reputation and excellence as that of his former command. When I found out about this it explained much of the attitude towards Saint Ursula's of the older boys and men (there were some grown men) in our outfit. It was a romantic feud and conflict of loyalties which impressed me powerfully.

Mr. Thompson was at this time securely in the saddle at Oakdale. In fact he was one of the most universally liked and respected men I've ever known. I guess he was then about thirty-eight, he must have been the same age as the century or thereabouts, because he had been a bandsman with the rank of Boy at the outbreak of the first war. He had served right through it, three years as a drummer and the last year-and-a-half as an infantryman. He was very, very short, not more than five feet one or two, but he didn't seem small because he had a solid square head and a big chest and a perfect, very striking, military carriage, shoulders well back, chest up and out. One never thought of him as small; I considered him enormous during my first years in the Band. He had a firm tanned red impassive face, and neatly clipped brown hair beginning to grizzle. Looking back, I would guess that he was not a highly intelligent man but he was purposeful and disciplined and so got by, which is all anybody can hope for.

In his other, less romantic, daytime life he was a salesman for Canada Packers, a moderate to good one but not the best or most productive. Away from the Band he had a pleasing natural diffidence that would have held down his sales. He was economical; the year I joined the Band he bought a new car, a compact Willys sedan, and he maintained this car superbly and was still driving it a decade later. Once a year without fee the Band put on a demonstration at the main Canada Packers warehouse out past St. Clair and Keele Street, in a sort of plaza bounded by loading platforms and railway sidings and dominated by a monumental stench. All the employees and, I suppose, some of the managers, maybe even J.S. McLean himself, used to watch leaning out of windows. It must have proved annually to his superiors that there were places where Mr. Thompson too was admired and obeyed without question. His uniform was always particularly regimental on these occasions.

He was buying a home in one of those Toronto districts where lower middle-class English people used to congregate. It might have been in lower Parkdale, or a few blocks west of Dufferin north of Bloor. But in fact, as I remember, his house was on Belsize Drive or one of the shorter streets parallel to it between Mount Pleasant and Yonge. Could it have been Davisville? No. Too much traffic, and he would have lived on a quiet street and a modest one. It was one of those five-room brick houses with a veranda and a wooden railing painted white, with Gothic cutouts in it, the veranda floor painted a sturdy battleship grey. There were shrubs and geraniums in front of the veranda and a big maple tree and a neat cement walk. We used to ride past his house on our bikes on Saturdays; it made us oddly confident to know that he lived there.

Mr. Thompson had at this time a great and overmastering ambition. He wanted to obtain new instruments for the Band and had been after the Brothers to buy them. Our old bugles, dating from before the war, were full of dents which impaired their tone. And the drums, though impressive in appearance, were the type which you tighten by adjusting ropes around the side of the shell. They were old and the ropes would not stay taut, which caused a lot of broken drumheads.

The Brothers were most reluctant to spend the several thousand dollars needful for the new equipment, and were looking around quietly for somebody to donate it to them. The high spot of my first few months with the Band was the evening at practice just before Christmas when Brother Willibald made a great announcement. The well-known public figure Senator Frank J. Mulhearne had agreed to donate half the purchase price if the Band itself would contribute the remainder from the earnings of its engagements. There was much cheering and noise and Mr. Thompson's face was a picture of joy and delight. Band outfitters' catalogues were passed around for us to stare at and of course the proposition was accepted by unanimous vote and the senator's generous offer taken up.

The new instruments were months and months coming from England. One of the major department stores jobbed the order. I don't remember whether it was Eaton's or Simpson's, but I have the feeling that it was the latter. During January and February of 1939, an individual picture was taken of each bandsman in his uniform with his instrument, and then these pictures were hand tinted and cut out and mounted on little stands, providing an entire miniature band. When the instruments were at last delivered, the department store set up an enormous window display, with a dummy bugler in full sergeant's uniform, pyramids of the new drums, great sweeping files of the silver bugles, their bells plated with fine gold, the regimental colours of the Oakdale Cadet Corps and Band,

and in the centre the cutout miniature Band in the act of executing a right wheel, so that each bandsman was plainly visible. The display was featured repeatedly in newspaper advertisements and was instrumental in obtaining the publicity which decided the Brothers to accept an engagement at the New York World's Fair, just about to open for its first season in Flushing Meadows.

The New York trip, which we actually took with huge success, was the second great event of my first year. My father used to go to New York two or three times a year, spending a great deal more than he could afford while there. It made him laugh, he said, to think that I was getting a free trip to the Fair by playing the triangle; by then I was almost old enough to catch the full inner sense of his joke.

"Wait until they hear you play 'The Star-Spangled Banner,'" said my father jovially. He had heard us practising and knew whereof he spoke. You couldn't really play a tune on our bugles, even the marvellous new ones—there just weren't enough notes to go round. We could eke out "God Save the King" because its intervals are easy; anything more recondite taxed our musicality excessively. But Mr. Thompson was determined that we should play the American anthem at the Fair, so he pieced out an arrangement using what notes we could command, and where we couldn't get the required tone he settled for a loud, positive, self-assertive BLAAATTT from all buglers together, thus:

> *Da-da-da, da, da, dee,*
> *Dee-dee-dee, da, da,* BLAAATTT.

It was a direful strain, and when we executed the number, bang in the middle of the Plaza of Nations at the Fair, there were shocked stares of horror and surprise from our hearers. Next day in two of the New York papers there were heated remonstrances; nobody seemed quite sure whether a joke or slight had been intended—the Americans are notoriously touchy about such things. Anyway wiser heads prevailed. Brother Willibald persuaded Mr. Thompson to drop the offending piece. He did so with reluctance, substituting "There'll Always Be An England," a tune just out and by no means as famous as it was shortly to become—for we were in the summer of 1939. We couldn't play "There'll Always Be An England" either, without disfiguring it with weird atonal—almost Schoenbergian effects:

Da, da, da, da, da, da-da,
Da, dee-dee, dee-dee, BLAAATTT.

But this song had no political, national, or warlike overtones as yet, and nobody at the World's Fair was offended by our rendering, so that the excursion went unmarred by further incident.

If we'd been so foolhardy as to use the same arrangement at the Canadian National Exhibition, say, next summer or any time in the next five years, we'd have been execrated and consigned to obloquy by our hearers, for the war was coming on, came on, engulfed us, and the Gracie Fields recording of the tune, unmistakable in its clear, true, unmusical clang, became the anthem of Toronto patriotism and remained so until the advent of the Bomb.

We had to give up playing it.

Mr. Thompson was not, you must understand, a man given to the frivolous adoption of novelties for their own sake:

Be not the first by whom the new is tried,
Nor yet the last to lay the old aside,

as Mr. Pope so beautifully says. If anything he erred in the direction of conservatism, and in the end it undid him. He would now and then introduce an outlandish and unplayable tune but he would never consider transforming the group into a brass band, for two reasons. One: he couldn't so far as I'm aware read music. Two: the Band had always been a drum and bugle corps; it was the best of its kind; he could see no reason for change.

Once or twice in the years at the end, and just after, the second war, he did make certain concessions to modernity. He got the notion somewhere, I believe from an American news magazine, that the Band should acquire what he called "bugle bells." I think he made up that term himself. I've never heard anybody else refer to them as "bugle bells." They're often called glockenspiels and sometimes bell lyres, but they remained "bugle bells" to Mr. Thompson.

It must have been late in 1944 when he began to talk about them at our post-practice NCO councils. I was by then a lance-corporal in the bugles, having outgrown (or rather outlived, I hadn't grown more than an inch; I was under five feet until my last year with the Band) the triangle and cymbal section.

"We've got to move with the times," he would say anxiously, casting an uneasy glance upon Brother Linus, who had succeeded Brother Willibald at the latter's death, "we can't get them from England on account of the war, but I believe I can get them made up locally." Ten years before, he had introduced leopard skins for the bass and tenor drummers and still thought of this as a greatly novel *coup*. He had the reverence for history that I admire, and no itch for the sensational.

He did get the new instruments made up in Toronto, and when we finally introduced them they looked lovely. If you think of a glockenspiel you'll know what I'm describing, a lyre-shaped, xylophone-type of instrument with a dozen metal bars which the player struck with a knobbed wooden hammer. Ours had a fatal flaw when we first got them. The bars were made of the wrong sort of metal; they gave the correct sequence of notes, but only very softly, having neither ring nor resonance. You couldn't hear them even when they played solo, and it was over two years before they were finally reworked into playable condition. Meanwhile they were carried on parade, the way band-singers in the thirties used to hold guitars with rubber strings, for the look of the thing. By the time the bugs were out of our glockenspiels everybody else had them, the war was over, we had failed to move with the times quite fast enough.

I grew through adolescence to young manhood during the last years of the war, being seventeen when it ended, too young to have served and probably just old enough to miss the next one on grounds of age, which won't make much difference, I'm afraid. While I was growing up, the complexion of the Band altered drastically, somewhat undermining it as an institution. In the late thirties there had been several young men in their twenties in the Band as senior NCOs. During the war they all disappeared; many of them were killed, like Johnny Delancey and Morgan Phelan, and the rest were almost middle-aged when they came back and wanted nothing to do with bugles and drums.

A whole new generation of bandsmen grew up, boys my age and younger, during the first half of the forties. None of us had any close touch with British Army traditions; we leaned if anything closer to the style of the University of Michigan Marching Band; there was a movement afoot to step up our marching pace from the conservative British step but Mr. Thompson wouldn't hear of it, and he had two powerful supporters, Perce McIlwraith the bugle-major, a man almost his own age, and George Delvecchio the quartermaster sergeant, only slightly younger and a family man who had not gone to war. These two chaps were the last of the veterans who had been in on the Band's first years and who had stayed with it out of loyalty to "Tommy" long after they had grown up. Perce McIlwraith in particular retained the enthusiasm of a child right into his forties. I can see him still—as Bugle-Major he marched at the right of the first rank of buglers—raising his arm at the end of a long drum section to signal us to put our bugles to our lips as one man. He was a tirelessly energetic second-in-command and a man of perfect, admirable, unquestioning loyalty. He used to lecture us at NCO Council when the drum-major was out of the room.

"I don't know if you realize how much 'Tommy' Thompson has done for you fellows. Who got us the Lindsay parade, the trip to New York, the new bugles? By God, there isn't a better man alive than 'Tommy' and see you remember it." I think that even then poor Perce had an inkling that an older order was passing away. He must have been close to fifty when he left the Band. His company transferred Perce to Windsor, and it nearly broke his heart.

As second-in-command, Perce McIlwraith was senior NCO and presided, ex officio, over our NCO Council, the strategic and disciplinary assembly of the Band. Before I became an NCO I often came before this body on various minor charges. I fell in with a crowd of older boys who congregated in the last rank of the bugles and horsed around during practice. Evil communications corrupt good manners. Mr. Thompson never appeared to notice our carryings-on but he knew perfectly how to squelch them; he gave us responsibility and finally gave most of us a stripe, that first treasured stripe, the lance-corporal's.

After I became an NCO I grew sober and mature at practice—we all did—we were all hoping for another promotion and then a third, if you made corporal you would likely make sergeant before you left the Band. A sergeant had the right to wear a broad red sash over his right shoulder and down across the chest, it was the ultimate accolade, only one or two men in the Band's history had risen higher. I finally obtained the long-coveted sergeancy in my last year in high school, in January 1945. I remember it vividly because the promotion came through suddenly and unexpectedly just before the annual Battalion Ball, the major dance of the year at Oakdale. As it happened, there wasn't an extra sash in the stores at the time, and I had to travel halfway across the city to borrow one from an unfortunate sergeant-drummer who was down with mumps and would therefore not appear at the dance. I had had mumps and wasn't worried about the communicability of the disease. My date caught them instead, most likely off the sash.

That was my last Battalion Ball and my penultimate stage with the Band. I graduated from high school in June 1945, in that uneasy period between VE and VJ Day, just before they drapped the first bomb, and at the annual Cadet Inspection of that year I was awarded the Most Efficient Band NCO Medal, which I wore on my chest for the first time on our VE Day parade, a riotous occasion.

The end of the war punctuated my love affair with the Band because I had to go to work. I meant to go to college of course, and eventually did so two years later; but I was short of money and there could be no question of my father's sending me as he was. then at the absolute nadir of his financial career. Like a good many of those who achieved a sergeancy, I decided to stay on, partly in the desperate ambition of earning an even higher grade, Quartermaster-Sergeant perhaps or even, if anything untoward should happen to Perce McIlwraith, Bugle-Major. It was an unrealistic and adolescent ambition because nothing was going to happen to Perce; several years elapsed before his company transferred him out of town, and by then the Band had so evolved that my love affair with it was long long gone.

I tried to keep up to practices even though I had a full-time job in the Civil Service; but there was a lot of reorganization going on at Oakdale and little by little I fell out of touch. For the first time, in the winter of 1945–46, Mr. Thompson introduced a wholly new kind of march, a complicated species developed during the second war, featuring rudimentary harmonies. The bugle section was split into four, two sections of open bugles, and two of crook. Each section had—and this was genuinely revolutionary and a great credit to Mr. Thompson—an independent musical line to play which required much greater prowess on the bugle than we had been accustomed to display. We regularly had to produce the sixth note on the instrument, and sometimes even the seventh, a thing extremely difficult to do. And we had to learn not to listen to what the other sections were playing and stick to our own line.

Our first march of this type was called "Field of Glory." It took us all winter to master it—it was like a symphony to us—and we meant to create a sensation with it, but there were two defects in the production. Everybody else in town, even Boy Scout bands, had the same number. And no matter what band played it, no matter how carefully rehearsed, it sounded crazily incoherent as though we had our signals crossed and were playing two quite different marches at the same time. For some reason, the harmonics simply wouldn't blend into a meaningful whole.

In vain did Mr. Thompson introduce variations on the idea; in vain did we practise and practise. It was a question of a search for a new musical form that didn't exist. I didn't understand then, but I do now, that Mr. Thompson was in the position of Haydn in 1792, confronted with the Opus 1 of the young Beethoven, those revolutionary trios. He knew blindly and obscurely that there were new forms to be created and explored, that the old forms had been worked up to their zenith by himself and Mozart (I mean Haydn, not Mr. Thompson) but he had grown too old to discover the new forms. Mr. Thompson might, with the aging Haydn, have written *hin ist alle meine kraft* at the last page of his latest efforts.

I left the Band in the spring of 1947, having decided that it was time to put away childish things, and having saved a certain amount of money, I started to college that fall. From first to last my love affair with the Band had lasted thirteen years, and I guess that was time enough.

I moved away from the immediate neighbourhood of Oakdale, and became involved with the usual collegiate misadventures. I took a flat on Sussex Avenue near the corner of Huron, so as to be near the centres of undergraduate activity. I began to drink beer and get around to the pubs with the boys, and I thought my twenty-first birthday the happiest day of my life. I acquired a card-sized birth certificate and started to tell the waiters in beverage rooms not to bug me about my age. I looked sixteen then but in the interval I've aged. Nobody asks me to prove my age nowadays, and I wish to God they would, such is the perversity of man.

Sometimes on a fine night in the spring or fall, I'd be sitting by the kitchen window in our flat on Sussex, drinking an ale with my roommates, and way, way off across town, softly at first as they marched down from the upper campus, and then with perfect clarity, I would hear the Band practising, and if I had had enough to drink, and sometimes even if I hadn't, I'd feel a wave of longing and nostalgia. I would want to sober up, hustle uptown on the Avenue Road bus, and take my old place in the last rank of the bugles. But I couldn't have done it; my lip had gone soft and I wouldn't be able to hit the sixth note.

I couldn't escape the Band though. Now and then I'd see them on the street during a parade, or in a newsreel of a Royal visit, or at a football game. Around the university there were always people from Oakdale with a similar sentimental attachment. Through one of them who'd been in a later class than mine I heard about the later stages of the Band's history, sometime around the summer of 1951. There had been a lot of palace rivalry within the group, between the Brothers and Mr. Thompson. The out-of-town engagements with the large fees had stopped coming, the Band wasn't the draw or the novelty that it had been fifteen years before. Perhaps attachment to the Crown and the British connection had generally been enfeebled, I don't know, but there was feeling among the Brothers that the Band ought to break new ground, that it should somehow look different.

Then around 1953 I heard that Mr. Thompson was out. I wish I could narrate that final interview. But maybe there wasn't any such scene, maybe he quit. But I don't see how he could have quit, it wasn't in him to do it. He couldn't have done it.

They replaced him by Warren Haggerty, an Oakdale grad, a former sergeant-drummer and ex-Air Force officer, a real punk. He lasted two years. After that they appointed a boy younger than I, who'd been in first year high school when I was doing Senior Matric, and was therefore five years my junior. I couldn't see then, and I don't now, how little Norm Hutchings could have the effrontery to stand up there in Mr. Thompson's place, but he was too young to have appreciated "Tommy" Thompson, he was a creature of the Haggerty regime and can't have known what he was doing.

They did a lot of things to the Band, to revive it as a Toronto institution. They discarded the bugles and drums that Senator Mulhearne had donated, and, my God, they'd only seen ten years' service, they might as well have been brand-new. Nowadays they have a slew of bastard trumpets; "valve bugles" they're called, soprano, tenor and baritone, and they try to play things like "The Tennessee Waltz" and "Tzena, Tzena, Tzena," and even "Rock Around the Clock" and they violate the integrity of the organization, the way Andre Previn plays jazz piano. I hope that Mr. Thompson can't hear the practices but I'm afraid that he can.

Last summer I met a group of Oakdale bandsmen on a Toronto streetcar; they were wearing what they call their summer uniform, a shoddy sweatshirt, a $2.98 item, and sleazy cotton trousers of a vile light blue, the colour of faded blue jeans. They don't wear gold capes anymore, winter or summer, and they have some sort of plumed shako, and they look like ushers in a second-run movie palace. Nothing endures.

So I imagine Mr. Thompson, as old as the century, which would put him in his early sixties, sitting in the summer twilight on the veranda of his house, which must be paid for by now. He'll be getting on to retirement age, if he hasn't already reached it. But perhaps he left Canada Packers when he left the Band; I don't know and I haven't any decent way of finding out. It would have been hard for him to carry on at the office, don't you see, because in a way he loved that goddam Band.

I think of him sitting upright in a porch chair somewhere on Belsize Drive or one of the little residential streets in through there, between Yonge and Mount Pleasant, impassive in the changing light, hearing the dreadful new sound rolling across the city, miles and miles, to remind him, sitting innocently there, of past glories, things that are utterly vanished, that will never come back again, his face firm, his chest out even though he's seated, his face sunburnt an even red, eyes unblinking in the growing darkness, listening to the young in action.

And as the summer darkness comes on, the children riding their bicycles noiselessly along the quiet street, going home, shadows in the dark, I almost feel myself sitting on the veranda steps beside him, and I want to tell him what we thought of him, Perce McIlwraith, Johnny Delancey, Morgan Phelan, Ted McGarry, all of us who loved him in return. It's almost time to go inside now, but in the darkness, oh, in this last time, I can almost reach out and take him by the hand.

RECOLLECTIONS OF THE WORKS DEPARTMENT

I N THE SPRING of 1952, six weeks after I finished my M.A. courses and involved myself in further graduate studies, I decided that I'd have to find a better summer job.

I had been working for the English publisher Thomas Nelson & Sons as a stockroom boy. The pay was low, and the work remarkably hard. I had only been on the job ten days, but after an afternoon stacking cases of *The Highroads Dictionary* (familiar to every Ontario school child) ninety-six copies to the case, in piles ten cases high, I saw that this state of affairs could not go on. These packing cases were made of heavy cardboard, strongly stapled and bound; they weighed seventy-five pounds each and they had to be piled carefully in a complicated stacking system. You had to fling the top row of cases into the air, much as you'd launch a basketball. I started to look for something less strenuous.

At length an official of the National Employment Service who handled summer placements at Hart House, a Mr. Halse, a man remembered by generations of Varsity types, suggested that I try to get on the city. I took an afternoon off from Thomas Nelson's and went up to the City Hall, to Room 302, a big room on the west side with a pleasant high ceiling. I was received with courtesy and attention, and after filling out some forms I got a job as a labourer in the Works Department, Roadways Division, payday on Wednesdays, hours eight to five, report to Foreman Brown at Number Two yard on College Street tomorrow morning, thank you! I stood at the counter a little out of breath at the speed with which I'd got what I came for.

"You're not very big," said the clerk at the counter. "Are you sure you can handle a pick and shovel?" As the wages were twice what I'd been getting, I thought I'd try it and see.

"I can handle it," I said. I've never seen anybody killing himself at the pick-and-shovel dodge. I asked the clerk for the address on College Street and, oddly enough, he didn't know it.

"But you can't miss it," he said. "It's next to the fire hall, three blocks west of Spadina. Ask to see Mr. Brown. And you'd better get on the job on time, the first day at least."

I thanked him and strolled back to Thomas Nelson's where I explained that I'd found something that paid better, and would they mind letting me go at the end of the day. They didn't seem surprised.

"You've got three days' money coming," said the stock-room superintendent dolefully. He sighed. "I don't know how it is. We can't keep anybody in that job." I said nothing about the cases of dictionaries.

Although it was the middle of May, the next morning was brisk, a bright sunny day with the promise of warmth in the afternoon. I was glad that I'd worn a couple of sweaters as I came along College Street looking for Number Two yard. It wasn't hard to find. It stood and still stands just west of the fire hall halfway between Spadina and Bathurst, on the south side of College. It's the main downtown service centre for roads and sidewalks, responsible for the area bounded by Bathurst, Jarvis, Bloor, and the waterfront. Any holes or cuts in the roadway, any broken sidewalks, or any new sidewalks not provided by contractors, are tended by workmen from this yard. It also serves as a reception desk for calls connected with trees, sewers, and drains from all over town. There's always a watchman on duty to attend to such matters, day or night.

I walked into the office and stood next to a washbasin in the corner, feeling a little nervous. Most of the other men on the crew were ten years older than I, although I spotted a couple my own age. None of them looked like students, even the young ones; they were all heavily tanned and they all discussed their mysterious affairs in hilarious shouts. There was a counter in front of me, and behind it some office space with three desks, a space heater, some bundles of engineers' plans of the streets hanging in rolls above the windows. It was the kind of room in which no woman had ever been, but it was very clean.

Outside, a green International quarter-ton pick-up with the Works Department plate on the door came smartly into the yard. A one-armed man got out and began to shout abusively at the windows of the fire hall. This was the foreman, Charlie Brown, who conducted a running war against the firemen because they persisted in parking their cars, of which they had a great many, in his yard. He bawled a few more curses at the face of the fire captain which was glued to a third-storey window, and came inside, immediately fixing his eyes, which were brown, small, and very sharp, on me.

"Goddamn-college-kids-no-bloody-good," he shouted irritably, running it all together into a single word; it was a stock phrase. He glared at me pityingly. "Where the hell are your boots?" I was wearing a pair of low canvas shoes of the type then known disparagingly as 'fruit boots.'"

"Cut 'em to bits in five minutes!" he exclaimed, quite rightly. I wore them to work one day later on, and the edge of the shovel took the soles off them in under five minutes.

"Go across the street to the Cut-Rate store. Tell them Charlie sent you. Get them to give you sweat socks and boots. You can pay for them when you draw some money." I tried to say something but he cut me off abruptly and as I went out I could hear him mumbling, "Goddamn-college-kids-no-bloody-good."

I had a good look at him as he banged noisily around the office when I came back wearing my stiff new boots. He was a burly man, about five-eleven, with a weathered face, a short stump of a right arm—the crew called him "One-Punch Brown"—a pipe usually in his mouth. He was the kindest boss I ever had on one of those summer jobs; there was no reason for him to care about my shoes. The workmen cursed him behind his back but they knew that he didn't push them too hard. And yet he managed to get the necessary minimum of work out of them. I found out, purely by accident, that the way to make him like you was to say as little as possible. It was fear that made me answer him in monosyllables but it suited him.

Charlie had four men in the office with him and three gangs of labourers out on various jobs, widely separated in the mid-town district he was responsible for. In the office were an assistant foreman named George—I can't remember his last name—and a clerk named Eddie Doucette who sometimes chauffeured Charlie around town. Usually Charlie drove himself, and how he could spin that little International, stump and all; he used the stump to help steer, along with the good arm.

Then there were two patrolmen who kept checking the streets and alleys in our district, reporting any damage to the roads and sidewalks, and the condition of any recently accomplished repairs. Johnny Pawlak was one of them, a slope-shouldered rangy guy of thirty-three or -four, a bowler and softball player, the organizer of all the baseball pools. The other was called Bill Tennyson, a lean, wiry, chronically dissatisfied griper, always in trouble over his non-support of his family, and half-disliked and suspected by the rest of the men in the office for vague reasons. Finally there were the three gangs out on the job: Wall's gang, Mitch's gang, and Harris's gang. Wall ran a taut ship, Harris an unhappy ship, and Mitch a happy one. I never worked for Wall, but I did the others, and the difference was wonderful.

When I got back from the Cut-Rate store it was already half past eight. "What are we going to do with this kid?" I heard Charlie Brown ask rhetorically as I came into the office.

"Aimé's still off," said George softly. "You could send him out with Bill and Danny." They stared at me together.

"Ever handled a shovel?"

"Yes."

"Go and help with the coal-ass."

"Coal-ass?"

"Do you see those men and that truck?" They pointed out the windows. Across the yard beside a couple of piles of sand and gravel a stubby old guy and a man my own age were sitting, smoking idly, on the running-board of a city dump-truck.

"Go out with them today. And take it easy with the shovel or you'll hurt your hands."

I left the office and walked over to tell the two men, Bill Eagleson and Danny Foster, that I was coming with them.

"What's your name?"

"Hood."

"All right, Hoody," said the older man, Bill, "grab a shovel." After a moment he and Danny stood off and studied my style.

"Do much shovelling?"

"Not a hell of a lot, no."

"Swing it like this, look!" They taught me how, and there really was an easy way to do it, one of the most useful things I've ever learned, a natural arc through which to swing the weight without straining the muscles. It was the same with a pick or a sledge; the thing was to let the head of the instrument supply the power, just like a smooth golf swing.

When we had enough sand and gravel, we yanked two planks out of a pile and made a ramp up to the tailgate.

"We'll put on the coal-ass," said Bill Eagleson.

"What's that?"

"Cold asphalt. It's liquid in the barrel and dries in the air. We use it for temporary patches."

Danny and I rolled an oil-drum of this stuff around to the bottom of the ramp. Then we worked it up to the tailgate and into a wooden cradle so that one end of the drum was flush with the end of the truck. Bill screwed a spigot into the end of the drum and we were all set.

"You're the smallest, you sit in the middle," they said flatly.

Apparently Danny and the absent Aimé fought over this every day. When we had squeezed into the front seat, Bill checked over the list of breaks in the roadway and we set out. It was already nine o'clock.

As we drove slowly along, the barrel bouncing and clanging in the back, they told me that our job was to apply temporary patches where damage had been reported by the patrolmen or a citizen, to save the city money on lawsuits. The idea was to get the patch down as soon as possible. They weren't meant to be permanent but they had to last for a while.

We stopped first behind some railway sidings on the Esplanade, next to the Saint Lawrence Market, to fix some shallow potholes. Bill filled a large tin watering-can with coal-ass and spread the black tarry liquid in the hole. Then Danny and I filled it with gravel. Then more coal-ass, then a layer of sand, and finally a third coat of the cold asphalt to top off.

"It dries in the air," said Danny with satisfaction, "and tomorrow you'd need a pick to get it out of there." He was quite right. It was an amazingly good way to make quick repairs that would last indefinitely. From the Esplanade we headed uptown to Gerrard Street between Bay and Yonge where we filled a small cut in the sidewalk. Then Bill parked the truck in the lot behind the old Kresge's store on Yonge.

"Time for coffee," we all said at once. We sat at the lunch counter in Kresge's for half an hour, kidding the waitresses, and I began to realize that we had no boss, that Charlie wasn't checking on us in any way, and that Bill had only the nominal authority that went with his years and his drivership. Nobody ever bothered you. Nobody seemed to care how long you spent over a given piece of work, and yet the work all got done, sooner or later, and not badly either. If you go to the corner of St. Joseph and Bay, on the east side, you can see patches that we put in nine years ago, as sound as the day they were laid down. By and large, the taxpayers got their money's worth, although it certainly wasn't done with maximum expedition or efficiency.

When we'd finished our coffee it was obviously much too late to start anything before lunch, so Bill and I waited in the truck while Danny shopped around in Kresge's for a cap. He came back with something that looked like a cross between a railwayman's hat and a housepainter's, a cotton affair that oddly suited him. We drove back to the yard, arriving about eleven forty-five, in comfortable time for lunch. We were allowed an hour for lunch but it always ran to considerably more. The three big gangs didn't come into the yard except on payday, unless they were working close by. It seemed to be a point of protocol to stay away from the yard as long as possible. Each gang had a small portable shed on wheels, in which the tools, lamps, and so forth could be locked overnight, and these sheds are to be seen all over the downtown area.

After lunch we fixed a few more holes. About two-thirty or three we parked the truck in the middle of Fleet Street with cars whizzing past on both sides. Danny handed me a red rag on a stick. "Go back there and wave them around us," he said. "We'll fix the hole."

I stood in the middle of Fleet Street, that heavily travelled artery, and innocently waved my flag, fascinated to see how obediently the cars coming at me divided and passed to either side of the truck. Now and then a driver spotted me late, and one man didn't see the flag at all until the last second. I had to leap out of his way, shouting, and he pulled way out to his left into the face of the oncoming traffic and went around the truck at sixty-five.

Pretty soon Bill and Danny were finished and we got into the truck and drove off. "Payday tomorrow," said Danny thoughtfully. "You won't draw anything this week, Hoody. They pay on Wednesday up till the previous Saturday."

"We'll buy you a beer," said Bill generously. He began to tell me about himself. He was an old ballplayer who had bounced around the lower minors for years, without ever going above Class B. Afterwards he came back to Toronto and played Industrial League ball until the Depression killed it. Then he had come on the city, and had now been with the Roadways Division for fifteen years.

"Just stick with us, Hoody, and keep your mouth shut," he said, repeating it with conviction several times.

"You'll be with us at least until Aimé gets back," said Danny.

I asked what had happened to Aimé. It appeared that he'd been found sitting in a car that didn't belong to him, in a place where the car wasn't supposed to be. He got thirty days and it was taken for granted that he'd be back on the job, same as ever, when he got out. Many of the men had had minor brushes with the law. A few weeks later Danny got caught, with two of his friends and a truck, loading lengths of drainpipe which they planned to sell for scrap, at a city maintenance station south of Adelaide Street. They just drove the truck into the station after supper and spent six hours loading pipe. They might have got twenty-five dollars for it, dividing that sum between them. It didn't seem very good pay for six hours' work; when I suggested this to Danny he shrugged it off. He hadn't figured out that his time was worth more than he could possibly have made on that job.

Bill Tennyson, the sulky patrolman, had often been charged with non-support by his wife, and with assault by his fatherin-law. He passed his nights alternately at his nominal place of abode, where his wife and children lived, and at a bachelor friend's apartment in the Warwick Hotel. An unsettled life, and an irregular, whose disagreeable circumstances he used to deplore to me in private lunch-hour chat. Charlie disliked him, and used to ride him quite a lot; he was the only man in the whole crew to whom Charlie was consistently unfair. He had that irritating goof-off manner which always infuriates the man who is trying to get the job done. Yet he had no vices, drank little, didn't gamble. No one knew how he spent his money and no one liked him.

He had his eyes on Eddie Doucette's desk job. But Eddie could type after a fashion, and had some sort of connection at the Hall which everybody knew about and never mentioned—he might have been a nephew of the city clerk or the assistant assessment commissioner—I never found out for sure. But nobody was going to get his job away from him.

Eddie wore a cardigan and a tie, and rode around in the truck with Charlie and George, while Tennyson wore sports shirts and walked his beat. The rest of us wore work clothes of an astonishing variety. My regular costume, after Aimé came back and I had to get off the coal-ass crew, was an old Fordham sweatshirt which my brother in New York had given me and which by protocol was never laundered, jeans, work boots, and the same pair of sweatsocks every day, and they too were never laundered; they were full of concrete dust at the end of the day and by September were nearly solid. I could stand them in the corner, and they never bothered my feet at all as long as I washed off the concrete as soon as I came home.

That first day we got back to the yard about four. We walked into the office, clumping our boots loudly and officiously on the floor. Charlie and George had gone out somewhere in the truck and wouldn't be back that day. Apart from Eddie, the only person in the office was a man who was sitting in Charlie's swivel chair, bandaged to the eyes. He seemed to be suffering from broken ribs, collarbone, and arm, shock, cuts, abrasions, sprains, and perhaps other things. He was having trouble speaking clearly and his hands shook violently. He and Eddie were conspiring over a report to the Workmen's Compensation Board.

This man became a culture-hero in the Works Department because he was on compensation longer than anyone had ever been before. Everyone felt obscurely that he had it made, that he had a claim against the city and the province for life. He would come back to work now and then, and after a day on the gang would be laid up six weeks more. They spoke of him at the yard in awed lowered voices.

"How do you feel, Sambo?" asked Bill solicitously.

"Not good, Bill, not good."

"You'll be all right," said Bill.

The injured man turned back to Eddie who was licking the end of his pencil and puzzling over the complicated instructions of the report. "It says 'wife and dependents,'" he said uncertainly. "We'll put them down anyway. If it's wrong we'll hear about it."

"I want to get my money," said Sambo.

"You'll get it soon enough."

I couldn't think where anybody could pick up that many lumps all at once. "What happened to him?" I asked.

"He was Aimé's replacement till yesterday," said Bill unconcernedly, "but some guy on Fleet Street didn't see the red flag. He was our last safety-man before you."

I thought this over most of the night, deciding finally that I would have to be luckier and more agile than Sambo. The next day was a payday, and in the press of events I forgot my fears and decided to stick with the job as long as I could. At lunchtime, the second day, most of the men expressed commiseration at the fact that I would draw no money until next week.

Bill Tennyson came out of the office with his cheque in his hand and an air of relief written all over him.

"Nobody got any of it this time," he said, as nearly happy as he ever was; his salary cheque was almost always diminished by the judgements of his creditors. "How about you, Hood, you draw anything?" I told him that I wouldn't get paid for a week and he stared at me dubiously for a minute, coming as near as he could to a spontaneous generous gesture. Then all at once he recollected himself and turned away.

Charlie Brown told me that if I was short he could let me have five dollars. I could have used it, but it seemed wiser to say "no thanks" and stretch my credit at my rooming house for one more week. He seemed surprised at my refusal, though not annoyed.

"You're on the truck with Bill and Danny, aren't you?"

"Yes."

"Stay out of trouble," he said cryptically and went out and got into the quarter-ton, holding a roll of plans under his stump and stuffing tobacco into his pipe with his good hand. All over the yard men were standing in clumps, sharing a peculiar air of expectancy. Some went off hastily, after eating their sandwiches, to the nearest bank. Danny Foster let his cheque fly out of his hand and had to climb over the roofs of several low buildings on College Street in order to retrieve it. A quiet hum of talk came from the tool-shed behind the office where the gang-bosses ate whenever they came into the yard. There they sat in isolated state, old Wall, ulcerated Harris, and the cheerful Mitch, the best-liked man at the yard, sharing their rank, its privileges and its loneliness.

The undertone of expectation sensibly intensified as the lunch-hour passed; payday was different from other days. The whole business of the gang-bosses on paydays was to ensure that their crews should be on a job proximate to a beverage room. One of the reasons that Harris was so unpopular was that he was a poor planner of work schedules; his men often had to walk six or even eight blocks from the job to the hotel. Mitch, on the other hand, seemed to have a positive flair for working into position Tuesday night or Wednesday morning, so that one of our favourite places, the Brunswick perhaps or the Babloor, was just up an alley from the job. I don't understand quite how he managed it, but if you worked on Mitch's gang you never had to appear on a public thoroughfare as you oozed off the job and into the hotel; there was always a convenient alley.

Bill and Danny and I left the yard sharp at one o'clock bound for some pressing minor repairs on Huron Street behind the Borden's plant. When we got there we couldn't find anything that looked at all pressing, except possibly a small crack beside a drain. We filled it with coal-ass, Bill laughing all the while in a kind of sly way. I asked him what was so funny.

"Johnny must have reported this one," he said. "He knows where we go.

"Go?"

"Oh, come on!" he said.

"Should we stick the truck up the alley?" asked Danny.

"Leave it where it is," said Bill. "Nobody's going to bother it." He was perfectly right. The truck sat innocently beside the drain we'd been tinkering with for the rest of the afternoon, with CITY OF TORONTO WORKS DEPARTMENT written all over it in various places. A casual passerby, unless he knew the customs of the department, would assume that the truck's occupants were close by, hard at work. Everything looked—I don't quite know how to put this—sort of *official*. Danny leaned a shovel artistically against a rear wheel, giving the impression more force than ever.

We walked up Huron Street towards Willcocks.

"Where are we going?" I asked, although by now I had a pretty good idea. Anybody who knows the neighbourhood will have guessed our destination already. I'm talking about that little island of peace in the hustle and bustle of the great city, the Twentieth Battalion Club, Canadian Legion, at the corner of Huron and Willcocks. This was the first time that

I was ever in one of the Legion halls. I had always innocently supposed that you had to have some kind of membership. Nothing could be further from the truth, and the knowledgeable drinkers of my time at the university would never be caught dead in a public place like the King Cole Room or Lundy's Lane.

It was a custom hallowed by years of usage that Charlie Brown, George, and Eddie Doucette should spend Wednesday afternoon in the Forty-Eighth Highlanders Legion Hall over on Church Street. It gave one a feeling of comfort and deep security to know this.

We went into the Twentieth and took a table by a big bay window. The houses on the four corners of Huron and Willcocks were then perhaps eighty-five years old, beautifully proportioned old brick houses with verandas at the front and side, and a lovely grey weathered tone to the walls. Like many of the original university buildings, these houses had originally been yellow brick, which the passage of nearly a century had turned to a soft sheen of grey. It was one of those beautiful days in the third week of May without a trace of cloud in the sky, the trees on Willcocks Street a deep dusty green, and now that most of the students had left town the whole district seemed to be asleep. That was one of the finest afternoons of my life.

"Are we gonna go back to the yard?" said Bill to Danny, really putting the question of whether they would take the truck home with them or not. They were deciding how much they meant to drink. And the nicest thing of all from my point of view was that they took completely for granted that they would take turns buying me beers. I was always glad that I had frequent opportunities to reciprocate.

There was an unspoken decision to make an afternoon of it.

Over in the opposite corner, fast asleep with a glass in front of him, sat the inevitable old Sapper who would revive later on to give us a detailed account of his exploits at Pass-chendaele. Next to him were two Contemptibles with identical drooping wet moustaches engaged in another of their interminable games of cribbage. All afternoon their soft murmur of "fifteentwo, fifteen-four" droned away peacefully in the background. It was a place where a man could stretch out and take his time. In all the time I was in the Twentieth after that, though I saw plenty of men thoroughly drunk, I never saw one really troublesome or nasty.

At a big round table in the middle of the room, all by himself, shifting a pair of small eyes in a head of heroic proportions, drinking mightily, sat a young man whom I vaguely remembered having seen around the university. This was the tenor, Alan Crofoot, now a favourite of Toronto audiences but in those days dabbling in the graduate department of psychology a block away. We grew to be good friends later on and I often reminded Al that this was the first place I'd seen him close to, though we didn't speak. Once or twice that afternoon he glanced across at our table, plainly wondering why I had FORDHAM lettered on the front of my sweatshirt. I let him work on it.

There wasn't a waiter; you had to go to the window. In a minute Danny came back with three ice-cold Molson's Blue and glasses on a tin tray. As a matter of fact we had had a fairly busy morning, we were sweaty, we had just had a heavy lunch—nothing ever tasted any better than a cold beer on a beautiful afternoon with nothing to look forward to but more of the same.

In those days I had a small local reputation as a better than fair beer drinker with plenty of early foot, though with nothing like the stamina or capacity of Al Crofoot, say, or any of half a dozen other redoubtable faculty members and graduate assistants of my time. But I couldn't even stay close to Bill and Danny, who drank two to my one, never appearing to feel it and never becoming obstreperous or downright disagreeable as I regularly did myself, and as my usual drinking companions often did. It was a great pleasure to pass the afternoon with them. And when five o'clock came they both pressed money on me, in the unspoken recognition that I would naturally go on to another beverage room after dinner. We parted on the best of terms.

Soon this comfortable alliance was dissolved by circumstance, when Aimé arrived back at the yard after doing his thirty days. He flatly refused to go out with one of the gangs; he had earned his place on the coal-ass crew, he felt, and no goddam college kid was going to get it away from him. Bill and Danny were indifferent in the matter, as was natural, and at length, about a quarter to nine the first morning Aimé was back, Charlie called me in from where I was sitting smoking to ask me how I felt about it. You see, he respected the prescriptive right that I'd already acquired in the job. There was an unspoken but very strong sentiment at the yard that once a man got his hands on a soft spot he acquired a kind of generally sanctioned right to it. Charlie peered at me sidewise as I came into the office and leaned casually, as I'd already learned to do, on the counter.

"What about this, Hood?" he asked sharply but, I sensed, half-apologetically. "Aimé wants his job back."

"Fine," I said. He looked at me with relief, palpably surprised that I hadn't made more of a fuss.

"You'll have to go out with Harris," he said warningly.

"Okay."

Aimé looked at me. "No hard feelings, kid, you understand."

"No," I said, smiling. He went outside and picked up a shovel. Soon I could hear him wrangling with Danny over who was to sit in the middle.

"Goddamn French Canadian bastard!"

"Shut your fat mouth, Foster!"

The three of them got in the truck and drove off.

I sat in the office wondering how things would be on Harris's gang. He had the reputation of being a driver, a tough man to please. He hadn't been a boss long and the responsibility bothered him, mostly in the stomach. He had a lean hatchet face and sunken cheeks, the face of an ulcerated man, with hysterical eyes and a marked Birmingham accent. Like many of the men at the yard he had a lot of trouble with his wife.

He and his boy had been piddling around with a tiny sidewalk installation on Bloor Street, between the Chez Paree and Palmer's, for several days. They couldn't seem to get the camber shaped right and the rain lay in a puddle instead of draining off into the curb. Twice now they had had to come back to the job to rip out recently installed bays of concrete. Bloor Street, you understand, was the street of all streets about which we had to be most careful—Toronto's Fifth Avenue—our display street as far as Charlie's professional reputation was concerned. He hadn't wanted to let Harris handle the job, but Wall's gang was tied up elsewhere and the work had to be done immediately.

As a finisher, Harris lacked confidence in himself and the resulting sureness. A concrete finisher has to be able to coax the water in the concrete to the surface together with as many air-bubbles as possible, smoothing the surface and shaping the sidewalk—sculpting it—so that it curves almost invisibly from a high point in the centre down to either side. This is all done by the eye and the hand, sometimes with the aid of a level and a piece of two-by-four, but always pretty crudely, and Harris didn't have a good enough eye. Concrete is an interesting medium, plastic enough to allow some correction but quickdrying enough to require a firm decisive trowel-stroke and what a draughtsman would call a good line.

Driving me over to Bloor Street, Charlie said little, but I knew he was embarrassed about taking me off the coal-ass truck. I didn't really mind because I'd expected to get a little light exercise on this job, but you'd have thought he was sending me to Siberia.

"Here's another man for you, Harris," he said when we got out of the quarter-ton in front of the Laing Galleries.

Harris eyed me with a great sourness; like everyone else at the yard he knew that while I wasn't weak, I was damned clumsy. I knew what he was thinking but he couldn't very well say anything; he'd been after Charlie for an extra man for weeks.

"Can you use a sledge?" he asked me doubtfully.

"Sure."

"Go and help them throw the broken stuff in the truck."

I said nothing and walked along the street to where the rest of the gang were cleaning out some bays.

"Got you working now, Hoody," said Freddy Lismore as I wandered up.

"Don't let Harris throw you, kid!" said Wally Butt, the assistant finisher. I grinned and, bending over, began to pick up pieces of broken sidewalk, the largest weighing not much more than thirty-five or forty pounds. Some of them had sharp edges though, and could cut your fingers badly if you weren't careful. Fortunately I had a pair of cotton work gloves in my hip pocket. I wasn't killing myself, but as I lofted a chunk of concrete into the truck Charlie came over and spoke to me.

"You're out of shape," he said briefly. "Work into it slowly."

"All right," I said, "and thanks." He disappeared in his little truck and Harris came back, giving me a highly critical stare. I took it easy all right, but everybody in the gang took it even easier. And as is always the case with any gang of workmen, there was one guy who pottered around between the toolbox and the job, doing absolutely nothing. On Harris' gang that would be "Gummy" Brown, always called "Gummy" to distinguish him from Charlie "One-Punch" Brown, the foreman. Gummy had a single black tooth on the left side of his upper jaw—all the rest was a great void, justifying the nickname. He had been drunk, it was held universally, since the world began.

If you counted Gummy, Harris had seven men under him, and the use of a truck owned by its driver and rented by the city. This truck-driver went back and forth from the asphalt-plant on the waterfront, bringing loads of ready-mixed concrete—we almost never had to mix by hand—and the art of managing the gang largely consisted in exhausting the last load for the day at about ten to four, leaving plenty of time to clean off the shovels and put up barricades and lights, moving at a sober and godly pace, before quitting time. At ten to five Gummy Brown would get the keys to the tool-box from Harris and we'd stick the shovels, picks, crowbars, and trowels in the box. Gummy would lock it with enormous satisfaction and we'd all walk off the job, meeting there by prearrangement the next day. While we were on that Bloor Street job, I had a twominute walk around the corner to where I lived and I used to be home washing my feet before five o'clock. And this comfortable situation lasted through the early part of the summer.

I stayed with Harris for about six weeks that first summer, all through the ill-fated Bloor Street job, then on Robert Street fixing householders' sidewalks a bay at a time, insignificant jobs, and finally around the Art Gallery and Hashmall's Pharmacy on Dundas Street. I broke out concrete, used the sledge, floated off—the works. The only thing I would never risk was swinging the sledge at a spike. I could never hit the damn thing—poor timing and eyesight, I suppose—and it was dangerous for the man holding the spike.

It might be of interest to the reader to follow a simple job from start to finish. First came the problem of getting the old cement up and out, which could be managed in several ways, depending on its age and hardness. If there happened to be grass or mud at the edge of the sidewalk, we took a long bevelled bar and worked it under the concrete, placing a rock under the bar for leverage. Then a couple of us would rock up and down on the bar to see if we could lift the slab; usually we could. When it was a foot or two off the ground, one of us would hit it in the middle with the sledge, splitting the whole slab into small chunks which could then be thrown into the truck to be disposed of at the waterfront as fill. We would clear out eight or ten bays at a time, shovelling out the rubble underneath and levelling the ground in readiness for the fresh mix.

There could be complications. At a ramp behind the bus terminal on Elizabeth Street we found that the old concrete was over three feet thick, to take the weight of the buses. Worse still, it was criss-crossed by heavy reinforcing wire which resisted pliers and had to be cut, strand by strand, by driving a spike through it with a sledge. This reinforcing wire had to be watched carefully for it was rusted and the broken ends were dangerously sharp; that small job lasted nearly two weeks.

When we had prepared the ground we would send the truck for a load of concrete. This always meant an hour's wait, either around ten-thirty or about two in the afternoon. It made a nice break. We would take things easy, cleaning off the shovels or sneaking a bit of leftover concrete to a home-owner to be used for a patio. The great thing was to melt inconspicuously into the landscape so as not to attract the attention of the ratepayers.

When the truck appeared, we either dumped the concrete into the road and shovelled it into wheelbarrows for delivery to Harris and Wally Butt, on their knees together at the edge of the new installation, or if we were only fixing scattered single bays, two of us would climb into the well of the truck and throw down shovelsful from on high. There was a certain amount of horseplay involved in this; more than once somebody down below caught a great lump of wet concrete in the pit of his stomach.

One morning in late June I was standing in the back of the truck about eleven o'clock, shovelling the stuff into a bay, sweating and feeling pretty loose, when Charlie Brown's head appeared out of nowhere at the side of the truck. The edge of my shovel just missed him and an enormous gout of wet concrete went whizzing past his ear.

"Watch what you're doing!" he said. That's only a rough transcription of what he actually said. In fact he was speaking the dialect that Alastair MacCrimmon and I used to call "cityese," an exotic English, rhythmic, heavily cadenced, comically obscene, with an unmistakable structure. If I were blindfolded in Rangoon and heard two men speaking "cityese," I'd be able to spot them instantly; there's something unique about the scansion.

Charlie got down off the truck and spoke to Harris.

"I need Hood in the yard," he said.

"Why don't you take 'Gummy?'" asked Harris protestingly. I felt proud.

"I want somebody who's alive," said Charlie disgustedly, motioning to me to join him in the truck. I looked at Harris inquiringly but he shook his head. He didn't know what was up.

On the way back to the yard Charlie told me about the watchmen. There had to be somebody in the office from around four in the afternoon until eight the next morning, as well as all day and all night on the weekend, which worked out to sixteen eight-hour shifts weekly.

Three old men approaching retirement split fifteen shifts amongst themselves, leaving an extra one to be filled in by one of the workmen. And each of these watchmen was entitled to three weeks' holidays a year for a total of nine weeks to be filled in through the summer. Charlie had decided that my combination of supposititious book-learning and puny physique made me the ideal replacement.

"You can put in the next nine weeks on this job," he said encouragingly. "That'll take you down through August, and then I'll find something else for you to do." I was due to leave towards the end of September.

Now the thing was, I'd been getting used to the work on the gang and enjoying it. On the other hand, every man at the yard would have given his eye-teeth to acquire this sinecure. I didn't want to turn down what was obviously meant as a kindness, so I said nothing.

Charlie looked at me curiously. "What's the matter? Don't you want to do it?"

"Sure," I said, "It's fine, Charlie." And it turned out to be an interesting job, each shift presenting novel problems. The four to twelve, and the daytime shifts on Saturday and Sunday, brought the most service calls. The twelve to eight was mainly a matter of arranging seat cushions from the swivel chairs on top of the desks, or on the floor, and trying to sleep. Once in a great while you might get a call in the middle of the night, usually from the traffic squad, to report that the barricades were down or the lights missing on a hole in the road. Then you had to call out an emergency truck from one of the yards—there was only one truck available, each yard providing a stand-by driver in turn—and direct the driver to the danger spot. The time of the call, the trouble, the location, the remedial action, and the precise time that the driver called back to say that the repair was in effect—all these things had to be noted down in a daily journal and initialled by the watchman. These books were sometimes produced as evidence in damage suits by city lawyers, and so had to be kept up carefully.

But most of the twelve to eight I spent sleeping, or talking to policemen who came in for a smoke and to warm themselves, or to nap for an hour or to hide from the sergeant. These men patrolled one of the toughest parts of town and were as eager to stay out of trouble as the rest of us. They hated the corner of Bathurst and Queen, for example, because of the half-dozen enormous taverns located there, which meant that

Friday and Saturday nights on that corner were real hellers. I'd often seen eight policemen standing in pairs on the corners of that intersection and wondered why. The answer, I was told, was that they just didn't want to come alone.

Many of these fellows were English immigrants, bewildered by the Toronto attitude to the police. They were always complaining about times when they'd been losing a fight and hoping in vain that a citizen might give them a hand. I remember one Englishman in particular who was leaving the force and taking his family back to England because of this kind of thing. He felt alone and threatened in a country where incivility and disrespect for the law seemed accepted and regular.

None of these constables knew much law; none had a clear idea of his powers, and these were constantly exceeded in some circumstances and allowed to lapse in others. They hated and feared all lawyers, and were easily cowed by them. I know one drunken lawyer, a driver of spectacular incompetence, drunk or sober, who despite his erratic behaviour awheel, and despite the dozens of times he's been stopped by traffic officers, has never been fined nor even summoned to court. He bounces aggressively out of his car, announces that he's a lawyer, and the policeman, unsure of his ground, backs off.

On the other hand, when the officer feels that he has the upper hand he is perfectly ready to exceed the limits of his mandate, and is apt to be quite cynical about it. One young constable admitted to me that he always bulled the College Street crowds around, pushing people and threatening them with arrest to persuade them to move on, when there was no conceivable charge he could bring. Most of the people in the crowds, Jews and DPs, had no notion of their rights and legal safeguards and were easily intimidated.

But most of the younger policemen were decent unassuming men, not too happy with their rates of pay and promotion considering the nature of the work, but proud of what they were doing and even of the opinion that it was a dignified public service. I asked them about favouritism on the force and they all agreed that there was very little, and that a man would normally be judged on his merits. Their testimony carries some weight too, because they were all in junior positions and there was nothing in my questions to put them on their guard.

Another instructive aspect of the watchman's job was our emergency sewer service. When there is a very heavy rain the Toronto sewers cause trouble; they are not equipped to carry off the excess water, being designed for normal conditions of flow. If there is an extremely heavy rain they back up, and the water begins to rise in cellars all over town, especially on low ground, in hollows and valleys and on the lower slopes of hills. And the only real cure for this abnormal state is the end of the storm.

Understandably enough, few householders are aware of this. When they observe the flood rising in the cellar, with its sometimes dismal and offensive accompaniment, they become alarmed and the result is a flood of calls at the yard, none of which distinguish between a genuinely blocked and defective sewer—with a tree root in it, say—and one which is in perfect shape but which is just too small for downpour conditions.

I remember afternoons, almost always on the weekends, when the phone rang as soon as I put it back in its cradle, for hours on end. I'd get panicky elderly ladies, people who raved in exotic foreign tongues, frightened children, Bohemians with basement apartments in which their folksong records floated soggily round and round—every imaginable strip of complaint. There was simply nothing to be done until the storm was over. I tried telling them so but it did no good and at length I learned simply to note the call, and imply, without actually making a commitment, that a service truck would be along. Of course no such service call was ever made unless there was a clear indication in the complaint of some genuine blockage or break. But I never told anybody that.

I channelled and re-routed calls of this and other kinds until the end of August, when the three elderly watchmen had all enjoyed leisurely vacations. By that time I was pretty much regarded as one of the office staff, and Charlie was visibly reluctant to send me back to Harris—it might create a dangerous precedent. The day after the last of the watchmen came back I ambled into the yard wondering how he'd work it out. He had, you see, a kind of problem in status, or prestige, to resolve. But he was equal and rather more than equal to it.

It was the Tuesday after Labour Day. The Scotch guy (a man never known by any other name, always "the Scotch guy," with a thick burr and a great genius for killing time) was sitting outside the tool-shed when I meandered in. He said nothing but grinned cheerily. When I went into the office Charlie handed me a small can of black paint, a small can of white, two brushes, a box of cleaning rags, and a set of stencils from zero through nine which could be fitted together to form any number up to 9999. He told us where to find a little ladder and the Scotch guy ran to get it. We threw the things in the back of Charlie's pick-up truck and he drove us to the foot of Jarvis Street, where we got out. I was still quite in the dark.

"I want you to re-paint the numbers on the lamp-posts," he said. I'm not joking, that's what he said. "When you get to Bloor Street, come into the yard and I'll give you a list of other streets." He got into the truck and sped off along Queen's Quay while we looked at each other, scarcely able to credit our luck.

We painted our way up Jarvis Street at a snail's pace—boy, did we take it slow! I'd go ahead and slap on a background of black paint. Then I'd walk back—we only had one ladder—and we'd work along, putting on the fresh numbers in a creamy off-white, a kind of eggshell or buff tint. We got up to Bloor Street on Friday afternoon, a matter of four days. When we appeared at the yard Charlie glared at us in extreme vexation.

"What the hell are you doing here?"

It would not have been possible to go slower.

"We finished Jarvis Street," I said apologetically.

"What, the west side too?"

"I'm afraid so."

He began to root around in his desk and finally drew out a few dog-eared sheets of foolscap with a list of street names on them. He flourished it in the air and then handed it to the Scotch guy.

"Do these!" he said. He looked at us and began to smile and at last to laugh. "There's fifteen hundred dollars in the estimates to be spent on this job," he growled. "Now get out and don't let me see you around here for at least three weeks."

So I finished out my first summer without any strain.

When I came back to the yard the next year, I had only two more years' work to do in the graduate school. I had held a good fellowship which took care of most of my expenses, I'd had a highly remunerative job at the CN Express, where you could log seven or eight hours' overtime if you had the nerve and could evade the foreman, so I wasn't hurting for funds quite as much as before.

I went back because I liked it and I even persuaded a friend of mine, Alastair MacCrimmon, to apply for a similar job. He was then an intermittent student at the university and is now a film technician at CBC. Every night in the Chez Paree from eleven till two, he and I would sit around that summer exchanging our observations of life on the city. He was working at Number Six yard and apparently things were managed there much as they were under Charlie. We used to amuse ourselves by playing a game which we called "Translate into Cityese." Alastair would feed me a line in ordinary spoken English, or I would feed him one, and the idea was to render it with the peculiar diction, cadence, and rhythm of the men on the gangs, getting the feeling as authentic as possible.

"Goodness me," I might say, "we filled that hole in the road yesterday, and there it is again." Alastair would translate this flawlessly.

"The men at the hall have not sent up our cheques," he would come back straight-faced, "and here it is nearly noon." This would stand a lot of translation.

"Someone has stolen all the lights off the barricades," or possibly "Itchy-Koo has been drinking and cannot work."

Or most enigmatic, even gnomic, of all: "The truck has stopped and will not go."

It was Alastair who created the legend, on the city, of what Itchy-Koo said when he hit his foot with the sledge, crushing the metatarsal forever. He said: "That hurt!"

It was understood that I would get back my night-watchman's job when the holiday time came; but I put in most of May and June on Mitch's gang. When you remember poor old Harris's anxiety-ridden behaviour, it was a revelation to see the difference in Mitch's methods. He was very relaxed and so was his gang. Everybody had a good time; we were always close to a beverage room. And though it was the small-est of the three gangs, we could handle a moderate-sized job much faster than Harris, and nearly as professionally as Wall. The first thing we did that spring, as I remember, was a major installation of double sidewalk on Spadina Avenue just north of College outside the Tip Top Tailors branch store. We were right across from the Waverley Hotel and that branch of the Canadian Bank of Commerce of which my father had been manager fifteen years before.

In those days Dad used to do a lot of loan business in the district with furriers and garment-trade people during the season, and with independent sales agents, small jobbers and importers, smallwares and novelties salesmen with tiny agencies, and the like. One of these freelance salesmen, a man called Earl Darlington, came to Dad one day with a peculiar request for a short-term note. Earl could sell anything—he could charm the monkeys off the trees—but he never handled the same line two weeks in a row and so had no established line of credit. However, Dad listened to the story, which was colourful and involved. He had a chance to buy the refrigerator in the Waverley for next to nothing because they meant to replace it. This was not what you and I think of as a refrigerator but an enormous thing the size of an apartment living-room, with walls in which the cooling devices were intricately cemented. The whole room had to be removed, walls and all. It was like transporting a small house.

Darlington told Dad that he had a buyer for this monstrosity, the old Hunt's Confectionery on Yonge Street, next to Loew's Uptown. All he needed was the money to put a deposit on the refrigerator and to hire a truck with a flatbed trailer, and a gang of men, to move the thing. Dad listened to this beguiling tale and thought it over, talked to the manager of the Waverley, and in short concluded that it was a chance for Earl to make a dollar, so he let him have the money. 119

After surmounting fantastic obstacles they got the refrigerator out of the hotel in one piece and onto the trailer. They had the necessary permit from the police to move it, after business hours, and they hauled it up to a lane behind Stollery's on the corner of Bloor and Yonge. In went the trailer and down the lane, but before they got to Hunt's rear door the refrigerator got jammed between the walls of two buildings abutting on the lane. They couldn't back up; they couldn't go forward though they tried their damnedest. They were stuck fast. In desperation Darlington told the driver of the trailer and the gang of labourers to go home and get some sleep—he could see his quick profit being eaten up by overtime—and they'd try again next day. Then he went home himself, leaving about four tons of refrigerator immovable in the lane.

When they came back next morning the trailer was parked where they'd left it but the refrigerator was gone, vanished. Stolen, by God! And it was never traced.

Eventually Dad wrote off the loan.

Watching the men on the gang slide across the street and into the Waverley reminded me of this story and I told it to

Mitch, who got a big chuckle out of it. He was then, I should say, about thirty-two or -three, which seemed middle age to me, though it doesn't any more. Everybody liked Mitch, even Bill Tennyson who came out with us for a day once in a while, moody, difficult, but after a couple of hours' joking with Mitch he would loosen up a bit and tell us about his latest crap with his father-in-law, an ex-bantamweight who liked to mix it with him now and then.

Then there was Frank Hughes, another nice fellow—Mitch had all the easy-going types out with him—a hockey player who had spent the previous winter in the Eastern League. He was going to the Detroit camp in the fall and was putting in the summer with us to stay in shape. I don't know how much good the work on the gang did him as far as staying in shape went; but at least, like the rest of us, he got a good tan. Frank used to play fastball with Sherrin's down at the beach and he was enjoying a very good year at the plate, which made him even easier to get along with. Like all ballplayers, he loved those base hits. He weighed around one-ninety and had one of the most powerful builds I've ever seen. He wasn't broadshouldered; he had low sloping shoulders and a cavernous chest and magnificent legs. He was a defenceman and though I never saw him play, they tell me he could really dig. I weighed around a hundred and forty, but the odd thing was, I had about an inch of reach on him. We used to spar around comically for the amusement of the gang and the passing girls who always had an eye on Frank—he was a very handsome man.

"You look like a pretty good light-weight, Hoody," he'd say. This always convulsed Mitch.

"Try and hit me," I'd say, dancing around jabbing, or pretending to tie him up inside. Like most students, I had terrible co-ordination.

"Going to get in shape on the city," we'd sing absurdly, and this was also good for laughs. Then we'd swing our shovels for a minute as though our lives depended on it. A girl would go by and we'd straighten up and inflate our chests, holding ourselves immobile.

"Who's she looking at, Mitch," Frank would say, "me or Hoody?"

The poor girl would blush and we'd gurgle happily and foolishly to ourselves. We never tried to offend or embarrass a passing girl but they never could resist a peek at Frank, and if we caught them at it, why then the joke was legitimate.

But life on Mitch's gang was too good to last, at least for me, though it went on and on for them and still does. When vacation-time came I went back on the night-watch at the yard, guarding the piles of sand and gravel and the tools in the shed, feuding with the firemen or throwing a football with them, depending on the state of our relations.

Early in June in the summer of 1953 there occurred the most momentous event of my career as a fill-in watchman, the Coronation of Queen Elizabeth II. There were weeks of preparation of one kind or another in case of crowds, but somehow the most weighty arrangements of the whole affair went untouched until seven-thirty on the morning of that eventful day.

It was a fit day for a Coronation, the sky an absolute crystalline blue, the air dry and soft, and College Street slumbrous and deserted at seven o'clock in the morning. I had promised Jimmy Baird, whom I was to relieve, that I would come on early so he could go home and get dressed up with his medals on for the parade. The bagel shops were silent—you could hear birdsong on College Street!

I was whistling "Land of Hope and Glory" softly to myself as I came into the office. The sound woke Jimmy who stared at me with infantine sleepy eyes, hardly recognizing me—the emergency calls never woke Jimmy—as he rolled off the top of the desk where he'd been lying, straightened his collar and tie, and prepared to leave.

"Anything doing?" I asked.

"Not a thing." There was never anything in the book after Jimmy had worked a shift. I suppose the sight of his lifeless body was enough to frighten marauders away, though; he looked quite dead when he slept.

"Tommy Cowdrey's the driver," said Jimmy as he left. "If anything comes in, call him." He slunk out the door. I stood in the gateway to the yard for a while, looking east and west along College Street, and there wasn't a sound, nothing stirred. Then, a long long way off, perhaps as far away as Sherbourne Street, I could hear a streetcar, the clicking of the points as the trucks passed over them and then the rumble along the street; it was coming fast and I could predict exactly from the sound when it would come in sight away along to the east about St. George Street. A car with an Alabama plate went slowly past with a tired driver slumped over the wheel. They must have driven all night. A single policeman idled in front of the Mars Grill.

Inside the office the phone rang suddenly, urgently. I caught it on the third ring. It was seven-thirty. "Number Two yard," I carolled into the mouthpiece, and then I got a shock.

"This is the commissioner," said a tense voice. "Is Foreman Brown there?"

"No, Mr. Chambers."

"Then you'll have to get hold of him. This is an emergency." The hair stood up on my head; there was real urgency, even fright, in the commissioner's voice. "We've got to erect a temporary comfort station in Queen's Park," he said. "The bandstand facilities won't be nearly enough. I've just had the parade marshal on the phone and he's furious." He began to give me explicit instructions.

"We'll use the same model we used on VE Day. Twenty-four compartments, twelve of each. Brown has the plans. He'll need workmen, lumber, paint or stain, buckets, chloride of lime, and the appropriate signs. Get him into the yard and call the crew. Then call me back."

"Yes, sir."

"Very good, Who's speaking?"

"Hood. Fill-in watchman."

"All right, Hood, I'm counting on you. Get busy!"

I called Charlie at once and he was galvanized into action. "You'll find the plans for the model in my desk. Do you know where the key is?"

"Yes."

"Call Eddie and tell him to pick me up. Then get out the plans. Then call Wall and tell him to call six of his best men and have them meet me at the yard. They'll draw double time, tell him, but they've got to come in. I don't know how we forgot about this." He hung up in great distress of mind and I began to carry out his instructions.

By eight-fifteen Eddie and Wall and six labourers were standing uncertainly in the yard. Charlie was inside on the phone like some great captain adjusting his tactics after a military disaster. "My right flank is crushed, my centre in full retreat, my left wing collapsing. Very good, I shall attack!"

"Send the partitions to the bandstand," he was shouting, "and some green stain, and don't forget the signs like last time."

At eight-thirty he and the men departed for the site of the proposed comfort station.

As you remember there was an enormous parade that day which was to assemble on the university front campus, the back campus, and in Queen's Park, and which was to move off at one-thirty. Besides the marchers and police and civil dignitaries, there would be great crowds of spectators, hot-dog and ice-cream vendors, flag and souvenir salesmen—altogether about seventy-five thousand people. I wondered if twenty-four compartments, even adding on the bandstand facilities, would be enough.

Soon there came an anguished call from a pay-phone at Hart House. It was Charlie. "No buckets!" he wailed.

"No buckets?" I echoed, thunderstruck.

"They're out of them at the supply department. Now look, Hood, we've got to have those buckets. There are ten thousand people here already and they all want to use the facilities. Call the commissioner and ask him to get them from Eaton's mail order. They're sure to have some."

I called the commissioner and he was aghast. "There won't be anybody there today. Maybe I'd better have it broadcast."

"Don't you know anybody at Eaton's?"

"I know Lady Eaton, of course," he said doubtfully. "I've met her at civic functions. But I can't call her."

"We've got to have them, sir."

"All right," he said, "I'll get the buckets. What size?"

"The largest," I said, "galvanized iron." He hung up and in a matter of seconds Charlie was back on the line. "What about those buckets?"

"Chambers is calling Lady Eaton," I said, and he seemed reassured.

At eleven the buckets arrived on the site and instantly the crowds swarmed around the workmen demanding access to them. But the walls and roof weren't complete yet, and Charlie was afraid of offending public decency; he held the besiegers off until the partitions were up and the roof decorously in place while the swarms of bandsmen, hot-dog vendors, and children with balloons grew thicker. At length the last nail was driven home, the last plank solidly in place, the buckets in a glittering phalanx.

The parade marshal blew his whistle, the drums rolled; it was one-thirty. The parade moved off and the crowds began to disperse, streaming down University Avenue towards the reviewing stand. In fifteen minutes Queen's Park was deserted except for a child chasing a floating balloon. The comfort station went unused.

Away off down on Front Street bagpipes skirled.

Muttering curses, Charlie ascended to the roof-tree, and taking a hammer ripped out the first of the planks. For him, for all of us, the holiday had been a magnificent fiasco. *"C'est magnifique mais ce n'est pas la guerre."* For weeks a pall of meditative, reflective gloom hung about the yard.

Nothing in my second summer exceeded the high adventure of that day. There were a few memorable happenings, but the glory seemed dimmed. There was the time that Charlie incautiously named Gummy Brown to fill in the extra watchman's shift. I had been on the job for eight hours prior to his arrival and had spent the evening watching the fights on television, on the third floor of the Fire Hall. After the fight was over I had a couple of cups of tea and a chat with the fire captain which was interrupted by a hail from the ground floor, which drifted up through the holes in the floors through which the brass pole descended.

"Gummy's here," shouted one of the hook-and-ladder men.

"Tell him to come on up for tea."

"I don't think he can make it."

The hook-and-ladder man was wrong because in a minute a red-and-black face hove into view on the stairs. It was Gummy, drunker than usual, if that were possible, and making heavy weather of the ascent.

"Chrissakes, Hoody!" he got out. "Whyncha in the office?"

"The fights," I said.

He began a disconnected tirade to the effect that one should never leave his post, seizing a stalk of celery as he eased along the table towards the teapot and inserting it in his mouth.

"Can't chew it," I heard him say before he slumped over.

"Come on, man," said the fire captain, "on your feet!" This captain was a bit of a puritan who disapproved of the freeand-easy manners which obtained under Charlie's aegis. "On your feet!" he said again.

Gummy lifted his head and squinted at him and then, discerning the voice of authority, he rose and lurched backwards out of the door of the lunchroom.

"Watch it there, Gummy!" I cried, but too late. He disappeared soundlessly, magically, through the hole which circumscribed the brass pole, falling freely three storeys to the cement floor of the garage and breaking both legs. Fortunately he was completely anaesthetized against the pain, which otherwise might have been very great. He lay there, the celery stalk between his lips, quietly gumming it like a cow with a cud, while we eased him onto a stretcher and waited for the ambulance.

"Take my shift, Hoody," he said as they carried him off. "Double time."

I saw the compensation reports on that one, and you'd have supposed that Brown, Norman, 37, married, was the very model of sobriety and conscientiousness. It was at length established that as Gummy's shift hadn't actually begun he was not entitled to compensation. The case was appealed on the grounds that he had been travelling to work, though how a fall through a hole could be construed as "travel to work" rather eludes me. The last I heard, the appeal was pending.

That damned old snake of a fire captain was a troublemaker. One evening when I was doing a four to twelve, a Friday night as I recall, four friends of mine appeared with a case of beer and an old car. One of these was later to become a reverend and dignified professor of law at a hoary academic institution and I won't embarrass him by mentioning any names. It was his idea that we should consume the case of beer during my shift and then hasten to the Chez Paree in the car to get in another couple of hours. There were two men and two girls besides me, and the girls drank perhaps a pint each, giving the rest of us a good start.

There was a good deal of singing and noise, and though I had drawn the blinds, a policeman friend of mine twice entreated us to be more quiet, not for his sake but because some people on Nassau Street, two blocks away, had lodged a complaint. And at that he drank a pint of our beer, carefully rinsing off his mouth and hands afterwards.

Now while we were enjoying ourselves in this innocent and peaceable fashion, that spy of a fire captain crept across the yard, peeked around the drawn blinds, and noted carefully what was going on. Having satisfied himself with what he considered enough evidence to obtain my discharge, he withdrew unnoticed. Next day he went to Charlie and told all, but without realizing it he had played into Charlie's hands. It was perhaps true that I was treated with coolness, even severity, for a day or two. There was even some talk of sending me out with a gang again. But Charlie knew, and I knew, and finally the captain knew too, that the folkways were too strong. The affair was passed over and, in fact, when one of the watchmen suffered a heart attack in September, Charlie kept me on till Armistice Day, a wholesome object lesson to the fire captain. I carried on my graduate work during the days. My last few weeks on the job, the nights were getting pretty chilly, and I had instructions from Charlie to keep the space-heater on all night. "I'm always cold when I come in at eight o'clock," he said, "so keep things good and warm for me, Hood." I promised him that I would. When I went off the job for the last time, on the cold morning of November the 11th, Charlie nodded to me curtly.

"We'll be seeing you, Hood," he said, his sharp little eyes looking all around the office to see that things were in good order. And then, amazingly, "Take care of yourself." I nodded silently and, leaving the yard behind me, I started for home.

I only ever saw them once more. Four years later I was on Richmond Street on Midsummer's Day, going in to be interviewed by Jack Kent Cooke for the editorship of *Saturday Night*, a job which I had no business applying for and didn't expect to get. As I came abreast of the Consolidated Press building, my throat constricted and I stopped in my tracks.

For there they all were, Mitch's gang, lounging around a dozen open bays, waiting for the truck. There was Mitch, grinning as cheerfully as ever, Gummy hobbling idly around on a cane, Bill Tennyson, who recognized me and came over to say hello. And there, parked across the street, was a new green International quarter-ton and in it, gripping a pipe between his teeth and puzzling out a roll of plans, sat Charlie. Everything was just the same; they were all the same and would always be the same. I said a word or two, jokingly, to Tennyson, and then he went away.

I glanced at the sky; it was a hard blue and there wasn't a cloud to be seen. I squared my shoulders and went inside to my doomed-to-be-mutually-unsatisfactory interview. And it struck me after it was over, that silly interview on which Jack Cooke wasted half an hour of his time and his indubitable charm, that I'd be wiser not to try for impossibilities but to set down records of things possible, matters like these, tales of the way one man paid for his education in the bad old, good old days before the creation of that warm featherbed for talent, the Canada Council.

LE GRAND
DÉMÉNAGEMENT

Suppose you move here the end of August, say. You arrange with your *propriétaire* for a lease which, no matter what your wishes, will terminate on April 30th the next year, or more probably the year after, giving you a *terme de bail* of twelve plus eight, or a total of twenty months. A lease in Montreal ends on April 30th. Useless to plead its inconvenience, if you only mean to stay nine months, or fifteen, because the custom is invariable. So God ordained it; so it remains.

That might sound like an exaggeration to a stranger, but in fact the custom of the great move on May Day is rigorously—I won't say enforced, there is no constitutional or legal prescription—but enjoined by immemorial habit. This has something to do with elements profoundly rooted in our people, a trust in the value of building, solid brick and mortar, the rental property. Sociologists assert that the impulse rises from the defensive instincts of a conquered minority. I don't believe that. I don't think any true *Québecois* ever resigns himself to such a status. This urge to acquire property is a constructive and aggressive force, not purely defensive. I can remember Professor Bonbourgeois, the economist, saying to me, "Put your money in duplexes, my boy. Nothing is so good an invest-ment." And this man is very very far from being a minority-group defeatist. He's an aggressive and daring leader whose debatable pronouncements make members of the cabinet tremble and grow pale.

"Put your money in duplexes. Be paid rent. Grow fat."

The *rentier* psychology is easy to understand, but where did the choice of April 30th (coincidentally my birthday, more about that later) originate? I've seen the question argued each year in the papers; nobody seems to know. It might have some quasi-ritual function. I suspect it does, something associated with the return of fine weather, the final long-deferred and patiently awaited coming of spring. The first of May is asso-ciated in many local devotional practices with the Mother of God, just as May is her month. Could there be something going on here that nobody has noticed, an assimilation of the new, unexplored and therefore slightly alarming domicile to the protection of Mary? I'm not sure.

The movers in Montreal have for years been trying to push through some modification of this practice of doing all the moving on April 30th and May 1st. You can see the complica-tions for them. I mean, think it over. Over seventy percent of their business is done in a ten-day period at the end of April, when you can't get hold of a mover for love or money unless you got a signed agreement months before, when you can't under any circumstances rent a truck. All reserved, booked up solid. The movers claim that they're in a ruinous business; they have to maintain equipment the year round at a level of investment only justified during the magical transformations of midnight, April 30th, when old *foyers* die painfully and the new are born. There's a suspicion of witchery about the whole rite.

What I want to know is this: what do the movers do the rest of the year, hibernate? Do they sit around in an enchanted slumber eleven months of the twelve, occasionally walking out zombie-style to handle an industrial move? And how the hell does it all work out so neatly without any displaced tenants left over? I worry about this, looking at it as an enormously sophisticated problem in statistics and operations analysis.

Sixty thousand families load their furniture into trucks, buses, station wagons, human- and horse-drawn carts, on April 30th, which means that there have to be sixty thousand open spaces waiting. But these spaces are still occupied by sixty thousand others who are waiting for the first ones to get out, so they in turn can occupy vacated space. No signal is given, like the whistle at the kickoff, to warn half of the populace to move out so that the other half can move in, permitting those already out on the street to move in . . . the mind boggles at the complexity of the operation.

I've always been haunted by the spectre of the last man to vacate, who at eleven fifty-nine on the night of May 1st, when everybody else is happily settled in, dust falling back to the surface of newly arranged bric-a-brac, finds himself wandering through the streets of Montreal with all the spaces taken, as in musical chairs. Some enchanter has sneaked in and removed one apartment and there he is, the final tenant, seeking a home.

You may object that each year new apartments come into being, but equally each year are older ones demolished. There may be a small net gain in units available, but you can't tell me that the whole undertaking isn't wildly risky, like kicking over an anthill. One of these years the movers will get everybody out in the streets and then find that a hundred buildings have unaccountably vanished, leaving the whole transition irrecoverably muddled. The city will then become the habitation of nomads, eternally condemned to wander up and down Maplewood or Saint-Urbain, looking for a ghostly four-and-a-half with garage, locker, taxes paid, heat supplied.

This conception alarms me deeply each time I'm forced to consider moving, something I'd put off for the remainder of life's allotted span, if at all possible. Whenever my lease gets down towards the end of the final year, say six months before, I begin to scan the document nervously. Finally, obsessed by the complexity of the whole nightmarish undertaking, I contact my landlord months before there is any need, begging him to renew and undermining my bargaining position, so as to assure myself of three tranquil birthdays without another move.

The last time we actually had to do it, I worried, my wife worried. In November we began to review the "Duplex to Let" columns and quite soon found one that was going to become available the end of February! Hallelujah. Now this meant that I paid rent on two apartments through March and April, but the peace of mind was worth it. Early in March we began to trans-ship stuff from the old to the new place, taking our time, after all we had nearly ten weeks. I used to load up our Volkswagen bus with junk from the locker, superannuated stuffed animals, picture frames, cartons of obscure and long-forgotten electrical devices, curling-irons and broken toasters. Three bicycles. I carried out and in, by my accurate count, thirty-two sixty-pound cartons of books. Then there were the records…

By my birthday we'd been in our new place for three weeks; God, but I felt smug. But on mulling it over, I see that I devoted a couple of hundred hours to the move; and figuring my time as worth a dollar an hour, approximately the local minimum wage, I didn't save as much as I thought.

But as I leaned back in my dining-room chair, took a deep breath, and blew out the candles, I thought that after all we were relocated awfully conveniently, while at that very instant all the streets of the *metropole* were crawling with insect-like totings of heavy bundles. *Fourmillante cite*: bet your sweet life.

In our house we celebrate all conceivable festivals, the kids see to that. The Jewish high holidays are very big with us, though we aren't Jews. When you work it out, we have a major celebration every second week: Christmas, New Year's,

Grandma's birthday, John's birthday, Valentine's Day, Lincoln's birthday because he freed the slaves, Saint Patrick's Day, Sarah's birthday, Easter, Dwight's birthday, taking us down to the end of April which is me.

Sarah came in one time from the parish school and announced, "Today is the feast of Saint Louise de Marillac."

"Yeah," I said, not too interested, "so what about it?"

"Aren't we going to have a cake?"

I thought it over. "I don't think Saint Louise de Marillac is close enough we have to have a cake."

"Oh, Daddy." She went off and took the matter up with her mother who, I'm glad to say, supported me in the issue.

So when I admit that I enjoy my birthday party, it isn't wholly from infantilism, it's really for the kids. We have party hats, the same ones we've used for everybody's birthday since Sarah was born, noise-makers, and those things that you blow into and they unroll with a whistling sound, a feather at the end to tickle your dinner partner's nose. After the first course is over—the kids don't eat much—we turn out the dining-room lights and Noreen goes for the cake. She brings it down the hall, we all sing, the candles are blown out, the cake is cut, and then there are the presents. Everybody knows how the feast develops, even the baby. Everybody gets the same intense pleasure from repeating the same sequence of actions regularly at the same time each year. Just like a secular liturgy.

Part of my birthday party that the kids aren't aware of is my annual late-evening tour of the streets to observe the movers and their problems, not entirely a sadistic enterprise. Full of cake and striped ice cream, glad not to be loading a van, I wander out after the children are in bed to see how things are coming on; the activity continues late into the night and all the next day.

An apartment, a *foyer*, grows an essence of its own as people live their way into it through the term of a long lease. It isn't just so many walls, so much raw physical space; the soul of the place is in the forming actions of its inhabitants—these are the true *lares et penates*. It is always sad to see so many patterns being broken all at once. Remember how you did things when you lived on South Drive? There was that peculiar low ceiling at the landing on the back stairs as you go up to the attic, where your wife always used to bang her head, carrying laundry baskets down from upstairs. You had a garage full of gardening tools such that you couldn't get the car in out of the winter weather. Your eldest boy, now in college, drew all over the living-room walls at eighteen months, and you made the mistake of hanging new wallpaper yourself. Remember how sticky the paste was, and how you howled with laughter when the project had finally gotten out of rational control?

End-of-April night, ten o'clock along Maplewood, families leaving, taking a last look around to see if they've forgotten anything. They have, but they won't find out for weeks.

"What happened to that fruit jar, the one I used to save pennies in?"

"Didn't you put it in the carton with the ashtrays, when you were cleaning out your study?"

"I thought I did, but I can't find it. I had thirty-seven cents in there. I know because I wanted to roll them up and didn't have enough. *N'importe.*"

I come mooching along the street, watching them go, feeling each backward glance. A young father comes out of 2225 Maplewood holding a canary in a cage, with a sleepy three-year-old girl clinging to his leg, almost tripping him. Further along, where we used to live, there's a studio couch sitting beside some garbage cans. Somebody has abandoned it and my wife would swear that it was almost new. I sit on it and bounce, wondering if I should go home and get out the car and pick it up. Scavenging like this, we've acquired a house full of interesting pieces.

Have you ever tried to throw away a worn-out studio couch? I mean really worn-out, with the ends bulging out and the springs down to the floor? Can't be done! You have to wait till you move, or are fleeing the country under a cloud, to dispose of the item. We had one around the house so long it started to go bad—it smelled. I think mice were living in it. With immense difficulty, I and a pal wrestled the thing onto the balcony and tipped it over, hoping it would divide on impact so the garbage men would haul it away.

But it didn't. We had to work it into the bus and drive to an open space miles across town, safe from detection, as we hoped. We drew up on a slight incline, hauled the damned thing out, and left it settling cosily into the mud beside a baseball diamond.

"Coast away," my buddy said.

For days I went skulking around nervously, expecting a call from the Sanitation Department charging me with trespass, littering, abandonment, whatever the formal accusation is. Better to leave them around your old apartment when you leave.

When we moved away from Maplewood, I sent the others off with the van and stayed behind for ten minutes with a broom, meaning to leave everything tidy. I swept up, borrowed a dustpan and emptied the sweepings into the incinerator, took a last look around at the four-and-a-half empty rooms (five if you count the dining alcove as a room). Motes of dust danced in slanting sunbeams. In that corner, there, Sarah sat for hours with her crayons making Christmas or Easter cards. Here in the kitchen was where Dwight cried for six hours one night, causing my wife and me to have our worst-ever fight. Dwight was long past that stage now. Sarah would never sit in that corner again; the apartment seemed haunted by actions irrecoverably lost. What is permanent, I wondered? Where did all that go? Once on a birthday night walk, I counted seventy-four moving vans along Saint-Urbain in half an hour. Think what is lost forever in all this.

Especially on Saint-Urbain do you get the impression of the evanescence of life. From Van Horne south past Rachel, the street must have the highest population density in town, thousands of small apartments in two- and three-storey buildings, a balcony for each apartment, from which soft voices buzz on dark spring nights. It's an old quarter and some of the buildings are untrustworthy. Once last year, just before moving day, a young woman fully nine months pregnant was sitting with her grandmother on a Saint-Urbain balcony when all at once it pulled away from the face of the building and they fell three storeys to the ground. They were rushed to the *Hotel Dieu*, fortunately not far off, and the miraculously unhurt young mother gave birth to a healthy infant, despite her understandable state of shock. I have the impression her grandmother wasn't quite so lucky.

On May Day, right after this unhappy accident, I was driving slowly past the place where it happened, looking in amazement at the raw scar on the front of the building. I stayed in second gear because of the crowds of trucks and other wheeled vehicles. Suddenly I saw an ancient man, bearded, standing in the gutter looking at a homemade wagon piled high with household effects, mattresses, bedding, pots and pans, half a ton of stuff. He had apparently meant to drag this weight unaided across the district to his new home, like a carthorse in the traces. But his intentions had been dashed by the collapse of the wagon. A wheel lay at a crazy angle near the curb, a ragged stump protruding at the end of the axle. His effects teetered gently on top of the wagon.

This man wore the most puzzled expression I've ever seen. Not angry, not despairing, simply puzzled, as though he were working out a complex equation in his head.

My Volks bus was empty. I felt a compassionate impulse, struggled with it, almost crushed it down, but then stopped and got out, meaning to offer to help. We could easily have put his stuff in the bus and moved it in one load. I spoke to him but he apparently didn't understand me. I guess he was a Polish Jew. I began to wave my arms, pointing at my bus. A look of profound suspicion spread over his face, making me feel foolish in front of a considerable group of bystanders. I'm no good Samaritan, anything like that. I just figured what the hell, I had nothing else to do that afternoon.

As I stood there trying vainly to reassure the old man, another bearded figure materialized and seized me by the arm.

"That's a nice truck you got there, Meester," said this man.

"It's not a truck," I said, "it's a station wagon."

He looked with contumely at my scarred and dirty car. He knew what a station wagon looked like, and this was not it. "By me it's a truck," he said. "You want to help me?"

I was certainly not getting through to the old fellow with the busted wagon, so I seized the chance to ease out of the situation.

"All right," I said, trying to ignore the laughing crowd, "what's your problem?"

"Two dollars."

"Huh?"

"I'll give you two dollars."

"No," I said, "I'm not in the moving business. Just tell me what you want."

This affected his composure slightly. "I want to move a sink. It's my tenant Swackhammer, oh my, you should have such a tenant, always complaining. It's got a crack; it leaks into the garbage pail and through the floor. He won't be responsible for the plaster, so I got to fix it."

"A sink?" I visualized something you'd wash your hands in, a little bowl about eighteen inches across. "Sure, I'll give you a hand."

"So come."

I followed him. He wore a heavy overcoat inappropriate for the season but easy to keep in sight, deep black. We entered a cavernous foyer and went up three flights of stairs into an enormous apartment running the length of the building and overflowing with all varieties of highly coloured furniture; there were framed photographs on all sides.

My employer waved a hand at the pictures. "He gets them wholesale from a nephew, a druggist. The sink is back here."

We went into the kitchen and there it was. I had been quite wrong in my estimate of its size. It was a bloody old battleship of a kitchen sink, divided in halves, one shallow for dishes, one deep for laundry. It was colossal, stained, cast-iron, and it sure was cracked. A deep fissure ran down the division between the tubs and across the bottom of the laundry tub; leakage might certainly occur.

"I'm simply protecting my property," the man said.

"You own the building?"

"A small thing, a nothing," he said evasively.

"How are we going to get this thing out of here?" It must have weighed over a hundred pounds and looked an awkward shape to move.

"Down the back. Go get the car and bring it round the alley." I figured this man was used to exercising a certain amount of authority, saying to one "Go," and he goeth, and to another "Come," and he cometh; he had a basilisk eye. As it turned out, he was a rabbi and a scholar besides being a property owner, and something in his manner commanded assent, and anyway I was feeling easy. "Bring it along Saint-Cuthbert and down the alley. I'll stand on the back balcony and stop you."

I had to laugh; he had it all set up. I went downstairs and out to the street. The old Polish waggoner was nowhere to be seen, but his belongings were highly visible all over the street and in the gutter. Children were picking up the pieces. I got into my car and wheeled it slowly up the street, round the corner onto Saint-Cuthbert and down the first alley. Soon I saw an overcoated figure standing on the balcony, well back against the wall, away from a rickety railing.

"Stop, that's it." He beckoned and I climbed the stairs again, feeling it in my legs. Tenants began to appear at windows to watch our descent, which was difficult. A very fat woman leaned out of a second-floor window and cried angrily, "Ha, Pachsman, I see you're fixing up Swackhammer's place."

"A minor repair, that's all, a little porcelain job."

"So what about the bugs?"

"They're being taken care of; it's no problem."

"Sure they're being taken care of, but who's taking care of us? It's time you did something for me. Just because I don't complain, like some…" Her voice trailed off angrily as we went lower. I had the bottom end of the sink, the heavy end, and at that the Rabbi was doing a lot of huffing and puffing. When we finally got the damned thing into the car, he climbed into the back beside it and began to give me directions.

"It's over on Saint-Gregoire past the park. Drive fast. You can go along Saint-Urbain and across Laurier."

"All right, all right. What's the hurry?"

"Swackhammer," he said moodily.

We drove east on Laurier and north to Saint-Gregoire, then east again behind the park, a part of town I hadn't seen before. In a few minutes he told me to stop beside the entrance to what looked like an old stable; there was a high, weathered board fence around it, and around the yard an L-shaped ramshackle two-storey loft. We leaped out and entered the yard. I noticed a sign saying *Rosemont Plomberie, Reparations, Service*. In a minute a foreman came out onto a platform on the second floor and lowered a length of chain with a hook on the end, meanwhile giving us elaborate directions. I had to back the car into the yard; then we had to lead the chain through the hole in the bottom of the sink on the good side. Then we had to work the hook through a link in the chain so the sink could be hauled up. It took a certain amount of time and energy, but finally we both heaved sighs of relief as this incubus was swung up into the sky above us and into the workshop. I turned to go, but Rabbi Pachsman had the last word.

"You're driving me home?" He had me there.

Next Monday night about twenty to six, I was eating supper with the family when the doorbell rang downstairs and the front door was flung resoundingly open. I stuck my head into the stairway and by God there he was, overcoat and all. I hadn't given him my address, and I still don't know how he found me. The car was parked outside. Could he perhaps have checked all the streets west from Saint-Urbain, looking for it, or did he simply take the licence number and check it with the Bureau?

"Meester, Meester, we gotta go quick, they close at six."

"The sink, you mean?"

"What else?"

I hadn't said anything about any return trip.

"Besides I haven't given you the two dollars."

"Oh, hell," I said to my wife. "Keep the coffee on the stove and I'll be back in an hour."

Driving across Van Horne towards the east end, he kept bouncing up and down like butter in a fry-pan. "Faster, faster."

"Look, I can't go any faster, this is a street full of traffic."

"They close at six," he said in anguish, "and Swackhammer..."

"Yeah," I said, "I know. Swackhammer is complaining."

"You got it," he said, "faster, faster, go east on Saint-Gregoire."

"Yeah, yeah, yeah."

We made it about one minute to six, and he hopped out and ·ran into the old barn and upstairs. In a minute I heard loud contentious voices which rose in pitch; then his dominated, the chorus died away, and very shortly the re-porcelained sink was swung out overhead and lowered. I stood at a prudent distance until it touched ground. Then we unhooked it, stuck it in the back, and had a look at it. They had certainly done a lovely job on the porcelain. It looked like a new fixture.

"Did they fix the crack?" I said. You certainly couldn't see it.

"That I can't say," he said.

We drove back to his place in relaxed and comradely silence, and when we had carried the thing to the third floor, again to the jeers of the tenants and in the inexplicable absence of Swackhammer (could he possibly have been a polite fiction?), Rabbi Pachsman drew a long black purse from the depths of his overcoat and extracted a crisp new two-dollar bill.

"For you."

"Aw, no, look, I'm not in the business. It was just a favour."

He stuffed it into my shirt pocket.

"All right," I said, "I'll send it to a charity, B'nai B'rith or the Knights of Pythias." He smiled cagily. I did send off the money too, I think to the United Jewish Appeal, but somehow I'm sure he'd never believe it.

Since then I park the car off the street.

LIGHT SHINING
OUT OF DARKNESS

SOUTH of Boulevard Mont-Royal as far as Rachel, from the Main eastwards past Papineau, lies the country of the *ruelles*. Close to the Main are streets like Henri-Julien, de Bullion, Hotel de Ville, one-way north or south, which in another place might be considered slums; not in Montreal. Going east past Christophe-Colomb towards de Lanaudiere, Fabre, past des Erables and Parthenais, you discover small enclaves which are clearly the homes of comfortable older citizens; the grocery stores grow imperceptibly more prosperous in appearance, their paint is fresher.

Ah, but Henri-Julien, Drolet, that's the real thing. Hundreds of young families with three or four children, the youngest a bare-bottomed infant creeping along the *ruelle* curb, already trained to evade the creeping delivery vans which sometimes bump along the pitted track, while his sister, maybe four, in a smudged undershirt, eyes him as he learns his way...

They are narrow blocks, buildings fronting on parallel main streets and backing on a shared alley. Each long block is made vertebrate by the crawling teeming *ruelle* life, traced out in the shape of an H, or a pair of goalposts, with a very long crossbar running up the middle of the block and two short uprights at the ends.

When these streets were laid out, before the turn of the century, there was no automobile traffic, and there are no private driveways in the district. The houses, and the enormous stately multi-family dwellings, not precisely apartment buildings, crowd against each other. Back of them are the alleys which once upon a time must have been long networks of stables. They aren't a convenient width for automobile traffic, though you can get a car in or out. Trying to ease into a former stable, you have to scramble around a very sharp right angle as you aim for the door. It's tricky in snow.

On the lesser thoroughfares, the houses will be painted brick, doorways flush with the sidewalk, three storeys high, and very often they will have ornamental cornices in wood painted light green, pale blue, most frequently pink. Atop these cornices there will be two or three little minarets or globes or vanes, all in woodwork. When you examine them closely, they are evidently not the work of master craftsmen who worked in extreme detail; there are no intricate carvings, no highly developed skill. They are the work of adze and plane, executed roughly, the same shapes repeated hundreds of times all through the neighbourhood, but never too close together. From the sidewalk there is an impression of delightful variety, heightened by the colours of successive thick coats of paint.

You enter the house directly from the sidewalk, there being neither areaway nor front garden, nor is there space between houses. The windows have snow shutters, again executed in rough but useful carpentry. In the poorer parts of the district, the shutters are sometimes missing, the windows inadequately boarded over and the house left empty. But mostly these places present a rich family life which, having no outlet in front but the sidewalk, tends to proliferate in the alley, safer for the abundance of babies. Sometimes back there you'll find a small, balding, grass plot with ten adults roosting on it and God knows how many kids hollering ... toy trucks with a wheel gone, orange plastic Really-Ride-'Em tractors.

The main streets east and west are (from the north) Marie-Anne, Rachel, and Duluth, and a slow summer bicycle ride east along any of them will display the variety of customs and of wealth. Go along Marie-Anne and your way east from the Main is at first narrow and crowded, the business in the small grocery stores done half in the street. Motorists are circumspect. Men load meat in trucks from some wholesale *salaison*. The slope of the street decreases as you come towards Saint-Denis, the pavement widens. If you were to ride as far as Fabre, you would spot on the southeast corner a line of half a dozen row houses which could have been built yesterday, they shine so with fresh paint and gleaming woodwork, and they aren't restored town houses for television executives either, though each has a television aerial. They are two storeys high, and the curtains have all been starched this morning.

North and south are some big important streets like Saint-Hubert, and here again you'll find a kind of dwelling that is perhaps indigenous. I mean those long rows of tall broad uninterrupted buildings that can't be called apartment buildings because the units are not connected by interior corridors, nor, very often, by heating lines. These huge piles are approached by outside staircases—the beautiful Montreal staircases—front and rear, so that you don't enter the building and traverse a hall to reach your front door. You climb an outside staircase and enter an independent dwelling, often totally separated from the rest of the building except by the plumbing. You will heat your home at your own expense with one or another of those space heaters which each winter effect multiple accidental fires and smotherings. There is something very *Montrealais* about such buildings, which combine independence with strength and bulk. Yet the staircases are often of an extraordinarily pleasing lightness and apparent fragility, front and back. Take a look at *Le Montagnard* which fronts on Saint-Hubert and backs on ... well it ought to back on an alley but actually backs on Avenue de Chateaubriand, which makes me think of rich bloody steaks, of Atala and Rene, and of the gypsies in Canada ...

Shvetz and I were sitting in the Gerard Marcil Tavern, corner Saint-Hubert and Duluth, *Repas Complets*, waiting for Lazarovich, in from Ottawa for a weekend. He wanted to talk to the Old Man, whom we could see plainly sitting across the room, but whom we didn't want to join till Lazarovich came, as he's the contact.

This tavern may have been successively a *caisse populaire*, a grocery store and a small warehouse for novelties and sundries before becoming a tavern. It's the corner property in a big building, a true apartment building, this one, painted in a matte shadowy silver colour over what might be compressed gypsum siding, a very cozy spot on an iron-cold deep February night. We had come there at Lazarovich's command, an hour before, so that he could combine an evening with us and a chat with the Old Man, Petroff, the patriarch of Montreal gypsies. Afterwards we would go around the corner and up de Chateaubriand, if we didn't miss it in the darkness, to see Tom. The cold held on hard, but the tavern entrances were screened by inner winter doors, and we were sitting at the back of the room.

Shvetz said, a bit restively, "He knows everything."

"Petroff?"

"He's been everywhere. We'll see if we can get him to talk."

About ten o'clock Lazarovich arrived in a rush. He's always in a rush on these flying trips; he may find the pace a little slow in Ottawa. He came to the table and said without ceremony, as though we'd seen him the day before, "Let's move."

We picked up our ten glasses and followed him across to the table where the Old Man was sitting, his beard fluffed out down the front of his overcoat to the third button, his bright large deep-set eyes looking slowly around the room like distant early warning radars, maintaining order by a searching glare, anticipating disaster.

"How are you, Mister Petroff?" said Lazarovich. He sat down, and after a moment we did too.

"I'm an Old Man," said Petroff; you could hear the capital letters.

"He always says that," said Lazarovich aside.

"Could we buy you some beer?"

"One or two, I think, no more. I'm an Old Man and I don't need as much as I did in the old times. This is good beer," he said generously. "I've always liked the Canadian beer, not like some. In Hungary, we find a native beer which is light but drinkable, but there, of course, there is much else to drink, and in the Ukraine, and among the Slovenes. The Slovenes are always quarrelling with one another, naturally, and haven't much time for drink, so the gypsies consume the excess." He laughed, took up a full glass and swallowed it. "These glasses are too small."

"I haven't seen you for a while," said Lazarovich, "not since my party when Vanya was born. Do you remember?"

"Very well. That was the last time I danced. I danced with your wife, and with Tom's." He stared hard at Shvetz. "You were there, with your jokes. You were very happy."

"I've given up joking," said Shvetz, "I've become a family man. I have responsibilities."

"That happens to all you young men. Look at me, now, I'm seventy-eight and have buried three wives, two in Europe, one in America, and I have no responsibilities except my position. I used to move around, a year in Sofia, a year on the road. Even after I came here I was moving all the time. I was with carnivals, with a Wheel of Fortune, then the Nifty Girlie Show, then with the Bingo 'Jouez-au-Bingo, sieurs et dames. Venez, venez, dix sous seulement, ça commence encore, ça roule tout en ronde.' I am never settled down." He gave Shvetz a hard stare. "What responsibilities have you?"

"Well I'm learning the clarinet, I . . ."

"You have settled down to learn the clarinet. Good. You will be a master, since you take it so seriously, but you will not travel, play in a village orchestra, for your dinner and a bed. You will never accompany a dancing bear. For a dancing bear one needs a small drum, about the size of the larger tambourine."

"Tambourine means 'little drum,'" said Lazarovich.

"Not at all the same; it is a mistake in the name. A tambourine is struck with the open palm, and has no base, no resonator. There are metal plates let into the side, which vibrate as the head is struck. There are different sizes."

"It's strictly a percussion instrument," said Shvetz.

"Not at all, not at all. If you have different sizes you can simulate chords, and you can vary the beat—there's much music in the tambourine. But you are right in this respect, that a single tambourine is a percussion instrument, not more."

"For a dancing bear!'

"No," said Petroff wearily, "not for a dancing bear."

"What then?"

"For a dancing bear," he began again, "a small drum is best, with a boy to play the bagpipe. You interrupted me. But in this country you do not have that sort of village entertainment. You will never go from village to village in that way, as I did for forty years. It is a kind of freedom you cannot hope to know."

Shvetz prides himself on being a free soul, and he began to protest. "There are other ways. I gig around. There are dates."

"Have you played Mascouche? Saint-Jovite? Amqui?"

"Well, no."

"I have."

They began a discussion of freedom and responsibility which was beyond me, my mind being too heavy and concrete for any flight of abstruse reasoning. I sat on, following the talk at some distance, sometimes getting ten cents' worth of pistachio nuts in a paper cone to go with my beer. After an hour's debate, Lazarovich went to the bathroom, and from there to call Tom, to see if we should come by.

"You must see him," said Mister Petroff, "see him, he is a fine young man who will replace me when I die. He has a wife and three daughters but he is free . . . free. He will not remain where he is."

Lazarovich came back from the phone. "It's all right," he said, "he's in. It's only a minute from here."

"I hope so," said Shvetz, clearly disgruntled. "It's bloody cold."

The Old Man began to laugh. "Dance, dance, that will warm you." As we went to the door, he lifted his hand in a grave salute. We went out into black cold.

If you blink you'll miss Avenue de Chateaubriand. In this part of town, it is really an alley with pretensions, too narrow for cars to pass. It starts at Roy and runs north just past 149 Marie-Anne where it is interrupted by the railroad right-of-way, the iron curtain of Montreal which severs the life flow of all the streets in the east end except the biggest, as far out as D'Iberville. North of the tracks it begins again somewhere back of de Fieurimont, running into the north end where it gradually becomes a real street.

Where Tom lives you can't park. To do so, you would have to climb right up on the sidewalk, and at that it would be hard for somebody else to get past. Sometimes at the north end of this block an undertaker parks a hearse for several hours, and then the street is effectively closed off. As in an alley, the big buildings fronting on the next main street present their backs to the passer-by. Tom lives in what must be the back part of *Le Montagnard* or one of its neighbours on Saint-Hubert: but for him the entrance is on de Chateaubriand. The approach to his third-floor quarters is embellished by a really beautiful spiral staircase with a delicate iron rail rising in a graceful curve. I don't deny the staircase is dangerous in winter, when you can't put your bare hand on the railing, and when you have to watch your footing very carefully.

As we ascended Lazarovich said, "A man fell down here one night straight to the bottom. He was a Hungarian, may have been drunk. Killed instantly." It was hellishly dark climbing, but as we came to the second floor, a blind shot up on the door to your left and bright light streamed out; a pair of female eyes glared angrily at us. Then suddenly the blind descended and it was as dark as before. On the third-floor platform, right at the top, you're apt to feel slightly dizzy if you look down at the black rectangle below, whose center, an oblong grass plot, is ringed by upwards-pointing metal spikes. There is the impression of an elevator shaft of indefinite length, without entry except from above.

It was very dark on the balcony. All at once a door flew open and we were flooded and surrounded by intensely bright light. Tom stood in the doorway, beckoning us in. Lazarovich went first, then Shvetz, then me. While introductions were circulating, I stood blinking and looking around, a little confused by the wave of light and colour. I had a rich, mixed impression of much pale electric light in which were splashed patch after patch of brilliant colour, high up in the room. I scarcely understood the introductions except to get the sense that I was meeting Tom and his wife, old friends of Lazarovich.

As my eyes grew accustomed to the light, I saw that all over the room, mounted on dully shining polished wooden stands, on top of the taller articles of furniture, stood a great fleet of what seemed at first to be children's toy sailboats. Examining them more closely, I could see that far from being playthings they were immensely delicate and detailed works of art, models of famous sailing vessels of the sixteenth and seventeenth centuries. Their sails, sometimes pale waxen yellow like old parchment, sometimes closer to an oily transparent brown, sometimes nearly white canvas stippled with almost invisible brown dots, were emblazoned with royal and naval arms, purple and red and blue and gold, gleaming richly in thick oil laid on the heavy fabric of the sails. The decks of these ships were hand-worked in strips of miniature planking fastened with nails so small as almost to disappear. Hulls were varnished in hard thick transparent coats, and sometimes the keels were coated in sheets of shining copper, polished and giving back an image of one's amazed inspection.

This was a fantastic dream of vanished fleets, Drake's Revenge, galleons of the Armada, Admiral Blake's flagship in his Dutch wars, Hudson's *Half Moon*, ship after ship, all famous, all worked with magnificent accuracy, all in splendid and royal colours. As I stood there saucer-eyed, taking this impression in, the others began to laugh softly at my amazement and talk began, and a potent fruit punch was served.

Sometimes a calm scene like this, a rounded period in the life of the imagination, will rest in one's faculties, stay, rotate, restate itself over and over in changing colours and meanings, exciting feelings, instincts, memory, imagination, seeming to have special powers to enlighten and give form to the rest of our lives. Standing there in the queer narrow living room, almost a scarcely enclosed balcony projecting over nothing, a bit drafty, a bit poor in its other furnishings, I was mysteriously overwhelmed by this various and splendid sight with feelings of a hidden and immense joy. I was smiling and transfixed, and the remembrance of the sight long after retains the capacity to direct and strengthen all my ways of feeling, so that the life of de Chateaubriand mixes itself irrecoverably with my suspicions of the possibility of goodness, of the memorable life.

Confusedly smiling and wondering, I felt grateful when Tom's wife put a glass of rosy punch in my hand. I drank it at once, and immediately began to feel sleepy. I found a seat beside her—I never learned her name—and began to look at her admiringly. She had small dark features, beautifully composed, giving her an exotic loveliness; she looked like an elf; she looked like the gypsy she was. As my eyes moved from her around the room and back, she laughed soundlessly.

"My husband is in the Marine Museum," she said, "and these are his work. He has a great collection, you know, one of the best in the world, all his."

I said thoughtfully that such work must require great powers of concentration and great skill.

"They've been written up and photographed. There was a big story in colour on them in *Weekend Magazine*."

I remembered having seen the story, but when I said so she was not impressed. "He could do this work anywhere, for the Royal Navy, for the Institute of Naval History, but these are his, and even so this is not his life work."

"What does he do?"

"Why, he leads us. Listen."

Tom was discussing Romany history, of which he was certainly a learned exponent. "The aboriginal home of the Tzigany or Romany folk, or as they are called in English the Gypsies, is shrouded in the obscurity of prehistory. Their English name ascribes to them an Egyptian origin, but this is certainly false. Their language—our language—is structurally of immense antiquity, being closest in its morphologies to Sanskrit, closer than any modern tongue except perhaps Lithuanian. From those primitive vocabularies we possess (unfortunately much mixed with loan-words), it is possible to hypothesize a location in Northwestern India. From there we made our way overland, south of the Aral and through Persia, appearing in recorded European history in early Christian times. We have always been travellers, free, moving." He broke off.

His wife said proudly, "Tom is preparing the first scientific lexicon of Romany."

"For English use?"

"Of course." She and Lazarovich and Shvetz began to talk to Tom about his chances of publication, of an offer from a great university press, and of some of his appearances on television. It seemed that he had done much, worked very hard for a long time, to redress some of his people's legal and political disabilities connected with citizenship, conscription, and taxation. I grew very drowsy. Once his wife said to me confidentially, "He's been interviewed on TV twice."

"I know," I said hazily, getting up to go to the toilet at the end of an extraordinarily narrow hall. As I poked my way past an undersized space-heater, past baby-carriages and playpens, three little girls popped successively out of three doorways. They were exactly like their mother. She followed me, glass in hand, and knelt among them, fondling them and crooning to them. Their appearance so late at night in this tiny isolated apartment intensified my earlier feelings of wonder. They smiled and began to sing sweetly to their mother, an old song in the minor about the larks in wintertime.

In the living room, a technical philological discussion had now begun. I drank off my punch, accepted a refill with misgivings, went to the bathroom, and got back in time for Lazarovich's reluctant goodnight. "I'm only in town for a day and a night," he said.

They stood, black silhouettes, in the doorway, warning us of the steps. I saw them framed in the brilliance of their room as we went back down.

"What's his last name?" I asked Lazarovich.

He paused at the bottom of the spiral. "It's very funny, you know that? I've known him for years. I can't tell you his last name."

Avenue de Chateaubriand grows deadly cold after midnight in February. We moved off, and parted at the corner. Much later in the year, coming back alone and unannounced to drop in on Tom and his wife, I discovered to my sorrow that they had moved on.

GETTING TO WILLIAMSTOWN

"Many a green isle needs must be
In the deep wide sea of misery."

D RIVING out of Montreal in the old days, it used to take me a couple of hours to get off the island—they do it in forty-five minutes now—and by the time I was up around the Ontario line I would decide to by-pass Cornwall, "smelly Cornwall," the kids called it, rightly. How it stank, that town, of sulphur and God knows what else! We got off the highway at Lancaster, jog right a hundred yards, jog left onto County Road 19, and away.

Mr. Fessenden ... Mr. Fessenden?

There was a creek we followed upstream for miles, Raisin Creek, was it? More than a creek, almost a river in places, but shallow. Broad but shallow, like a lot of things, with trees bending over in the summer so they almost formed an arch over the water. We always meant to stop and wade; we could have done it easily. The children would have loved it but we had to get on. Raisin Creek there, with the little bridges and culverts, and from time to time in the distance to the south a view of the main line, and beyond the glitter of the river. It seemed to be always sunny back then.

The road wound back and forth, not a modern highway, badly engineered on the curves so that you couldn't go over forty without braking suddenly at every new curve. I taught the children what the highway signs meant, a cross, a curved line to right or left, railroad tracks, intersections at various angles. We were surrounded by rolling, beautifully cultivated fields with the only interruption a few lines of maples bordering the farms, the road, and the river. The fields were expansive and rich, peaceful, ah, God!

I see it now, projected on my walls as though real. Five miles west of Lancaster, about two-fifteen in the afternoon, we pass a gas-pump and a refreshment stand, abandoned for the last few seasons. The pump has a globe of opaque white glass for a head, with three red stars on it. Underneath there is a transparent glass cylinder with gallonage calibrated from zero to twenty, and below that the pump, with a long handle at the side. As the attendant gives you gas, the level drops in the glass cylinder and the clean brilliant red fluid splashes and foams while the children watch fascinated. I pay him, and stand for a moment as he pumps gas back into his apparatus, until at last the cylinder is that beautiful red clear to the top, no nonsense about premium quality or tetraethyl.

Beside the abandoned gas-pump there's this old refreshment stand. In the late twenties somebody used it to sell pop and ice cream in the summer, and farm produce around harvest time. The shingled walls were green and the roof red; but now in 1934 the paint has flaked and peeled and I can just barely make out the colour. We made up stories about it; it was a little house or an enchanted castle. In truth the stand and pump sat there in overgrown grass, amid wildflowers, lonely and haunted.

Now we are coming to Williamstown; the trees are growing plentiful and the children need, they say, to stop. Deep,

deep in the countryside. They can wet in the ditch at the roadside if they must, for there's no-one to see or mind very much. But they hope for ice cream at the general store, so we don't stop by the side of the road. The trees thicken; bright sunlight glances on the green. I see it on these white walls.

The town lies tranquilly in a tiny valley beside the creek, in an island of green under the sun. We dip down in our Chrysler Airflow—there weren't big enough windows in that car; it was too experimental! Down we sail as the highway narrows and becomes King William Street, steep as we come into town, swooping toward a dangerously narrow bridge at the foot of the hill. As we descend, the foliage obscures the sun. We pass fields on our left, and on our right I have the sense, through the narrow windows of my Airflow, of a white building standing the width of a field from the edge of town, a building in a field that I have never really seen, but shining, always freshly painted, in the last sun before the shade trees crowd in on King William Street.

Careful turning onto the bridge. Cars cannot pass here but in twenty years I never had to dispute the passage with anyone, certainly not with a citizen of Williamstown. Once, I recall, I came to the bridge, going west into town, just as a farmer arrived, going east and homewards. He had a Model-T truck with a load of crated chickens; the crank stuck out of the face of the Model-T like a pipe. We smiled at one another and I backed off. When he drove past, he waved and nodded politely. Across the bridge we take a right, passing the few houses this side of the stores. This is where my heart stopped, every trip for fifteen years.

Just this side of the stores stands an old house that's for sale, has been ever since I've been driving through. It's yellow, or would be if the paint were restored; the porch sags somewhat. The windows are comprised of sixteen small leaded panes apiece; some are broken. It is a heavenly place. The backyard opens on fields, as do all the backyards in town, and the house will be maybe a hundred and thirty years old. There is a small lawn in front which someone cares for, perhaps the long-dead realtor whose bald sign penetrates the turf. Going by, I sigh and yearn. But for some reason, we never stopped just there. We proceeded to the general store, grocery store, variety store, butcher shop, what would you call it?

Outside Williamstown the highway is paved, but in front of the cluster of stores, for whatever reason, the street is always dusty with a light haze hanging in the air. BUSTIN'S DRUGS: pharmacist's globes dim in the window. DEVLIN'S HARD-WARE: a display of CCM bikes and a cream separator. In the window of the grocery store appear the name of the propri-etor and the words SALADA TEA arranged in an arc, in white tin letters appliqued to the glass in some mysterious way. Here we stop, taking no special care to park in this or that direction.

The kids have used the toilet here so often, at least six times a year, that the proprietor believes he knows us. He gives them extra large scoops of ice cream, dipping it from a cooler with big round holes in the top, and truck lids like gladiators' shields. Then he sprinkles orange and red and chocolate flakes of candy on top of the double-dips; this costs a nickel. He has a glittering and lethal meat slicer with which he cuts boiled ham and pork for picnic lunches, and a superb coffee grinder, and the place smells of spice and coffee. The showcases are bound in a beautiful walnut. I can't smell that smell. I can think of it but I can't recreate it. Later, perhaps.

"That's quite a car, Mister."

"Yes, that's what they call streamlining. It came in this year."

Into the dark hot car, then, and down King William Street westwards past the District Catholic School, just where the sidewalks end. It's three o'clock and we'll have to make up time if we're going to be in Maitland for dinner. The highway straightens and we get up to fifty, going straight west away from heaven.

Time for Mr. Fessenden's injections.

But you couldn't get in and you couldn't get out, in those days. It took half a day to get to Williamstown and another three hours to Maitland, in all a seven-hour drive, a hundred and thirty miles, what with lunch in the car, stops for the toilet, occasional car-sickness. I dreamed of commuting, for it can't have been more than sixty-five miles from the city.

"I could go in by the day."

"No you couldn't, Henry, you'd be exhausted. No, don't begin to explain it to me; there can't be any question of driving in and out of Montreal every day. Think of it! Your heart would never stand it."

"But I'm a young man, Irma, and there's nothing wrong with my heart. I've just had my checkup and I'm fine, just fine. And only think of the peace in the winter, alone, a couple of feet of snow. Black dark and little lights in the parlour windows; there's a school, a good one I'm sure, and later on we could send them into Lancaster on a bus, or they could come with me."

"And you seriously propose to bury me in that place with the children? Who would they play with?"

"I imagine there are children living there; there must be five hundred people in the place."

"And what about me? What would I do for amusement, with the car gone all day? I'd go mad in a place like that."

"It might be good for you, Irma."

"What are you insinuating?"

"Oh, nothing, nothing. I love you, Irma."

She would have a lightning switch of mood.

"I don't know how you put up with me, Henry, I'm such a mess."

"Well, we all have faults, dear."

"Yes, but think, Henry. No movies, no friends, no theatre."

"We don't go to the theatre."

159

"But we might sometime, and we *can* if we're desperate. No concerts, no public transit."

"You don't need streetcars in a town that size; you can walk to church and the store. And I want to live there. It wouldn't be like this."

"There's nothing wrong with this. You're doing splendidly. You have all your friends in the office and inside of two years you'll be a trust officer. You'd have to get up at five to drive into Montreal, and you wouldn't get home till nine, which exactly reverses your present hours. It would kill you."

"I could make better time than that."

"We don't have enough money to fix up that ruin."

"Now that's not fair. You've never even been inside it."

"Have you?"

"No. I've never been there but with you, driving through on the way to your mother's."

"Henry, you have no idea what it costs to fix up a place in the country; that house looks good to you, seeing it for the first time from the outside; but it'll be full of dry rot and structural faults; there's no plumbing."

"How do you know?"

"There's a little house in the backyard."

"I didn't notice."

"No, you wouldn't! I'm the one who'd have to nurse the children through typhoid."

"I'll bet there isn't any more typhoid, per capita, in Williamstown than here."

"We'll wait till they're a little older before we run the risk!"

She always closed a discussion by tabling the children's needs; we moved from the condition of my health to the children's needs and back. They were the poles of her dialectic. And about most points in the argument, she had fact and reason on her side. I *did* have friends in the office and almost nowhere else, and I *did* become a trust officer in charge of important portfolios, and I didn't have to go to war on account of the family and my public responsibilities as a trust officer. In Montreal, the public responsibilities of a financial officer are taken to be great and pressing.

"Mother, how can my friends come to an upstairs duplex? It was all right when I was small; I didn't understand. But look at the difference between us and the Lewises. It makes me so ashamed. Why can't we have a house like everybody else?"

"Ssshhh! Mustn't disturb your father, Frances. He's lying down before dinner."

"He's always having his rest. What does he have to lie down for?"

"It's better, dear, when a man is middle-aged, for him to conserve his energy. Come into the dining-room." Their steps recede.

"I want to have a skating party with coffee after."

"Aren't some of the children young for coffee?"

"Oh, Mother!"

"We can call it a coffee party anyway and no harm done. What sort of house do you think we should have, dear?"

"Mother, I want to live in the Town of Mount Royal!"

"So do I, dear!"

Oh thickening trees, oh shady sunlight, leaded panes and quiet dusty street.

There are no trees in the Town of Mount Royal; this is a fact. Here and there one finds a stunted shrub or two; but when they laid out the developments during, and just after, the war, they bulldozed down all the trees, a bad mistake that nobody seems to regret. Without noticing it, the citizens live on an arid plain where the grass yellows in May. If the land were clear prairie they would see this; but amidst the ranch houses the desert effect is half-obliterated. That you can't sit in your own backyard in July because of the glare seems to be taken for granted by all but me. It takes me an hour and a half to drive two miles to work, because of a bottleneck at a level crossing. In wintertime, it takes much longer.

"Everybody else has a television aerial."

"Some people put them up without a set," says Bunker.

"Oh, your father would never do that, would you, darling?"

"What is it, darling?"

"Frances and Bunker think we should have television."

"Everybody on the street has it but us."

"Then I'll order one today. I hadn't noticed. Are there good programs?"

"I believe it depends on your aerial, dear."

"Ah, like the radio. I'll see about it this afternoon." At this, the children—and wonderfully they aren't children any more—are silently pleased, as they should be. I've never denied them anything. Irma hugs me, and they observe us indulgently, gratified.

Yes, comatose, a terminal case, I'm afraid.

Terminal, that's what they said when Irma went and the house was empty, Frances married and living in Toronto, and Bunker in Maitland. He's a real grandmother's boy, that one, looking after the store and the farm properties, and seeing about Irma's flowers now and then, something I couldn't do myself from Montreal.

"That's quite a car, Mister."

"Yes, that's a French car, a Citroen. Most comfortable car on the road, you ought to try it sometime."

I can go back and forth to Maitland in under three hours now, with 401 connected to the Metropolitan Highway and only one traffic light between the Town of Mount Royal and Toronto. I don't have to have a fast car; the Citroen isn't what you'd call a fast car. I just average a comfortable sixty miles an hour and I'm there in no time. Why, Bunker might just as well have been living with me, we've seen so much of each other, and he's been in to see me . . . to see me here.

401 follows the river pretty much, about half a mile inland. You pick it up at the Ontario border; you don't go into Lancaster, and naturally you don't go anywhere near Williamstown. I haven't been through Williamstown since before Irma died, I don't believe. Maybe I'll go, one of these days. But I've been going out on 401, and for a while it's pretty country down by the locks and the islands; every few minutes you can see the sunlight on the water. But soon, northwest of Cornwall, the geography changes; you can't see the river and the land is swamp. Scrub timber, marsh, cattails, and the occasional concession road running north into the scrub. There are probably plenty of flies in there; but I've never stopped to see. Coming back down at night, it's black as a yard up a stovepipe along 401; there isn't the traffic to justify a superhighway through there but it had to go in because of Montreal and Toronto. There are only the two gas stations between the border and Maitland, and the province has to subsidize them, and the food is bad, especially the coffee.

Going along in my Citroen between the railroad tracks and the river, I can always tell when we're passing Williamstown because I can see the steeple of some church peeking up out of a clump of trees a few miles to my right, a rectangular white tower with a pointed lead steeple on top; the town must be five or six miles off the highway and one of the county roads connects. One of these days I'll take the ramp, turn off north in my Citroen and astonish the grocer, though the children won't be with me.

"You'd be better off to come and live in Maitland, Dad, where you'd be near Mother."

"Well, but Bunker, she's dead. I mean, I can't see that it matters where I am, relative to where she is."

"Haven't you got any feelings on the subject? After all, the DeVebers have been established in Maitland almost a hundred and fifty years. Grandmother used to tell me, and she showed me pictures."

"I'm not a DeVeber. And I'm a Town of Mount Royal man, if there is such a thing."

"You don't like it in the Town, do you, Dad? Think what that big house is costing to keep up, now we're all out of it. And maybe you'd enjoy helping me with the business; there's talk of a shopping plaza out by the 401 cloverleaf and I'm considering putting a store in there. Naturally there would have to be additional capital."

"DeVeber capital, I hope."

"Oh now, Dad, it would be a good investment. You could put in what you get for the house without liquidating any of your other holdings; that might be enough. What do you suppose the house is worth?"

How does he seem today, nurse?

Bunker has been in to see me right along; he drives down afternoons and has his supper in the city. Then he goes back after nine o'clock. He's attentive all right, and it's cheerful to have somebody here, although I can't work up the strength to discuss the house with him. Perhaps we'll sell. I never liked it, and it looks as if I may be here some time. No use having it standing empty and a tax charge. But I don't feel up to talking now. It wouldn't be good for me. I mean, I'm not well.

"Bunker, if you've brought me all this way on a false alarm, I'll kill you. You think you're the only one in the world with business to look after. Thursday night is Debbie's school play, and I haven't finished her costume. Tomorrow night Butler has tickets for the O'Keefe Centre, and you drag me to Montreal on a wild goose chase. Look at him, he's as comfortable as he could possibly be. They're doing everything they can for him, not that there's much they can do, in his condition."

"He'll hear you!"

"No, he won't. They've got him sedated. They have to because it's very painful at the end if they don't. I don't suppose he's felt a thing for days, poor Dad, but at least he isn't in any pain."

"It's wonderful what they can do with drugs, these days."

"Sometimes they don't help though. When I had Debbie, they had me doped right up and it still hurt like mad. I screamed my head off. But with this, it seems to work."

"He's quiet enough, all right, poor old man. He was never the same, you know, after he lost Mother. He went right downhill, just as if he'd lost part of himself, and it isn't as if he were that old, either."

"He's sixty-five, isn't he?"

"Sixty-six. He quit the Trust on his sixty-fifth birthday."

"I remember. I guess they'll look after . . . uh . . . things, won't they?"

"Yes, they're the executors, with me."

"With you?"

"If we're going to discuss this, let's whisper, Frances."

"Why you, Mister Smartie, why not me? I'm older."

"I'm a man."

"I don't see it makes much difference. Anyway you're not that much of a man."

"Frances!"

"Ah, I'm sorry, Bunker, I'll take that back. Who named the executors?"

"Dad."

"Why did he leave me off?"

"I have no idea; he probably thought it didn't matter. When you're making a will, you likely think all will be harmony and concord afterwards."

"Just you try any tricks, Bunker Fessenden, and I'll harmony and concord you!"

"There'll be no tricks; the whole testament is as plain as day. The office wrote it up for us, and as far as succession duties go, it's a masterpiece. We get everything and the government gets nothing."

"Nothing?"

"Practically. The minimum, and you can't do any better than that. The estate is divided equally between us. That's fair, isn't it?"

"I'm older. And I have Debbie."

"But you've got a husband to look after you."

"Hah!"

"Butler supports you, in spite of everything. Nobody supports me, and I've been thinking of getting married."

"You?"

"Yes, me. That's a big house you know, and with grandmaw gone I'm all alone."

Alone in a big house. Our house was the first California-redwood ranch in the Town of Mount Royal, with the refrigerator hung on the kitchen wall—too high to reach comfortably but very stylish. There's much glass, too much. When I wander through the house alone nights, with all the lights on, I'm always exposing myself accidentally to the curious stares of passers-by. It's a house where you have to be careful how you quit bathroom or bedroom; there's always somebody looking at you from out on the sidewalk. The recreation room gives on the main street; it's the shape of a small bowling alley, with a tiled floor which gives your steps a curious dead ring. Walking back and forth in there at night, with a vast expanse of plate glass on one side of me, and the television and bar on the other, I'm unutterably solitary, like some aquatic creature in a tank, going purposelessly round and round. Now and then I throw darts at the wall; it must look very strange from outside, the brightness, the solitude, the aimless activity. It's a good thing we had that window in the recreation room, because that's how they found me.

Banging on the window, rap, rap, rap, reverberations in the sash.

Feet upstairs, then coming down.

Indistinct shapes beside me.

"You were right, Mary, it's Mr. Fessenden, and he's sick."

"Should we get mixed up in this?"

"We can't leave him here."

"We can call the police and wait till they come."

"I'll call them."

"Don't touch anything, and be sure to get a release."

Feet going away and then, later, being carried gently.

"What's his trouble?"

"*Sais-pas*. Some kind of a deep coma."

"No fractures, no hemorrhaging? Careful how we handle him; it might be anything."

"What do you think?"

"Heart or malignancy."

"Yes."

"The tests will show."

"Yes."

"Off we go."

What is this, this heavenly feeling of being carried, this lightness never felt before, lie back and float into the white room and the level bed, and afterwards the pictures flashed on the walls and now and then a voice or voices. Being carried, ah, ah.

Bunker lives in a stone house; they'll never find him when comes time; he'd better get married, start the whole thing off again in Maitland; but I won't come to the wedding. I'm going to take the ramp when I see that white rectangle, that leaden tower, in the sun above the trees five miles to the north. I see the sun on the walls now, and now coming through the walls. The trees bend over as we glide along beside the river; the walls open and fade and give on the country road and the rich cornfields, a line of trees in the distance and coming closer, lustrous in the sun.

Look after the Fessenden business, orderly!

Being carried along at the top of the hill and we swoop downwards as trees thicken, a green island, around us and here at the edge of town I see the white building gleaming in the sun under the soft sheen of the tower, one narrow field from town. Being carried gently in by men in white to the porch of the white building in the bright sun. Blaze of glory on leaves moving in the windows as these six bear me kindly up the aisle.

THE
TOLSTOY PITCH

"OOK at all the Volks buses."

"That's the one to have, all righty."

"Turquoise and white, red and white, brown and sand."

"Lady antique dealers. Look, there's one, and there's another . . . or maybe dog-raisers."

"Not here. What's the name of this place again?"

"It used to be called Hitchcocksville, but they changed it to Riverton."

"Because of the river," said Squires acutely. "What river?"

"I think that's the Farmington."

"Christ, it can't be the Farmington, or else every river in Connecticut is called the Farmington. Maybe it's the Housatonk."

"The Housatonic is bigger. Pastore will know."

"I'd have thought he'd have a Volks bus," said Jed Squires, picking up the loose end. "That's his image, isn't it?"

"Not exactly," said the agent. "You haven't quite caught the tonalities. He's trying to be very simple and ordinary and unaffected—it's a most involved concept."

"But he is simple and ordinary. At least ordinary."

"No he's not. It's a very clever act, if you ask me. Once upon a time he was simple and ordinary, twenty years ago. Then he was a polished sophisticate about ten years back, when I took him on." The agent laughed softly. "And now he's ordinary again, but not the same way. Take his wife now."

"Yeah, yeah."

"Sandra, that's no name for anybody; that was a name for movie stars around 1948. Nobody's used it since. But the fact is, her name really is Sandra. In these Connecticut mill towns..."

"...like Riverton?"

"No, Riverton is an antique village, not a mill town. Winsted is a mill town. In the mill towns like Torrington or Bristol, the Italians might very well call a girl Sandra for real. Straight. It's just short for Alessandra. Alexandra. So she has numerous choices; she can be Sandy, a clean-cut WASP, or she can be Renaissance Alessandra, or movie-star Sandra, or old fashioned Edwardian Alexandra, all on the one name."

"So what is she really, besides a smart writer's wife?"

"Right now, or ten years ago, or twenty?"

"Sir John Hawkins' stockings, eh?"

"The problem of identity. She's a kind, keen girl who wants to help her husband."

"Langley, for gosh sakes."

"I believe that, Jed. I think that's the consistent element." He took Squires by the arm and moved him gently across the smooth lawn. "She wants us."

"Frank's back in the warehouse, Langley. Can you spot the flaw? Come here a minute." Sandra held one of the chairs upside down, frowning. "They're practically giving this one away. Twenty-one ninety-eight, and it looks perfect to me. Could there be some catch?" She was unaffectedly eager to have his opinion, and he took the chair from her, feeling the fine hard surface of the wood with unaccustomed pleasure. The chair was wonderfully made and very good looking, the wood under the finish an almost buttery golden colour, over which the characteristic pattern lay like light on an autumn pond.

"These are seconds," said Sandra to Jed Squires, "and at these prices there's always a flaw. They tell you so with perfect frankness; there's a sign somewhere, displayed, but not displayed with oppressive candour."

Squires gave Langley Benton a sudden look but the agent pretended not to notice, pushing tentatively at the chair with his forefinger. "It's the glue," he said abstractedly, "there's a tiny blob of glue here where the rung fits in. I think that's the flaw. Would that affect your wear?"

"They won't sell them if they won't wear. I'm going to take this one, that makes four."

"All the same colour?"

"No, I got one gold, one oak, two black. I wanted them in odd colours, not a set. A set looks too composed, and in any case they're for the kitchen." She gave Squires a confiding grin. "We live in the kitchen," she said, and turned away toward the salesroom to place her order.

"'In any case,'" quoted Squires. "This is an Italian girl from a mill town?"

Benton said, "Don't be too hard on us. We're all trying to grow and remain ourselves at the same time."

This made Squires writhe in discomfort.

"Awful, ain't it?"

"Awful."

"So why do you want Pastore?"

"He has exactly the right kind of name."

"Well certainly, there you go, you're doing it too, you calculating bastard."

Squires started to clown around in a self-parody. "We'll get this poor slob's name on the jacket, and if it doesn't go, he's to blame. If it goes big, we're shrewdies for signing him, and anyway it was our property right along." He looked back at the door to the salesroom. "If I had a big black cigar I'd wave it around. The fact is, and I should never say this to an agent, Frank Pastore is perfect."

"Not small, not really big; artistic but not obscure; neither avant-garde nor book-dub."

"Respectable. Lives in Greenwich. Safe, ah, safe, safe. You know, there's nothing so comfortable as an established artist."

"Here they come."

Squires shut up and faced the writer and his wife who advanced hand in hand across the astonishing lawn. They looked young and in love.

"They're putting the chairs in the car," said Pastore, "and look at these for ninety-eight cents on sale." He showed some tea-towels in a coarse weave, done in Colonial motifs. "God, I love a bargain."

"What about lunch?" Benton never cared to be long away from food.

"All set up, all arranged. I'd never drag you fifty miles without food, Langley. We can pick up complete box lunches and cold beer right around the corner; then we'll go and have our picnic. There are two beautiful picnic grounds right near here, one just down the river, and one further along by Barkhamsted Reservoir. Look at the day. What a day for a picnic."

"I think they're ready," said Sandra. "Let's go to the car."

"Have you been up this way before, Mrs. Pastore?" asked Squires.

"We used to come here on picnics. I was born in Bristol, about twenty-five miles from here by the back roads. It's an ugly town, nothing quaint or New England about it, not even a Colonial Howard Johnson's. So we were always glad to get out here. We used to come on Columbus Day."

"Kind of late in the season."

"Oh no, no, it was often fine. It's a real beauty spot in a way. We'll pick up the lunches and you'll see. Here's Frank."

Frank drove an ordinary medium-priced Ford station wagon in an ordinary medium-blue. The chairs, nested in pairs and tightly tied with heavy twine, lay enfolded in paper in the rear deck. The agent, the producer, and the writer's wife, an unholy trinity, clambered into the back seat together, and sat chattering idly while Frank drove around the comer and stopped at the restaurant. There was a short wait while their lunches were boxed up, and then they drove along a narrow country road that led to the picnic spot.

They were on the east side of the river and in about two miles the paved road curled away to the left, heading off east and south to Route 44. Pastore turned to the right onto a sandy track that went down to the riverbank, where the picnic tables were. In a few moments they were in a little shady grove, almost a wood, that was fitted out with tables, green oil drums for the disposal of waste food and paper, and some stone fireplaces.

Frank ran the car up into a perfect natural parking space formed by intersecting rows of trees, and they got out and took the beer and sandwiches down to a picnic table on the sunny riverbank. First thing, Frank and Sandra took their shoes off and dug their toes into the warm sand. In a couple of seconds, Benton and Squires found themselves, to their bewilderment, doing likewise. The four of them sat around the table, bare feet in the sunlit sand, salting hardboiled eggs and looking inside chicken sandwiches.

"Put the beer in the river," said Squires knowledgeably. "The movement of the water will cool it."

"I wonder if there are fish in there?"

"Too shallow, Langley."

"Couldn't small fish live in it?"

"Perhaps. I've never seen anybody fishing right here. Lower down."

"Oh, come on now, Frank. Papa used to fish right over there, beside those stones." Sandra hitched up her skirt, took an egg in her hand, went down to the water and waded in. Mud swirled in the water around her ankles, hiding her pretty feet. She went a third of the way across the river, about twenty yards or a little less, and the water came up to her knees. She stood there nibbling at the egg and smiling happily in remembrance.

"He caught a little fish once," she called, "and I was so excited I fell down and got my bloomers soaking wet."

"I remember hearing," said Frank, "but there's no fish now. Come and have a sandwich and a beer." She waded back, half-unwilling, and they went on with their meal.

It was one of those immensely sunlit days in the late summer when the sky is off-white instead of blue, because of the glare. Sitting out in the sun, they were glad to have the trees and the green promise of shade just at their backs. Sometimes a car drove slowly past on the road on the other side of the river, but most of the time their picnic was intimately quiet. Squires felt rivulets of sweat under his arms; he unbuttoned his top two shirt buttons and tilted his head back to stare at the sky as he drank his third beer.

He had not done anything like this since he could remember—they did not get these colours in California. For long afterwards this afternoon stayed in his mind as one of those rare, mysteriously beautiful instants of quiet in modern life. He felt so much at ease that he hardly took any account of it when Sandra Pastore, having finished a heavy meal and fought off the temptation to sleep, put her head close to his and asked in the accents of intimate friendship: "Is Jed Squires your real name?"

"We take the West Side?"

"Aw, no, listen, go in on the Major Deegan if you don't mind? It's quicker, and I'll be down there all morning."

"It's all speculative, you realize. He doesn't know about it yet; he thinks you want the two short stories."

"If necessary I'll take the two stories, just to get him. When Lazenby hears what the arrangement is, he'll be wild to do the book."

"Oh, he wants to do the book, Jed. It's just that we can't be definite about Frank until I've talked to him. I've got plenty of other clients, you understand." He caught the nuance crossing Squires' face and developed his idea. "I'm not undercutting Frank, but if he doesn't do it, somebody else will, and I just hope it's a client of mine. That's a lot of money."

"Uh. He's the one we want. Will Lazenby go to bat for us?"

"For a big best-seller over his imprint Lazenby would do most things. Not absolutely anything, but most things."

"He's all right; he's like us; he can't afford the luxury of choice."

"But Frank can."

". . . why I want him, elementary psychology. I should tell him to forget it but I can't. It's that easy authoritative independence. Did you hear that girl of his? 'Is Jed Squires your real name?' Nobody ever asked me that in my life before."

Benton laughed. "Did Sandra say that? It sounds just like her."

"Was she kidding or what?"

"Sandra? No. She never kids like that. Not just like that. She really wanted to know. You got to admit, Jed, your name sounds like a stage name." The expression on the producer's face was mixed, but he let the point go.

"When you have lunch," he said, "underline how strong the storyline is. He doesn't have to do a thing but set it and dialogue it; it's all there ready in the line. He could do it in six months or less. The book can appear next August, and we'll be shooting by then. We'll give the movie sale to the press well in advance of publication, and the thing will be in the discount houses by the carload, while we're shooting. It's an enormously strong property, and when Pastore and Lazenby are through with it the market will be pre-sold at all levels. Nobody needs to know the idea didn't originate with him."

"He'll know."

"My goodness, yes, that's his trouble."

"I use a parking garage over off Second Avenue. Is this all right?"

"Perfect, I'll take a cab from here. Thanks for the ride in."

"Oh, a pleasure. We'll be in touch. Say hello to Lazenby for me."

"*Ciao, caro.*"

Pastore came along a tunnel from the station through the Roosevelt lobby and out onto Madison at 44th, wondering if he should bother with a cab. His lunch date was ten blocks uptown, but they were short blocks and he had plenty of time. In Greenwich he walked everywhere but in the city he found himself taking cabs hither and thither and becoming involved in picturesque—excessively picturesque and therefore unusable—conversations with cab-drivers. He loitered along; as it was just on noon the street was briefly sunny and very crowded. There was much to observe, styles in haberdashery, skirt lengths, ugly new construction, graceful new construction, friends and acquaintances passing, unnoticing, in the throng. He came to town very infrequently and, not expecting to see him, these men would attach other names to his face. It made him feel invisible, not dead but gone before, especially when Langley Benton's partner passed him and looked obliviously through him. He wasn't Benton and Zaslow's best-known client, but he was unquestionably their most prestigious (he felt that their best-known client was not a serious writer) and he had been to lunch at least fifty times with Morris Zaslow, though they never met socially, and here the agent didn't recognize him when they passed on Madison Avenue.

He thought: I'm becoming invisible. What's going to become of me when I've reached the point where I never come into the city, never leave the house or at most the garden? I know it worries Sandra but it isn't the onset of madness or even neurosis. I'm not afraid to go out. Here I'm walking down a very crowded street and I don't feel vertigo, I don't feel nervous, my palms are dry and I'm not terrified of meeting somebody. It isn't that I refuse to go out. I just haven't any reason.

All I want to do is mind my own business, keep my mouth shut and do my work. A close-mouthed writer, that's a lunatic program. Hmmmn! The trouble is patent, obvious, what we have here is the classical first stage of the religious life, the gradual detachment from sense. I love my friends, I love my wife, I love God, but *things* are beginning to melt on me and run off the table. What am I going to do if they go altogether? Who the hell ever heard of a writer in this fix? What has happened to that minute obsessed interest I used to have in the details of physical life, skirt lengths, peoples' incomes? A writer cares about the world and the flesh, by definition. He must. What happens to him if that goes? *A Serious Call to a Devout and Holy Life.* No, no, spare me that, for Christ's sake. I mean, I'm not ready.

He stepped off the corner as the light changed, and was almost beheaded by a length of pipe, as a truck beat the red around the corner.

You see? I'm not ready.

When he had come ten blocks he walked a few feet to his right and entered a passageway leading to some elevators and a cigar counter. He bought a pack of cigarettes and threw away an old one which had been lodged in his pants pocket for several days, crumpled and crumby with tobacco. He noticed uneasily that he had been smoking progressively fewer cigarettes.

Flipping the crumpled package into a canister of sand between the elevators, he crossed the small lobby, passing two old female residents of the hotel with their Pekingese in tow, and stood in the doorway of the dining-room. Far down at the back, solitary at a big table, sat Benton. They waved at each other. Smiling at the manageress whom he knew slightly by sight, he nodded toward his agent, and went to join him.

The table was littered with Langley's belongings, a briefcase, three books, a wrapped bottle of liquor. He always took a big table, claiming that he needed space to spread out contracts, and it was true that much of his business was done over lunch and/or drinks. The New Weston staff were used to him now, and as he rarely came in when they were busiest, they indulged him. He opened his briefcase as Frank sat down, extracting what looked like an enormous insurance policy.

"Here's the contract," he said.

"What contract?"

"With Squires."

"Oh, that's it, is it?"

"Yep. I guess I'd better put you in the picture."

"Waste of time."

"Ah, you don't know."

"Yes I do."

"What then?"

"He has a story idea that he thinks will make an important film," said Pastore patiently, as if he were humouring a small child. "He values my name and reputation highly because I'm a prestige writer. He knows that I've never had a movie sale and that by his standards—I guess by any standards—I don't make a lot of money. So he proposes that I take his story, write it up as a novel, hypothetically a best-seller, as my own conception, if you'll allow the expression, publish it with Lazenby, issue a fictitious press release about its sale to the movies—lots of ink— and in short create public interest and a market for his picture. This is done. Other writers have done this, even some proficient ones. I don't use the word 'good' in this connection, because this isn't a moral issue. Also, it has nothing to do with my pride."

"But you won't do it?"

"No, but it doesn't affect my opinion of you."

Benton stuffed the papers into his briefcase with a hurt look, almost a pout, on his face. A waitress came and took their order and went off. Waitresses loved Benton; he had superficially the traits of an adorable small boy.

"He'll buy the two stories anyway; *he's* magnanimous."

"He can afford to be magnanimous," said Pastore smiling.

"Oh come on, Frank."

"I'd like to oblige you, Langley."

Benton perked up a bit. "It really is a strong property, and perfect for you. You can really come on with the Tolstoy pitch."

They stared at each other silently for several seconds. Finally Pastore said, "Pitch? I don't understand. What do you mean, pitch?"

"Ah well, you know, the Frank Pastore image. What we're selling."

"Pitch," said Pastore, deeply offended, "the Tolstoy pitch. I see what you mean. I'll have to think it over."

"Yeah, think it over," said Benton, as their food began to arrive, "and don't hold it against me, Frank. It isn't a sin to want to make some money."

"No, no. I do see that."

That night in Greenwich, pacing up and down the carpet and around the divan, he gave her a rundown on the lunch, and a depth analysis of Benton's shaky position. "I have no axe to grind," said Frank from time to time in the course of his tirade, "nothing to sell, no pitch."

"For Heaven's sake don't worry about it. What can it matter, what a silly man says? He's a silly man and he has silly ideas, but we needn't pay him any attention, and then, he does sell your work."

"Sell, sell. It's like the money changers in the temple. Do you know what he wants?"

"What?"

"Well, this lout, this Squires."

"He's not so bad."

"No, no, he has to live, like the rest of us."

"So what about him?"

"He wants me to take some story he's thought up, a story, you know, a *plot* for God's sake, and write a novel on the basis of his *plot* so that Lazenby, that strait-laced conservative old family-held prestige image publisher, can publish it to hosannas and fanfares. Then we sell, or pretend to sell, this object to Megalopolitan Mighty Art and World-Wide Sound Films—that's Squires—so that he can capitalize on the prestige and the publicity."

"I don't see anything wrong with that."

"There's nothing *wrong* with it. Morally speaking a work of art can be published, broadcast, circulated, sky-written, in any way short of deliberate deception of the public. I'm not objecting to the mechanism of publication."

"Then what?"

His voice began to sound like a snarl. "Don't be such a dumb bunny, Sandra, and stop it with the Socratic method. I don't have to 'talk it out.' That's just tea-table psychology."

"I want to hear what you think."

"You know what I think." He trotted a fast circuit of the divan. "Do you remember that Huckleberry Hound cartoon about the Spud?"

"I don't study them like you."

Frank laughed. "If I were a learned literary critic, which thank Christ I'm not, I believe I'd write a book. *Aspects of Huckleberry Hound.* No, that's not modish enough for a title. Let's see? *Image and Pursuit: A Rhetoric of Bestiary in Late Hanna-Barbera.*"

"That sounds great," said Sandra. They had at one time read much university-press criticism. "Or how about *Animate Satire: Splendours and Miseries of Hound and Bear*?"

This made him chortle, as she'd wished. "Tell about the Spud."

"We open in an Idaho potato patch. It seems that there's this one potato—you ought to hear it in the Huckle voice, which I can't do—who didn't just have eyes. That little feller, he also had a brain. We see this potato lying in a pile with the others. He sprouts legs and stands up, and then arms, and then he addresses the other potatoes, inciting them to revolution. No reply. So he says, 'All right, I'll do it myself, I'm gonna grow. GROW: BIGGER AND BIGGER AND BIGGER.' He gets enormous. Then in the next scene we see a lot of people milling around and shouting 'Run for your lives. The Spud is coming.' It's just fine, great, I tell you."

"I don't see the application."

"Damn it, Sandra, don't be dense. You must see it."

"Nope."

"He wants to grow, see? And to do it, he just plants his two little potato leggies solidly on the ground, and sort of shrugs his shoulders and grits his teeth and grimaces and goes uhhh-hhh, and he gets as big as all hell, just by the effort of will."

"Ahhh."

"I'm a good writer of the middle rank and I'm forty years old and I want to grow."

"You don't propose to lead the revolt of the potatoes and terrorize the world?"

"I don't know. Such a program has attractive aspects, but I guess not, I just want to get bigger. I don't want to be stuck at this point for the rest of my life—I'd be better off dead, and the really dreadful part is that it's out of my hands. I just have to sit tight and see what develops, and do what I think is right." He shrugged comically and gritted his teeth and grimaced. "Am I any bigger?"

"No."

"Which of us by taking thought can add to his stature even one cubit? It can't be done. I'll simply have to wait it out, and in the end I'll be like that writer in *The Seagull*, a good writer, but not so good as Turgenev."

"Tolstoy."

"Ah, you're on my back too. *How Much Land Does a Man Require?* What a title! It takes a lot of guts to start writing parables—you have to rate yourself mighty high, mighty high."

"That had been your intention?"

"Partly. What I want to do is affect the attitudes of a great and simple man, precisely what Tolstoy did. He wasn't a great and simple man to begin with, but he nearly made it."

"By striking attitudes? I don't believe it. The fact is, Frank, you aren't a great and simple man."

They looked at each other with sad affection. "I know," he said, his face a touching parade of emotions. "I'm neither a saint nor a great artist."

"Then you haven't their responsibilities; take the money."

"I don't know that I can work from somebody else's idea."

"At that hourly rate, you can give it a good try."

"I'll call Langley in the morning." He paused. "I wonder who Tolstoy's agent was ... or if he had one."

"Ah, darling, darling, come and kiss me!" Their embrace was heartfelt.

Benton and Squires were sitting in the agency office on Thursday morning, waiting for the call. It had been an exhausting week for poor Squires, who hated sleeping out of his own bed. He was a man of unimpeachable sexual morals who beguiled his free time when in New York in studying shipping. He had always wanted to go to sea, but had become a major producer instead, almost by mischance. One of his oldest friends in New York worked in the office of the Moran fleet, and on his introduction to a captain Squires had spent Tuesday and Wednesday out around Sandy Hook. It had been marvellously relaxing and instructive, but tiring, tiring, and now he looked like the stereotype of the big producer, pouches under the eyes and a papery skin, as though he had been living in nightclubs, an irony whose nuances he didn't bother to dispel.

"Oh, sleep," he said, looking out the window, "thou art a blessed thing."

"You look awful," said Benton candidly.

"Yes, and I got ten hours last night. I can't sleep on foam rubber."

"You ought to come out and stay with us."

"That would be in violation of the conflict of interest rules."

Benton's phone rang and he fidgeted jumpily while the girl on the switchboard cleared the call with him. "Sure I'll take it, Muriel," he said, rolling his eyes expressively at Squires.

"Pastore?"

He nodded and started to talk. "Frank? You in Greenwich? Listen, Jed goes back this afternoon. Yes, that's right, he's talked to Lazenby and the house is entirely agreeable. Matter of fact they think it's a big break for all of us." He spoke as if to overcome objections by erosion and didn't seem to listen at all, which made Squires most impatient. "What does he say?" he repeated. "Let him tell you what he thinks." But Langley wasn't to be diverted; he developed his keyed-up harangue. "... right here with me now. We all think this is the biggest opportunity in your career, not that your own ideas aren't always great, they are, they're just great, Frank, you know I don't have to tell you that, and I wouldn't want to see you write in any other way than what you do. We just want you to use that fine Pastore technique, the good clear prose, the clean dialogue. You know? It'll be your book from beginning to end without question."

"Let him tell you what he thinks," begged Squires.

Benton listened at last, and then he turned to Squires with a joyful face. "He's going to do it," he said, "I never thought he would. My goodness, but I'm glad." They could hear Pastore's voice, shrunken and metallic in the receiver. "Talk to him," said Benton, "this is a turning point; this is going to make all the difference." He handed the receiver to Squires and sat back in his chair looking dazed.

"Hello, Frank? Jed Squires here. Look, Frank, have they 'told you any of the storyline at all? Uh-huh, uh-huh, no. No, that's not quite it . . . no. Look, it just came to me a couple of weeks ago, all in a lump, the whole story, and it will make a perfect film, perfect. I'll give you a quick summary now and I'll tell Langley to get the mimeograph out to you. Now listen closely: there are these two sisters, see, around twenty-six and twenty-two. The older one doesn't care for men; she isn't Lesbian but she's all balled up emotionally and can't love. The younger sister is full of life, outgoing, pretty but not beautiful. The older sister is a beauty, but frozen stiff. Okay? Now here's the angle. The older sister is always on the lookout for a husband for the young one, at least ostensibly. She screens all the young men who visit them with an eye to marriage, but not her own marriage. Crazy, eh? What's that, Russian? It sounds Russian? You're damned right it sounds Russian; it's a great story. I can't do it justice on the phone, but Langley will have the copy out to you this afternoon." He listened to Frank for a few seconds. "Right. Great. I'll be looking for it every day." He hung up and turned to Benton. "He says he'll have a ten-thousand-word outline for our use in two weeks, with a complete scenario. He thinks he can have a draft ready for the end of November, and he's working toward publication in less than a year." The two men looked at each other solemnly and then, actuated by common feelings, they shook hands gravely.

"You'll be shooting next June. Boy, when I think! Lazenby, you, me. The publicity! I had no notion he'd do it. I'll bet there'll be a play in it, television, everything. I tell you what it is, Jed, I've finally managed, after ten years, to do something for him."

"I had him all wrong," said Squires, "all wrong. I had him figured for a posturing phony from the word go. I was wrong. He wants to work. He says he wants to do the screenplay. He turns out to be sincere. A real pro, that's all." He rose to go; he had a plane to catch and he left the summing up to Langley Benton.

"A great guy," said Langley as his confederate left the room, "a real pro, sincere, and a great guy."

A SOLITARY EWE

"*P*OTAGE *aux oignons*, is there plenty of cheese floating in that?"

"It's thick and hot, sir, and good. It's a specialty."

"I'll have that," Peter said, "with cretonnes."

The waitress smiled at Charlie over her order book. "He always says that," she said, "and he always has the onion soup."

"It's how I stay thin. It's a meal in itself, with bread and something to drink; see what it does for me?"

Peter looked handsome and well fed, but not overfed. He had always had that look, Charles remembered, at school and then at McGill, the look of one whom the gods had blessed with every gift, intelligence, health, modest wealth, a clear conscience.

"You mean *croutons*," said the waitress. "Do you want curtains in your soup?"

"Slipcovers," said Peter, "nice chewy ones, cretonnes. And lots of bread and especially lots of butter. Will we have a bottle of wine?"

"Not for me. I've got to read scripts all afternoon. These are all Public Affairs scripts on the Defence Committee, and I can't understand them at all."

"But you'll put them on, won't you?"

"Yes, certainly. Nobody listens to radio."

Peter preened himself. His own show was only local, but it was a television show, very popular in Montreal, which had done much for his reputation. Soon, surely, he would be moved up to something more worthy of his real talents, and for the moment he enjoyed his status of big frog.

"The Defence Committee? We haven't done anything about that."

"It's a sitting duck," said Charlie. "Don't waste your time!"

They were eating in *Le Normand*, a little place with a liquor licence hidden away in a bad block on Metcalfe behind the Mount Royal Hotel. Just across the street, a door in the monolithic grey mass of the hotel admitted members—Peter and Charlie among them—to a club in the subbasement. Most of the club members knew about *Le Normand*, which was not much publicized, maybe because a lot of people who did publicity ate there. The restaurant had a cluttered little window with Calvados bottles and tearsheets of ancient A.J. Liebling articles in it, a number of pictures of Canadian troops at Caen in 1944, and a deceitful menu which was never revised.

Once you got inside, you were disappointed or pleased, depending. There was a cigarette machine with a lot of QUEBEC LIBRE stickers on it, a cash desk where they sold gum and candy, and an undistinguished hatrack. The place hadn't an atom of *panache*, and was popular and patronized in a peculiar subterranean way by people who knew what they were about. When you came back to the half-lit area next to the washrooms and the kitchen, and got snugly seated with a yard of dirty tablecloth in your lap, and were greeted by Marthe, a terribly pretty girl, or by Madame or Monsieur, who would debate the choice of a bottle willingly for an hour, you were gradually made to feel like one of the family in an insidious way.

When you had been there three times and Marthe's husband Victor came out of the kitchen to show you a new knife, you were a confirmed habitué. The restaurant employees plainly had no notion of what they were doing; but the image they projected was as distinct as if they'd had the place designed by a top consultant. They displayed the inimitable freedom of speech and behaviour, not seeming to care if anybody ate there or not, and all this without being discourteous or over-casual: they were just right, and Charlie went there as often as he could, almost every day. He knew Madame and Monsieur much better than Peter did, but hadn't the ability to impose himself.

When the soup came, it was what Peter had called it, a meal in itself, with tremendous body. Not simply *soupe* but a genuine thick *potage* with oil on top, coils of half-melted cheese swimming in it with soaked bread, good and hot. They broke bread together—they were old valued friends—and began to eat hungrily, though neither was in a hurry to get back to work. There was a companionable silence lasting maybe three or four minutes, and then Peter took up the thread of the talk.

"Like the man said, Charlie, 'if you have to ask, I can't tell you.' I'd love to help, but I can't coach you."

"I know, I know."

"Tell me more about her. How does she spell it, J-E-A?'

"No, without the E—Janine." He repeated her name. "Janine!" A shy, pleased look crossed his face; he was not an ugly man. "Janine," he said again, musing.

Peter rapped his knuckles on the tablecloth. "Hey, hey, come back here! You know, I think you're in love."

Charlie looked at him blankly. "What is that?" he asked. "What is 'in love'? Nobody we know talks like that; that's from nineteenth-century novels."

"Not at all," said Peter, "it's a perfectly natural, normal state; it has to do with the glands and glandular secretions. It has happened to me about six times, since I've been a man. It's a co-efficient of the activity of the adrenal cortex."

"No. No. I'm not 'in love'—uggh, how hard that is to say—like somebody in a Hollywood film. The Hollywood stuff is all false, and so is what you say."

"Have some more bread?"

"God, yes, it's fine, isn't it? Let's have that wine anyway. I feel better just talking about it. I'm not an adolescent, Peter, I just don't seem to know what to do."

Marthe came over in response to Peter's fond wink. "*Ma mie*," he said, "will you give us a bottle of the nice cheap white Bordeaux?"

"A Government bottle?"

"*C'est bien ça.*" He watched her go in amusement.

"Prettiest waitress in Montreal," he said. When she brought the wine, he poured it out quickly and they drank. It's been a little heavy and sweet the last couple of years, that dollar bottle, and with their meal the effect was opulent.

"It's odd that something that costs so little should be so good," said Charlie, "fifty, sixty, cents apiece."

"I'll pay for the wine."

"I asked you."

"That's right. You wanted to talk about love."

"Oh, come off it!"

Peter grew serious. "Tell me what it is you want, Charlie, and I'll do what I can to help."

"A few pointers, hints on behaviour. I'm a year older than you; but at school you were the one who told me how to make babies."

"This girl *is* bothering you! Describe her, so I'll have an idea."

"Upper Outremont. She might live on Stuart, facing the park."

"But she doesn't, does she?"

"No, but that gives you the tone."

"Mmmm, I can't see you getting anywhere with such a girl. Does she speak English?"

"Some. She's in the International Service; her office is two doors down."

"They really have you segregated over there, don't they?"

"Yeah, we never see anybody from International. But she keeps making excuses to consult me."

"And what does she talk about?"

"Diplomacy, external affairs, parliamentary affairs."

"Well, but that's you, isn't it? That's your pigeon?"

"Yes, but it isn't just a matter of expertise. This is hard to get across but she seems to ... look up to me. No, I mean it. She really does. She seems, I don't know, simple."

"Retarded?"

"Unaffected. Good."

"And you say that she's lovely?"

"Yes."

"Perhaps you'd better follow this up. Tell me more."

"Ah, you know how these girls are. She lived in Paris for a couple of winters, and then she went down to Ibiza in a duffel-coat and nothing else. Wine eight cents a litre. Speaks Spanish and Italian."

"As well as French and English?"

"Well, they all do."

"Uh-huh. How come somebody hasn't snapped her up?"

"She's very intelligent. Perhaps she's resisted the snap."

"And she likes you, and you don't know what to do?"

"Yes."

"It's very delicate, this; it's a matter of the texture of your feelings, both of you. I wouldn't care to interfere."

"I ask you. I shake when I pick up the phone. It's so silly, I'm a grown man."

"Yes, and you'll die a bachelor if you don't get over that. Tell you what you do, ask her in the office. Just blurt it out. All you have to do is get out the first five words, Charlie, 'Will you go out with me?' That's six words. Then, since you're such a good fellow, the rest will follow naturally. She'll be easy on you; the attachment will ripen."

"Where should we go?"

"Somewhere simple. A free concert. Do you ski?"

"Uh-huh."

"Skiing would be a bit much. Skating would be good."

"I've got an old pair of skates; we used to play hockey together."

"You and she?"

"You and I."

"Take her skating; that would be an excellent move."

He heard her. There she is, he thought, listening to the sweet soft womanly voice, and longing. These French girls, what is it they have? They stay so slim; they have these enormous eyes; they treat you like a man, not a teen-aged basketball player. Janine.

There was a drinking-fountain twenty feet down the corridor, and men's and ladies' lavatories just beyond, which caused a considerable amount of traffic past his door. The network had rented a jumble of miscellaneous office space in an old building on Stanley just up from Sainte-Catherine, where several minor projects were housed—some International Service types, talks producers in Public Affairs, one or two obscure continuity writers, and to give the place balance and tone a couple of sensationally important senior administrative officials, very close to the President, or as close as you could be in Montreal. This congeries of swarming activity went forward in a strange nest of wallboard partitions constructed on the principle of a Snakes and Ladders board or some sort of Chinese puzzle, partitions within partitions, cubbyholes without number separated by a thin layer of fibre, between which communication might only be established by tunnelling under, by climbing over, by drilling holes, or by following out several hundred feet of mazy corridor.

The arrangement of these offices very strongly intimated itself as an accurate model of the consciousness of the network's governing body.

Janine's cubbyhole was fifteen feet from Charlie's but their duties were separated by infinity, and according to departmental directives they were officially unaware of each other's existence, a curious Romeo-and-Juliet relationship—except that interfamilial relations hadn't quite reached the point of violence.

Should he go and get a drink, or go to the bathroom? He had used either pretext numberless times since he became aware of the lovely girl, and they were beginning to seem unbearably transparent. The typist whom he shared with three other producers, who dwelt in an even smaller room next to his own, was starting to make wisecracks about his bladder which he thought very unbecoming in a young girl. 191

"Not again?" she said behind him, as he sidled out the door.

"If Elspeth calls, tell her I'll call back," he said, "I'll only be a minute."

"Want me to come and hold your hand?"

He ignored this and walked quickly to the fountain, where Janine stood with her back to him. She was wearing a dress which no English girl could have worn in the office. Not that it was over-elaborate. It simply wasn't sensibly drab. It was silk, or some silky material with a soft sheen; it was a beautiful fit with out in the least calling attention to itself. It made it discreetly plain that Janine was a grown woman, not a length of cordwood with a woman's head and feet. He had the sense of some kind of subtle flower pattern in greens and blues, a curiously marine motif. She turned around as he came up, and smiled.

He smiled back, dazed, looking with delight at her breast. Not her breasts, in the technical sense, but the plane of firm and rounded muscle that lay across her chest below the collarbones. The silk of her dress lay on this beautifully shaped sloping surface in a way that struck Charlie as almost intolerably beguiling. At that instant, there was no question of sexuality, he thought, in his apprehension of her beauty. The soul and body are one. Body manifests soul. It was the humanity of that gently curved, lifting and falling surface that drew him, the curving line presenting the life beneath. It gave him an intuition of the inner movement of her being, quite as much as her face (which he could barely bring himself to look at) could do. To his intense surprise, he felt himself close to tears, for what reason he couldn't judge.

"Oh, say," he said, "I have the figures you asked for, on Embassy personnel in Moscow."

"Already? It's very…" she hesitated over her idiom, "…very decent of you. *Très complaisant.*"

"We have wonderful researchers."

"So do we," she said loyally, "but not so many. We don't have the subventions."

"Appropriations."

"Don't you say 'subventions'?"

"It's just coming in," he said, gasping. "I wonder. Will you go out with me?"

"Yes."

"When?"

"When you wish." She laughed at him. "Ask me!"

"Friday night?"

"Ah, that's not a good night. Were you going to give me something to eat?"

"If you like. Anything."

"On Fridays, I have to eat fish and I don't like fish. Thursdays?"

"Thursdays are fine. Thursday is my easy day, and this makes it even easier." He had never realized it was this simple. "Would this coming Thursday be all right?"

"Yes, it's perfect. What are we going to do?"

"Would you like to go skating, if it isn't too cold?"

"Or too warm."

He judged from her face that his proposal was highly proper, neither too emphatic nor too offhand, just a pleasant evening's sport. Peter knows his way around, he thought.

"Of course, or too warm. Is there a rink near you? You know, I'm not certain where you live. I know you're in Outremont."

"I live on the northwest corner of Hartland and Lajoie, just across from Joyce Park."

"Then we can skate there."

"No. That ... *patinoire* ... rink?"

"Yes."

"It's for children under eleven."

"I almost qualify," he said ruefully.

"But there's another park near us, Pratt Park, which has a pretty little rink for pleasure skating only, no hockey. When I was a young girl, we always had to chase the boys off the ice."

"I'm sure you did," he said, laughing happily, "but you're a young girl now. I hope I won't be chased off."

"Ah, just leave your hockey stick at home."

Corner Hartland and Lajoie, across from Joyce Park, he mused, coming along the street toward her home. What a singular address! He was sauntering along slowly, for they had arranged to meet at eight-fifteen, to give themselves an hour and a half's skating before the rink closed. All this district was gentle, well-bred, comfortable, expensive. He had passed some houses that had obviously been done over without regard to cost, some of them clearly way way up in six figures. Janine's house was a family home, he knew. She still lived with her parents who were, happily, out for the evening. There would be that ordeal to go through another time. His skates bumped on his chest—he'd slung them around his neck—and he felt absurdly young. Going skating, he thought, something I haven't done for ten years. He had tried his skates on a couple of days ago, and had them sharpened. His feet seemed to be about the same size as ever which was peculiar, since the rest of him was larger. Something to be proud of, he thought, medium-sized feet!

He came along by Joyce Park and stood across the street from her house, analyzing his sensations with amusement and annoyance. His knees were trembling. Getting on for thirty, he thought, and my knees are trembling at the idea of entertaining a pretty girl.

But he knew it wasn't the abstraction "pretty girl" that troubled him. It was *this* particular girl, the one lurking with her figure skates behind that front door over there. This is love, he realized in amazement, Peter was quite right. He had never felt anything like this before, and saw plainly that it had nothing whatsoever to do with adrenal secretions. It was a singular experience, unlike anything to which he might relate it. It was not like wanting something, or wanting to be with somebody whose company he enjoyed. It wasn't quasi-religious; it didn't seem to be especially sexual, and it wasn't painful. The difficulty lay in specifying it, except that it was certainly love.

You could say that without it I'm missing a leg or an arm. That wasn't quite it either. Across the street in that big comfortable dimly lit house was a person from whom he could scarcely bear to be removed.

He went across and knocked on the door, and she opened it at once. She was wearing a pair of dark stretch pants, a red and white striped sweater, and one of those dizzy fur hats, the enormous ones, that look like a crazy wig. She caught him smiling at the hat.

"Aren't they silly? And really too warm for skating. But I have nothing else."

"When is your *anniversaire*?" he asked quickly, and then wished he hadn't.

"In the summer," she said vaguely, crossing the porch with him and going down the stairs. On the sidewalk she put her mittened hand in his confidingly, and they walked the block and a half to Pratt Park.

"It's the prettiest little park in Montreal," said Janine with the air of a proud proprietor. "I was brought up in it. Isn't it charming? Look at the bandstand."

He had often had the same reaction, driving past the park. It comprised a large city block, sloping from Lajoie at the south end to Van Horne at the north, in a series of small rolling hillocks and mounds. At the upper end was the miniature bandstand, with the park attendants' rooms below. Then there were some artfully arranged small clumps of trees, some rivulets and ponds and toy stone bridges, all slowly inclining toward an open level area at the north end, where a cement walk encircled what was in summer a tiny lake and in winter the skating rink.

In their idyllic innocent summers, children came from all over Outremont to sail boats in the pond. Mothers and grand-mothers and nursemaids drowsed through long afternoons chatting idly while the stiff white sails crossed and re-crossed the clear shining surface. Sometimes the attendant would come along with a seine and a pair of hip-boots and, to the children's delight, would wade around in the lake, seining out leaves and refuse and recovering becalmed sailboats.

In wintertime there was a small temporary *cabane* with heated changing rooms for boys and girls. Charlie led Janine to the door, feeling a pang at the momentary separation. "I'll meet you outside," he said, fumbling with his skate laces. She threw him a smile and disappeared into the girls' dressing room as he undid the knots and went to put on his own skates. The building shook and reverberated with the shouts and laughter of the dozens of youngsters who came and went, teasing the attendant and stealing each others' gloves and shoes. The confusion and the noise heightened Charlie's feelings of renewed youth. He turned his head from side to side as he tightened his skate laces, smiling at the boys in the room and at the harrassed attendant.

"*Salut, Monsieur*," he volunteered, and the attendant, an elderly Parks employee, gave him a beleaguered nod. He tied his skates and stood up, not too shakily. He walked to the door, went out, and stood waiting in the clear night.

All around the hut were straight black trees, their boughs stark and intensely black against the sky. All the stars were out. There were a few clouds, grey, slaty in texture, whizzing over the black sky. The grey-on-black tones were strangely rich and soft, not bleak and repellent and wintry, but full, lively, the tones of certain dresses and laces in the paintings of Goya, a paradoxically warm range of tones. And all along the walks and stone stairways were lamp-standards whose globes resembled Japanese lanterns because of their soft orange-yellow hue. The park always had a romantic Hallowe'en aspect, and was a favourite haunt of lovers in the spring, summer, and fall. The darkness was palpable, thick, encouraging. The cries of the skaters on the pond came to him like birds' calls.

Janine wobbled out of the hut; she was none too secure on her blades. Together they inched carefully down to the edge of the ice, nearly falling once or twice, and reinforcing each other's laughter. At the edge, it was necessary to step down about eighteen inches to two feet, pushing off and launching forward on one blade. The skaters went round and round in front of their very noses, whizzing past—you could hear the air in their clothing, and there was a certain difficulty in getting into the stream of counter-clockwise traffic. And as usual there were a couple of high-school kids who were skating clockwise and throwing the pattern off.

"Let yourself go!' said Charlie hopefully.

She gave him a shaky frown. "My first time," she said, and letting go of his supporting hand she stepped down and onto the ice, gliding forward through the flow of skaters, cutting across the centre of the pond with her arms extended to either side. He clambered down himself and pursued her. She was making a turn, clumsy, but to him inexplicably beautiful, and trying to get the rhythm of the others.

"Just go slow, and in a minute you'll get on to it."

"Oh, I've skated before," she boasted, and he noticed that her skates were old and dirtied, "but this is the first time in years."

He thought of the Queneau novel and relished his surge of mirth. For a minute or two they skated side by side, pushing hard and bending, and breathing in long sighs. Then in unspoken agreement they straightened and took each other's hands, skating as a pair. He had his right arm around her waist with her right hand in his, and his left arm across his chest, holding her other hand. He had a vague sense that this wasn't exactly the classic pairs position; but anyway they weren't figure-skating. They had a hard time getting their legs to work together.

"There's an extra leg," said Janine finally, "one of us has a leg too many."

"It's simply that we don't know what we're doing."

"Shall we rest?"

"Yes. We can study the others."

They glided slowly toward the snow-covered rocks at the edge of the ice; they were breathing heavily. As they slowed and stopped, he turned and looked her full in the face, or in what he could see of her face under the fuzzy hat. She was silent, her lips in a slight pout. Then she smiled again.

Instantly he felt an enormous solid spasm or wave of desire, which crossed him like an electric shock or an actual physical pulse, greatly magnified. It felt hot and made him tremble. Her face seemed to quiver. "Did you feel that?" he asked in amazement, and she nodded wonderingly. They sat on the rocks and waited for breath to come back, watching the skaters and enjoying their antics. A pattern began to emerge from the bright flow, the courting couples, the thirteen-year-olds who should have been doing their homework, the sixteen-year-olds bent on minor mischief, the consciously good skaters, the consciously speedy.

Then they rose and worked their way back into the pattern, holding hands almost casually, and skating more surely than before. He held her as close as he dared, and looked up now and then at the deep sky, which seemed blacker than before, with rich deep greys splashed on it. The great black disk of sky turned slowly, and at the edges of his vision yellow-orange Japanese lanterns on the walks came slowly by. What he saw, the yellow, orange, grey, and black, and what he felt, contentment and peace, merged in a single indescribable experience and they went on skating slowly around, around...

As it grew later, the crowd thinned and one began to pick out individual personalities. There was one speedy figure in particular, a new arrival, who skated in a racer's crouch, who sped around at a sickening pace and seemed always to be on the other side of the rink, going like hell. He wore ski-pants, a windbreaker, and a long-tasselled toque. The plume of the tassel streamed out behind him on a cord, fluffed by his slipstream; he skated very expertly. Janine and Charlie watched in admiration and then, all of a sudden, Charlie perceived with a slight shock that the speedy one was Peter.

"That's a friend of mine," he told Janine, "he's awfully good, isn't he?"

"He skates wonderfully," she said, "and he doesn't bump into people and knock them down."

"Let's stop a minute and let him come up." It took Peter perhaps thirty seconds to execute the circuit; as he swooped down on them, it seemed to Charlie that a satisfied expression crossed his face. The plume of his tassel swung down across his shoulders as he stopped beside them.

The tassel was orange and yellow. "That's quite a cap you have there," said Charlie.

"Keeps me warm. Fancy meeting you here!"

"Fancy!"

"I come here all the time," said Peter, "the park attendant is a pal of mine."

"I didn't realize you lived around here."

"I don't, quite. I live up by the *Centre Social*, but this is the nicest park around, and it isn't far. Who is this?"

"Oh, excuse me. This is Peter de Beauvoir, Janine." He almost thought Peter was going to kiss her hand. "And this is Janine Flon."

"Ah! Related to Suzanne?"

"No," she smiled, "Related to Simone?"

Peter winced slightly. "No, I'm what they call an Uncle Tom."

"An Uncle Tom?" She wrinkled her brow.

"He means that he's an Anglicized Frenchman who went to Lower Canada College and McGill."

"Oh, one of those," said Janine dubiously. Charlie felt glad.

Peter held his head in mock embarrassment. "*Hélas!* But I can justify everything, if you'll only let me explain. Are you going anywhere from here?"

They looked at each other. "I thought we might have something to eat. We both have to work tomorrow."

"Tell you what," said Peter, "we'll go up to the Gourmet."

"What?"

"The Gourmet Delicatessen, wonderful kosher stuff."

"Is it far?"

"Just up the hill. This park is right on the border, you know. This is French, that's Jewish, and there's a very orthodox temple on the corner."

"We'll give it a go," said Charlie without enthusiasm.

The food was marvellous, particularly the herring, cole slaw, and potato salad, the imported chocolate bars and pastries. They sat in the back room for over two hours, while the room filled around them with the skating crowd, gradually emptied and then filled again with the aftermovie crowd, older and slightly less noisy people. Peter spoke animatedly about his projected new show on the network.

"We'll call it either *Janus* or *Gemini*—they're the same in both languages."

"A two-headed program?" asked Charlie, not without malice.

"Well, not for people with two heads."

"For cultures à deux têtes," said Janine, "*pour un pays biculturel.*" She was very interested in the idea.

"That's right. We'll put it on both networks, and we're going to have acts and material in both languages, without any hoke. No cute translations! Anybody who wants to watch—and it's going to be the most attractive show on the continent—will have to put up with acts in the other language. In effect we'll be doing what we should have done a century ago in this stupid country—ignore ignorance and force the ignorant to meet our conditions."

"Maybe you should call it *Mélange Adulteré*," said Charlie. Janine gave him a thoughtful look.

"Nothing of the kind. Imagine a show where you can see Jacques Brel, Aznavour, Wayne and Shuster, Robert Goulet, Sylvie Vartan…"

"God!"

"All right now, plenty of people like Sylvie Vartan. Paul Anka."

"Is it going to be just variety?"

"No. We're going to have political personalities, writers and artists, all kinds of interesting people and no interpreters."

"Is this show definitely scheduled?"

"Almost, not quite."

"Do you have a script assistant?"

"Not yet." He looked at her appraisingly. "Would you be interested."

"*Bien sûr!*"

"I might be able to work you in. It helps to have intelligent people around. That's the trouble with talent—the talent are never very intelligent. They have no common sense."

"*Le gros bon sens. J'en ai assez.*"

"*O, ça se voit.*" Charlie began to feel ill at ease.

This dreadful uneasiness grew and grew, and made him frantic in the next week, for he couldn't find her anywhere, couldn't hear her voice in the corridors or over the thin partitions, had only the vaguest notion where she might be. He didn't know who her boss was—their acquaintance had flowered at the water-fountain, and though he knew of course what section of International she was in, he wasn't sure what local to try, or who he should ask to speak to. No matter who he asked, he would look ridiculous, not that he would care about that. But he could vividly imagine the muddled exchange of misinformation, and remembered with intense irritation that IS and PA were not officially in touch.

"To whom did you wish to speak, please?" This in a rich accent.

"Miss—I mean Mademoiselle—Flon."

"Who is calling?"

"Oh, uh, a friend. I mean, I'm in Public Affairs. I'm right next door."

"Was it on business?" Whatever he answered would be wrong. If it was a personal call, he was wasting corporation time: if business he was by-passing some injured authority. The Slavic tones would grow stiff and cautious. "I am sorry, Mr. . . . uh. Mademoiselle Flon has been seconded to Television Network Programming. You will have to try to reach her there."

Sitting at his desk, clenching and unclenching his fists, he meditated some desperate course of action, he wasn't certain what, something spectacular. He got up, put on his hat and coat, and went out to lunch, intending a long solitary lunch at which he would mature his strategy.

When he came out onto Sainte-Catherine, it was windy and very cold, and without thinking he headed over toward Metcalfe, meaning to eat at *Le Normand*. He was glad it was so close because the wind cut at him, making his eyes smart and his nose drip. He trotted up behind the great bulk of the hotel, grateful for the protection it gave him. Then he crossed the street in front of the restaurant, raised his eyes involuntarily and looked through the crowded window, and there they were, heads together, sitting in his customary corner. He blinked, lowered his head, and read for the hundredth time the lying menu. Lies, he thought, lies all around us.

He turned up Metcalfe, walking toward Burnside, trying to think of another place to go. When he came out from behind the hotel, the wind shook and almost staggered him, and he turned up his coat collar. It was so cold that his sinuses hurt and made it hard to think coherently. I'll fight, it kept running through his head, this time I'll fight, this time I want my rights, I'll fight, I'll fight.

THE FRUIT MAN,
THE MEAT MAN,
AND THE MANAGER

A GROCER named Morris Znaimer managed the Greenwood Groceteria, up on Greenwood Avenue next to the
university, for over seventeen years, in partnership with
Jack Genovese, fruit and vegetables, and Mendel Greenspon,
an experienced butcher but not kosher.

Mister Znaimer took care of grocery inventory and the
beer, and he also did the accounting and book keeping, supervised the cash desk and checkout counter with a girl named
Shirley to help, and decided about charge accounts and bill-
ing; he had hardly any bad-debt items because he was a
shrewd judge of credit.

Jack did the buying for fruit and vegetables, going daily to
the markets before dawn, and usually getting the pick of all
local crops. And Mendel Greenspon was an expert in his line,
a butcher who could have worked anywhere, with a surgeon's
hand with his knives and an exact honesty about weights and
measures. The meat at the Greenwood was famous for blocks.

The store was half a block from Ballantyne and the competition had the better location, right on the corner of Greenwood and Ballantyne, *Marché Boisvert*, with a pharmacy and
a hairdresser in the same building drawing customer traffic.

Both groceries served a high-class residential quarter and a funny thing was that often the Jewish store got most of the French trade, and the French store got most of the Jewish. Why would that be?

"Boisvert, Boisvert, they stole the name from us," Mister Znaimer would often say to his partners. Both stores were precariously located because of the closeness of the university, then in a period of expansion that threatened to consume all the available frontage along Greenwood.

The Greenwood Groceteria wasn't a big store; it had a thirty-foot frontage, two show windows that weren't often re-arranged, except for the sales announcements lettered in black and red by Mister Znaimer, two main aisles and a single cash desk, no windows on either side of the interior, and usually a lot of soiled sawdust or sweeping compound on the floor, particularly in winter. At the front there was always a traffic jam of shopping carts. If the store was crowded it was hard to get your cart in and out through the people.

Mister Znaimer and Jack and Mendel kept abreast of the competition, maybe a bit ahead, by maintaining high standards or goods and services and fast free delivery—two trucks and a succession of more or less reliable drivers, a continual worry to the manager. They had a big packaged-goods inventory and a storage problem. They had very good Christmas trees, better than the competition, standing peaked with snow in a rich-smelling heap next to the delivery trucks, all through December. They made a special display of Hallowe'en pumpkins and drew kids in.

Sarah Cummings would go there for some of her groceries through the middle of the week when there was no time for a trip to the supermarket, or at the end of the month before her husband was paid. Sometimes she felt that she was taking advantage of the small tradesman, buying from him only when convenient, using credit with no carrying charge, which you couldn't get from the chains, now and then picking up two or three loss-leaders when Mister Znaimer had clearly been thinking of one to a customer. On the other hand, she paid more at the Greenwood. Meat was higher, though trimmed right down and more tasty than the artificially tenderized supermarket meat. A few prices were competitive.

She liked to take Stephen and Brent for a walk along Greenwood around ten-thirty in the morning, Tuesday or Wednesday, to get a pound of butter and two quarts of milk and cigarettes. The boys loved the store and would talk for indefinite periods to Jack Genovese, who was very fond of kids. Once when she was first going there, she caught sight of Stephen out of the corner of her eye, standing down by the fruit next to a basket of plump, succulent pears. The basket stood on a carton and Stephen's nose was flat against a pear on the top of the pile; they were wrapped in silver paper, high-quality party goods.

"Get your little nose out of there, Stevie," she said, not unkindly, while she looked in her purse to see what money she had. She saw a glance pass between Mister Znaimer and Jack and then the fruit man said, "Naw, naw, Missus, that's fine. Here, can I give him one?"

She said, "Oh, you shouldn't. They'll both have to have one." Brent came running up.

Jack picked out two pears, peeled the silver paper, rubbed them against his sleeve, bent down and gave the boys one each. "The best," he said. "Melt in your mouth." The boys took them politely and went outside, enjoying themselves a lot.

Mrs. Cummings said, "I'll pay for that please, Mister Znaimer; would you total them in?"

"It's goodwill," he said. "We don't ask you to pay for goodwill. That'll be three dollars and seventy-nine cents, including the two cigarettes and not including the pears."

"And would you charge it, please?"

"Certainly, that's on a charge, three seventy-nine. Can I send that down for you?" Without looking he plucked her small shear or charge bills from the pile behind him, and added the latest.

"I don't want to trouble you."

"That's no trouble, that's what we're here for." He picked up the small bag and walked with her to the door. Stephen came over and handed him the core of his pear, and the grocer laughed, and flipped it into a trash carton.

Sarah began to think of him as the fatherly type; he was stern in appearance, very erect, and he rendered his accounts very precisely at the end of each month. When she asked, as she sometimes did, if she could carry part of the balance forward, he was prompt to agree, and at no time suggested that she put a limit on her balance. The highest she ever got was once before Christmas, a bill of around two hundred dollars which her husband discharged as a Christmas present; he pinned the receipted bill to the tree and made a joke of it.

"I'm glad it's paid," she said, "I'm a little afraid of him."

"Who?"

"Mister Znaimer. He reminds me of my father. He isn't disapproving, but I think he expects good behaviour."

"So do I," said her husband defensively.

"Oh you, you're a woolly lamb."

"I see what you mean though, he's impressive."

Maybe even just, Mrs. Cummings thought, maybe a just man. She looked forward to her talks with him.

"If we didn't have the beer, we'd be out of business, Mrs. Cummings. The supermarkets aren't allowed to sell it, for that reason, to keep the small stores going."

"My husband said that was socialistic."

"It may be, it may be. Look, just give me a chance, let me handle your groceries for a month, one month, it's all I ask. What do you spend a month, a hundred and eighty? Forty, forty-five dollars a week? You spend a third of that with us."

"I know it's mean," she said.

"It's not taking advantage; it's the way things are. But you let me have all your orders for a month and I'll beat the chain stores. I deliver free—you save on gas. I don't have a service charge on accounts, and anyway you can't get one in a supermarket. I'll match their prices—if you can get it cheaper over there, come and tell me and I'll match it. I can do it. I know I can. You want pink stamps?"

"I wasn't going to say that."

"I know you weren't, you're a nice lady. Tell you what, we don't bother with stamps or booklets; you don't need to lick them or paste them. Keep your register slips. When you've got a few hundred dollars in slips, bring them in and I'll rebate two percent, same as them. Here, come and look." He led her to the show window in which a few items of soiled merchandise were carefully arranged, looking like they had been there for some time. "You want pots? A nice pot with a copper bottom, cost you seven dollars? I'll have it for you. A lamp? A little coaster wagon for your boys, red with white letters? I know what you're spending. I'll fix you up."

An old man stood next to her at the cash desk with a jar of Yuban in his hands, staring at her in mute appeal. She smiled at him and let him go through, and Mister Znaimer looked at her with approval; she felt pleased.

"Personal service, that's what we offer. Where can you find butchers like Mendel? Today we have rib steak, ask him about it, a good buy. When it comes off his block, it's clean; you aren't paying for bone and muscle, you're getting all meat. For two-fifty you can serve your family steak that you can't match anywhere, aged properly, none of this chemical tenderizer. Go and ask him about it, all red brand, the best."

"I wasn't going to buy meat, but for a treat perhaps I should see it."

"He's right there waiting, Mrs. Cummings. There's no line-up."

She went down to the meat counter and asked to see the rib steaks, watching Mendel Greenspon as he whisked a chunk of meat out of the cooler. He held it up on a sheet of bloodied brown paper and prodded it.

"Big enough? Right thickness?"

"I thought of two adult servings and another piece for the boys."

"About two and a quarter pounds is what you want." He walked into the big refrigerator and came back carrying a large beef rib. He laid it on the block and sliced, and it was wonderful how exact, how sure, his movements were; first the cleaver; just the thickness her husband loved; and then a long thin knife of extraordinary sharpness which cut like a laser beam; boned it; trimmed it, threw in a lump of suet for free. In a second he showed her two large pieces and two child-sized. They reminded her absurdly of the Cummings family walking to church.

"Just right," she said.

"It weighs a bit more, but we said two and a quarter pounds. That'll be two twenty-five," and he handed her the parcel. When they ate the steak, her husband crooned endearments at her.

"Better than filet. Boy, what a buy!"

She said, "They can't really match prices, not for long."

"We'd better keep the account paid up, if that's any help."

"I think it's only fair."

Once when she went in to pay up her account, Mister Znaimer wasn't in the store, and Jack came over and took the money.

"Morris is out with the truck," he said, "one of the drivers has been out since payday; they aren't dependable. That's Mrs. Cummings, isn't it, sure, got it right here." He fumbled through the file of accounts hanging beside the register, and a letter in a legal-sized envelope fell onto the open cash drawer from somewhere behind the accounts file. She noticed the university emblem on the envelope, the same kind of envelope her husband's salary cheques came in. Jack picked it up idly, looked at the address, stood silently for a moment, and then took the letter and read it; his face changed expression, darkening. She had never seen him look so grim.

"Mendel," he called, "come and look at this. Excuse me a second, Mrs. Cummings." He strolled to the back of the store and said to the butcher, "Your hands clean?" Mendel wiped them on his apron and took the letter, and Jack came back and gave Mrs. Cummings a receipted cash slip for the balance, smiling and half bowing.

"Always a pleasure," he said. "I'll tell Morris you were in." He mentioned Mister Znaimer with a shade of embarrassment.

After that Sarah began to feel hints of impending changes; the atmosphere in the store was not as happy as before. The give and take among the partners had not the familiar ease; the drivers booked off drunk more often. Shirley the cash-girl would talk discontentedly from time to time of quitting. Always described as "the girl" by the partners, she was really a plump, tired-faced woman in her late thirties with hair that escaped from pins and straggled against her cheek. She wore a white coat that was none too clean.

"My husband wants me to retire," she would whisper to Mrs. Cummings. "He never wanted me to work."

"I didn't realize you were married."

"Oh yes, a long time. I've got a little boy, older than yours. He has eye-trouble."

Once she did quit, but it didn't take. After three or four days she was back in the store with a salary increase, but still gloomy.

"I'm glad to see you," said Mrs. Cummings.

"It won't last."

"What?"

"The store. It's folding up pretty soon now, I think."

"What's wrong?"

"The university wants the land for a new sports centre. They made a good offer and Jack and Mendel want to take it. They own two-thirds of the business, so Morris can't buck them. He can't afford to buy them out, and he can't talk them into fighting expropriation."

"But it's a good store. Wouldn't they be crazy to quit?"

"I don't know. It's a living, that's all. They might be able to fight the university for a while, but they'd lose in the end and the offer might even be reduced. Mendel and Jack are afraid, and I guess they're right; better get out while the getting's good."

"I don't understand that. I always thought they got along so well."

"It's just business, Mrs. Cummings, that's all it is."

"Well, if that's all it is…"

She felt that there should be more to it, and out of loyalty stopped dealing at supermarkets, to give the Greenwood all her business; she urged her husbands' colleagues' wives to shop there, and might have been responsible for a slight up-turn in sales, nothing you'd specially notice. She felt baffled and sorry that she couldn't help to change matters. She was in and out of the store a lot, and naturally Mister Znaimer noticed it.

One October morning he mentioned it. "I appreciate it. I've been glad to have the business. I tell you what it is, Mrs. C., I like to do business with people like you, with some sense of how to behave. I could tell from the first day you came in— there's a nice lady. You can tell from the children. No complaints about substitutions on phone orders. A lot of people, to hear them talk you'd think we always sent a higher-priced item on a substitution. It isn't true. If I take a phone order I try to come as close as possible to what the customer wants, and I'll say this for Jack and Mendel, they're the same. We fill the order the way we take it."

"I've never complained."

"That's what I'm saying." He looked at her with affection. Then he had to pick up the phone and she moved to the back to negotiate a roast with the butcher. When she had made her choice, Mendel came around the corner of the meat counter and spoke to her confidentially. "I want to show you something, just so you'll know where I'll be." He handed her a business card:

HIGH QUALITY PROVISIONS
Superior Supermarkets, Corner Darlington and
Soissons, are happy to announce the appointment of
MENDEL GREENSPON, formerly with Greenwood
Groceteria, as Manager, Meat and Poultry Department,
effective November 1st, 1967. Come in and meet
MENDEL. Always ready to serve friends old and new.

"You're closing so soon?" she said, feeling very sad.

"Last week in October."

"Where is Jack going?"

The butcher mentioned a well-known gourmet grocery in Westmount, and Jack came over to them and shook his head affirmatively. "I'll have to wear a clean smock every day," he said, "I'll look like a doctor. Do you ever get down there, Missus?"

"Not often. That's an expensive store."

"It is," said Jack, "but such fruit! Oh my, it's a pleasure."

"Does Mister Znaimer know about this?"

"We haven't told him officially."

"Oh, you ought to tell him."

Jack said, "It's hard to do."

"But we'll tell him," said Mendel.

Then they began to cut back on everything, the shelves showed bare in places, through the final weeks of October. When the drivers booked off drunk they didn't bother to come back, and the last week the store was open Mister Znaimer took the deliveries himself in the only remaining truck, an old Chevrolet with a ruined clutch.

The store was to close on Hallowe'en, so this year there was no festive display of pumpkins and black and orange candies, no need to attract children. What remained of the packaged goods would go back to the jobbers. Jack hadn't re-ordered on fruit for days; the meat was right down, no loss on useless inventory. It had been quite a delicate trick to cut back the stock, while retaining enough to fill orders till closing date. Mister Znaimer thought they had done a smart job of it. When he packed up the last delivery orders, he could just about fill them and that was all.

He put the truck into gear with some difficulty and drove to the corner of Ballantyne. A group of *Marché Boisvert* employees stood on their steps. He waved a hand at them and they nodded back solemnly. They'll miss us, he thought, this part of the street will be dead for retailing in another year. We drew for them; they drew for us.

He drove north, down the slope of the mountain, and made his rounds, the truck making terrible noises. Have to turn this one in, he thought, and then remembered that there was no need to replace it. It took him only an hour and a half to deliver; in the old days two drivers had been out all day. Urging the expiring truck up back the slope toward Greenwood, he noticed how bare and cold the trees looked and how the sky was steely. He was in his own place in this neighbourhood and could not bear to leave. He felt that nothing holy was left in his life.

In the store he couldn't find the partners, who were perhaps cleaning up the cellar while Shirley swept out the storage room in back. He spoke out loud: "Fools, fools to leave this, they could never have forced us out. Close one store and leave the other alone? They'd never have dared, never. Haven't you got any pride in what we have here? Seventeen years!"

Over a year later, when she had almost forgotten the three grocers, their store long since levelled, Sarah Cummings got a Christmas card from Mister Znaimer, not a business card, a personal one with a short handwritten message inside.

> Dear Mrs. Cummings: how are you and the boys? It's a long time since I've seen you. I retired, you know, when the store closed, and I'm living just a few blocks from you on Greenwood. I hope maybe I'll see you and the boys on the street sometime. I'm not sure—if I go back into business. I might someday, if I could find a place.
> Yours sincerely, Morris J. Znaimer

Maybe other people got cards from him too.

GOING OUT
AS A GHOST

THE CHILDREN were preparing for Hallowe'en, a festival they preferred to Christmas. The sombre mysterious end of October, when it grows colder and nobody yet knows how cold it may become, had always seemed more inviting to them than the steady weather of the solstice. They set great store by their costumes—had in different years presented themselves as Laurel and Hardy, four Marx brothers, knights in armour and hairy serfs, the two ends of a horse. They were a quartet agreeably near in age inclined to form pairs, liking to complement one another: master and slave, fat man and thin.

Their father, a confused man, joked with them about the reach and complication of these conceptions. "Going to go out this year?" he would inquire as they grew older. "What are you going out as?" The boys would argue between themselves, the girls exchange secret smiles, giving nothing away.

"I'll throw a sheet over my head and cut holes in it," their father would say at the very last minute. "I'm going out as a ghost." And the entire family would laugh uproariously, for this struck them as the lowest deep of impoverished fantasy. "Going out as a ghost," they all sang together, laughing, but inwardly troubled by the concept of dressing up as a clown or a cowboy. Such children could—probably did—miss altogether the intense, absorbed September and October during which the dress-up box was emptied, filled, emptied: old organdy and silk from costumes of years past held to the light. They had also a property box filled with daggers, stilettos, swords, false noses, wigs, grotesque false ears. Theatrical make-up was available, nose putty, crepe hair. A family half sunk in show-business. All this began in late summer with vacation still in progress.

"If you're going into town, bring back my gorilla mask," said the older of the boys to his father on a Wednesday in late August. "I want to compare the fur."

"Where is it in the house? In your closet?"

"It's hanging on the light fixture in our room," said the younger boy. "I hung it there to make it look like a head sticking out of the wall."

"There should be a gorilla's hind-end sticking out of the wall in the next bedroom," said the father. He chatted amusingly with the children, but the image of the gorilla mask stayed with him disagreeably as he drove into the city. One of those rubber, over-the-head, monster disguises which can be found at theatrical costumers, it had been a birthday gift to his son, who had a collection of them: Dracula, Frankenstein's monster, the Wolf-Man, the Gorilla. In a poor light the thing was genuinely horrific and might prove shocking to householders on that dreary night nine weeks in the future. He was troubled by the human cast of the bestial shape. The coarse red of the cheeks, upturned snout, matted dangling hair, the powdery texture of the pliant rubbery skin. The boys played up certain simian characteristics in their movements; they liked to lower their hands around their knees by flexing the knee-joints. They would gibber in simulated ape-language. The younger boy often hung head downward in trees. With the gorilla mask over either head, full disguise was at once effected, a whole transformation of behaviour threatened. "Now I'm going to tear you limb from limb," they would say.

He had further worries, minor repairs impending on his automobile, which gave trouble as he drove along; the radiator leaked, spreading the odour of coolant through the passenger compartment, the smell of ethylene glycol, and some sweetish, doubtless wholly poisonous, additive—radiator cleanser or sealer; there might be holes in the hoses. Late in the day he arrived in his city neighbourhood and left the auto with a local service man who at once, before his eyes, dismantled it, rendering it inoperative. "Tomorrow, one o'clock," said the mechanic, a highly trustworthy man.

"Going back to the country in the afternoon."

"You can have it by one. Not before."

He was glad to leave his car sitting on the lot, always felt better about it at such times, as one does about the seriously ill member of the family who is at last "in good hands." As he walked the short distance to his empty house, it began to rain, then in the next hour settled into a steady downpour. He let himself in, stepped over the pile of mail lying on the floor below the letter slot, into the quiet hail. He had always liked the look of this house in the late afternoon with no electric light on; what light there was entered freely through large windows front and rear, then diffused itself into the corners of dark halls. He mounted to the second floor and standing in the doorway of his sons' bedroom he saw the gorilla mask hanging over the light socket, from which the bulb had been removed. Outside the rain continued to fall; it was now very dark for this time of year. The house was shut tight and stuffy, yet the mask moved and lifted slightly in some faint air current. He stared. He decided to have his evening meal delivered, Chinese, or barbecued chicken, no need to go out again. He might call a friend, see if he wanted to watch a late movie. What else had the kids asked for, was it masking tape?

Later he shuffled through the mail, discarded almost all, phoned for chicken, phoned David, who agreed to drive round at 9:30. Unmarried, self-employed, chronically at loose ends at night, David seemed pleased to be asked. "There are two good films on tonight," he said. "I hope my car starts." He came a little early, barely past nine, surprising his host, who was ensconced before the TV in the basement, picking chicken from the spaces between his teeth, listening to the rain, not making much sense of the program he watched, which was loud. The doorbell rang several times before he grasped that it was not part of the soundtrack, which might well have had bells in it.

He switched on the porch light and peered out at the rain. Might as well be Hallowe'en, he thought, and opened the door for David. "You're early."

"You said anytime. You're alone, right? How much do you charge to haunt a house anyway?"

"What makes you say that?"

"I just thought of it. Your house is always a little haunted, you know." This seemed a disobliging comment which he could only ignore; they descended to the TV which they watched with pleasure for over an hour, until the telephone rang. This bell, different in tone from the doorbell, could not be assimilated to the sound of TV, had to be answered at once or attention would stray. He climbed unwillingly to the ground floor and went to the telephone in the studio at the very back of the house, where he fondled the clamorous instrument, gazing through the huge window at shining wetness. He put the receiver to his ear.

"Bet you don't know who this is," said a melodious voice. The line clicked and crackled strangely; the voice echoed, seemed familiar, then wholly unrecognizable. He had heard it, he knew, but how very long ago. "Bet you don't know who this is ... this is ... is ... who?"

"We were in school together," he said firmly, shutting off the unsteady echoes.

The voice cooed, "You're getting close."

He listened harder; he had heard the voice somewhere in the past. There was a *castrato* music to it, high, sexually elastic though certainly male. "It's Philly White."

"Who?"

"Philly White. We went to parish school together, don't you remember the Whites, my brother Bob, my sister Pauline? We made our First Holy Communion together."

"So we did. So we did. Of course I remember. You had smallpox when we were in the third grade?"

He could remember the effects of the disease vividly, the spoiled face, the depth of indentation of the small round scars, about the size of a flake of confetti. His complexion had been like his name, white, the holes in his face changing colour as embarrassment or exposure moved the boy. He had often been in trouble with the teachers, hadn't been heard from in forty years. The voice was irrefutable testimony, when linked to a past and a name.

"I'm here at the Prevention Centre on Parthenais Street." The voice in the receiver pronounced the name wrong, as an Ontarian would, and translated the name of the institution too literally. *Centre de Prevention* doesn't mean "prevention centre," it means "detention centre:" a quasi-jail where persons are held to await trial or, in certain cases, sentencing after conviction. Until now he had never heard of the place or seen it, knew nothing about it, couldn't have identified it from glimpses at a distance. It is a deceptive building. It is the embodiment of a lie. It doesn't look like what it is; suicide is routine inside. Men have spent fifteen months there awaiting trial, the presumed innocent often treated far worse than the proven guilty because the innocence is purely formal and presumptive. Most inmates are habitual offenders. None of this was familiar to him. "What are they holding you for?" he asked.

"Some trouble about a cheque. Well, actually two cheques. Three. You knew my family, you knew Bob was ordained, you knew . . . I was married there for a while; then I moved out west. I had a car business in Vancouver and then came back east. Two little girls. We're separated now of course . . . you're the only one here in the city . . . I don't want my wife to know yet. I was hoping for a reconciliation. I want to get straightened out and start again."

"What's the charge?" He felt proud of the way he phrased the question; he had no contact with police, courts, criminals, or even people who were being held, detained, prevented. "Have they got anything to go on?"

"Actually. . ." Indecision floated into the quavering voice. "I can't talk any more; they're taking me back. They might let you see me. Could you try to see me?"

"The charge?"

"Matter of two years . . . I've been sentenced. . ." He never found out whether the term of the sentence was two years, or whether a longer term might be reduced to two for good conduct. "They're deciding whether to send me to a dry-out clinic. There's a problem of alcoholism. And they're waiting for information from Vancouver."

"What sort of information?" He felt damp; the studio was damp.

". . . conviction for fraud . . . not serious."

"What else?"

"Hotel bills in Dorval. They brought me in from Dorval. I was there a month. I have to go now." It sounded as if the call had been cut off at the main switchboard. He put the receiver into its cradle and took several deep breaths, then called downstairs. In a few moments, David appeared from the depths. "You're missing some good takeoffs," he said.

"Will you do me a favour?"

"Yes."

"My car's in for repair and I have to go out unexpectedly. Would you do me a great kindness and drive me across town?

I'm not sure exactly where to go. Do you know where Parthenais is?"

They had to unearth David's street-guide in the glove compartment, then consult its small print as they drove along Sherbrooke in the persistent rain; the windows kept fogging over; it was difficult to see. Parthenais was well out toward the east end, past De Lorimier almost at D'Iberville. They turned south when they came to it, down the steep hill toward De Maisonneuve. In a few minutes a massive dark shape stood up indistinctly before them, an ultra-modern office building fourteen storeys high, in glassy black plastic siding, standing on a small plot of land surrounded by chain-link fence topped with multiple strands of shining barbed wire. It reminded him of a shiny polished dark monolith seen in some science-fiction film. Some sort of object of perverse worship. Close up, the building looked like most others built around 1969. They parked across the narrow street and approached the main entrance which opened into a spacious glassed-in hall two storeys high, with an elevator bank to the right and a reception desk nearby. One or two guards idled in corners, paying no attention to them. He asked at the desk if he would be able to see Philly White, and the receptionist—perfectly agreeable and forthcoming—laughed jovially.

"Tomorrow, 1:30. Come back then."

"He seemed in pain or frightened. Could he be afraid of something?"

"Tomorrow, 1:30. Come back then."

One of the guards moved indecisively.

Time to get out of here while we still can, he thought. He felt great waves of imaginary fugitive guilt washing over him. Hundreds of movies lodged in his memory now rose up to frighten, to accuse. He thought of the fearful ending of *I Am a Fugitive from a Chain Gang* and hastened away. "What do you do, how do you live?" "I steal."

Driving homeward, David said, "I didn't care much for the atmosphere…"

He had to force himself to return the next afternoon. Just before he left the house, he got a call from a police sergeant in Dorval. "…heard from Philly White this morning—he's not a bad fellow, Philly, he wouldn't hurt anybody. He has no violence on his record."

"Record? What record?"

"Oh a long, long record. Four convictions in BC. Fraudulent auto sales with forgery. Fraudulent roofing contracts. But no violence, I was glad when he told me he found a friend to help him out. If I come by your house, can I give you his radio? He left it in the cells here and I know he'll miss it. That Parthenais … it isn't like the Dorval Jail. It's no picnic, you bet." He recited a series of calamitous occurrences which had taken place at the detention centre. Group suicides, self-mutilations. "So you see if old Philly has a friend to help, I'll be glad. His family won't do nothing."

"His family aren't here. His mother is dead and they all live in Toronto."

"Did he tell you that? His mother lives in Montreal with one of his sisters and one brother. They don't go to see him. His wife and kids are here too."

"Does his wife know he's awaiting sentence?"

"No, she doesn't know a thing … nobody knows anything about Philly White for sure. Can I drop off his radio?"

"I'm not sure I'm going to be here. I have to go to the country. I have to go pick up my car. I don't believe I can make it; the family's expecting me back. I have to go and …"

"He'll be disappointed. He said you were coming down."

"He seems to say whatever he likes."

"That's right."

"Mail him the radio. I'll be away."

"No. No. I think I'll deliver it by hand."

The car was ready when he went over to get it. "It's ready; it's ready. You said it would be," he said happily; the garageman looked at him in surprise.

"It always is."

"A pleasure ... a pleasure."

The building on Parthenais looked more horrible in bright sunshine than in rainy darkness. Huge, slab-sided, far too glassy. Your gaze went right through it and out the other side. He went in, explained his errand to the man on the desk— the same man as the night before; didn't he ever sleep?—and ascended to the tenth floor in an ordinary elevator. At the third, fifth, and eighth floors it stopped automatically; he peered out without ostentation. Each floor seemed perfectly normal; you could see across the hall and out the windows. Ordinary office space. The view grew progressively more distant and spread-out as the car rose in the shaft. He was prepared for a hand- some prospect as he stepped out on ten, and was chilled and repelled by the barred, electrically locked gate, the approaches beyond it to heavy steel doors. The four top floors of the build- ing form a maximum security jail. There is no exercise yard. There is no sports program. Prisoners may use one of three small recreation areas for periods of up to one hour, every sec- ond day, if they aren't receiving special discipline.

"... you are not permitted to see him. What gave you the idea you could see him? Are you a relative?"

"No, he told me on the phone that..."

"I'm sorry, sir. His case is awaiting disposition. Only rela- tives."

"He told me he had no relatives nearer than Toronto."

"He told you a lie."

"Does his wife come to see him? How long has he been in here? I want to try to help."

"You aren't an officer of the John Howard Society?"

"No, nothing like that."

223

"Not a lawyer conferring with a judge about the sentence?"

"No, no."

The walls of this dreadful bullpen—a long counter or booth like that in a government liquor store or customs house—were painted a very pale grey-blue which did nothing to conceal their metallic chill. He began to look around wildly.

"What is your name, sir? Why did you come here?"

"This man called me on the telephone last night and told me he was in trouble; he didn't say how serious it was, but I gathered that he felt pretty desperate..."

"...they'll all tell you that."

"Yes, I'm sure they will. I would myself, I think, if I had to stay here. Can't you tell me anything at all?"

"I've never seen the man."

"How do you know so much about him?"

"I'm simply following general regulations, sir."

"And he has no right to a visitor, like he claimed?"

"Certain relatives, his lawyer of record, officially authorized prison visitors."

"All right, then, a sergeant from Dorval is bringing in his radio. He left it there. Would you see that he gets it?"

"I don't know anything about that at all."

He left the bullpen and walked quickly through the massive doors. He felt very glad that they opened for him, that the elevator came, some time after he pressed the DOWN button. All the way out to the street and into the driver's seat of his car, he felt as if a hand might descend on his shoulder. There was a parking ticket under the left windshield wiper. The rubberized gorilla mask smiled up at him from where he had dropped it on the front seat. He felt intensely happy to see it there, happy that he'd remembered it, that his children enjoyed having it. He made the best of his way out of town.

The mask alone was not enough, naturally. Four imaginative new costumes were required. The boys decided to go out as soldiers of the American Civil War, one in blue uniform, one in grey; design and fitting of these intricate costumes occupied much of September and early October.

"What are you going out as?"

"Soldiers of the War Between the States, as they would have been dressed at Gettysburg." The younger son was a student of Civil War history and a bitter partisan of the North, an admirer of Lincoln and Grant.

"But don't you think Lee was the greatest general of that war?"

"He lost, didn't he?"

Not much to be said to that.

And of course, he reflected, on the essential issue of slavery the North had been in the right. He was certain of that; what could possibly be urged in favour of slavery, of imprisonment, detention, referral to clinic? He felt mixed up, his head crowded with civilized misgiving. He started to get letters addressed to Philly White, in his care. He wouldn't open them and couldn't decide what to do with them. Some were postmarked Vancouver. One looked like an Income Tax refund cheque. A month after the first phone call, there came another. "Yes, it's me. I want to thank you for everything you've done for me. Sergeant Bastien told me how you helped him."

"The man from Dorval with your radio."

"He said how kind you were."

"Were you actually talking to Sergeant Bastien?" It had become important to extract some unambiguous, verifiable statement.

"Not actually talking to him in so many words ... exactly."

"How then?"

"Well, he got through to me all right. These veteran police officers have ways of dealing with things that you and I wouldn't think of."

"I didn't do anything for you, White. I have no intention of doing anything for you." He at least could be unambiguous, or hoped he could.

"But you came down to the Prevention Centre to see me, didn't you?"

"I did. Anybody would have done that."

"But you came twice, didn't you?"

"How do you know?"

"I know." There was a noxious appeal to this way of talking. He felt himself being drawn into the position of co-conspirator and even accomplice. He had enough free-floating fear of having done something criminal in his imagination without this.

"Just handle my mail for me," begged White.

"Why can't it go directly to jail?" He felt dreadfully like laughing. He thought, "Go directly to Jail; do not pass GO; do not collect $200"; he remembered the cards in the pile marked "Get out of Jail free."

"Would you like your wife to have to send her letters to such a place?"

"No."

"Do this for me then, for the sake of the old days."

"What old days? Do you know, I can barely remember you. That's forty years ago. I don't have any responsibility for you."

"We are all responsible for one another," said White.

"Then why did you ... never mind."

"I can use your address?"

"I'll forward anything that arrives."

The call was abruptly ended by that strange echoing click suggestive of constant switchboard surveillance. He wondered who was listening, and thought of making misleading and ambiguous remarks the next time White telephoned, just to give the listeners something to think about, realizing at the same moment that such an action would cause them to set up a dossier on him, which would then have the assured and interminable existence of an official file.

A flood of correspondence ensued, much of it from distant provinces, all addressed to his quiet Montreal street, all for

Philly White. He would wait for three or four days till he had a dozen or so items, then bundle them together in a single large envelope and forward it to Parthenais Street. Certain letters obviously got through to White, who discussed them in later phone calls. Some were perhaps suppressed by the authorities or censored by them, but on the whole White seemed well abreast of his outside affairs; he had now been at the Centre de Prevention for August, September, most of October—almost thirteen weeks; this was nothing compared to the detention of other unfortunates. The top floors were designed to hold 250 inmates, all in one way or another of special status. Either they could not be brought to trial because the prosecutor's case was incomplete, or the dockets were overburdened, or their lawyers were evading the event for tactical reasons: those in this last category might wait forever without their process coming on. Many died on Parthenais Street without receiving either condemnation or justification. And there were always more than three hundred crowded into the cells.

There were many like White whose guilt had been legally established. Convicted, criminals in the eyes of the law, sentenced, as yet undisposed of, they could not be conveniently put away and forgotten in this or that prison because a humane penology wished to "cure" them—in White's case apparently to dry the liquor out of him and begin treatment for alcoholism. A cured alcoholic, he might no longer be a fraud-artist and con-man, but this was doubtful. The alcoholism and the pathological addiction to lying might be elements of deeper ruin, probably were.

Nobody knows what is truly criminal, who are culpable. There are legal definitions, always abstract, inexact. There is observably bad—at least socially unacceptable—behaviour: what is called the "psychopathic personality" where social responsibility is rejected together with the possibility of truthfulness. What oppressed the listener to Philly White's phone calls was that he never, even by accident, said the plain truth.

Disguise abounded; cold came on. Toward the end of the month the boys completed their Civil War costumes and began to parade around the house in them, looking from a short distance wonderfully authentic. The younger lad had constructed one of those flat, forward-slanting Confederate caps with a badge of crossed rifles over the peak, and the letters C.S.A. sewn into it irregularly. The effect was truly persuasive. He had a cardboard musket and a water bottle. He kept saying, "Pickett's charge represented the high-water mark of the Confederacy," and his father never managed to establish what that meant. The other boy had decided to approach the northern infantryman's dress with less historical correctness and more freedom of interpretation. He carried a powder-horn—more appropriate for the Revolutionary War—and wore a shaggy false beard made of stuff chopped from an old Borghana coat of their mother's, which gave him an unexpectedly Russian air.

The girls hovered over alternatives. Then in a late fury of artistic creation they evolved two superb and original designs. For the younger girl, the baby of the family, they made a horse's body from a painted and draped cardboard carton fitted around her waist like an Eskimo's kayak. This was completed by floppy artificial legs hanging from a painted saddle—a caricature of a circus equestrienne. Her sister had then simply to dress herself as a ringmaster: red coat, tall hat, white breeches, riding whip, and the illusion was perfect and striking.

Mixed images of strangely caparisoned, smallish persons capering around him wound their way into their father's worried judgment. All day on the 31st of the month he lazed around the house among orange and black festoons, expecting some sort of resolution of the affair of White the bunco steerer. The weekend before, all clocks had been put back. It was full dark by six p.m. The children departed for their exciting annual night walk, gangs of neighbourhood kids beginning to press the doorbell. The phone rang in the midst of other urgent pealings, as he raised his coffee cup to his lips. Of course it was his old friend on Parthenais Street, with his first concrete demand for money. "If you'll just make the one payment for me, $184.80, we can retain ownership, they won't repossess. It's in the wife's name. I'll tell you where to send your cheque, and thanks for what you're trying to do. I really mean it."

He felt great anger squeezing his throat. "You don't mean it at all," he said, "you're just trying it on. I knew it would get to this point. A hundred and eighty from the poor sucker for openers, eh? It's finished, White, you get me? That's it. Don't call again and don't have any more mail sent here. I thought you needed me. I thought you meant it. All just a big con. You're still at it even though they've locked you up. You've been sentenced. How come they don't put you where you belong?"

"*They're* trying to help me."

"Let them! Whoever *they* are."

'I'm only trying to make contact."

"Good-bye, White. Don't call again."

He hoped the listeners got it all; there wouldn't be any more calls. The doorbell rang and he walked through the house, opened the door and confronted a small visitant dressed as a ghost. He handed this person many sugary treats, then shut the door. I did right, he told himself, I did right (wrong), I did right, right (wrong), I did right...

I'VE GOT
TROUBLES
OF MY OWN

ROM first to last she never saw them. Entertaining angels unawares, she thought, gritting her teeth, giggling. She didn't know a thing about the law of landlord and tenant but she knew that she had to have somebody living in the house to carry the running expenses, immediately, before the mortgage charges and the cost of oil and the wear and tear on her Toyota, driving back and forth three times a week between Kingston and Sweet's Corners, ate up all her earnings, leaving her without enough pay for her apartment and to feed Freda and herself. I asked for it, she remembered, single-parent status, an old country house up Highway 15. And I got it. Pray that you never get the thing you want most; it will bankrupt you. This shining flawless shard of cynicism galled her, enforcing its accuracy as she thought of it. Take what comes that you don't much want; take that. Forget wishes!

Well shit, it was easy to get there; that was the lure. She could slide out of the *Whig-Standard* offices most days by late afternoon on any of a wide selection of pretexts; then she would collect Freda from the day-care centre on Division Street, go out 401 to the Highway 15 exit, and be in Sweet's Corners in forty minutes tops. She had pictured herself going into Freda's room at seven a.m. in the stillness of winter, unbroken snow-crust gleaming in the last starshine and first light, waves of hot air billowing from the register next to the child's bed, familiar drafts around her slippered feet as she crossed the wide planking of the floor. An old farmhouse. A country retreat. Single-parent status. You brave brave girl, how can you ever manage? (Who was the father anyway?) You're so self-sacrificing. (She does everything for that child, who would have guessed?) Oh how gallant you are, how much the new woman.

From old lady to new woman in a single leap. She wasn't sure who the father was; it could have been somebody on the paper; it could have been a man in a bookstore; it was probably a zoologist at Queen's. There seemed no point in sharing the baby around so she took it all for herself and was, she thought, the first or second (actually she was the seventh) woman in Kingston to give birth while unmarried, in a public hospital, without using an assumed identity. She had imagined herself "bearing the shame" or "facing up to her disgrace" but there wasn't any shame or disgrace. People applauded. Brave girl. Gallant new woman. Freda was now four and getting to be a problem; there were difficulties with the milk-products enzymes; her spit-ups dissolved pantyhose.

The two of them would have their breakfast next to the kitchen range, would eye the old dry sink and the dim form of the unworkable pump beside it. The first extra expense—in itself almost ruinous—had been the digging of a new well on the other side of the house, the installation of the uncloggable foot-valve and an adequate electric pump. When she remembered what that had cost, she always thought of S.J. Perelman's definition. "A farm is an irregular patch of nettles bounded by short-term notes, containing a fool and his wife who didn't know enough to stay in the city."

The sentence, while not entirely applicable to her own situation, nevertheless possessed a considerable element of truth. At least she had not gotten lumbered with the land from the farm; that had been sold away from "the old Kelsey place" a dozen years before to a neighbouring farmer who now claimed an inalienable right-of-way across her front lawn. She only found this out much later, when the question of re-sale surfaced; nobody said anything about it when title passed to her. There was no irregular patch of nettles but there were plenty of short-term notes which grew harder and harder to meet.

She used to get demand-note loans from the Royal Bank branch near the office at a preferred-client rate; when she bought the house she'd been able to raise a quick $1,000 at any time by this means, paying twelve percent for the use of the money and repaying the loan in ninety days. At that rate and on those liberal terms, the bank manager assumed—arrogated to himself or was allowed by her—she never quite knew which—a father-figure status which was probably psychologically inadmissible. He treated her like a little girl who had been bad and now stood before him drawing her toe across the carpet and hanging her head; then he would pat her on the cheek, pass the note across the desk for her to sign, dismiss her with a paternal nod. He did not look like her father, a man with entirely different paternal characteristics; the only fatherly attitude the two men shared was their refusal to admit alarm, disappointment, resentment, any of the traditional emotions at her free-form pregnancy.

Her bank manager had once patted her distended stomach in a comradely way as he leaned across his desk and proffered a promissory note. This gesture had offended her right to the sources of her being. But what could she do? She took the note and signed beside the pencilled X. She needed the money for the foot-valve and the black plastic piping and the new sink and toilet. She had ninety days to pay him back for that pat on the tummy and she had only one resource, her other father-figure, her real father who sent her in turn to *his* father, an old man still deeply involved in the family furniture business, factory, warehouse, retail sales outlet, in Napanee. This old man, whom she hated and feared, said a few forthright things about bastards and gave her $1,000 which she accepted with a mixture of reluctance and eager relief. She would never have gone near her grandfather, she assured herself, if he weren't still living in the elegant family home on the bluff which overlooks the river just where it widens and enters the bay, the most superb house in Napanee. And that's saying a lot.

She wanted to live like that. Everybody knows that nobody lives like that anymore but she was going to try. She wanted a house like her grandfather's, filled with the kind of furniture that his factory hadn't turned out since well before she was born. If that old man could stride around those wide verandas kicking porch furniture out of the way while he complained about other peoples' morals, then she was equally entitled to wide verandas and a view. At least her grandfather was decent enough to insult her straight out; her father only looked his reproaches; the sleek manager of the Royal branch near the office just patted her and approved. Fuck them!

After the new well, the rise in oil prices. She never got to inhabit the house for a full winter; there was always something in the city that kept her on the go: a war among the theatrical companies in town, each clamouring for her support and space in her column on the local scene or a secret council hearing on the location of the new sewage farm. She spent days on that assignment, finally winkling a sheaf of most-secret memoranda out of the mayor's secretary who had just had an abortion and admired her for walking around with her navel out to here. It turned out that raw waste would have to be trucked to Belleville for treatment and disposal at inadmissible cost to the taxpayers until a new disposal plant could be put onstream four years in the future. This revelation almost cost the mayor his chair and she got a raise at the *Whig*.

God, the house, the house. She had to pay to heat it for three winters in which she almost never went there. It just sat on its tiny knoll up above the road next door to the Anglican church and drank up heating oil like Freda swallowed expensive formula. She had to have a tenant!

But who? Where to find one she could trust to look after her plants, to devote time to the continual attention the house demanded: pointing, weatherstripping, adjusting the thermostat night and morning, keeping an eye on the sump pump, seeing there was oil in the tank, laying more insulation batts in the attic, watching out for traces of water damage through the roof. God, the house!

She called Babs Cornford at the local Century 21 agency and begged for her help. Babs had sold her the old Kelsey house in the first place and continued to send her a booklet each month containing mouth-watering photographs and loving descriptions of other old country houses in case she felt like trading up.

"No possible way, Babs. I'm a single woman. I only have one income. A pretty small income."

"You're unionized, right?"

"I'm what? Oh right, sure, I'm in the guild, but that doesn't make me a rich lady."

"I don't have any union going for me," said Babs. "Anything I have coming in, it's because I got out and hustled for it."

This did not sound like the old Babs Cornford who had been kissing her bum before the closing date.

"Is something wrong?" she asked.

"Wrong, wrong, wrong. I just lost a sale I thought I had locked up. These things happen." Babs started to weep, explosively, chokingly, at the same time reading from her list of properties.

"There's a place on the road in to Chaffee's Locks that you'd just adore (*sob, sob*) and you could move right in for the equity on your present home. Let's see, your down payment was what, $10,000?" Sniffles and gasps from Century 21.

"I put $20,000 into it, Babs. You should know that better than anybody and I'm not in the market. I want you to get me a tenant."

But there was no money for the agent in a search for a tenant.

"All I get is the first month's rent . . . what were you thinking of asking?"

"Just enough to pay the mortgage, the insurance, the oil, and the taxes until I can afford to live in it."

"When would that be?"

"I don't know, maybe two years, maybe three." Maybe never, she thought. "Say $300 a month. That would just barely cover it and it's a low rent."

"Could you slip me a little extra if I get somebody good? Three hundred would just pay for my gas and phone."

"Why should I pay for your phone?"

"Give me two months' rent and I'll find you some good people."

"I guess I've got no choice." Dear Jesus, let some big story break, a six-alarm fire, a sex scandal at the university, anything for some overtime.

There wasn't much response to the ads for a tenant. The kind of people who were looking for low rents were definitely not the same crowd who admired mid-nineteenth-century brick farmhouses. Prospective tenants had one thing in common: low income. They were mostly retired couples from the surrounding villages who thought $300 rather a high rent. A barber and his wife who was in a wheelchair; an old man who had sold his hardware store too long ago and now had a poverty-line income; folks like that.

"Really, Babs, I can't let chronic losers into the house. I might never be able to get rid of them when I'm ready to move in."

"Back to square one," said Ms. Cornford pensively.

And then she unearthed the Megarrys, Tom and Lila. "These are real folks," she claimed on the phone. "All they need is a bit of a helping hand to get themselves back on their feet."

The phrase made little waves of apprehension shiver her spine.

"But have they got any money?"

"They can pay the rent, if that's what you mean, if you would be willing to shave your price just a little bit."

"How little?"

"They could manage $250."

"For an eight-room house with a new well, new pump, new sump pump? You're joking."

"These are the best prospects I've been able to locate. Tom is getting compensation regularly."

"What?"

"His workman's compensation."

"You mean he's not working?"

"Not right at this moment."

"When does he expect to start working? He has worked now and then, I suppose. He's managed to get himself onto the welfare rolls."

"Welfare isn't the same thing as compensation. He suffered an injury on the job so he collects a monthly payment from the board."

"How much?"

"He says around a thousand a month. We could easily check on that."

"How can he pay the rent I'm asking on $1,000 a month?"

"That's why he's asking you to drop it fifty bucks." This reply had a savage logic which was compelling.

"You feel he can pay $250?"

"Cross my heart."

"What sort of injury?"

"Injury? Oh, Mr. Megarry, yes. He was hoisting a truck engine out of its bed when the block and tackle let go. He took all the weight of the engine in his arms and back. Tore the muscles right out of his lower back," said Babs. She repeated the last phrase with gloomy relish. "Tore them right the hell out of there." It was clear she was quoting somebody.

"Have they got any family?"

"Two of the sweetest little girls you ever saw."

"Hmmmmm."

"I've got the first month's rent here, in cash, and a cheque for the December rent. After that they'll simply remit cheques to you. We won't give them a lease. I know you don't want a lease. We'll write up a month-to-month tenancy agreement and get her to sign it."

"Her?"

"The wife, Lila. She signs the cheques."

"Why?"

"No doubt they have their reasons."

"And you're certain they can make it?"

"As certain as I've ever been about anything."

"Okay then. I'll draft a tenancy agreement and give it to you tomorrow and you can get them to sign it. Do I get any of the first two months' rent?"

"No, that stays with me. But I'm paid in full and you can enjoy your rental income without further payments to your realtor and good luck!"

"Oh, stop it, Babs. You better tell them I want my cheque for the January rent on or before the first of the month and no fooling. Maybe they'd better give me a series of post-dated cheques through the end of May."

"And why not?" said Babs.

The new tenants were to move in just after the first of November which left a single fall weekend free for country amusements. She bundled Freda into the back seat of the

Toyota under a pile of sleeping-bags and a hot-plate and took the child to spend a restorative weekend with her—perhaps the last for many years—on their property. There were some good moments. When she'd bought the place, very little land had come with it, about two acres. What there was lay well back from the road with cart-tracks of her neighbour's right-of-way running across it to the south towards his fields and woodlot. There was a tacit agreement that she could use his fields for walking or cross-country skiing in return for the regular passage—questionably legal—up the track past her place with a wagonload of fodder or hay or horse dung. This neighbour used to cut her grass from time to time, often when she was staying in the house. A sunburned man with a striped locomotive-engineer's cap and underneath it a bold look. He made her grass look pretty good using a big power-cutter and he let her wander around his own 239 acreage with complete freedom. She had an inkling he knew all about her single-parent status, which was in certain ways more and more a prestige symbol or a species of invitation.

She took Freda out on the Saturday afternoon for a brisk walk across the back fields and along the edge of the woodlot which lay several hundred yards back from the road running along behind the Anglican cemetery and the shining little church. They bumbled around back there until Freda grew tired and began to beg to be carried; as she was almost five and a chunky little Ms. she made quite an armful. It seemed wise to take the shortest way back.

They struck out towards the little cemetery and came to an almost invisible fence which had formerly marked off consecrated ground. It had been down for some years and was extremely rusty though not barbed. You could just barely make it out; two or three old headstones lay there on their backs entangled in the growth of wildflowers and weeds. Some of these stones gave birthdates in the mid-eighteenth century for those whom they commemorated. She hadn't realized people born that long ago had lived out the balance of their lives to die in Sweet's Corners in the 1830s and 1840s.

The Anglican pastor, Mr. Marjoribanks, stood some distance away in the middle of the cemetery, his head bent in an awkward and unfamiliar attitude. She saw with relief he was wearing ordinary clothes; once before she'd met him outside the church when he'd been wearing a clerical collar above a dark-grey shirt, an aspect of dress he found repellent. She set Freda down—there was protest at this—and walked over to greet Mr. Marjoribanks, hoping uneasily that he wouldn't bless her or do anything silly. But he only looked up and smiled vaguely. He obviously had no idea who she was.

"I am your neighbour," she said, then wondered if the simple words suggested parody of some Biblical utterance. "From the house next door."

"Mrs.... Mrs.?"

"Mzzzzzzz," she said sturdily.

She realized that he didn't even suspect what Ms. stood for and decided not to follow up on identification. Let him think what he liked. He probably figured she was Mrs. Mzzzzzzz.

"I own the house next door, the old Kelsey place."

The minister extended his hand and she clutched at it. The palm was firm and dry with a faintly powdery texture; there were many liver spots on the back. He looked to be about seventy-five, as old as her grandfather. Was she always going to be surrounded by old lawgivers?

"I knew the Kelseys well," said Mr. Marjoribanks. "Baptists, most of them, otherwise well-behaved."

She wished he hadn't introduced shop-talk. Another minute and she would be interviewing him for a page in the weekend magazine:

Aging clergyman mourns decline of faith.
Exquisite temple unattended.
What shall we do with our tax-free church buildings?

Pictures of the interior of Saint John the Divine, Anglican, Sweet's Corners. It was a very handsome building, paintwork shining white, pews deeply reflective of fifty coats of varnish, elegant tower, some indifferent glass.

He walked her around the interior, made small talk about local notables lying in the churchyard. One of them had been in the provincial cabinet a century ago; another had lived to be a hundred and ten. She had to get out of here, she saw, or be sick. Already Freda was dribbling something that smelled bitterly of sour skim milk. As she passed out towards the front porch she gave the minister her news.

"I've rented the place to a young family, the Megarrys. Perhaps they may become members of your . . . flock." She felt pride and amusement at remembering the technical term.

"But they may not be Anglicans," said Mr. Marjoribanks.

"I don't suppose anybody insists on doctrinal purity any more. Or do they?" She corrected herself, seeing a look of pain on the man's face. There might be a story in this, she thought, for a small old audience.

"We try not to force our attentions on anyone to whom they may be unwelcome," said Mr. Marjoribanks. "Good-bye, Mrs. . . . Mrs. . . . I hope we meet again soon." He had picked up on her lack of a married name. The hell with that anyway!

The Megarrys moved in on the Monday and for some time she heard nothing more about the house. Around the second week in December an envelope arrived at her apartment with a series of post-dated cheques in it, drawn on a branch in Lyndhurst, dated January through May. She examined the handwriting on the cheques inscribed in defective ballpoint, a pale, almost untraceable mauve. Whoever wrote them had pressed down hard on the pen when writing the signature; some of the other writing, including the amount on the face of the January and March cheques, was hard to make out. The numbers were generally clear enough.

"Lila Megarry," said three of the cheques. The other two were signed "Mrs. L. Megarry."

She wondered if there were any specific reason for this. It was the handwriting of somebody who had been taught to write in primary school but had not done much with it afterwards. The letters were childishly formed; at the same time they had a faded elegance like the handwriting one might expect to find on packets of correspondence found in Victorian chests. All the cheques were dated on the first of the month.

She deposited the first one directly after New Year's, intending to pay a couple of important bills with it, but it came back from Lyndhurst under a cloud. She studied the "refused payment" stamp on the back of the wrinkled slip of paper—it was the first time she had ever been given a rubber cheque—and wondered if there were anything she could do with it. An indecent phrase suggested itself; she dismissed it immediately. She rang up the offending bank in Lyndhurst and asked to speak to the accountant, a Miss Belvedere, who assured her that there could be no harm in re-submitting the cheque for payment later in the month.

"It might just get through," she said.

"Might?"

"A proportion of them do."

"When should I try again?"

"Whenever the utterer of the cheque is likely to receive payments. I don't think there's much point in depositing it more than once more; after a couple of refusals a lineup has formed."

"I see."

She did not like the sound of this one little bit. She would have to do without something while those people (they were assuming the aspect of *those people*!) lived in her house for a full month rent-free. In an agony of frustration she crumpled the worthless cheque into a ball and flushed it down the toilet. At ten o'clock in the morning on the first day of February she was standing at the door of the bank in Lyndhurst, first in a small lineup, every member of which, she felt certain, held a cheque signed "Lila Megarry." She shoved the February cheque through the window of the first teller she saw and a *mauvais quart d'heure* ensued.

"The account can't quite cover this."

"How do you mean?"

"I can't tell you that."

"Can't tell me what? All I want is to cash the cheque."

"I'm not allowed to tell you anything that would reveal the customer's balance."

"You've already let me know that it's under two-fifty. What we have to determine is how far under. I mean, is it close?"

The teller screwed her head around on her neck very uneasily. "It's fairly close."

"Within ten dollars?"

"Not quite that close. Almost."

"Then cash the cheque and give them a ten-dollar overdraft."

"I don't think Mr. Ellenbeck will hold still for that."

"Could I talk to him?"

"I'll see." She went away again and as there were only two tellers working the lineup began to lengthen out. There were mutinous grumblings from other customers. In a few minutes the manager came to the counter and asked her to join him at a point somewhat removed from the cages. Bloody bank managers control our lives, she thought.

"They're short again," he said dolefully. "I nursed them through the last three months and now this."

"I didn't get my rent for January," she said, feeling close to tears. "I lost $250 I was counting on." She blinked, staring at the manager. "I have problems. I've got a little girl. I can't afford to have my house sitting empty. Couldn't you pay the cheque and subtract the OD from their next deposit?"

"I might do it for you, but don't, for God's sake, let it get around. I can't do it for everybody. I suppose they do have to have a roof over their heads. And a little food."

"Are there many others?"

"The Bell and Hydro, that's about it. God knows how they're heating the place. Is there any wood on the property?"

"There are trees."

"They won't fell the trees because they couldn't burn them for six months. Or maybe they won't think of that. You might take a look as you drive past."

"Cut my trees?"

"I'll pay this cheque through at its face value," said Mr. Ellenbeck, "but I don't know how long I can go on doing it. I hear he's having trouble getting his compensation. You have to have some sort of income after all, don't you?"

He led her back to the teller and oversaw payment. She just snatched at the money and ran without thanking him; it was her money; it was coming to her. She drove out the sideroad toward Highway 15, past Saint John the Divine, Anglican, and her place. It did rather look as if a couple of the trees at the back were missing. A clothesline hung very slack between the house and a nearby sumac; there were tiny faded dresses hanging on the line like thing in a horrible Shirley Temple movie. She sped on, gained the highway, retreated to Kingston, and went in to work in the afternoon; her grippe had miraculously cleared off, she said, and she couldn't bear to be away from work a whole day. And they believed her, even sympathized with her. Megarry didn't sign his own cheques, she saw clearly, because the fucker couldn't write. An illiterate. I've saddled myself with an illiterate and his brood, back-country hicks. She shook with an unidentifiable emotion of great intensity.

The March cheque sneaked through. At the same time however rumblings of discontent began to reach her in the form of phone calls from the Bell and the Hydro. Was she in any way connected to the Megarrys by blood? Would she make herself responsible for accounts left unpaid by them? There was a strong, if tacit, suggestion in both inquiries that she would have the dickens of a time getting the phone and the power turned back on once her tenants finally quit.

"You mean I'd have to pay for them?"

"Certainly," said the nasty voice of Bell Accounts. "You could scarcely expect us to restore service unless previous billings were met."

"How much do they owe?"

"They haven't actually paid us anything since installation but you can put your mind at rest; they aren't making a lot of long-distance calls. It's mainly a matter of service charges on three instruments."

"Three?"

"They've got three coloured phones and jacks all over the house. They're like beads and trinkets to them, you know."

"Them?"

"Mr. Megarry is part-Indian."

"I won't pay!"

"You'd be wise to think about getting them out."

Though it was late March, and the weather about as horrid as it could possibly be, wild wind, deep snow, deadly cold, she made up her mind on the spot. "I'll throw them so fucking far out they'll bounce; I won't put any backspin on them either. Do I make myself clear?"

"I think you'd be doing the right thing," said Bell Accounts.

"Bet your ass!"

This was when she began to learn the law of landlord and tenant, to realize that the drift of legal interpretation over the past decade had favoured the tenant. If you wanted to hurl somebody out, you had to show that no lease existed, that one month's notice was mutually recognized as the instrument of termination, that the tenant clearly undertook to vacate at such a time and was thus responsible for the payment of utilities and fuel bills incurred by him. You had to be able to *show* this. Just to claim it was so would not satisfy a rental board. There might be hearings. This made her quail. She had so often acted the part of the crusading investigative reporter ready to crucify an elected official, reveal the nervous shrinking egotism of an actor or director, the fumbling negligence of a school administrator. She had been fearless in uncovering injustice in fairly high places. Now she was cast in the role of landlord and it appeared that Lila Megarry was pregnant again; that placed her in the position of putting a penniless member of a persecuted minority—positively one of the Dene Nation—on the street with his pregnant wife and their infant family and nowhere to go. Oh, terrific!

She would not swerve from righteousness. She was entitled to rent. January rent had not been paid. April rent had not been paid. When that cheque came back, there was little to be gained from it but the bank's notation in the characteristic green stamp-pad ink on the reverse of refusal to pay. In the sheriff's office, that notification on the worthless cheque stood for something, perhaps almost everything.

The Sheriff of Leeds County, a mild and quiet elderly man, wore no tin star, carried no six-guns, resembled a lawyer or your dentist. He fingered the bad cheques and her lawyer's letter and the unpaid Bell and Hydro bills which had mysteriously come into his possession.

"No problem," said the mild sheriff. "You've got enough here to hang him. I'll issue notice to quit this afternoon and after he gets it he has till the end of May to leave. If he isn't out of there by the thirty-first, my men will put his furniture on the roadway. Show me again exactly where the building is located."

"Don't let them hurt my house plants," she said. "It's right next door to the church of Saint John the Divine, Anglican."

"Right next door to Mr. Marjoribank's church?"

He pronounced the name "Marshbanks."

"Is that how you pronounce it?"

"What?"

"Marjoribanks."

Some slight confusion ensued.

"Never seen it written down, I don't believe. Always called him Marshbanks. Everybody does," said the sheriff.

"I see. My house is next door to the house of God," she said, yielding to some imp of perversity.

"We'll take care of you," said the sheriff. She had a hunch he knew she worked for the *Whig* and had something he wanted to hide. Almost everybody does.

So the Megarrys were overmatched; they didn't hang around to be evicted, just vanished in the night, sometime during the final week of May. Her lawyer phoned the glad tidings on the twenty-eighth of the month, advising her to get right out to the place and start the cleanup.

"Cleanup?"

"The Sheriff says the place is a mess. If you want to rent it or get rid of it, you're going to have to clean up after them."

Driving out from Kingston she predicted dirt and found shit, all different kinds. Mouse shit. Rat shit. Dog shit. Cat shit. Human shit. Shit shit. Smeared and strewn around piled-up green plastic bags in which reposed the detritus of a terrible winter: newspapers, cooking grease, diapers, sanitary napkins, tampons, broken dishes, countless bodies of insects, dead rats, live rats, ashes and clots of other unspeakable substances whose textures repelled her.

She had to clean it all up. She couldn't show the place to anybody—what would they think? How banish the stench? She hired a trucker for the last Sunday in May and together with him and his helper she carted three truckloads of tenant shit to the dump where it was burned.

Then, late in the afternoon, trembling with exhaustion, she determined with fanatic resolution to hose down and sweep out the summer kitchen where the mound of ordure had been stacked. It would take weeks for the odours to disperse. As she played a powerful jet of water over the walls and floor of the infirm frame structure, she saw Mr. Marjoribanks standing not far off, just across the property line. She turned the hose off and walked over to say hello, hoping inwardly for comfort and encouragement.

"You wouldn't believe what I've trucked out of there," she said as she drew near. "Filth! But I don't think they'll bother you anymore."

"They weren't any bother."

"They weren't?"

"No, they'd had a very hard time. Mr. Megarry was a cripple and there were interruptions with his compensation money. They were expecting another child and they had nothing."

"I can't help any of that," she said. "I've got to think of myself. I'm not your mean landlord, I'm a person with problems too. I've got a little girl. I work for a living. I have to get income from my house. I can't provide anybody with free rent. Nobody's entitled to a free ride through life. I'm not listening, I tell you. I'm not listening, do you hear?"

BREAKING OFF

J UPITER LIFE and Casualty/Canada (with home offices
in East Tonawanda, NY) were locked into a term lease
in Commerce Court that had been one of the keys to
the financing of the complex, four tower floors, the twenty-
second to the twentyfifth: Executive Offices, Finance, Legal
Department, Sales, Advertising and Publicity, Computer Centre, Records and Statistics. There was intermittent gossip in
the offices about a new building on the 401 service road in
Oakville, which scared everybody on junior staff. The move
to Oakville would cost half of them their jobs, for it would be
a testing commute. The Commerce Court lease, however, was
in the opinion of the legal department an ironclad document.
It had looked unbreakable when it seemed favourable to
Jupiter, and it looked from an unfavourable angle even more
likely to hold water. No move seemed imminent. The lease ran
through 1987.

Overcrowding was an eternal office menace, which implied
continual shuffling round of desks and fragile partitions; small
rooms were always being re-assigned to persons in modest
authority. Every six months a new wave of design efficiency
would sweep through some department, washing away bulletin

boards and water coolers, rearranging the positions of graphs, charts, files. Only the computer banks remained impassive. Very extensive, anchored to special power-cables, they could not be shifted to any area not serviced by reinforced flooring, special shielding, and sophisticated circuitry.

This sempiternal fluxion contrasted sharply with the tone of the chaste and perfectly clean quarters in which it evolved. The office tower was a marvel of simple, natural illumination, efficient heating and cooling. The interior temperature remained at an equable seventy degrees winter and summer, and there was none of the faint susurration of air-conditioners that tore at the nerves of personnel in office complexes completed in the 1960s and the earlier 1970s. As far as mere irreducible living conditions went—lighting, heating, smooth silent floor tiling, portability of partitions, colours of walls, durability of door hardware, ease of building maintenance— the tower was an unqualified success. It seemed the correct solution—or anyway one of the possible correct solutions— to problems of inner-city work-force comfort. Overcrowding must be avoided or this elegant solution would suffer a credibility loss. The architect—a western visionary—had stipulated in the final contracts the number of workers allowable per given square-footage of area space according to function. His provisions were rigorous, and the executives felt obliged to observe them.

Sometimes it seemed that in order to keep the four floors functional and elegant they had either to restrict the amount of business done, or overwork their employees. Perpetual juggling of assignments, farming out of a certain quantity of legal work and some publicity consultancies, and regular updating of information storage and retrieval systems, helped in part to preserve an attractive environment, always in delicate balance.

Enormous quantities of paper had to be disposed of daily, because the photocopy centre spewed forth an unending stream of pamphlets, booklets, memoranda running to many pages, and statistical breakdowns of remarkable subtlety and advanced mathematical character, all designed to be disposed of as soon as read, sometimes sooner. This was a part of an ongoing revolution in the technique of office management, which was replacing heavy, unwieldy, bulky filing cabinets, and punch-card or drum-type retrievers, by disposable records issuing from memory-banks of relatively compact physical proportions.

The photocopy centre, for example, tucked away between the computer centre and Records and Statistics, possessed two distinct copying systems—the small and the large—which were in operation all the time, staffed by two permanent women, and a temporary boy who did nothing but empty the OUT trays as fast as they filled. This boy, or rather this series of boys identical in manner and costume, and facial configuration, for all practical purposes a single specimen of the type, nameless but potent, sometimes found himself inadequate to this rapid flow. Confidential reports often fell to the floor to be covered by piles of other more or less recherché documentation. Information proliferated: knowledge became obscure: wisdom was inconceivable.

When too much paper had accumulated, the young women who operated the copiers, Olive Honeywell and her leg-girl Emmy Ivey, used to have to send a hurry-up call to other department and section heads, beseeching them to come and get it, the latest massive publication, the weekly claims breakdown, monthly policy registration, quarterly statement, annual report. Then the other departments would send around their youngest staff members to bear away what seemed relevant. In this way, Olive and Emmy acquired a wide acquaintance with strongbacked, usually male messengers. Theirs was a useful command post, a kind of redoubt whose walls were solid bricks of heavy white photocopy paper piled in stacks sometimes seven feet high. The photocopy centre had originally stood right out in the open, but over-production had walled it in, and now it was effectively a small cave of fact in which two fatal sisters and a malignant elf plied their shuttles.

They had copiers of the utmost sophistication. The big one could not only copy at unprecedented rates, but could sort the sheets as they burst from the entrails of the reproduction system, spraying pages into individual racks, lining them up, then stapling them. You could set the copier's memory, for example, such that the title page would be copied forty-eight times and distributed in the racks, then the table of contents, the opening page of text, the following pages, the appendices, a regular little book produced miraculously out of nowhere in seconds.

The little copier, Emmy Ivey's special pet, could not do these wonderful things, but it was very quick on single-sheet reproduction. If what was wanted was six hundred copies of two facing pages from *Actuarial Review*, Emmy could have them ready for distribution in five minutes.

Naturally with this production capacity they were up to here in high-quality, expensive, white photocopy paper. Supplies began to be ominously heavy; there was a serious question about weight distribution. The centre started to spread out after a while. Olive used to say jokingly, "I don't have secretary's spread, but my department does." She certainly did not have the characteristic poor posture and inferior muscle tone of a stenographer chained to a desk. Long practice in sprinting about the confined space available while carrying heavy weights had kept her lissome and markedly underweight, though approaching thirty. As for Emmy, she was a phantom of delight, her head with its bouncy aureole of tightly permed blonde ringlets all that was visible to the exterior world, the entire length of the twentythird floor, a sea of bent heads at light spacious attractive desks, spreading towards the far region of separate offices where, it was whispered, actuaries and logicians dwelt, and beyond them again in larger rooms, vice-presidents.

From vantage point at the feed-slot of the small copier, Emmy occasionally sallied forth with material wanted immediately, which some person would actually read. For some reason such publications were infrequent and small in print-order. Very rarely were more than fifty copies required of something which would be studied with care; these fifty rarities were invariably circulated to a restricted list of folks who were required to possess literacy, which was comprised of policy-making senior staff and department managers. Emmy could easily distribute an entire edition in a rapid forty-five minute tour of the four floors which the company occupied, sliding single copies into the appropriate IN trays as she passed, like some ministering angel of the Old Testament, a type of Passover messenger delivering saving signs.

She gave much pleasure to those who witnessed her passing. The golden head commanded high visibility; she earned a surprisingly large salary for a young single woman with a highschool education, and spent most of it on her clothes. She was still living at home but thinking about her own apartment. Clothes, potential apartment furnishings, and her stereo and records were what she spent her earnings on; she had no thought of saving. She wore casual, laid-back styles, wraparound ankle-lengths, the vests of men's suits found in secondhand and Junior League stores, frilled shirtwaists, occasional middy blouses, men's neckties loosely knotted, scarves in figured silks. Before the movie came out, she had achieved an Annie Hall look which was first queried by her bosses, then highly approved of by them, once they recognized it in advertising. Emmy was the office pet.

Often on these peregrinations she would meet one or another of the boys who came to the sequestered photocopy section to pick up heavy piles of stock. Les Pargiter was one of them, from the legal department, the most junior lawyer on their staff, not ashamed to act as a privileged office boy, possessor of two university degrees and unexpectedly youthful looking. Les was always puzzled to find how little his university background meant to Emmy; she had had almost no contact with professional or university people, and their learned attainments meant absolutely zero, zilch, zip to her. Most people she knew were working for a big company with a pension plan and a hospitalization scheme tied into OHIP and offering extra psychiatry as a fringe benefit. She had no knowledge whatsoever of other kinds of lives lived in other parts of the city besides the office or her home on Albany Avenue near the Bloor/Bathurst subway station. Everybody had the same kind of stereo, in the same price range between six hundred and fifteen hundred dollars. Most girls in the office tried to look like her, and she certainly wasn't going out of her way to look for Mister Goodbar.

Basil Mossington was more interesting than Les Pargiter or Motil Panilal or Sandor Ferenczi, though equally from some distant region which her imagination could not penetrate. He lived way off somewhere forty miles across town. When he went home at night he took the Yonge Street line all the way up to Finch, and a bus from there to someplace out back of Black Creek. He worked in Finance, in the budget section, and like Les Pargiter was one of the most junior employees, without Les' advanced professional training. Basil had answered a want-ad to get his job. He had one year at Ryerson behind him; classroom education meant nothing to Basil. He thought that work was better than school. Like Emmy, he enjoyed having money to buy things.

None of the grave questions which twenty-year-old people used to ask themselves ever crossed the minds of Emmy and Basil: whether or not they should save up to buy a home—an idea which would have struck either of them as bizarre. Nobody they knew had any idea of doing that. Everybody lived in onebedroom high-rise apartments, which you could furnish in high style for very little money actually paid down. You could have the ready use of five or six major credit cards.

You could pick up what you needed to eat every night after work at a Mac's Milk. You could wear new or secondhand or old clothes strictly according to your taste, as long as you could dig it. Neither of them had thought through this fate, but it was there, discoverable, somewhere in the backs of their heads. Two people with no commitments and twice their individual earnings—an extraordinarily large amount—could have an apartment in a brandnew building with big closets, full-length mirrors, a crystal roomdivider between dining and food preparation areas, and a twentieth-storey balcony with a view of the lake, posters from Marci Lipman Gallery, colour TV, twenty-one-day vacation excursions via Sunflight to Greece or St. Lucia, forever and ever, without having to learn or unlearn anything.

About two months after Basil began to be seriously and steadily aware of Emmy's orbitings, he went to a stylist in the bowels of Toronto-Dominion Centre and had his hair blown and waved, which gave him the look of a pro football player, a cornerback. Hardly anybody at the office noticed the change in hairstyle, because most of the older guys in Finance had already had it done. Even some of the actuaries were into far-out stylings and disco.

Emmy noticed it. She started stopping beside his desk instead of whizzing past with a brief backwards look over her shoulder and a bob of the head.

"Here's the constant-estimate-adjustment sheet for the third week of the current quarter, and the departmental breakdown, oh, and the extrapolation for the remainder of the quarter, and the . . . let's see, what is this . . . the in-field operations costings, and this is the divisional operations summary with three-previous-year comparison parameters. That's all, I think." Business of looking under arm. "Yes. That's all."

"That's a lot of paper. Don't you ever get tired?"

"I don't know. The whole thing comes to, what is it you've got there?"

"Runs about twenty pages."

"Well, times fifty, eh? Gives you five hundred sheets of paper. I'd be a pretty poor physical specimen if I couldn't carry that much weight, wouldn't I?"

"You look in pretty good shape to me. What are you doing, running? I mean, do you run? Tennis? Do you belong to a health club or something?"

"Well, I don't yet actually, but I'm considering it. I've been thinking about Super Silhouette."

"Super Silhouette is just for girls, I mean women, right?"

"No, it went unisex about last January. A lot of guys go there."

"What are they, mostly gays?"

"I guess there's some gays. I don't really know. I only went the once, with a girlfriend. I noticed mostly black guys."

"Why would that be?"

"I don't know. Maybe they've got more money."

"It could be that, yeah … but you haven't joined yet?"

"No. That month I went to a new stereo, a Sansui top of the line. I'm up around fourteen hundred dollars now."

"Who do you like?"

"Queen, Pink Floyd, Kate Bush. I like Leon Redbone too."

"Redbone?"

Emmy giggled. "I have to go. You'd better take those in to Daffy Duck."

They both laughed. Daffy Duck was the head of the Finance Department, called that by everybody who worked for Jupiter because of his heavy lisp in moments of excitement or annoyance. His true name was something quite different. Emmy stood on the tiptoes of her left foot, lining up her pile of papers.

Basil said suddenly. "You look like a bird poised for flight."

"I also own a parrot," she replied unexpectedly.

"You probably get it from him."

"Get what?"

"That look of being up on a branch, ready to fly away."

This remark pleased Emmy. It seemed stirring and romantic, and stayed in her mind, though she didn't exactly think of it as gallant. She didn't know that word, but had an idea of the thing it named, an agreeable and deferential readiness to serve, to protect and defend. She might have called it kid stuff, or male chauvinism, depending on her attitude to herself and to young men, or 'class' or 'cool' or merely 'being nice,' the simplest and least precise signal of acceptance and approval. She had no moral vocabulary, but she had a complex moral life, which went on throughout her waking hours without her being in the least aware of what was happening; she lived in a riot of difficult questions and stern judgments, which she could neither propose exactly nor form finally.

She knew that she was doing something to and with Basil which depended on her attractiveness, but she knew she wasn't a tease and didn't want to get serious. She didn't know that the four generations immediately previous to her own had called this 'flirting,' and if anybody had decribed her as a flirt she would have felt demurely old-fashioned and girlishly sweet, and she would have been at a total loss to identify a model for her behaviour. The closest she might have come was one of the girls in *Charlie's Angels*, probably Jaclyn Smith, or the Cindy Williams character in *American Graffiti*. She had no language to cover her behaviour, and this deficiency made her self-consciousness very intense.

She often wondered where her life was going, as she grew a bit older but, she felt, no wiser. As the shape of her body changed, grew less girlish and more womanly, thickened slightly at the waist and hips and grew fuller in the bosom, as she stopped being a size-eight, she might expect to change inside too, in her head, but what kind of change should she expect? Would she keep this job? Or become head of the photocopy department when Olive left to get married? As far as Emmy knew, Olive had no such plans. Her life outside the office seemed to consist in going with other girls to places to eat lunch, or have a drink after work; then she vanished into the city and her own mysteries. In three years or five or seven, Olive might disappear for good. Emmy had no way of telling; either of them might outlast the other. It was very unlikely that they would remain where they were until they were old. Nobody like them had done this; there were no old people in the office. Some strange process of selection and elimination kept the visible range of people around her at Jupiter Life no more than thirty-eight at the outside. Almost none of the women in the office was older than, say, thirty-four or -five. Where were all the oldies?

Suppose she were to try and make some sort of connection with Basil or somebody like him. What would that be like? The words "get married to" drifted through her head now and then, but she couldn't connect with them. People still did that, she knew, but what was the point to it? Nobody minded if you lived together two by two, or two guys and a girl, or two girls and two guys, or any of the other possible combinations. She had been in apartments shared by all numbers up to eight, in most of the possible combinations, and nobody minded or cared or paid any attention to who lived there and who didn't or for how long. "Get married to" rang no bells. She knew everything there was to know about IUDs and pills and about the state having no business in the bedrooms of the nation, and cared nothing about these matters. She had been clinically de-sexed by current history.

She was still living with her family in the brick house on Albany Avenue, two blocks north of Bloor. The old-time family structure which had ruled her parents' lives was still highly visible around her. Her grandfather lived in the house; he had the best and biggest bedroom in the place, the front room with the canopied balcony which monopolized the morning sun. This was because he owned the house and allowed his son's family to live there for a moderate rent. Old Mr. Ivey had been a barber with his own shop and four chairs—three lesser barbers in his pay—at the corner of Brunswick and Bloor from around 1928 till just a couple of years ago. He had bought the Albany Avenue house at the bottom of the market in 1933. His wife was dead; one of his boys was dead; the girls were married and living in other parts of the city, but his younger son and his son's wife, two grandsons and young Emmy, were all comfortably installed in his house, earning huge amounts of money and carrying the heating, insurance, and taxes for him, as their rent. The mortgage had been paid off years ago and the book value of the building was now enormous, a far larger amount than old Mr. Ivey had ever imagined himself possessing.

For his granddaughter, this very comfortably off, dignified, neatly dressed old barber didn't exist. She saw him every night but he wasn't real. She couldn't even begin to guess what his life had been like, or was like now. She could barely understand what her parents said to her, although their sporadic remarks made more sense than her grandfather's disconnected, almost demented—as they seemed to her—observations and suggestions. All the same he had given her Crackers, the parrot, the nicest present she had ever had. She often wondered what he'd been thinking of when he'd bought it for her eighteenth birthday, more than two years ago. Had he always wanted a parrot in the house and picked her birthday as the time to acquire one? It was impossible to say. She loved the parrot, had named it herself, and passed whole evenings watching it and trying to get it to talk. She was certain that it could say its name, "Crackers," and also perhaps "Where's Emmy?" but there was widespread disagreement about this in the family. Her brother Marshall claimed that Crackers had once said, "Come on over!" to him. The notion that her bird said things to Marshall that he didn't say to her troubled Emmy deeply.

Between the kitchen and the dining room in the Ivey house there lay an extra downstairs room, not the living room, which was at the very front of the house, but more of an expanded passageway, a cloakroom or butler's pantry, of whose original function nobody in the family was certain. The house had been built at a time when rather formal dinner service was still customary in well-to-do families; this room might have been some sort of serving room or buffet. It was difficult to identify. The passage of time had made of it a peculiar no-man's-land where old furniture collected in clumps. There were two prehistoric sofas in there and an ancient Zenith TV with a twelve-inch screen, and among other crowded items an enormous cage, a kind of terraced apartment block for parrots, in which Crackers swung from his perch, making eager noises in the early morning and peaceable split-tongued gurgles in the evening, as the time approached for his retirement to rest. With the installation of the parrot, this room had been definitively identified as Emmy's. It was shady and retired; there was a glasspanelled door through to the dining-room and a curtained archway to the hall. Here she used to entertain young men who came calling, and it was a settled matter of family policy to let her strictly alone while these entertainments were proceeding. Her father and mother and even her brothers were aware that the young women of today live lives completely different from those of women in earlier times, freer lives, more self-determinate, void of conditioning.

When Basil Mossington started coming to the house there was none of the low comedy that in times past was often associated with patterns of courtship. For one thing, nobody, not even Emmy and Basil, had any clear idea of whether or not this was a pattern of courtship. They hadn't studied anthropology and didn't know that almost any form of conduct can be a courtshippattern in the right context. The whole damn family, the brothers, the retired and withdrawn grandfather, Dad, and vivacious and noisy Mrs. Ivey, knew that they'd better keep their hands off and their tongues still if they didn't want Emmy to disappear from view forever; they knew she'd been buying apartment furniture at odd moments. There was a brand new Simmons Hide-a-Bed and loveseat in an oat-meal twill, sitting in that middle room no-man's-land, which Emmy had bought on impulse at a sale. It would look pretty smart in the living-room of a one-bedroom somewhere. It certainly didn't go with any of the other furniture in there, the superannuated chesterfields and hatracks, the parrot cage.

Crackers the parrot supervised Basil and Emmy in stri-dent and vociferous tones, sometimes so like human speech miniaturized that they were hallucinatory. They would be strolling around this room, wondering what it was and what they were supposed to be doing in it, poking at the stuffing of the chesterfields, sofas, divans, davenports, whatever those old relics were, or peering at the backs of books in the ranked wooden bookcases—there seemed to be an almost complete run of *Reader's Digest* books, with titles like "Annapurna" and "Kabloona" printed on the spines. Or they might tinker with the old Admiral electric record player and the Mart Kenney records that were strewn about, always in a sleepwalker's blank failure to apperceive what these objects were.

A lot of their time in there was spent in overtures to the parrot, passing him bits of celery or apple, changing his water, trying to stroke his tail feathers, an endearment which he sternly resisted. One night when they let him out at the top of the cage, where he could perch in his "poised-for-flight" stance, Basil began to snort and grunt uncontrollably. At length Emmy realised that he was laughing.

"That's where you learned to stand like that."

"Where? What?"

"He looks just like you, standing on the edge like that."

She wasn't sure how to take this but felt certain that the learning process must go from her to the parrot and not the other way around. After all, she antedated the parrot. She held up a finger with a chunk of apple stuck to the tip. Crackers shifted an uneasy foot and cocked an eye, inclining his head towards the fingertip.

"Shhhh shhhh shhhhhhhh."

"Gwock wock wock. Gwock."

"Come on, little Crackers!"

The bird bent and snatched the fruit in his beak, crushing it audibly.

"Muppetational," exclaimed Basil, and feeling moved by unfamiliar impulse he stepped briskly forward to kiss Emmy on the back of the neck or behind the ear. He remembered seeing this done in a recent movie. But she stepped aside unawares and he found his face pressed against the tiny cold bars of the cage. He was not a surefooted suitor, hardly a suitor at all. One of those fumbling types who don't swing the bat crisply and with attack, he found it hard to ingratiate himself with the Ivey family, not knowing what kind of people they were. The two brothers, Marshall and Clem, were visible but rarely. Marshall, the oldest child, was a chief flight attendant for Air Canada who spent more time over the Caribbean than in Toronto; he had much seniority and flew on preferred routes, always to warm countries. Clem was a recording engineer in a studio on Yorkville Avenue of such technical sophistication that he could give no adequate verbal account of it. He really was an intimate of many recording stars, didn't boast of it, scarcely mentioned that Joni or Carly had been using up some of their tax-break in the studio the day before yesterday.

Mrs. Ivey had perhaps the most unreadable character of them all. She looked to Basil pretty much what the mother of a family ought to look. She prepared meals, and sometimes wore an apron in the kitchen. The first time he came to the house, Mrs. Ivey happened to let fall some observation about games of chance, and Las Vegas. Thinking to make a favourable impression though he had no specific feelings one way or the other, Basil had piously remarked that he held gambling in great disesteem. He thought it a vice, a serious flaw in character, the wish to get something for nothing, an impossible distortion of the real. He would never think of gambling, not he. He had too much respect for his earnings to throw them down the toilet. These last two observations were true.

Rather to his discomfiture it immediately turned out that Mrs. Ivey was an ardent and inveterate horse-player and purchaser of lottery tickets. She followed the *Morning Telegraph* and Jimmy the Greek's sports line religiously. Her great ambition was to get back to Vegas where she had once passed a never-to-be-forgotten week on some excursion flight with hotel and meals included, which Marshall had given her as a Christmas present. She eyed Basil with mistrust. He saw that his halfhearted protestations of what he thought was virtue had gone for nothing.

He was a nervous guy. No matter how hard he tried to keep off coffee when he was going to visit Emmy, he found that he gulped two or three cups of the stuff during his evening meal, then was apt to spend much of the evening wondering where the bathroom was. The coffee had a marked effect on him, especially if his feet were cold, which made these evenings very mixed in the impression they left. If he and Emmy were out somewhere, he always spotted a toilet first thing, in the theatre before the movie started, or at a weird place they used to go to, over near Ossington along Bloor, which had been a Macedonian restaurant for forty-seven years before suddenly metamorphosing itself into an early Toronto copy of a Jackson Heights disco.

It was one strange scene—crowds of people shooting their arms alternately in the air like convulsed wind-up toys—wearing vests and shiny high boots while rhythmic choruses of soprano voices chanted indecipherable syllables which rerurred hypnotically. There was an operator on a dais, back in the recesses of the long room which had been the kitchen of the restaurant. Where he sat had been the location of the cookstove and a powerful smell of fries and gravy lingered there, oddly harmonizing with the flickering shadows and the sound of many sliding dancing boots. There was a toilet in this place which Basil detected effortlessly—he had a light-ning-quick eye for men's room signs—and the descent to the facility, down a staircase at the side of the room, was magical in the suddenness of the stylistic transformation from the sounds and sights of the late seventies to the conventional stinking basement washroom of those district restaurants called things like New Idea Lunch, Arlington Grill, Osgoode Café, featuring Devon Ice Cream and canned chicken noodle soup, which had been characteristic of the mid-century in the city: standup urinals which dripped and sweated, with G.H. Woods germicidal cakes of unearthly violet hue strategically seated in their recesses, conventional inscriptions delivering highly unlikely messages, phone numbers, names of theoretically enthusiastic sexual partners.

Basil would have to visit the toilet three or four times in the evening, no matter how much he sweated upstairs. This gave Emmy a peculiar impression of him as a friend actuated by sudden opaque impulses. She didn't know where she stood with him, or when he might disappear somewhere, muttering an unconvincing excuse. He would reappear holding two drinks, but never consumed his. This struck her as odd indeed. She knew nothing about him except what could be picked up in the most casual surveillance in the office, at her home, and in the uncertain shadows of the disco. He seemed a creature of the subway, in the sense that he and millions like him were strung out along the criss-cross of the main subway routes like crystalline atoms clustering around the nodes of the stations. From the Finch station multiple lines of structure shot jaggedly forth towards King City and Richmond Hill, places to which Emmy would never travel, any more than she would visit Madagascar or Tierra del Fuego. When Basil abandoned a paper cup of fruit drink behind a loudspeaker, the act seemed loaded with unreadable significance.

Much later he took her home and sat with her under the watchful eye of the parrot, leaning close to her for moments, then looking wildly around and plucking at the collar of his sweaty shirt. He was terribly uneasy, crossed his legs, stood up and sat down, then murmured endearments which lacked conviction. Towards one in the morning he shot erect and abruptly excused himself, pacing away into the adjacent kitchen with rapid agitated movements. In a moment she heard him running the taps at the sink. There was a pause. The sound of rushing water grew. Perhaps he was looking for a glass.

She pushed through the curtained archway and stuck her head around the frame of the kitchen door. All the lights were on in the room and for a second or two Basil was just a vibrating dark outline in the glare. Then her eyes focussed and she saw him jump back from the edge of the sink with his hands clutched convulsively at his waist. He turned towards her with a smile of frightened guilt.

"Hi," said Emmy.

He brushed the back of his hand across his mouth and cleared his throat. Then he bent his back and stuck his head under the taps, drinking convulsively and getting water in his ears. There was a quiet metallic buzz which she couldn't identify. He turned off the taps and faced her. "Thirsty!" he said.

It wasn't until two or three days had gone by that she worked out the explanation for the extraordinary furtiveness of his manner. He'd been too shy to ask where the toilet was, and she'd surprised him peeing in the sink.

After that she couldn't feel the same, naturally, and she ignored Basil in the office, keeping her head averted in an affected way when she had to pass his desk. He tried to speak to her, smiling in the same way he'd smiled the week before the incident, when she'd considered him attractive and worthwhile, but everything was altered. He seemed much more real to her now, much more there, and distinctly contemptible. The minute he'd emerged from the shadows he'd done something silly. Was everybody going to prove to be like that? Basil started

calling her at home, which he'd never done before, and she had
to listen to her mother taking the calls.

"I don't want to talk to him."

"Why? What's he done to you? I thought he was a nice boy,
a little tight-assed maybe but kind of sexy."

"For goodness' sakes, Mother!"

She wished her mother wouldn't talk in that style; it
reminded her too much of Ellen Burstyn and Cybill Shepherd
in *The Last Picture Show*. She wasn't a dumb teen-aged tease
like the girl in the movie. Her mother wasn't a smart, tough,
hardbitten broad either. The whole recital bored her, and it
made her mad when her mother insisted that she speak to the
young man.

"No, I'm busy tomorrow night. I'm staying downtown
with Olive; we're going to the ballet. And no, no, I'm busy all
next week. I'm sorry, no."

He claimed he had a birthday present for her, which he
wanted to show her, so she went as far as to agree to meet him
after lunch, in the treed space between the towers of Commerce Court, where personnel sometimes sat when the
weather was fine. There were potted shrubs and a few strug-
gling plantations of slender maples down there, a pool and a
fountain. He sat perched on the edge of a bench and showed
her the birthday present, and it really was nice. An excellent
piece of costume jewellery, still in the People's box, a pin or
clip—she didn't examine the fastener—in gilt paste in the
shape of a slender, feminine hand and wrist, with long, stylized, tapering fingers, a minute shard of genuine ruby tipped
onto the third finger—it was a right hand—to simulate a tiny
ring. She thought it might be from one of the better lines of
junk jewellery, Coro or Schneiderhan, or perhaps *Nuit de
Noel*. He pressed it on her but she wouldn't accept it.

"No, I'm sorry, no, I just couldn't."

"I don't understand."

"I just don't feel about you in that way."

The item probably cost him a hundred dollars, she thought. He put it away in the little blue box—rather a sweet box—and as it was time to get back upstairs they rode the elevator to the Jupiter suite and parted in silence.

Basil came to the photocopy centre now and then in the following weeks, but never when Emmy was there. He seemed to be avoiding her deliberately, which was fine by her; it spared her embarrassment and perplexity. She had survived a first encounter with another live human being with totally confused notions of conduct. When she heard what the man was doing with that stupid pin, or clip, she almost choked.

"Raffling it?"

"Yes, he won it in a contest, he says, and after all he might as well get the money out of it. Fifty cents a ticket or three for a dollar. I bought six, so I've got a pretty good chance."

"But Olive, you don't know where it's come from. It might be stolen. Have you thought of that?"

"He offered to show everybody his receipt for it."

"How could he have a receipt for it if he won it?"

"Well, I don't care. It's a pretty piece and it would look great on my mohair cardigan if it doesn't damage the stitching."

"You seem to think you'll win."

"I'll bet I do," said Olive. "I think I'll buy another dollar's worth of chances. He claims it's worth over a hundred and fifty dollars."

Emmy gritted her teeth, saying nothing more, and, wouldn't you know, Olive did win the raffle, which was strictly on the up and-up. Daffy Duck did the drawing one Thursday afternoon, lisping and drooling and laughing at Basil, whom he liked. "A wise young man," he kept braying, "a wise young man." He selected the winning ticket from a ceramic bowl which usually adorned his inner office. The event was exceedingly public, and Emmy, who did not attend, was sure that everybody there was laughing at her. They weren't. They knew nothing about her.

Olive Honeywell wore that clip—or pin—around the office for eighteen months, until she quit to get married. Basil Mossington got promoted and vanished. Severed hands, and other separated members, became permanent properties of Emmy's visions.

THE SMALL BIRDS

B Y THE BEGINNING of June the black flies and mosquitoes were so thick that Marian was trapped on the sunporch. Nobody quite knew why, but if there were one bug in a building it would go straight for her, forsaking all others, and bite or sting or fly around and around her head. It was impossible for her to concentrate on what she was doing, either shelling peas or reading *Cosmopolitan* and laughing at it. Sometimes a heavy fly would land on the crown of her head where the hair parted and exposed her scalp—they were attracted by the natural oil—and she would shiver with repulsion. She might pass the morning swatting and spraying, then sit all afternoon out on the screened sundeck, listening to the radio or reading or watching spring activity on the water.

Just before dusk a pair of blue herons would make two or three passes down the lake; often they flew back north with visible fish flopping in their mouths. The loons wouldn't make their appearance until the herons had nested successfully; there might be some rivalry between them or some element of ecological stress. Do herons eat loons?

Purple martins eat mosquitoes, she remembered. Two years ago the boys had cleared away a lot of piled-up brush at the back of the property, near the parking spaces, and had laid down an expanse of sod for a picnic ground. Now there was thick grass, a big picnic table, and a string of Japanese lanterns in the shagged beeches where nothing but huge split rocks, chipmunks, and juniper mulch had been. She still couldn't go out there till August or September: she'd get bitten to death and it was no fun.

The boys had built a birdhouse for purple martins (widely reputed to keep down mosquitoes), from a design on the vacation page of one of the Saturday papers. They did not reproduce the shape of the entryways correctly; flocks of birds who were plainly not purple martins had promptly moved in to stay. There may have been one or two purple martins in the crowd, but the mosquito count continued unnaturally high. They had had a wet runoff and a wet early spring. One could do nothing about the black flies.

So Marian waited on the sunporch for the later summer and felt pleased at the immensely wide and high view of the lake and the shore which the snugly screened windows allowed. In the old days at her grandparents' cottage at Beelzebub Lake the screens had been made of wire mesh which rusted, broke, and left dangerous needlepoints projecting around the holes. Wear-and-tear corrupted old-fashioned screening; the new nylon net was an enormous improvement. The filaments of the mesh were extremely fine but also extremely strong; they conceded nothing to wind and weather, wore for years without corrosion or breakage, and interfered only minimally with the view. If they were looked through, they blurred and ran together so that instead of an impression of criss-crossing lines, a vague sense of some impalpable invisible substance ran across the eyes' surface, something like the onset of glaucoma but not so menacing.

The sundeck projected forward from the cottage on tall stilts and there was about six feet of storage space underneath, open in front and gradually closing at the sides where the rocks on which the building stood humped up gradually under the flooring. There were old rowboats stored under there, a lot of plastic sheeting (used to seal the porch windows in the fall), and a sketchy collection of garden tools. Marian's gang didn't make a fetish of gardening at the lake. Now that they had a picnic lawn out back, they were satisfied to share it with martins and swallows and an occasional much-admired pileated woodpecker.

When the cool August nights killed the bugs, Marian would start to go out, but the first two months of summer were hard time; the marshy, swampy spring had sentenced her to sixty days. She would know when her incarceration was approaching its end by the phases of the summer light, the gradual progress of June and July to that point about the beginning of August when the mid-afternoon sun would dip low enough in the west to flood the porch with shine and heat and the gleam of the individual ripples as they came onshore brilliantly white, iridescent like oil paint fresh from the tube, thick and creamy.

There was shade and coolness on the porch for several hours and an even lemon colour washed around and through the field of vision. The sun was back behind the cottage at this time of year until very late in the day; the shady dark green of the evergreens was sunk all day in lemon glow. In this genial harmony it was possible to pick out individual birds, identify them, almost name them as pets. She would sit there watching the antics of various tumbling, flipping creatures, slowly realizing that they too had their daily routines, like hers and those of the larger birds, especially that masterful quartet of crows who woke her every morning with their bellowed threats at enemies far down the lake.

The small birds were more rigorous in their patterns of instinctual behaviour, their cautious short flyways, their choice of favourite trees, their aerobatics. It became clear that the orchestration and the melodies of their songs changed from one hour to the next around the clock: waking sounds, assertions of territorial right, feeding and mating calls, warnings, shouts of mere fun, information about food, signals to rest. All this was a musical score.

Marian came to be able to tell the time of day by the mingled harmonies of the birdcalls and the radio which sat close to her tuned to CBC-FM until it was time for the Expos' game that could barely be reached on a signal fading in and out.

Birdcalls, broadcasts, ballgames. How alliterative, she thought, how naturally formed. Flight. Some of the birds kept doing something in front of her, winding around five particular evergreens, two tamaracks, a spruce, and two dead pines which still stood up stiffly with spiny bare branches twigged in smaller and smaller points towards invisible tips. Sometimes a bird would stand at the very end of a branch, poised airily on a filament of support so dry and stiff and thin that it would seem balanced over nothing. Then the bird might make a sudden stab at its toes and curve in rapid flight down from the branch directly towards the face of the cottage. Marian would stiffen involuntarily, but no bump of small body against plywood siding ever shocked her. Those aerial swings and rushes, ending somewhere under her feet, finally brought her to realize that at least one bird was up to something under the porch.

She began to take a close interest in what was going on, would arrive at her watching post after a late breakfast about the time that CBC's "Mostly Music" came on the air. She associated the theme music, and the names of the program's announcer, Bartley MacMillan, and its producer, Roma Angus, with the nesting activities of two specific birds whom she christened Bartley and Roma. Unusual, slightly phantasmagoric names for swallows. They were certainly swallows, but to which sub-group they belonged she could not say. There were the usual bird books in the cottage (rainy day reading for idle inquirers), but even the superb Peterson line drawings could not finally make clear to her whether Bartley and Roma were barn swallows or cliff swallows. They didn't seem to have quite the right shape to their tails for barn swallows. An extra bar of grey around their bodies above the wings didn't seem correct for cliff swallows. She concluded that they must be barn and/or cliff swallows, Roma and Bartley.

Sometimes she fancied that she could hear the movement of their wings underneath her feet; the notion disturbed her. If there were to be birds underfoot, what might dwell in the skies? They kept flying right at the cottage, coming hard, dipping and vanishing at the last moment. They were up to something. The radio hummed and burbled. The one p.m. news came on, followed by the familiar theme and brisk loving voice of Bob Kerr from Vancouver with the broadcast of classical music. He sounded so friendly and likeable that Marian plucked up her spirits, rose from her chair, and sounded the back bedrooms in search of children. Only Ruth, her daughter, was in the house. Busy in the bathroom applying an experimental coat of make-up, Ruth was about thirteen.

"How come we never go down under the cottage like we used to?" said Marian. Ruth burst out laughing. "We could get up some kind of game with lumps of coal or something."

These were bits of dialogue quoted from James Thurber, familiar to everybody in the family and particularly loved by Ruth, a Thurber enthusiast from infancy. She looked over her shoulder at her mother, nodded once, then turned back and squinted at the mirror. "I'll come in a minute." Her eyelid flickered. "Damn."

"Language!" said Marian mildly. Both giggled. Ruth wiped a trace of mascara from her lashes and turned to face her mother. Her *maquillage* was elaborate and bizarre. Bright plumage. Unrestrained.

Marian said, "Did you know that the swallows are nesting under the porch?"

"Everybody knows that but you, Mumma. They've been going in and out for days. You should see them circling around in there."

"Have you found the nest?"

"No, I haven't looked. Do you think we should disturb it?"

"We won't disturb it, darling, we'll just have a little peek. We've had them nesting before, you know. Maybe you won't remember. It must be ten years ago. Before we screened in the porch."

"I remember," said Ruth, though she was uncertain about it.

"You would have been just a tiny girl at the time."

To this observation, Ruth would make no rejoinder. The mother and daughter strolled around to the front of the building and underneath the open face of the porch. They were now in sunny-shade, out of the direct line of the sun, right below the picnic table on the deck. A piece of music came to an end and the comfortable voice of the broadcaster explained the peculiarities of the record, its loved and special place in his huge—monstrous—collection.

The charming, friendly voice, the warmth without glare, the half-light, the absence of insects, the presence of Ruth. Marian felt so well that she almost felt sick.

"Here it is," said Ruth. "In under the floorboards, tucked up on the beam. I think they may be trying to hide it."

"You and your premonitions," said Marian, and they giggled again very quietly. The nest was cleverly concealed in a corner formed by two main supporting beams roofed in by the plywood flooring of the sundeck. Only an informed seeker or one of the swallows could have spotted it because the sunlight could never get in there at an angle acute enough to illuminate the crossbeams. It was a small nest, about the circumference of a softball, delicately and precisely put together with pine twigs and juniper needles. Dried now to a russet brown, the juniper shone in shadow.

There were four eggs in the nest, each the size of a green grape, but very different in hue, a pale grey or grey-blue found in expensive stoneware, neither polished nor shiny, chalky. Ruth pointed at them with a forefinger. Careful not to touch.

"Yes, four," she muttered.

"We'd better get out of here," said Marian. "They'll be wanting to get back on the nest."

And pat on cue, like the poor cat in the adage, a bird hurtled into the crawl space beside them like a projectile, whizzing past Marian's ear and out through the narrow opening at the side of the cottage with extraordinary speed. Marian stood up in shocked amazement and bumped her head noisily and painfully on the firm plywood.

"Fuck!"

Ruth said, "Language!"

The presence of the nest explained the perpetual comings and goings of Roma and Bartley, perhaps of their friends and relations too. It didn't seem possible to Marian that two small birds could give so readily the impression of a crowd. It wasn't that they were noisy; rather, they were around all the time, circling and diving, peeling off in echelon or sitting motionless in front of her at ten yards' remove on bare spiny twigs or hidden in thick pine boughs. Their speed, their surety, their swift instincts confounded her and caused a terrible commitment to their survival to rise up in her breast, Nothing must happen to them but good, she resolved, and she was desperately, bitterly, dashed to learn from one of her sons that the baby swallows had all died.

"Ohhh, no, don't tell me..." she said.

"I saw the broken shells, Mum. Maybe I shouldn't have said."

Neil could recognize the signs of his mother's genuine sorrow. He took a spoonful of Captain Crunch and shivered; the cream was chilled and the morning fresh. "Why not go and see for yourself?" he said, not unkindly. "I might have been wrong."

"How are the mosquitoes?" she said morosely.

"It's cool. It's cool." So she went.

The fascination of the process, the cycle, pulled her under and into the shade. The nest was visible, but only just, at this hour. There were—oh, damn it—half-shells and little bits of broken shell lying here and there on the rocks just below the nest. She picked up a half-shell and stuck it on the end of the little finger of her right hand. It looked like a terribly smart cloche hat of the 1920s, such a chic colour too! She wiggled the finger then forced herself to peer into the dim light trying to see what lay in the nest.

She was able to make out what looked like a pile of slimy mucous, a kind of muddle of bones and half-formed feathers and semi-liquid greyish matter without vital form. The look of the mess almost made her gag. She withdrew her head and started back outside. A swallow—possibly Bartley—passed her as she left, heading gracefully towards the nest with something hanging from his beak. This detail didn't light up in her head for several days, well on towards the beginning of July. Those slithery glistening minute exposed tendons, that liquid, the failure of generation. She strove to put the matter from her mind.

One Sunday afternoon she received better news. She was monitoring a double-header from Pittsburgh for Neil, Ruth, Daisy, and John who were down at the water. She caught sight of Ruth climbing slowly from the dockside and called down to her, "Pirates leading by two runs in the third on Parker's double, Moreno and Foli scoring."

Ruth turned to relay the news to the beach and Marian sat down and let herself relax in the sun. Insects buzzed outside the mesh. Broadcasters exchanged rhythmic dialogue. Crowd noises in the background. Impressive recurrences of between-innings commercials. Sleep in the heat.

"Mumma Mumma Mumma, they're not dead," shouted Ruth from somewhere underfoot, "they're not dead at all, they're sitting in the nest; oh, they look so funny, come down and look. Hey Mumma!"

Marian roused herself. A huge powerboat passed in front of the cottage, the discharge of its spark plugs causing a rasping buzz on the radio like the roar of a power saw.

"Come on, Mumma," urged Ruth, "down by the nest."

There was thrilling vitality and certainty in the child's call. Marian's shoulders were covered in a fine light sweat. She trembled, blinked, then trotted out the side door and around to the front of the building where Ruthie beckoned to her from the crawl space. She was crouched beside the nest making a lot of noise, while Roma and Bartley buzzed around her angrily, trying to drive her off.

"You're frightening the mother," said Marian.

"I know, I know, I know, but you've got to come and see them this one time; they're so funny with their little heads all in a row."

This description charmed Marian. She decided that one quick examination would not be traumatic. She inclined her head and climbed in under the flooring and there, sure enough, the four nestlings sat piled up on top of one another with very little room—none—to move about.

They were an absurd sight, feathers forming thickly, heads almost circular, all in profile. They had minute, whitish yellow bills which opened and shut avidly and they were all, without doubt, very much alive. They bore a farcical resemblance, in their insistence on remaining strictly in profile, to much mediaeval religious art whether in mosaic, fresco, or painting. Marian was reminded of dozens of groups of saints, viewed in right profile and superimposed one upon the other, with geometrically regular round haloes piled up like gilt coins on a dark plate. Some Biblical incident was insistently recalled, most likely from Ottonian representation in gospel book or fresco. All at once she had it: in the way the pulsing bodies were heaped together, in the pattern of unblinking eyes, working mouths, perfectly round little skulls, the small birds evoked the attitudes of the apostles rocked about in the stern of the fishing boat when Christ stilled the waves. There was the same awareness that something unexpected was about to take place. The same profoundly human confusion.

Bartley and Roma screamed in busy anger. Ruth and Marian withdrew. The radio hooted in excitement. Somebody had just got the go-ahead run ...

Coke adds life, Coca-Cola adds life ...

Maybe Bartley and Roma were feeding the kids on Coke. The nestlings got bigger and bigger and their home bulged. Once or twice in ensuing weeks, Marian surprised one of the parents in the act of shoring up the side of the nest, working fresh twigs into a space which threatened nestling-fallout. The grown swallow was perched nervously on the crossbeam, pecking away at shreds of twisted woody stuff, working it into the crevices, making everything tight. Under here, rain was not a problem.

How clever of them, thought Marian, then she remembered that the action was, after all, dictated purely by instinct. The birds could be conceded no moral credit for their sense of parental responsibility. They were always around the nest now, feeding the next generation with bits of matter almost invisibly small. Marian never saw any worms, but was able to identify the act of feeding. The parents would post themselves beside the nest with their backs to her. They would make that funny unmistakeable dip of the shoulders. Competitive pipings from the young, almost inaudible. Should be on film, Marian thought. Disney would make a killing with this. She never actually witnessed the passing of food from mouth to mouth.

The small birds grew and survived, crowded and hampered in their movements as they were. How would they learn to fly, Marian wondered. How would they ever find room to move their wings; how could they see at all? What could they hear, how receive instruction in the difficult art of self-powered flight?

By mid-July crisis impended; there was no more room in the nest. In a day or so they would start falling out. The nest was balanced over bare, flinty, ancient rock. A fall would make mush of infant bones. She worried, knowing that this was absurd, that the species would perpetuate itself with losses according to statistical norms. A couple of the young would fail to negotiate first flight, but so what? We all have to take our chances. It made her laugh to imagine that the classical music, the commercials, and the baseball broadcasts would form part of the inherited natural sound patterns· heard and instinctually assimilated by the next generation of barn and/or cliff swallows. Maybe the Coca-Cola jingle would turn up in their territorial calls next summer. Fusion of art and nature.

On Saturday, 19 July, she was lurking near the nest, thinking she might anticipate some infant attempt at flight, catch the creature if the attempt should go badly. She might retrieve some squeaking Icarus before he hit rock, a basket catch like those the outfielders kept making in National League play as described in the summer-long sequence of Expo broadcasts going on in the swallows' sky. In a bird's mind, the account of the game would seem like the voice of God, superior to the visible order, coming from elsewhere. Something given, a part of pure life.

She moved over to stand looking at the infants. They were fully formed, she thought, all set to go. Above her on the porch came one of those irregular broadcast interruptions and the game faded away into a distant blur of competing signals from thousands of miles off. Invisible influences crossed in the upper air. She turned her head to look out from under and then she heard the strange sound.

A swift-running rushing breathy sound, blurring, whistling, like being kissed by the angels, whispering, running past her hair.

When she looked back, the nest was empty.

There was nothing on the rocks.

She began to sniffle, then repressed the impulse.

Now there would be six particular swallows to be picked out of the circling crowd. She wondered if she would be able to recognize them. Could she draw them home by familiar sound? Would the voice of Bob Kerr call them to himself? It seemed a better than fifty-fifty wager. Afternoons on the sunporch lengthened; she began to struggle with binoculars, trying to focus directly on the branches close to the cottage. It ought to be possible to get a look at one of the birds in tight closeup, almost as though perched on the end of the glasses. They were too quick for her. Every time she got one of them into focus it would dart away. She would swing the glasses to try and follow the flight but the milky and confusing impressions caused by the nylon screening made her blink and lose track of the motion.

Eventually Marian's nature studies began to decline in interest. The glasses were more an impediment to observation than anything. She would catch herself mumbling, I could see perfectly well if it weren't for these damn glasses. The annoying element of the situation, which she recognized as fundamentally comic, was that the life of the birds grew more fascinating and complex just as she began to be bored with it because of her natural incapacity. This paradoxical relation struck her as exceedingly lifelike. She let the glasses alone after that, content to enjoy the weather.

It was almost aggressively warm and sunny on the sunporch in the August afternoons. The illumination that flooded the space reached an unmixed golden tone which it retained very late. It was hot and sweaty, not just in a light perspiration but in big drops which stood out on the forehead, arms, and neck and ran down inside bathing suits. Marian felt she could almost swim, certainly slither around, in this homestyle sauna. She would put her head down on her arms and sit there, wet, hot, solitary, and happy.

She kept hearing wings, wings, and the ballgame on the radio and new recordings of ancient instruments playing the infant symphonies of Mozart. Birds all over sitting on pine branches right outside, closer. Very close as though listening to baby Mozart or the game fading and returning. Swimming in the heat and the gold light. She moved her head idly, turning a cheek down into her bent elbow and feeling the wet in the hair on the back of her neck, warm sweat on her shoulder blades. Pipings. Soft calls. She lifted her head from her arms and opened and shut her eyes, trying to clear them in the blurring sunshine. The birds clustered just outside, listening to the game in their own space.

Marian whispered, "They're all around me." She glanced to the right and caught a glimpse of a young swallow motionless in the corner of her eye. Directly in front of her hovered a plump little dark silhouette, changing size in the wash of intense gold and blue. She blinked and looked again from left to right, picking them out one after another looking in at her and listening, leaning, tiny bright eyes gleaming in at her through the net.

THE GOOD TENOR MAN

ANNON, of Irish extraction, nominally a resident of
Paroisse Saint-Germain, worshipped regularly at Saint
Kevin's because he had grown tired of trying to go to
Confession in French. Twenty years in Montreal had taught
him the names of six of his favourite sins, but the seventh
eluded him. He could never remember how to say "take the
name of the Lord in vain."

"*Je me suis mis en colere avec ma femme, deux fois par
semaine,*" he would declare sadly, when he was obliged to seek
Absolution at the French parish church. Though his translation was accurate, the words did not sound fair or just, and
he felt that they didn't honestly describe his mean actions. He
had become attached to his Saturday afternoon recital, his
customary faults, those in which he had a proprietary interest, the neglected morning prayers, the irritable family quarrelling, and he didn't care to struggle with them or re-think
them, or try something new in the line of petty vice. At a certain stage of life a new vice is as unthinkable as a new virtue—
too damn much trouble.

He was a man of immoderate attachment to habit and
routine, which he held to have preserved him from much

sorrow, much pain and inconvenience. He would change his razor-blade every fourth day, religiously, and would buy a dozen pairs of shoelaces at a time, storing them in his chest of drawers and feeling vexed when his reserve stock fell below six. He had a great affection for the permanent and unchanging; rather than adjust himself to unfamiliar circumstances in a distant city he had thrice refused promotion in the bank where he was employed as an accountant, preferring to remain in the branch at the Wilderton Shopping Centre on a permanent basis. Advancement in the great Canadian banks depends on one's readiness to go anywhere and do almost anything (on the order of legitimate business practice), a condition that barred Hannon from higher places.

Monday the brown suit, Tuesday the blue, Wednesday the grey, Thursday the brown, Friday the blue, slacks and a sweater around the house on Saturday, and on Sunday the fine grey suit which had been rested since Wednesday. His brown and blue suits wore out faster than the grey, probably because they didn't get the extra day of rest. During his two peaceful decades as junior, ledger-keeper, accountant, accountant, accountant, he had had four blue, four brown, but only three grey suits. And only two tweed jackets to go with his Saturday slacks, his costume for Confession. There was a jarring quality about this sliding scale of consumption which gnawed at him. It was the fault of the calendar and the week—the fault of men, not of the solar round. He had four outfits; there should be either four or eight days in the week; or some larger multiple of four. Such a shred of detail will lodge in the mind of a man like Hannon and in the end prepare him, almost, for madness.

His sanity depends on a delicate balance of the processes of change, and their retardation, half-conscious, nearly buried, fearfully complex, and threatened at every turn by the mutability of the weather or the outrageous number of Chevrolets that might drive along the street in a given fifteen minutes, whereas the number of Chevrolets should only slightly exceed the number of Fords, and somewhat more exceed the number of Plymouths. Hannon would stand in front of his apartment building and count cars until he began to feel his blood pressure rising. Then he would adopt some desperate self-deception for equalizing or at least explaining the statistics he'd collected.

When he went inside he might protest bitterly to his wife about the irregularity of things. If he'd counted twice the number of Chevrolets he should've, he'd assail her for hiding his newly darned socks or for sending his shirts to the laundry a day late, throwing off his rotation so that one shirt received more wear than another. Perhaps he would notice that they hadn't had spaghetti this week, or if they had, that the sauce tasted slightly different.

"Bay leaf," he would mutter, "whoever heard of bay leaf in spaghetti sauce? There should be no green things in a sauce. You'll be putting spinach in next."

Aileen Hannon was a great user of leftovers, and here she gave a guilty start for the green in the sauce *was* spinach, not bay leaf at all. It had been bay leaf one night in 1947 and her husband had never gotten it out of his mind. She blushed modestly and said, "This *is* spinach."

Her husband glared at her morosely and picked up the *Star*. "Another riot at the penitentiary," he said absently, turning the pages. His wife made no reply. "Duplex for rent, corner of Côte-Ste.-Catherine and Hudson, taxes paid, $185." They had been thinking of moving since their second child arrived, to get more space, but the child, Michael, was now sixteen and was never at home; the time for moving had gone by. Hannon had successfully deferred or evaded his wife's entreaties for so long that the problem had solved itself.

What he couldn't defer or evade was death.

In the form of almost imperceptible change, another grey hair, a new blue suit, a bank merger and the ensuing new cheque forms, a birthday, the temporary disappearance of a child, the final disappearance of an old friend, panic picked away at Hannon daily, and he daily grew more frantic inside, redoubling his efforts to stabilize things. He bought a living-room carpet.

"It'll last forever," he said to Aileen. "We'll never wear it out."

"It'll outlast us," she said maliciously, for it was very ugly and she knew just where to take him.

"Not me, it won't."

"Oh, you'll live forever," she said, relenting.

He brightened and walked possessively across the rug two or three times, scuffing his shoes in the heavy tight pile and raising such a charge of static electricity in the dry living-room that he got a fearful shock when he touched a metal coat-hanger.

"Jesus," he said, and then more quietly, "Mary and Joseph! What's that thing doing there?"

"You left it there when your pants came back from the cleaners. I didn't know whether you wanted it there."

"Oh—" he said, mollified, "do we have lots of hangers?"

They had dozens of them.

"Yes."

"I'll throw this one out." She heard him march purposefully down the hall to the incinerator and back.

"Twenty-four average-sized steps from the door to the incinerator," he observed when he came back, "time to go for my candy bars." Every weeknight during the year except during Lent and Advent he ate two Neilson's Crispy Crunch candy bars about an hour before bedtime. They had been his favourite as a child. He knew exactly which spaces between his teeth would retain the tacky, slightly salty, filling of the candy and he spent a serene twenty minutes each night revolving the taste of the sweets in his mouth. He thought they gave him energy, perhaps mistakenly. Despite his tendency to coddle himself, he was endowed by nature with an enormously energetic, wiry body which easily overmastered his inclination to self-torment, and so he usually felt very well.

He did deep-breathing exercises before retiring, putting his head and shoulders out his bedroom window, inhaling the fresh air, even in the dead of winter. He would watch the red warning beacon atop the university tower, signalling to the planes making their passes at Dorval that they'd better avoid the seat of learning. As the spring came on, he had to crane his neck this way and that to spot the little red light through the foliage. At last, on the first of June or thereabouts every year, he could no longer see through the leaves and knew that summer was nigh. The beacon had never become invisible before May 28th or after June 3rd since he'd been looking out that window. If there is ever a new Ice Age, Hannon will know it's coming long before the geologists.

He used to get his candy bars from the Maplewood Grocery; they were sometimes stale, more often than he liked, because they didn't get much call for them. Then one year, along about 1959, a small frontage three doors down from the grocery store, which had been untenanted since just after the war, began to exhibit the signs of someone's intention to give the location another try. It was only a tiny storefront, maybe seven feet wide, maybe eight. Enough as it turned out to take a passageway and a pinball machine. Say seven feet.

For three months Hannon watched suspiciously as the narrow store window was coated with cleanser which hid the interior from view, as the paint was burned off the woodwork and replaced by a bright green. He walked past nights on his way to the grocery wondering and feeling assaulted; he had been so used to the store's being vacant. Who could be coming in? It couldn't be a dry-cleaner because there already was one. A candy store, perhaps? No, not enough trade. A newsstand? Everybody had the paper delivered. What?

One soft spring night, as he came along the street, he saw that the mystery had been resolved. The Coca-Cola Display

Department had been there that afternoon to install a sign, suspending it over the storefront with a complex crisscross of metal pole and guy-wires.

SAUL RASHER'S DELICATESSEN, he read in the standard display lettering, and underneath the soft drink sales message, and lower still the words HOT MEAT, CANDY, SOFT DRINKS, SUNDRIES. Hanging below the sign was a streamer that said WATCH FOR GRAND OPENING; it also said COORSH and there was a picture of a hand holding a sandwich.

Somebody had passed a polishing cloth over part of the window and as he passed Hannon spotted people moving around inside. He heard a faint snatch of music and wondered if they would have a jukebox or a television for the customers to look at.

It'll never go, he thought soberly, who needs it? Nobody around here eats out.

He was wrong. He had never owned a dressing-gown in his life, scorned them, laughed at them as effeminate when he saw them advertised. Then one Christmas his sons clubbed together and got him a dark blue and green Viyella tartan gown, warm and soft, with a nice loose rope to go around the waist. He never afterwards had it off when he was at home after dinner. He loved the thing, and inside of a month would have been deeply shocked if anything had happened to it. When he put the first cigarette burn in the material he cried, and paid seven dollars for invisible mending.

It was like that with Rasher's. He passed and re-passed, waiting for the "grand" opening and the speedy grand closing. He knew all about small businesses, having witnessed dozens of loan transactions at the bank; he knew all about under-capitalization and when he heard in the neighbourhood that Saul Rasher was a retired dance-band musician he felt sure that the venture wouldn't last six months.

For six months he refused to go inside, afraid of the contaminating properties of failure. If the Rashers were going to go broke, he didn't want them to know him or that he was a bank official, or that he sometimes sat in on credit applications, very rarely nowadays. Years ago, when his bosses had believed that he might one day be managerial timber, he had been encouraged to listen to the branch manager's reasons for this or that refusal to grant credit. Now that he had no more chance to become a manager he was only consulted when he knew the applicant.

The Rashers didn't bring their credit needs to his branch. Maybe they didn't need a loan, maybe somebody in the family was helping them. Anyway they hung on through the first six slim months of their operation marvellously and all at once in the middle of their first winter, that would be around 1960, everybody in the neighbourhood suddenly discovered that they couldn't imagine life without Rasher's. The store had made a place for itself. If you were hungry at night and didn't feel like cooking, you would phone in, and ten minutes later walk over, and your sandwich and pickles would be waiting for you on the counter.

Hannon found that the Crispy Crunches were fresher at Saul's place; that was how they hooked him. After three visits he was their most loyal customer and would be to the death.

Rasher sat in the back of the store most days, or upstairs where the apartment was, and played the saxophone, the tenor saxophone. He was a solid greying man who often wore green tinted glasses. Sometimes he played the pinball machine which stood on your left at the front of the store as you came in, and he showed a supernal ability to extract free games from the machine. Often he would play it for three-quarters of an hour, smiling and talking to the machine and giving the customers his spare free games. The narrow interior of the store rang cheerfully with the sound of the machine's bells and buzzers and rolling metal balls. Red and yellow lights flashed on the shadowy walls.

"We're not making a dollar with this box," Saul would say cheerfully, "but it gets a crazy sound, man." And he would tilt it gently back and forth, humming to himself, "Ba ba ba ba dee do dee da da da deelllya oo." He didn't talk in extreme argot but you could certainly see he'd been a working musician. He and the family used to "man" each other all the time.

"Please take out the garbage," Mrs. Rasher would say to her son Sam.

"That garbage is like gone, man," Sam would answer, and then the whole family would laugh and chatter in a friendly way to each other.

When Hannon had been in the store perhaps fifteen times, Rasher said, "You're making it with the Crispy Crunches, Dad," and it gave Hannon an indescribable pleasure.

"That's right," he stammered.

"Nervous!" said Rasher, picking up his horn and going to the back of the store to run a few scales.

Hannon told Aileen about this, saying that it made him feel good to be known and to know others in the neighbourhood, going on at some length about his feelings of human solidarity.

"I can top that," said his wife. "Do you know that crazy woman, the one who hangs out by the taxi-stand, with the black hair and the sunburn? I think she's an Indian, but she speaks both French and English."

Hannon said that he knew her.

"She stopped me on the street today," said his wife. "I was pulling the bundle-buggy full of groceries, not thinking of anything, just going along wishing I was already home, and out of a clear blue sky comes this Indian lady."

"What did she say?"

"That's the funny part. She said, 'You are a good woman, I see it.' But I can't get her accent. 'You good woman! All the time you care for your husband and sons. I see this. I know. God will reward you.' Do you know, that's about the first time she's ever spoken to me."

"I wonder what prompted it?"

"It makes you feel like you belong," Aileen said.

They missed their sons and wished they weren't eighteen and sixteen and almost gone. Paul was at McGill and Michael was finishing up at Loyola and somewhere, perhaps at a dance, he'd met Sam Rasher, and knew quite a bit about the family.

"Saul used to play with good bands," he told his father, "and he sat in with everyone who came through. He taught Sammy and Sammy's really good, better than his father. But Saul was a good tenor man in his day."

"In his day," repeated Hannon sadly. He was about the same age as the good tenor man. "Has he had his day?"

"You know what I mean," said Michael, taking money from his father and getting ready to go out.

"In his day," repeated Hannon. Saul seemed like a child to him.

Most of the real work in the delicatessen was done by Mrs. Rasher, who stood behind the counter all day, smoking interminably and getting to know the customers. She was a small woman with grey hair and a very pale skin who looked older than she was. At first Hannon had taken her for Rasher's mother and it was with a slight shock that he realized that she was his wife, and also that she was quite blind. She knew the layout of the store so well that she could put her hand on the Crispy Crunches without fumbling or turning round, and it wasn't until he offered her paper money that she faltered.

"What is this?" she asked brightly.

"Money," said Hannon, "what else?"

"Is it a one or a two or a five? I'm blind, you know."

"I'm afraid it's a five," he said, feeling for no reason as though it weren't really a five and that he was trying to cheat her. It *is* a five, darn it, he told himself, it is. She didn't question him or call Saul to examine the bill, although there was no one else there.

"You're the Crispy Crunch man," she said, "that's how I know you." She gave him change for his five. Later he was in the store when a youngster tried to cheat her, telling her that a one was a two.

"That's a single," said Hannon hardly, the force in his voice shocking him.

The boy looked at him, wondering whether to contest the statement, and then, seeing the hostility in Hannon's eyes and stance, backed down and claimed to have made a mistake.

"Sure, you're right, that's what it is, a one. I made a mistake."

"You made a mistake," said Hannon loudly, and watched him out the door.

"Thank you," said Mrs. Rasher.

"Does that happen often?" He gave her a useless smile, feeling that they understood each other.

"Not very often. My customers would never do it and strangers usually don't realize that I can't see. Perhaps he made a mistake."

"That was no mistake," said Hannon, "that was a little smartalex trying to cheat you, but he won't try again." He liked Mrs. Rasher very much and felt oddly protective toward her. Upstairs somebody was playing the sax. He thought it was probably young Sam; he was starting to be able to tell the difference in attack.

On his way home, his wife's Indian lady friend popped out of the parking lot where the taxis wait and laid a hand on his coat-sleeve. Against the dark sleeve her hand showed veined and tanned, almost a claw.

"Hello Mister," she said. "You go home to your wife?"

"Why yes," said Hannon, "where else?"

"Nowhere else," said the woman. She smoothed her intensely black oily hair with the other hand. "Your wife, she's well?"

"Oh fine, fine!"

"You tell her about Mrs. Rasher, eh?"

"What about Mrs. Rasher?"

"Cancer."

"What?"

"Inside, she's like lace!"

"What are you talking about? How do you know?"

"Same doctor. Saul doesn't know, he's like a child, that man. Tell your wife, Mister, she'll want to know. Like lace!"

He felt half-sick going home and he wondered where he'd get his Crispy Crunches if anything happened. But he said nothing to his wife. He didn't want to go elsewhere, to the grocery store or the drugstore, and he took to buying sandwiches at the delicatessen, a thing he'd never done before, watching fascinated as Mrs. Rasher moved slowly around behind the showcase, cutting the steaming meat in slices. She put in a lot of meat for him, though not so much as to lose money. He saw that she had some small brown marks on her face and hands and neck, which he'd never noticed before and which turned him to water inside when he considered their meaning.

One night about six weeks ago, just about the time that the leaves hid the beacon on the university tower, around the first of June, a Saturday night it was, he came slowly along the street toward the store. He would have enjoyed the night, the first full summer night in a season that arrived late, with the air moving the heavy bunches of leaves with that whistling sound one associates with the country and vacations, but he kept thinking about Mrs. Rasher. When he came close to the door, in the still evening, he heard a saxophone, the notes floating one by one out into the air and opening like flowers. He knew that it was Saul, not Sammy, because Saul didn't produce the tight phrases and the driving sound that his son got. He played simpler and looser like an older man, and tonight he played an improvised line, a long thin arc of sound that wound out into the summer night like a sudden exposure of private grief.

The music came thinly and airily out. Hannon strained to hear, the cars kept going by and he lost it in the sky.

He stepped compulsively into the store and saw that Saul was alone behind the counter, cradling his horn close to his chest. He glanced over his shoulder at Hannon and said roughly, "What'll you have?" and then more gently, "Oh, it's you. The way you came in I thought it was some neighbourhood kid."

"I was walking softly," Hannon admitted, "just taking my time coming along."

"I didn't recognize you," said Saul, and Hannon wondered if he too might be having trouble with his eyes. Saul handed him his candy bars without being asked, and turned away. He didn't put his horn down: Hannon asked for a sandwich—he'd had no intention of eating a sandwich—and when it was made and he had it steaming hot in his hands, he reached over and chose a dill pickle from a convenient jar, offered Saul some money, and stood there waiting and eating his sandwich.

"The Madame's in the hospital," said Saul, "and I'm minding the store."

"The Madame?"

"My wife. She's very sick." Behind the foolish dark glasses his eyes were unsearchable, but his voice gave it all away. "It's an obstruction of the intestinal tract; they operated this afternoon, and when she's strong enough they'll have to operate again."

"When?"

"In about ten days, they say."

Hannon wondered if Saul knew what it really was.

"I'm worried," said Saul, "I don't trust the doctors. I don't think they're telling me the truth, I'm worried it's her kidney. She's only got one kidney, you know."

"No, I didn't know that."

"The trouble that woman has had, you wouldn't believe. If it's her kidney, she's in bad trouble, she's only got the one.

I think that's what it is. I hardly recognized her when I saw her tonight, she was so weak. She didn't want to see anybody, she didn't even ask who was looking after the store. Of course, she's in pain. They keep giving her drugs all the time."

"What about this other operation?"

"They can't do it till they get her temperature down and they're sure her heart can stand it. If it really is her intestines, that is. They say in about ten days, but I'm keeping my fingers crossed. She wasn't like herself tonight." He stared moodily out the open door and blew air through his horn. "She lost her sight from a brain tumour, you know."

Hannon felt his scalp crawling.

"If she has half a chance, she'll get better," Saul said. "She's strong. Nobody knows how strong she is. She had a brain tumour removed, she lost a kidney, and she's never had what you'd call good health, I mean really good, but she's strong like you wouldn't believe it."

"When did she get sick?"

"She's been sick for a month but she wouldn't do anything. When she started to vomit last night, I made her go in."

Hannon held onto the counter surreptitiously, feeling his knees quaking. I don't want to listen to this, he thought, why should I have to listen to this? His palms were sweating.

"She'll make it if she has any chance," Saul said, and then with a flash of hilarity, "She's gonna cool it, man."

"I'll say some prayers for her," said Hannon faintly.

"Fine, that'll be fine."

Putting down the other half of his sandwich, which had cooled while he talked, Hannon walked hastily out of the store and off down the street, trying not to hurry.

The woman died, naturally; it made him furious. He went into the store every day for two weeks and every day Saul would report on her progress and Hannon would nod, ask a leading question, get the expected answer, but Saul never noticed that the questions were leading, that the temperature ought to go down but hadn't, that the high fever and semi-coma were not indicated in a recovery pattern. Saul's kids were in and out, the pinball machine rocked and rang for free. Her temperature wouldn't go down and one Sunday the Hannons parked across from the store to pick up ice cream. He crossed the street and read the pencilled placard. CLOSED ON ACCOUNT OF DEATH it said in rude lettering.

"She died," he said, getting back behind the wheel. "Did you know about her? I don't think I mentioned it."

"Certainly I knew," said Aileen.

"Where will we get our ice cream? Everything else is closed." He drove home slowly, with exaggerated care.

Monday night he examined the obituaries in the *Star*. "She's not in here," he said queruously, "I don't see the name." Aileen came and stood over his shoulder. "What do you want to know for?" she said, putting her finger on the place. "There it is, Rashevsky, they must have shortened it for the sign. 'Bertha Rashevsky, wife of Saul.'"

He read the entry over carefully. "Shiva private," he said. "Does that mean nobody should call?"

"I don't know. What do you want to get mixed up in that for?"

He was thinking of his own tribe's customs. "I'd like to go, or rather, I think I should." He didn't know why.

"Then call the funeral parlour and ask."

"Weinstein Mortuary on Côte-des-Neiges. I'll give them a ring." He dialled the number and an accented voice answered.

"You've got Mrs. Saul Rashevsky, er, resting there?"

"Yes."

"I'd like to call and pay my respects," he said, feeling like a snooping interloper, "but it says 'shiva private' in the paper. I'm not a Jew, you see, and I don't know what that means. Does it mean I shouldn't come?"

"No, nothing like that," said the voice. "The shiva is a prayer of leave-taking at the end. That's for the family only, but you can visit the deceased at any time."

"I'll come over after supper." He was glad that he would miss the final leave-taking.

Driving into the Weinstein parking lot on Côte-des-Neiges, he noticed that it was right across the street from Saint Kevin's, his church insofar as he went to Mass there, but not his really, not geographically his parish. I'm always in the wrong place, he thought. He expected to hear the saxophone as he entered the funeral home, but there was no music. "For Mrs. Rasher, I mean Rashevsky," he said to the attendant who approached him. The man handed him a folded triangle of black silk. "What is it?" he said, and then saw that it was a little hat, a skull cap in fact.

"It's a yarmulka, it's for mourning." The way he said it sounded like "yawmukka."

Hannon looked at the thing doubtfully, wondering whether he might be forbidden to put it on by Canon Law. Then he thought, what the hell, and stuck it on the back of his head feeling daring and not like himself. They rode upstairs in an elevator big enough to take a coffin on wheels. On the third floor they got out and walked down to the back of the building, where the attendant handed him over to a solitary mourner, a professional mourner by the look of him. There didn't seem to be anybody else around. The room was dark and bare, no flowers, none of the apparatus with which he was familiar at Catholic funerals, none of the hovering priests and sisters, family connections, no distant relatives of the departed sprung from nowhere, no kneeling benches to the pews, if they were pews. He sidled into one and started to go to his knees and realized that without the kneeling bench he would hardly be able to see over the back of the pew in front. He sat down irresolutely and put his head in his hands in an attitude of devotion. He started to bless himself and stopped as if stung.

Behind him the professional mourner was reciting, or half-chanting, what sounded like a litany for the dead. That's what it would have been across the street at Saint Kevin's, but this mourner sang it in a cracked plaintive old voice. He droned on for several minutes while Hannon stared at the plain black closed coffin, counted the candles on the two Jewish-style candelabra, curved at the bottom, not pointed at the top, and wondered what prayers to say. He recited the Our Father mentally a few times and then rose and left, pushing blindly past the mourner who held out an arm as if to block him. They had nothing to say to each other, there was no book to sign, nobody around, and he escaped unobserved.

A long time afterwards, he found out, purely by accident from a client at the bank, that the whole family had been watching him through a screen, furnished them by the undertaker, a regular part of the Jewish custom. When he heard this, he felt acutely resentful, as if he'd been robbed of his generous unobtrusiveness.

There was never after any question of his going back to the delicatessen; he even toyed with the notion of giving up candy for good. Then one night Aileen came home from a quick trip to the grocery and proffered some final information.

"That Indian knows everything," she said. "She's always by the cab stand. She must be married to a cabbie."

"What is it this time?"

Aileen began to giggle unbecomingly. "She said the weirdest thing. She was talking about the family."

He did not ask what family.

"She has it all laid down. She said, "Saul's like a different man. The family is all broken up." And then she said this odd thing. "I guess they'll move to the States."

Hannon gazed at his wife with revulsion, not from her, from the whole business. She began to laugh loudly. "Don't you see?" she said. "Of course that's what you do when everything is ruined. When it's all over. You just move to the States."

In spite of himself he laughed, the phrase had such a pat elegiac tone, the underworld, the happy land, Sheol. "They'll move to the States," he said positively, "they must have relatives there. Probably in California."

Each day he looked for the signs of their going off, but the signs were long in coming, haven't come yet. Hannon is still slinking past the open door to the delicatessen, he misses his Crispy Crunches. Music from two saxophones pursues him, one louder than the other.

GHOSTS AT JARRY

MARIO at the big O, a man who likes company. Squeezed into the 400 level up and in and remote from the *volti-geur de gauche*, not too many people near him in the four-dollar seats, filling for a cement sandwich, like being on a slab. Cold concrete. The 400 level is indeterminate space, neither a good seat nor a bad, too far away to hear the cries of the infielders like lonely birds swooping over green, too near to shave the price. That April afternoon he saw *les bouca-niers de Pittsburgh* take the Expos as the home forces booted the ball repeatedly. Fresh from Florida the unmeshed infield found the home weather too cold for fumbling fingers, base-balls rolling hither and yon, none penetrating the 400 level. No *fausse balle* enlivened the narrow precinct. Mario decided not to sit there again; it would have to be *le niveau 200, Section 18, Section 20*, or nothing, and it would cost.

He looked for friends, found none, though they were there for sure. They had told him they were coming, Ti-cul, Kurt, Silvo, present but invisible. After the fourth inning he went in search of Silvo, who used to sit out past third base at field level, but there was nobody in his seat, only vast stretches of unoc-cupied metal pigeonholes, roomy, chilly, in their thousands.

He couldn't find his way back upstairs; the arrows and signs confused him, and he watched the rest of the game from 106, a vacant seat downstairs, not having paid the full price. He felt nervous and guilty but no cheerful attendant asked to see his stub; nobody banished him from the third base line. Mario never got away with anything because he never tried to. Nobody came around selling peanuts; the vendors seemed lost in the empty reaches. Parched at the seventh-inning stretch he quit his usurped bench and found a nearby kiosk where nobody stood in line. He was served immediately, then had to find a lavatory, luckily next door. Mario blessed the *Regie des Installations Olympiques* for wise care of their *concitoyens*, but found the lavatory a maze of reverse-swinging doors. He had a hard time escaping, a belated rally in progress along the basepaths. Cash scored, the home forces appeared ready to carry the day. Mario fought his way to freedom in time to see the *Devinez l'assistance* figures flashed on the big board: 21,063, 19,750, 18,322, 20,004.

He thought: those are mistaken. There can't be twenty thousand people here, or eighteen thousand. I would guess maybe seven, he thought, maybe eight thousand. There is nobody buying beer, nobody helped me when I called. I might have perished in there. The board flashed the official figure: *Assistance d'aujourd'hui, 19,750.* He peered around incredulously. Had they counted sold empty seats perhaps? At Jarry such a throng would have stretched service beyond capacity. He'd never have been able to walk straight to the counter and demand a beer, not even after the game was over. Here there was infinite space, and it unsettled him. The long eighth inning continued; extra innings impended; afternoon stretched into early evening; people began to leave; the big O emptied; Mario got frightened.

He wondered if he would come back. It was so close to home, that was the thing. For his whole life, he and Ti-cul and Silvo and Kurt had been hoping for something in the east-end besides the Angus shops. Now here it was, five minutes from Rosemont, and it gave him vertigo. He looked out, squinting through the late shadows, at what-the-hell-was-it, sward? Turf? He wasn't sure of the word. *Gazon? Domtarturf?* It wasn't anything like grass, being a bright emerald, a colour never seen in the natural world, out of a laboratory, bottled. Such green as might be seen in a film about the distant future. He could see where the individual rolls had been zippered together and laughed when a tenth-inning ground ball, out past Parrish, suddenly bounded into the air as it hit one of the zippered seams in the gleaming surface and assumed a long incredible arc, hurtling past the amazed left-fielder towards the warning track. Two runs scored. Expos failed to even the count in their half of the tenth, and the game ended that way, towards six o'clock.

The players vanished like wraiths; never had Mario seen them disappear so fast. He used to stand close to the field after the final out, to watch the inept homesters make their exposed way out to the foul pole in left and into the clubhouse, exchanging discontented repartee with certain regular fans. Once that disgusting, off-speed-pitch-specialist Howie Reed had flipped a baseball into *les estrades populaires* as he sauntered, cursing freely and indecently in words Mario failed to recognize, into the sheltering clubhouse. There had been a scramble. Children had injured themselves. Such a thing would be impossible under the new dispensation, contact irretrievably lost. Mario felt specks and points tickling the curling hairs on his neck and looked up. Unbelievably a warm spring rain was finding its way to him from on high, hardly a rain, more a mist, spitting. Nobody was visible but a nonlingual youth who scuttled past turning seats up, mute arguably from birth; nobody could have decided on the evidence. He would have to look for Kurt and the others at the tavern; he was sure to find them there. He moved up the steps and in out of the rain; spring night enveloped him. In the dark, strange patterns defined themselves on the concrete walls as wetness slid down pocked textures.

Roofless, open, the giant structure admitted natural flow of water, perhaps its most grateful feature. He pondered this matter as he made for the main gates, wondering whether he should go home or go downtown to eat. What would the stadium be like in heavy rain, in snow, roofless or roofed? He had heard from a friend in the air-conditioning business that huge conduits, giant circulating pumps, were being installed in the building, which would in time be completed as an all-weather sports palace. But here imagination failed. How heat it in winter? Who would sit in caverns of ice to watch what? Should Expos ever make it into *la serie mondiale* they would have to play night games in mid-October; his Mediterranean blood roiled and thickened at the thought. A roof would inhibit free circulation of air. How dank, how chilled it would be, pressed up against that cold stone in late autumn! What could be done about it? And he thought, as he thought most days about the way things went on, how fix?

His feet had decided for him, leading him down the tunnel towards the Metro station. Nobody on the first flight. Nobody on the second flight. Silence along the terraces, solitude beside the newsagents stands. Inside a sandwich again, he thought, eaten by a giant. One solitary man in a glass booth opening a vacuum bottle. Steam escaped from its top, making him think of the roofless big O. In this rain, in these temperatures, there would be puffs of steam from the hole in the top, possibly even rings of vapour as if expelled from the cancered lungs of a colossal cigarette-smoker. He passed onto an almost silent train; a solitary passenger wasn't anybody he knew.

When he rose up out of the Metro at the Berri-de-Montigny station, he found the same spring rain falling into the lights of evening. He thought of the plastic emerald rug; this rain would not promote its growth, false surface. He had heard that the players preferred true grass which grew long, sometimes giving them a break on a hot grounder. Long growth might then be cut to surprise visiting teams with porous infields, a bit of baseball larceny less and less available to canny groundskeepers. Too bright. Too green.

And then there was the look and feeling of the oddly shaped hole in the roof, a shape that made him peculiarly uncomfortable, something wrong about it. He wasn't a poet; he wasn't an architect; he had a labouring job and didn't want to know about art, but he knew that the hole in the sky was quietly askew, wrong. It shouldn't curve that way because there was nothing in the curve to remind him of women's bodies. If something curved, thought Mario, it ought to curve in a useful or encouraging way.

He wouldn't go back in there; it wasn't like the old park, which had been like a village, close, warming, with the usual run of village characters. There had been a man who brought his goat to twenty games a season, and the club management connived at the smelly invasion, to court press photographers. At the opening game of the 1971 season, Mario's children had carried a huge homemade sign into the bleachers: BIENVE-NUE A NOS AMOURS LES EXPOS. At two in the afternoon a pressman took a picture, which appeared in the final edition of the *Star* that same afternoon; neighbours phoned excitedly during dinner to tell the family about it. The children had remembered it ever since and there was a copy of the picture still pinned to his bedroom door.

There had been that man who sprang up in the middle of rallies and danced like a dervish up and down the steps of the grandstand, executing unheard-of jigs and reels to an accompaniment of handclapping from thousands of enthusiasts around him, a lean man, crazy-looking, known around the National League as "the Dancer." His steps could not have been danced at the *Stade Olympique*. The pitch of the seats was too gradual, the stairs insufficiently raked. Some sort of classical pavanne would suit them, not the gyrations of the native Quebecker.

In the twentieth row of the bleachers, right behind the third base foul pole, had sat night after night an unspeaking man in a short-sleeved shirt, grey-headed, immobile, stumpy cigar always in place, not a word to say for himself but always there. No cheer escaped this man, no violation of the careful probabilities of baseball by fledgling expansion team could make him wince. Mario missed him terribly, searched for him during intense moments at the big O, realizing finally that the man had gone forever. He might just possibly be seated somewhere in the new building for his perpetual Buddhist posture but this seemed against all odds, the betting prohibitive. What is to be done, Mario wondered, how can this be restored?

Ballplayers—on the whole an ungenerous group of men—had hated Jarry Park for sound professional reasons as well as from personal pique. Not really great and good ballplayers, most early Expos wished to avoid the inspection of nearby fans, disliked the trudge along the track to the clubhouse, finally prevailed upon management to erect a cement-block tunnel from dugout to clubhouse, rendering themselves unobservable, incorrigible. A very few who for reasons of their own wished to court public favour continued to take the outside walk; but these were popular players apt to be fringe performers, a Ronnie Brand, a Marv Staehle, Jose Herrera.

The old park had the world's crappiest outfield, frosthumped, deceptively grassy, stippled with rabbit holes, hell to run on. It had no foul area; the bullpens were in the laps of the fans. Visiting relief pitchers endured coarse taunts during rare Expos rallies. Expos firemen grew accustomed to the stagey resignation of the home supporters.

"Attention, Attention. Le numero vingt-cinq, Dan McGinn, lance main tenant pour les Expos."

At this ominous declaration, Ti-cul, Kurt, Silva, and Mario would groan, make retching noises. The Buddha of the bleachers might shift one buttock's width to right or left, or he might not.

I will go back and look at Jarry Park, Mario decided. He had clipped a panoramic view of the old place from some special issue of *Le Dimanche*, park packed beyond capacity for some extraordinary occasion. Taken from an altitude of seven hundred and fifty feet, probably from a helicopter hovering above the parking lot to the northeast of the playing field, the photo emphasized the ramshackle, spurious, ad hoc, temporary, incredible cheapness of the silly building. It had cost three million dollars. But no public facility of the contemporary scene could possibly cost three million dollars, the thing was unheard-of. It was eight hundred million or zilch— there is no other way. When Jarry had been built, not all that long ago, Mario recollected hardly a decade, there had been 307 no cranes sitting idle on the site over weekends, at overtime rates approaching sixty thousand an hour. Overtime for idling cranes alone had cost more at the Olympic site than the entire cost of Jarry Park, three million. How fix?

The players hated it, and it made sense: two strikes. He thought he'd go and have a final look before they started to tear it down; there was no conceivable use for the facility. All he did was work. It looked horrible. The metal flooring of the stands had leaked copiously. If you stood under it during a rain-delay, the precipitation poured down your neck and into the dank bun of your hotdog. Those hotdogs had always been dung-like, inert, without form and void. Soggy, they constituted an offence against nature. No. There was nothing to be said for the former home of the Montreal National League Baseball Club Limited.

Somewhere around the house there was a portable radio, useable on house current or batteries, a discarded Christmas gift with exhausted power pack. Mario located it, dusted it off, supplied the requisite D batteries, and took it with him across town on an indifferent, coolish, Sunday afternoon with the Cards in town.

At fifteen hundred feet a familiar Cessna 150 banked, trailing a long streamer which delivered the Gospel according to Parkside. ALWAYS A BETTER DEAL AT PARKSIDE MOTORS. The plane hastened away as Mario squinted aloft. Perhaps the pilot had forgotten himself; returned to his old flyway mistaking the open space below for the true ballgame, then found it empty. The drone of the engine faded. Jarry was really desert.

He sidled towards the exiguous metal structure. One thing about it, though lonely, deserted, vacant, boarded over, it hadn't corroded. The metal facade shone dully, white in the uncertain atmosphere. It was an afternoon of ill-defined light, little sun, light overcast, a genuine Montreal uncertainty of observation. There was nobody in the park. He passed along the chain-link fencing looking for entry. Surely some boy or dog or vandal had effected the necessary hole—and there it was, back along the third base side—near the rickety ticket booths and the press gate, a gaping tear, edges bent backwards, big enough to drive a Jeep through. Somebody had been at work with a pair of wire-cutters. The edges of the severed strands were shiny-fresh and could hurt you. He passed inside.

What is quieter than an abandoned ballpark, unless the tomb? He shuddered to think where all the voices had gone. Once this place had shaken and resounded with the shrieks of fifteen thousand maddened kiddies on Bat Day, fifteen thousand miniature Louisville Sluggers pounding in unison on the metal flooring; it had been a hellish event. Householders for blocks around had complained to the authorities but the promotion had become a recurrent event. Bat-Day at Jarry Park was like the Last Judgement, sounding deeply impressive.

But unlike the judgement in this, that it was not still impending. He stole across the flat paved open area between the fence and the refreshment counters. A blue souvenir stand leaned ready to collapse, doors locked. From between the doors a feather protruded electric blue. Mario tugged at the feather end, and the whole article slid noiselessly from between the locked doors, a celebratory feather dyed red, white, and blue. The other end stuck in the door—perhaps attached to a hat inside, too big to fit through the crack. He could do nothing to release it and left it floating solemnly in the faint breeze, passed up a ramp and into the deserted third-base seats, once the best place in the city to see a game. He idled along towards the foul pole, clutching his radio. The day around him grew imperceptibly warmer, the grey lightened. Vacancy. The seats were all before him and he was at the extreme outfield end of the park, immediately over the gateway to the abandoned clubhouse. He sprawled in one seat, then stood up, chose another, put his legs out in front of him, and switched on the radio.

". . . and after the pre-game show we'll have all the action for you right here at Radio 600, the voice of Montreal Expos baseball. I'm Dave Van Horne and I'll be right here with Duke Snider to keep you up to date on the out-of-town scores and the other developments around the majors, right after this message…"

The sun came out. Mario drowsed and listened. He saw that this was life as it ought to be lived. The game came to him with perfect clarity and form over the radio. With his eyes shut he could fancy the whole place alive around him. Nothing was gone. The Gautama of the bleachers would be right over there twenty rows up, if he happened to glance in that direction. If the Expos happened to get something going—as they did almost immediately that afternoon—the Dancer would get his legs going too. The air would be filled with flying bags of peanuts. People would be passing hotdogs along the rows in a fine comradeship. All he had to do was listen, and keep his eyes shut tight.

". . . opened the inning with a single, went to second on Cromartie's roller to the right side. Valentine homered, his

sixth home run of the season and his nineteenth and twentieth RBIs. Perez reached on an error..."

Expos won that first game in Mario's resurrected Jarry,
a shutout victory for Rogers, and after that there could be no
question of viewing the games in the flesh. He started to come
to the old park all the time, nights and Saturdays a well as on
the Sabbath. He felt in control, as though the whole happening was invented by him. The conviction grew on him that he
could influence the course of the games by wishing, command-
ing in imagination. He knew that this was not strictly so, but
all the same the home club seemed to rally more often when
he really willed them to—balls found holes in infields, defensive replacements offered models of anticipation. Rookies
blossomed—three of them, almost a miracle—all through
closed eyes. He now began to think about bringing his portable
Sanyo along. If the atmospherics were right and the power pack
strong, he might be able to watch the games on TV, listen to the
expert radio commentary, have his eyes opened. Would the
TV picture be an adequate surrogate for all he could imagine?

Night games would tell; they were the best of all because
the tall poles no longer supported myriads of hot arcs. All
was still, but not dark. Those night games in May and June at
Jarry, the longest evenings of the year, had always been vexed
by the slow disappearance of the sun behind the bleachers to
the northwest. He remembered Ron Fairly refusing to scamper onto the playing area when the umpire called "Play ball!"
because of that late sun, dead in the eyes of the first baseman.
Fairly, always an intransigent ballplayer, had been able to persuade Dick Stello to delay the game until the sun disappeared,
an unlikely twenty minutes. At Midsummer Day it didn't get
dark in the park until the sixth inning or even later, while
across town the actual play would be shadowed in shroud-
ing concrete, no illumination relieving the cavernous gloom.
Night games were best.

Just about Midsummer Day, with a long brilliant evening light promised, he brought the Sanyo along and sneaked into his usual spot. For a while he contented himself with the radio and the fading summer sun on his tight eyelids, but a the light waned he grew curious, and when darkness descended very late, past nine-thirty, he turned on the TV and focused his gaze on the small picture, like some mystic concentrating on his mandala:

CARTER. 11 HR. 29 RBI. .268

The emission of light from the small screen was the only sparkle in the park, thought Mario. He leaned forward, the sounds of the city in the night drifting almost inaudibly overhead. He watched the final three innings, willing them to win, and they did. And as he switched to the post-game show on the radio, just as he turned his TV off, he caught a gleam of light almost the mirror image of his own at the extreme other end of the stands, over by the first-base foul pole. A line drawn from where he was sitting through centre field to the distant glimmer would form the base of an isosceles triangle whose equal sides would extend through first and third to home. He had no intention of launching himself into the deep well of darkness in centre. But he felt drawn along the shining metal gangway which ran the length of the grandstand.

The main bank of seats in Jarry was formed in the shape of an enormous letter L, the two equal sides of an isosceles triangle with its apex behind home plate. A fan sitting in Mario's position sensed this shape as a long line extending away towards home, with the other leg of the L running out of the corner of his eye in the direction of the visitors' dressing room under the first-base stands. The whole mass had something the look of an opened penknife, as used in the boy's game of "baseball" early in the century.

The distant figure on the other side of the park now followed Mario's lead and extinguished whatever light had been showing. The whole park lay under the night sky empty, glowing with night-shine off the aluminum seatbacks. A breeze moved quietly in the grass. Mario inched his way silently towards home in the darkness, and peering through the dark he had the sense that somebody else was coming in from right-field. A faint metallic sound drifted above the pitcher's mound, shoes on metal plating. Small shoes, by the sound.

He eased forward along the runway, which stretched out in front of him like a white dusty road in the country under starlight. The towers of extinct arc-lights stood up around the park like sentinels. There was the billboard advertising cigarettes, unreadable in the dark. Out to his left the old scoreboard, which had never worked properly, loomed with comforting familiarity. Clink of shoes on metal. He strained his eyes to see across the narrowing infield. Somebody was there. He caught a glimpse of a pale face in dim reflection. Then he heard swift footsteps and saw a slender form move in the dark like the ghost of a batboy. He ran along the third-base line, reaching home at the same moment as the ghostly figure. A girl in a dark blue halter and a pair of jeans threw herself unresistingly into his arms. This terrified him. Mario had held no girl but his wife in his arms at any time these twenty years. He drew back and tried to see her. Like himself, she carried a small portable TV and a radio.

"I thought you were a ghost," exclaimed this stranger. "Heavens, how you scared me."

"I thought so too," said Mario.

"That you were a ghost? How could you think that?"

"No. That you were."

"That's silly," said the girl scornfully. "Anybody can see that I'm not a ghost. I'm a very popular girl."

"I'm sure you are, Miss, but I can't see you very well in the dark."

"Why are you here?"

"I like it better here."

"Oh, so do I, so do I. I hate that other place with a passion."

"And so you started to come back here, just like me, to listen to the games and watch them on your TV. How long have you been coming?"

"This is my first time."

"I hope it won't be your last," said Mario with a gallantry which astounded himself. It would have astonished his wife too.

"But we're ... all alone in here?"

"There's certainly nobody here now, not even a security guard."

"Would I be safe with you?"

"Would one Expos fan insult another? And besides, now that there are two of us, others will come. I'm certain of it."

"Oh, I hope you're right," said the girl in a beseeching tone.

"I know I'm right," said Mario. "This is exactly how a house gets to be haunted." Afterwards, when he recognized the supreme justice of this observation he wondered how he'd hit on it. He considered himself habitually, by a kind of unthinking reflex, to be a stupid unfeeling person, but in this adventure he had shown, he saw, powerful imagination.

Many came after that first encounter; they came by ones and twos, then in troops, finally in hundreds. The abandoned park sprang back to a loony bootleg life all the sunny summer. People would bring their own hotdogs and beer, their radios. Somehow a cap and souvenir vendor found out about the secret congregation, and he came too one July evening with a trayful of hats and dolls and pennants. Nobody bought anything from him; they were afraid he'd disappear. Obviously the Montreal National League Baseball Club Limited knew nothing about him, a phantom souvenir salesman with phantom goods.

None of them revisited the big O. Not ever. And in the earliest hints of autumn they would laugh, and people in neighbourhood apartment blocks would wonder where the laughing was coming from, as the plangent tones of the Duke of Fallbrook oozed from the radios collected at Jarry.

". . . now we know, Dave and I know, that the club is playing a bit off the pace, but really you know folks that doesn't explain the dropoff in attendance. There has to be a big audience for Expos baseball out there somewhere, and I'm appealing to you—it's the old Duker talking. . ."

"That's right, Duke," said the voice of Dave Van Horne, "we've got a great home stand going here, so come on out to the Olympic Stadium and watch the Expos try to play the role of spoilers in this season's tight race in the National League East. Hope to see you real soon, right, Duke?"

"Right, Dave!"

But the ghosts of Jarry merely guffawed, an immense throng they were by now. And the first of them looked again at the wide heaven. No, he would never go back. He would spend no second afternoon in mental trouble excited by that crater in the air, gazing through the gaping enormous ellipse—was it an ellipse?—in the sky.

AN ALLEGORY
OF MAN'S FATE

Bronson kept seeing them tacking back and forth, sometimes in pairs, occasionally in squadrons, on the blue surface of the lake. The pretty scene moved him obscurely—roused some atavistic, long-repressed need for space, sun, shimmer off the water, silence. In the early autumn he bought a kit, intending to attempt to assemble the boat in his basement—conveniently large—in the city over the winter. In mid-October, just after the family had returned from an exceptionally fine Thanksgiving weekend at the cottage, a very large red truck appeared in front of the house about five o'clock in the afternoon, disruptive of the cocktail hour and dinner. There were two cumbersome, terribly heavy, cardboard cartons to be wrestled off the truck and into the recreation room. They would not go through the side door because of the angle; the driver and his helper were inclined to bugger off at once. They wanted their evening meal, like anybody else. It was only by giving them five dollars apiece that Viv Bronson, who looked awfully pretty with her cheeks flushed in annoyance, persuaded them to hang around and shift this heavy weight or that, up on one end, on its side, on the other end, around this way. Back. Crash; tinkle. Oh oh.

"They won't go in that way."

"No."

"What's in these, missus?"

"A boat. The parts for a boat."

"Parts only?" The implication was clear to Bronson who now hove into view—the nautical expression seems appropriate—behind the delivery men.

"Won't it go down?" he asked, and the others turned to gaze at him.

"No."

"Have you tried it up on end?"

"Yes."

"Have you tried it on its side?"

"Yes."

"We gotta go now, sir, Missus. Gotta go, yes, the truck is out on a lease basis, see? The boss don't own the truck, just leases it on a lease basis from nine to six, eh? Has to be back in the yard by six or goes on the overtime rate. We're going now, goodbye now." Off they went, leaving Mr. and Mrs. Bronson standing beside the long, heavy, wide carton jammed in the side entryway. The other, longer, thinner, not quite so heavy, rattling carton lay in the driveway in puddles of overnight rain, cardboard going soggy, Bronson saw. Both cartons were bound by metal stripping with viciously sharp ends and edges.

"Where are the kids?"

"How should I know? Where are they ever? Probably down the Azlex shoplifting."

"No need to fuss."

"…not fussing…"

"We'll try through the front hall then." He found rising to his lips an observation he had never needed to record in his tranquil life, until then, and said without thinking, for the first time, "There is no difficulty that cannot be overcome." His wife nodded. Feeling an enriched married mutual understanding, they first lifted the longer, now melting carton from the puddles and bore it, afraid that their hands would punch holes in the sodden cardboard, along the driveway to the front of the house, up the stairs onto the verandah.

Mrs. Fletcher next door happening to emerge from her home that moment, looking for the *Star* carrier, as usual very late, looked startled when she saw them.

"Somebody's getting a new mattress," she called.

"It's the spars," said Mrs. Bronson through her teeth.

"What, dear?"

"It's the spars."

"Aha. Aha. The *Star*."

They let the carton down carefully and began to pull it through the door.

"Have you had your *Star* yet?"

They got the box into the hall, where it filled the space at the foot of the stairs. Bronson now began to wonder whether the thing would go down the cellar staircase and into the rec room. He saw that a command decision would be involved and tried to think ahead. From the verandah, Mrs. Fletcher called in through the doorway, "Have you had your *Star*?"

"No, spars. The *spars*."

"No, have you had your *Star*? Has the boy been by?"

"Oh. No. Well, actually we don't take from the carrier boy any more. I just go over to the corner before dinner. I should go soon before he closes. Would you like me to get you a paper, uh, Alice?"

He never felt easy about calling the neighbours by their Christian names.

"No," she said, after deliberation. "I'll chance it. He's almost always late."

Bronson said to his wife, "Going for the paper, Viv."

"What, and leave this great thing here? And what about the one stuck in the side door?"

"I'll get it when I come back. Only be five minutes, darling."

Walking to the neighbourhood variety store, he felt doubt gathering in his mind. If he took the two huge objects downstairs as they stood, this would give him a rough idea whether or not he could get the assembled boat out again when the time came. This was clearly a paramount matter, requiring immediate clarification. The finished boat might very well prove bulkier than the boxes, probably would. The phrase "eleven feet long overall" came to mind, recollected from the newspaper advertisement that had incited the purchase. How wide? If a dinghy was eleven feet long, about how wide would it be? He found himself passing through Joe's doorway. He bought the paper and a Doctor West nylon-bristled medium hard, as a wedge for the conversation. "You live over the store, right?" he said to Joe, the owner.

"Yeah, correct, why?"

"Doing anything tonight?"

Joe's face slowly acquired a threatened expression; this was the first time in over seven years that Bronson had ever said anything to him apart from requests for this or that article—razorblades, paperbacks. He said, "What were you thinking of?"

"Involves heavy lifting."

Joe moved away from the counter, spreading his suitcoat open, plucking at his shirttail. For an hallucinated instant, Bronson thought he was going for a gun. "This is it," he told himself. Actually the storekeeper was opening his trousers. "See?" he said.

"What?"

"Triple hernia," he announced with satisfaction.

That hard leather lump down there, Bronson realized, was some part of a truss. He felt relief. "I thought I'd ask," he said, picking up his change and his toothbrush. He looked at the toothbrush absently; "Maybe I'll have yellow instead," he said.

"Take your pick . . . or there's the Py-Co-Pay line with the rubber tip, at the same price."

"Got what I want."

He folded the paper into a tight flat package and strolled back to the house, where Vivianne had dinner already on the table. "You want a sherry, or do you want to go ahead?" she said.

"Let's eat."

They sat through the meal in silence, oppressed by sober reflection. Though the weekend weather had been idyllic, it had rained on Tuesday. Now it was cooling. From time to time the aluminum side door creaked in the freshening breeze and gusts of air chilled Bronson's ankles. Once he almost got up to go and shut the side door, then remembered that it was propped open by his purchase. He sneaked a peek at Viv, at the other end of the table; she held a lamb chop in her fingers, nibbling delicately, close to the bone, a pink crinkled pantie dangling insecurely from the gnawed end. She smiled at him over the chop.

She said, "It'll be all right."

Later in the evening they were able to work the tall narrow box of spars into a permanent standing position, on end in the staircase well, such that one end extended upward almost to the second floor, like the brass pole in a fire hall. Bronson stood at the foot of the stairs, looking up and estimating how the mast would look when stepped in place. It would be tall and straight. He imagined a gentle swell, deck lifting under him, conversational water.

"There's the other one," said Viv breathlessly.

It was harder to extricate the heavier carton from the frame of the side entry, where it had caught on the hinges and the hook for the latch; there was breakage; the carton was punctured here and there; from its interior came disquieting sounds of shifting bits of heavy stuff, each time they moved it. But there was no way—it had to come out and back and along the driveway and up and inside when, exhausted, arm muscles aching, Bronson and his wife began to quarrel and insult one another. It was in the middle of a pitched battle that their teen-aged children, boy and girl, arrived home from different ends of the city.

"You're a feeble fool!"

"And you're living on the earnings of a feeble fool. So take care!"

"I should say. I should say."

"So you should."

"I will, then."

"See that you do!"

"What is all this?" said their daughter, Irene, sticking her bead in the door. Behind her, Gary, fifteen, heavily mous-tached, sideburned, leather-jacketed, could be heard demand-ing, "Is it safe to bring my mandolin in? Or will they wreck it?"

Bronson had once smashed a valuable antique, a blue crystal pitcher, in a fit of rage, shouting out that the spout was wretchedly designed and slopped over. Gary, sitting next to him at table, had been powerfully impressed by the violent action, never forgot it, and used to keep wooden, fragile things out of his father's way. From long witness of silent movies and cartoons on children's TV, he had gotten quite used to the idea of smashing ukuleles and mandolins over people's heads—this happened all the time on the little screen. He could imagine his father, in the grip of impulse, grabbing his cherished man-dolin and lowering it on Mother's pate with disastrous effect.

Vivianne started to laugh weakly. "Yes. No. It's this boat of your father's."

"It's for all of us." Bronson said. "We'll all have fun building it, and then sailing it." Afterward he wondered if this speech had exhibited the savage, unknowing pride of strength and power called *hubris* by the Greeks—an attitude that delivers punishment in its very structure. He got to his feet, made room for Gary to enter, and invited his son to help him store the second carton; they decided in the end to slide it in behind a breakfront buffet which stood in the dining-room and almost concealed the box. It stayed there the whole winter. The family decided after long consultation not to open the boxes and build the boat downstairs.

"That would make the basement unusable for any other purpose all winter and maybe longer," said Irene sagely, and all agreed.

"We'll build it at the lake," said Bronson. "We'll carry it out right in the cartons; no need to mess with it here."

By Christmas he had stopped thinking about his boat as such, as boat-in-being. Instead the form of the tall narrow carton of spars grew in his mind, taking various shapes and traces of suggestion as he imagined it from time to time: as scaffold in western film, as totem pole. Finally it assumed and retained the dark vague shape of a grandfather clock, perhaps because of the dim light lying along the stairwell, coming in the end to embody in Bronson's imagination the powers of ancient law.

In spring wide-flung doors dissipated this dimness; curtains around the window on the landing were drawn well back, admitting pale sunlight and good air. With May Day at hand, the family rented a U-Haul for their annual first weekend at the lake, loaded it with mattresses, extra oddments of cottage furniture and, this year, uniquely, their potential boat. The drive out by no means a short distance—was accomplished with surprising ease, the cottage fittings carried conveniently into the cedar-smelling small building. Then with gratifying rapidity the four of them hustled the two cartons onto the sundeck overlooking the shore, set up a pair of sawhorses presumed to be essential to the construction project, then stood back and gazed fearfully at the never-yet-opened, battered, holed objects. They had certainly managed to take on a heavy charge of *mana*, Bronson conceded, a load of family spirits and folk narratives that dwelt on and in them. To open them would be a very serious business. That weekend they recoiled; they covered the tabernacle with tarpaulin and returned to town to meditate.

The actual unveiling took place much later. They had hoped to get up over the twenty-fourth, but this proved impossible. June was dissipated on a business trip Bronson had to take, an annual affair. This time he asked Viv to go with him, an unprecedented request, possibly with concealed motive, and they spent a happy two weeks in and around Toronto. No boat-building got done that month.

On Canada Day weekend, Bronson steeled himself to cut. He sent Gary and Irene off to the landing with their pals for the day, then persuaded Viv to stand and watch as he tore the end off the big box, the one with the parts for the hull inside. He slid out many—many—long sheets of marine plywood. Bottles of starter fluid. Cans of glue powder. Strips of mahogany. Long strips of ash. Spindles and cutouts and plugs and blocks. "Good wood in this anyhow," he said, panting.

There was a clear plastic sack of white ropes.

There was a second clear plastic sack of brown ropes.

And another one full of strong, slender wire cables and rings and shackles.

There were many tiny clear plastic bags of different-sized nails.

And screws.

There were the sails, mainsail and jib, beautiful orange-red nylon with the sailmaker's logo in their corners.

"Red sails," said Viv, pleased, "how lovely."

Bronson didn't answer. He had found a pair of instruction manuals deep in the recesses of this carton, one on sailing, one on assembly. He forebore to open them, instead lining up the legions of parts; fitments, forms, indisputable shapes, on the sundeck. He upended the ragged carton and shook it for several seconds. A tiny square-headed copper nail fell out. He had a terrible fear that if he threw out the carton he would accidentally dispose of some essential irreplaceable piece, lodged in one of the folded ends. He carried the cardboard tenderly in his extended arms around to the flat, sun-drenched rocks behind the building, where he proceeded to tear it into little squares, with convulsive energy, removing first the flaps, then the sides. Every morsel of cardboard was shaken vigorously, as Viv stood by watching with anxiety. In the end, he was satisfied. No fugitive nail would lose this battle.

There was the second, or long and thin, carton to be gutted. This proved a simple matter, as only the mast, the gaff, the boom, and the oars were involved. These handsome, already half-shaped and dressed, wooden pieces slid neatly along the rafters of cottage interior until they were required, an age to come, while along the floor of the sundeck lay the other bits of boat. Hundreds and hundreds of them. I never thought it would be like this, he told himself, an exceeding great multitude. Behind him, plucking repeatedly at her lips with one hand and holding a manual open in the other, his wife checked through a complex list.

"They're numbered," she said slowly. "Every piece is stamped somewhere and if two or more bits serve the same purpose, they've got the corresponding number."

"I guess what we ought to do now," he said, working it out as he spoke, "is check over the list and make sure we've got everything." He could feel rationality reviving in himself, like an engine warming on a cold day, and was comforted. As Viv read off the list, he scrambled around on his knees, locating the objects numbered and so oddly named. At first things were easy, early numbers referring to the great sheets of lusciously grained plywood which would in the end form the boat's hull. Of these there were more than a dozen, none more than eight feet long. Bronson wondered how the boat could possibly be eleven feet long, if no piece extended so far, and was speedily enlightened. These extensive sheets were grouped together and stacked against the front wall of the cottage, where they remained until actual construction began.

"What the hell is this?" Bronson demanded at large, holding up a long, silky, ravelling roll of pale silvery tape.

"Appears to be fibreglass," said his wife, in her W.C. Fields voice, as she bent her gaze on the manual. Eventually they figured out what it was for.

"Don't you dig things out and ask me," she complained, "let's go along by the numbers."

"Yeah, yeah, what the hell is this?" He held up a metal object in light alloy, of decidedly suggestive shape.

His wife blushed. "It's an upper pintle."

"So you say."

"But it is. It is. Come on, sweetie, let me call them out."

"Oh all right."

"Looking for number 47. 'Boom-kicking-strap-chock,'" she chanted.

"What is that? I don't even know what I'm looking for. What would that look like?"

"Don't know."

"'Boom-kicking-strap-chock'?"

"That's what it says. Number 47."

It was a little cube of hardwood, no bigger than an Oxo cube. "What can it be?" marvelled Bronson. "What can it do?"

"Number 79. 'After-deck-batten-support.'"

"Is there only one?"

"One only, correct."

"Got it."

"Number 80. 'Quarter knees.'"

"How many?"

"Two of these, I think, yes, two."

"What would they look like?"

"It says they're mahogany, would this be them? Yes, here they are."

"All right, Viv, you read the book, I'll find the pieces. Okay? These are hard like rock."

"Number 83." She paused, staring at the text in alarm.

"What is it?"

"'Plate-case-packing-pieces.'"

The total opacity of this phrase excited paroxysms of horror and despair, and they took off for the rest of the day. Dinner at the landing with multiple drinks partially restored their spirits; the next day they persevered, finished checking their list, and read off a little surprise note at the back of the manual which informed them that their tool kit was wholly inadequate for the task impending. They drove at once to the nearest hardware store and bought Surform tools in various shapes, a large, solid, hand plane, an electric drill, an electric sander, drill bits in many sizes. Finally they owned everything necessary.

"And after, we'll have them," said Bronson.

Construction now began; they learned straightaway how an eleven-foot boat materializes from eight-foot pieces of ply. Butt-strapping! Now I know what butt-strapping is, Bronson thought, something learned, new valuable experience, never to be forgotten. I am enlarging my range, confronting and overcoming obstacles; nothing human is alien to me. Without realizing that he spoke aloud, he said, "There is no difficulty that cannot be overcome." His wife, sitting down hard on a glued butt-strap join, now drying, twisted round and stared at him.

"Don't move for a minute," he said, "it's almost dry."

"Now for the nails."

"It says to back up anything you're driving nails in by something solid like a piece of iron or block of hardwood. I wonder what it means."

Viv said, "It means if you don't you'll nail your piece of wood to the floor."

"Ha ha, very funny." All the same, he dug out a kiln-dried beam-end left over from construction of the cottage and used it as a back-up. Kneeling on the ply, feeling the solidity of this support and noting that the wood didn't bounce and recoil under hammer blows, he understood the instructions, and said to his wife, "When I read it in the book, I didn't understand, but after I'd done it, I could see."

Life continued. When the long hull forms had been glued, trimmed, nailed, hundreds of small holes had to be drilled along their sides to allow them to be *sewn together* with copper wire. This seemed a simple task, but after cutting 250 wire bits, Viv found that the tip of her thumb and forefinger on her right hand were abraded, blistered, then cut and bleeding; it was the bright end of each shard of wire, coming away from the snips, that kept nibbling the fleshy tips. She sucked them and stared resentfully at Bronson, busy drilling holes along the hull form edges. "You took the easy job," she said.

He lifted his head and wiped dripping sweat from his eyes. "Give you the hell of a stiff neck, this does. Want to have a go?"

She had second thoughts.

In a day or two they laid the plywood sheets on top of the sawhorses and started to lace them up tight with the lengths of wire, twisting and knotting them with pliers. This proved a relatively easy matter to begin with, growing harder the closer the edges came together; there was the artistic problem of forming the chine of the hull, as the later bits of wire drew in tight. The plywood edges were nipped in hard against each other; one person had to mold the desired form into the wood by main force, while the other threaded the cutting and irritating wires through tiny holes. At the end of the week they had four sore thumbs and four lacerated forefingers. And the formed hull standing bravely on the sawhorses. They shot a roll of film of themselves standing beside it, patting it.

Then the really hard part started.

Bronson said later on that the deception involved in the proceeding was that you had something looking like a completed boat very early, but it took months—possibly years—to finish it off. He considered this a rude parody of the conditions of human existence. They had to learn how to handle the liquid resin and strips of fibreglass that sealed tight the boat's sewn seams. This involved timing the hardening process of the resin, a stinking, poisonously blue goo. The first few times they did it, it snapped solid, BANG, like the lid of a closing trunk, before they had time to use it. Then it refused to harden because they didn't put in enough hardener. Then they got it timed right for a hot dry day and the weather turned cold and damp, throwing them off; paranoia threatened, but they learned, they learned. They got so much fibreglass on the hull they had to write to the city for more.

Virtually nothing was simple. They found that the sun beat down on them fiercely in the later part of the day, but they had so much junk stacked on the deck that there could be no question of moving to a shadier place. From time to time they broke small pieces. Bronson learned to improvise. "It's all educational. There is no difficulty..." His wife and children cursed under their breath and he let the remark trail off.

One day it took Bronson and Viv five desperate hours of sanding, smoothing, whittling, trimming, to get two small wooden pieces into place and securely glued. The further they went the closer the tolerances were, and the smaller the margin for error. Once they got a pleasant surprise. The deck tops, four imposing large pieces, fell into place as if they had been tailored to fit by master boatbuilders (of course they had). They grinned at each other, may even have exchanged kisses— their first in many days. Bronson thought: we will endure, we will go on to the end. They had managed every fitment but the last; only the inner and outer gunwales remained.

"Now for these we ought to have clamps," said Viv. "We're not strong enough in the hands to glue them, screw them, and hold them against the hull by ourselves."

But Bronson had spent more than he could admit to himself on extra equipment, and now called a halt. "We'll do without," he said, and they were able to glue the outer gunwales into place by the unaided force of their thumbs. There were cracks where the fit wasn't dead flush, but on the whole the correct curve of the hull was followed. It was the inner gunwales that brought disaster. As they were trying to force the first of them to fit, there was a frighteningly loud crack. The piece snapped at the stress-point. The kit had come from Great Britain.

Bronson felt his eyes bug in his head. Minute points of light danced in them as he shut and opened his lids. He said, "There is no difficulty that cannot be overcome."

His wife said, "If you say that once more, at any time, I'll leave you."

He looked at her. He saw that she meant it.

"This afternoon if necessary."

"We've done enough for this summer," said Bronson. "I don't want to spoil everybody's vacation." His wife made no reply. They gathered up the fragments in silence, and put them away for the winter. The following spring, they were able to have a replacement gunwale shaped locally by hand. They bought a dozen large clamps. They fastened those last few pieces to the hull with loud and cheerful cries. Then they sanded it down and sanded it again and again. Fitted the rudder together. Screwed on oarlocks, pin ties, eyes, varnished, varnished, sanded, painted, sanded, painted, painted, painted, painted . . . rigged. Hoisted their burgee.

The next summer, reaching and running on his blue lake, Bronson remembered nothing of what had passed.

NEW COUNTRY

THEY'D been staying in a borrowed apartment at the corner of Lawrence so the simplest thing to do was go straight up through Hogg's Hollow and get onto 401 going east from Yonge. Early Saturday afternoon, bright and cold in mid-March, with a rush of wind along the flanks of the car making it judder and fishtail at highway speeds, a light car, bouncy and jumpy and peppy. Lester didn't like to spend money on big cars, always drove a Nova or a Fairmont, changing them every October. He could always rely on his car.

He swung the six-months-old Nova across the service lanes, working his blinker lights and reading the rear-view mirrors expertly, and entered the eastbound through traffic at sixty-five. Molly never spoke while he was executing this manoeuvre. She liked to watch his face as his eyes flicked from the road to the mirror overhead, then to the left window, then across her to the right. He had had extra-large mirrors installed on every car they'd ever owned; you could see almost all the way around behind you if they were properly adjusted. Delivery of a new car each October meant an afternoon spent adjusting the mirrors for maximum visibility to the rear.

She waited for him to say something. When they first used to make this trip he would start to chat, on the way back to Stoverville, somewhere around Morningside Drive where the freeway drew away from the suburbs. These days he took longer to thaw. 401 spanned six full lanes of brisk traffic as far as Oshawa, and was being widened there, strewn with construction signs and warnings, and suddenly disappearing shoulders, arbitrary ramp-closings sprouting where wholly unlooked-for. Lester liked to hold his peace until the traffic thinned perceptibly, often saying little or nothing as far as Ajax or Whitby, then initiating a conversation only to lapse into glum silence as he negotiated the cramped outmoded underpasses of Oshawa.

"Ritson Road," he said suddenly, sighing. They were already almost forty miles along their way home. "Well, and how was she?"

"Brenda?"

"Just a minute till I get around this idiot."

She sat and waited; the seat-back punched powerfully at her shoulders; the blinker arrow came on; the car swayed.

"Brenda."

"Bad. She was bad, Lester. I think it was what we thought. She doesn't know. She didn't say anything about that; all she wanted to do was talk about her fibroids. I wanted to laugh, God forgive me. You know, Lester, I used to have this funny image of fibroids, like little pieces of candy. Like chocolates. I don't know why that was. Women talk about these things all the time and I don't suppose any of us has ever seen one. So you kind of make a picture in your mind of what they look like, and for years I've always imagined fibroids sitting in a row like fancy chocolates in a tray in an expensive candy store. In little crinkled brown paper pants. I think I've been seeing them as a lot of little Laura Secords. And I don't even know what a fibroid is."

"It must be made of fibre, judging by the word."

"I guess it is, but that doesn't tell me a thing. I believe they're little tumours of some kind. 'My fibroids were benign,' she kept saying, and she'd give me this awful grin. I think she suspects. I think it's what we thought. Way inside. I wish you could have seen her. I'd have liked to know what you thought. She had a poor colour, very very pale, very dry skin. And she used to have that lovely skin without a mark or a wrinkle on it. I wanted to cry, but I didn't dare show what I was thinking. All her clothes are two sizes too big for her and the worst thing is she suspects. I mean she sounded so beat-up and awful. She said her gynecologist was just awful to her, wouldn't call her by her first name on account of the feminists; it was 'Mrs. this' and 'Mrs. that.' Never a friendly word, and the usual comic insults. 'We'll just take a little tuck in it to tighten you up,' he said, poking in her vaginal canal. It was so offensive. She said she felt she was the size of a motorman's glove inside, too big for fun. 'I'm all saggy in there,' she kept saying. 'I'm so ashamed, I'm so lapsed and saggy that Irving can't get any purchase. No wonder he never wants to do it anymore. It isn't that he's too small. I never felt he was too small. I've got a hole in me the size of a circus tent.' Then she started to cry buckets. 'Oh Molly,' she said, 'never let them do it to you. I don't know how I let that man talk me into it. I think he just does them for the money. The government pays, so why not? It's like tonsils; they used to do tonsils routinely but they don't anymore. Now it's hysterectomies. They see a woman fifty years old, and they want to gut her just because it's the in-thing to do. Don't let them try it on you, Molly. The cure is worse than the disease.' And she laughed. I don't know what disease she was thinking of, maybe pregnancy."

"At least they did have kids."

"They never see the kids now. Neither of the boys visited her in the hospital, and when Arlene came they had a shattering argument, according to Brenda. She said Arlene said she was faking it, can you imagine? I mean the day before, practically, they'd removed the poor woman's womb surgically, and her daughter accuses her of malingering. Maybe she expected to see it in a bottle on the bedside table, for proof. They've never got along, and the boys are off somewhere, and nobody knows where. Irving is worse than useless about it. He can't control them."

"I think Irving has his own problems."

"Yes, and poor Brenda has them to think about while she's lying there. 'They do this routinely,' she kept saying. 'They recommend it for everybody. It wasn't as if there was anything seriously wrong. Wait till I get up and around. I'm too thin. Everybody tells me I'm too thin.' Like that. Now tell me, was she just kidding me? Or herself?"

"I'd say she probably doesn't know for sure."

"Well nobody does."

Lester kept his eyes fixed on the big camper in front of him, a home-on-wheels with a high centre of gravity and a tendency to sway in a crosswind. He eased into the passing lane.

"Lester, did Irving say something to you?"

"Just a second."

He flipped the right blinker on.

"She's my sister. I've got a right to know if anybody does."

"Molly, when they got inside she was like fishnet. All they could do was sew her up and forget about it. I talked to Irving on Thursday night while you were at the hospital."

"My God! Where?"

"Oh everywhere. Liver, womb, ovaries."

"She's younger than I am."

"Yeah, what is it, about two years?"

"I don't think she's fifty yet, honey. I was born in May and she was born in early June. The fifth. The fifth of June. She'll be fifty next June the fifth."

Lester said nothing and Molly quavered, "The poor thing." They covered a short distance in heavy silence. Then the car mounted an elegant rising curve, five miles east of Oshawa along the shoulder of a knoll which overlooks the lake. At this point the shoreline curves in under the hillside, and motorists have a view of the water across a bay or inlet—technically perhaps a bight—which always seems calm. It is the last place on the highway to present a prospect of the water before Kingston, a hundred miles further down. Lester used to enjoy the sight of the lake; today he ignored it.

The car sped inland towards Bowmanville and the Flying Dutchman Motel.

"Sam didn't look any too good either," said Lester. "I don't think he's a well man. His hemorrhoids are a curse, he says, and you know, you can tell from the way he walks. He has this air cushion in the office. I used to think it was funny, but it isn't funny really. All he wants to talk about is his proctologist. I was forty-five before I knew what a proctologist did. Now it's all I hear about. He can't concentrate on the line. How can you talk to buyers when all the time you're afraid to sit down? It's undignified; it's painful; it's on your mind and you wonder if they'll have to cut you. He told me this horror story about some friend who had the operation for hemorrhoids, and was he ever sick? When he woke up he couldn't go to the toilet. Either way. After a couple of days they had to introduce a catheter; otherwise he'd have got kidney-poisoning or uremia or whatever. I'm no doctor. They shove this long tube up through your thing, you know, and it drains off the piss. It hurts like hell. Just from the shock of the operation, it's no picnic. I don't know about Sammy. He hasn't been the same since Phil went. It was Phil who created Style-Made Sportswear. Sam was always really more of the accountant than anything. He doesn't know how to talk to buyers, or dress a display suite; he doesn't have the feel for it. He's anxious all the time and the customers can sense it; they know they've got him over a barrel. He has to do business so he can discount the orders and keep his cash flow in line. If the paper isn't available the bank gets upset. Sam is an accountant; he can judge to a second when the credit man from the bank is going to be on the line. He's always had this line with the Commerce, oh, years and years. Now they say that the industry is going to be phased out. They don't trust what the government says about imports, and nobody knows what the hell is happening. Getting goods into the stores is like a sport; you have to relax and swing easy and not frighten them off by pushing. It's hard to go on shipping to somebody who's in that frame of mind."

"Lester, he's your own brother."

"He's not the same. He hasn't been the same for two years, not since Phil died. Imagine the shock! They were sitting in the office in the factory around ten-thirty in the morning..."

"I don't want to hear this again."

"... and Sammy hears the canteen wagon roll up. He says to Phil, 'What'll I get you?' They used to take turns buying, I mean for thirty years. 'Get me a coffee, no cream, and a roll of plain Tums,' says Phil. 'Okay.' Sam goes out, gets the stuff, a doughnut for him and the Tums for Phil, and he goes back into the office and there he is, lying back in the chair with this look on his face. Gone. Like somebody switched out the light, and Sam says he didn't look peaceful. He looked like somebody hit him one hell of a smack on the side of the head. Sammy's standing there with this roll of plain Tums and the coffee getting cold in his hand. It stays in your mind."

Molly said, "It doesn't have to stay in your mind. It's not your affair."

"It's as much my affair as Brenda is your affair. He's my brother."

"You've never been as close as we were."

"He's a big account. Half our production goes to Style-Made. Almost half. Thirty percent anyway. I should have seen it coming. I blame myself."

"What could you have done about it?"

"It was losing that cutter did it. Some people might think I just wanted to unload every possible yard of goods on Style-Made, but it was never like that. You can't be greedy. You've got to supply quality in a good selection of widths; you've got to stay abreast of design trends. I admit it, I hate polyester. It makes me feel cold all the time. But it has definite uses if you're trying to produce sportswear at a price, so we have to be in a position to supply cotton and poly at any time in nice colours and patterns, no matter how I feel about it. I've given the trade maximum convenience and I've had plenty of customers. Maybe I made a mistake by selling so much to Phil and Sammy but they were always right there asking for our product. You don't say to your brother, 'I can only let you have so much this season. I've got you on a quota.' The effect of it is, I'm very tightly linked in with Style-Made, in a tough marketing situation, and they've always got maximum yield from our fabrics. That old man was a wonder."

"Highlands of Hastings," said Molly.

"What?"

"You missed the sign. 'You are now entering the Highlands of Hastings regional vacation area.'"

"Already? We're making good time. We'll be home for dinner."

Molly shrugged her shoulders up and down vigorously, and wound her head on her neck. "It's around three," she said, "it won't be dark for hours and hours; the days are getting longer."

"Old Everett Stapleton. He was a wonder. He could cut more pieces from a length of goods than you'd believe. You never used to see their factory knee-deep in remnants. He could look at a length and see, right in the flat cloth, how many garments could be made up out of it, including sleeves and gussets, like some kind of a sculptor. The designers used to take instructions from him. If the design couldn't be cut economically from the goods, he'd show them how to re-work it.

He'd re-do the sketches, right in the cutting room. Phil used to talk about him with tears in his eyes. Then he died, and they've never been able to replace him. After that, their ordering was less precise; they bought more, and I'll bet they produced fewer dozen garments from what they bought. A cutter like that . . . almost an artist, you'd have to say. I think it was losing him that brought on Phil's coronary. It isn't as though Phil was an old man. He was younger than Sam. I think Phil and I were about the same age. He always used to take good care of himself, then to go just like that."

Across the highway above the westbound lanes, a high ridge loomed up in a long gentle arc along the roadside, cutting off the view of the sky. They could see a long way ahead, perhaps two miles. Then the eastbound lanes banked down into a valley and were lost from view. The movement of the car and the presence of the high ridge beside them gave the impression that the car was floating idly and slowly towards a whirlpool.

"Highlands of Hastings," said Lester suddenly. "I wonder what the Highlands of Hastings are exactly? I wonder what they look like." He gave a sharp yank at the wheel. The car veered into the passing lane, then back to the right. Molly stared at him doubtfully.

"I've been going up and down the 401 for twenty years," he said discontentedly, "Stoverville to Toronto, Toronto to Stoverville. I've gotten to know this run too damn well. Glen Miller Road, Wooler, Salmon River. I might as well be on tracks. I never see what's off to the side. I've never had a look at the Highlands of Hastings."

He stared fixedly at the high ground swelling up on the other side of the road.

Molly said, "Keep your eyes on the highway, Lester."

"I wonder what's happening in the Highlands of Hastings tonight. Is there really anybody there? Sometimes I get the impression that big ridge up there is nothing but a canvas drop. Here! Let's go and have a look at what's behind it." They passed a sign which said, *Hwy 30 North-South Brighton Next Exit Only 2 km.*

"Kilometres, kilometres, why couldn't they have left it miles? Messing around with everything. Can't keep their hands off anything." He put on the right blinker and turned onto the exit ramp. The car slowed abruptly, running down to the stop sign at the sideroad, deep in a cupped hollow to one side of 401. They sat at the stop sign, the car idling quietly in neutral, looking around them at the wholly foreign scene.

"Left," said Lester, "we'll go left; we'll have a look at the back country."

"It's past four o'clock."

"You said yourself, it won't be dark till late. It's almost spring—according to the calendar—and the fields seem clear. Come on, we've seen 401 too many times. We'll go up to Highway 7, and go home the back way. It'll be something to do for a change. It doesn't really matter if we get in tonight." He paused, then said as if amazed at the notion, "We could get a motel room; we could go the rest of the way tomorrow. After all, why not?"

A car drew up behind them and honked softly. Lester gave a slight start, then put the car in motion, turning left. The ground began to rise at once; they were climbing up a steep hill as they came out of the underpass on the other side of 401. The highway narrowed abruptly as they came up the hillside, and a tight curve around a spur of high ground concealed the freeway from sight behind them. The motor whined, and Lester shifted into second. He said, "I haven't done that in years." The car continued to climb for some moments.

"We're going up through that ridge," said Molly suddenly. "It isn't a piece of scenery, it's quite real." The road wound slowly upwards to the right for another mile and a half; they might have climbed three hundred and fifty feet. Then it emerged into a terrain which was utterly novel to them, perfectly unlike the open countryside around Toronto or the limestone ridges, the granite shelves and narrow beds of good soil north of Stoverville. This was a central Ontario landscape seen by fewer and fewer people. They felt transported back to the 1930s. Highway 30 had the grassy ditches and narrow shoulders and Queen's Highway markers, the cracked surfaces and sudden, poorly-marked curves and intersections of the thirties. Molly felt the pace and rhythm of the car slow and adapt itself to the altered driving conditions. She felt no apprehension. Lester was, if anything, a better driver at these speeds than at seventy. She began to enjoy the deliberate motion, staring out into the deserted fields—what she could see of them—with curiosity, and real surprise at their unfamiliar aspect. Shown them in a photograph, perhaps on a postcard, she would not have been able to identify them as any part of the province she knew. She had a vague impression that they resembled some part of France. Even the earth tones in the fields, where small snowbanks lingered in hedges and along the depressions of drainage ditches, seemed darker and more distant, oddly withdrawn. There was a slight peculiarity to the lie of the country which at first perplexed her.

An elderly International pick-up, with a homemade stake body rattling loudly, came at them all at once around a curve, passing very near. Its front wheels had a pronounced shimmy. Lester took a quick look over his shoulder, disturbed by the narrow margin for passing. He dropped to forty. "Close enough," he said in a low voice, "maybe even too close. I wonder where we are exactly. Could you dig out the map? There's an Ontario road map in there somewhere."

She opened the glove compartment with an increasingly intense sense of *déjà vu*. When they had been an engaged couple, and for some short time after their marriage, Lester and Molly had made the usual weekend trips around their countryside along the back roads, on picnics and an occasional hayride. She always used to read the map for him, she remembered. She always had the customary comic trouble about re-folding the free road maps from the gas stations. They were no longer free, she reflected. Most stations couldn't be bothered to stock them, and those which did charged a dollar for a map.

"We're going north on Highway 30," she announced a moment later. "In a minute we'll be—no, here it is—we're going through Orland."

They passed a corner where a green arrow pointed east-wards. It said "Wooler."

"My gosh," said Lester, "so that's where Wooler is. I've never actually believed in the existence of Wooler. I wonder if there are five proofs for the existence of Wooler?"

"I'm enjoying this," said Molly. All the same she felt certain distinct qualms. She was not entirely happy with the prospect of the high, short fields. They were curiously broken and folded and they fell away out of view disturbingly, to reveal sudden deeps and shadows. It was still bright afternoon on the upper ground where the highway ran along between the small farms, but to either side the fields slanted away and down into obscurity. Here and there the entire rectangular outline of a field could be seen, a quarter-mile away from the road, lying athwart the pitch of neighbouring small hills, like a wet hand-kerchief draped on a radiator to dry. These fields had a convo-luted up-and-down shape. Nearer the highway the enclosures seemed—and doubtless were—smaller, humped up beside the road. The fields were in work already, most of them, freshly turned furrows awaiting the seed, perhaps already seeded and concealing new growth from her inexpert eye. There were no people visible in the fields, not so much as a tractor. It's late Saturday afternoon, she thought, and they've all gone into . . . into . . . she consulted the map. Where would they go on Satur-day night? Codrington?

They went through Codrington as this question crossed her mind, and it was at once evident that Codrington was not where the crowds went on Saturday night; there was nobody

339

in town. One or two farmhouse lights began to contest the late sunshine. Soon it would be time for dinner. She thought of Brenda and Sammy and Phil, briefly considered the prospect of reviving that conversation, rejected it, and waited for Lester to say something. He was concentrating on the road.

"My God, what country," he muttered. The car bounced and swerved. "We ought to be out of the high country pretty soon. Isn't Campbellford somewhere around here? I seem to remember..."

"Just a minute, just a minute." She rearranged the unhandy map. "There isn't room for this thing."

"It ought to be somewhere up ahead. We ought to look for a place to spend the night. I'll tell you, I wouldn't want to come up this way in the dark. I'm having to fight to hold the car steady."

"We go through a place called, just a minute till I get my glasses on, called Meyersberg, that's it. It can't be very big, so you'd better keep an eye open. After that we ought to be down out of these hills—which make me feel uncomfortable. Highlands of Hastings indeed! We ought to hit the Trent system somewhere up around Meyersberg, and after that it can't be more than a few miles to Campbellford. What makes you think of Campbellford particularly?"

"I just happen to remember it's around here. I saw a picture in some book. And there's your precious Meyersberg, look at that! It's a ghost town. I noticed in the paper the other day, last Saturday, an advertisement for a book called *Ghost Towns of Ontario*. It kind of made me think."

Molly folded the map carefully and put it away. She felt the car begin to descend. All at once, off to the right, a long stretch of water came in sight, broadening out as they approached, with huge shadows lying across it. As they came down the side of the hill—in second gear—they lost the sunlight, and the water looked flat and black and very cold.

"It isn't moving at all," Molly whispered.

"Is that a lake or the river?"

"I don't know what it is," she said, "and I'm not going to struggle with that damn map again. There's no current in that water. Look! Not a ripple."

"We'll be into town in a few minutes," said Lester. "I can see lights ahead. Oh, somebody else I forgot to mention dropped dead in Toronto while we were there. Do you remember Lionel Breitbart?"

"No," she said, "I don't and I don't want to talk about it. What's the matter with you, Lester? Where did the middle of our lives go? When we used to take this trip what we talked about was who was getting engaged. Who was getting married... having a baby..."

"We'll find a place," he said through his teeth. He speeded up, heading into a blind curve.

CROSBY

J ANIE ended with a conga line—soldiers and teen-aged girls weaving in effervescence through Edward Arnold's house—his house in the movie, not in Holmby Hills. Robert Hutton embraced Joyce Reynolds as Ann Harding shed motherly tears and Richard "Dick" Erdman kicked the edge of the rolled-up carpet in sexual disappointment. *The end* said the final title and the lights came halfway on in the Rialto, Manning Avenue at College Street, the traveller closed, a baby spot focused on it suddenly and a man carried a microphone and a trailing cord onstage, *shreeee, shreee, shhh, shhh, ting.* One two testing one two. *Shhh ting.* The spotlight switched to the pit placard: *Henny Mendrick and His Blue Boys.* Mendrick, a small, contorted pianist, stood, bowed repeatedly, sat, counted off in four-four and the band attacked "I Don't Want to Walk Without You." Half an hour till the second show starts and four contestants tonight, ladies and gentlemen, four, and here they are. Let's give them a big welcome.

From Harbord Collegiate, that teen-age cutup Mocky Raphael!

A skinny kid bounded from the wings into total silence.

"Hi everybody," he said in a shaking voice, "say, you know, the mice in my apartment. I mean. My apartment. My apartment is so small, my apartment is so small that the mice have to hunch up. The mice are round-shouldered, get it? My apartment...

And from Trinity-K Club, that popular fugitive from Borrah Minnevitch, Jeff Terpko and his chromatic mouth-organs.

And cute little Sherry Church from Clinton Street with her million-dollar tap shoes.

Loud applause, confused whispers.

"I don't understand. What does he mean? 'My mice are stunted.' Is this funny?"

"Be quiet, don't embarrass the boy!"

First prize, a twenty-five-dollar War Savings Certificate. Second prize, a ten-dollar War Savings Certificate. Third prize, a five-dollar Certificate, and every contestant will receive a two-dollar page of War Savings Stamps as an entry prize.

"Big deal, there are only four of them."

"Shhhhh!"

And finally, to get things rolling, our fourth contestant, from the Mars Grill, the singing cashier...

"The singing what, what?"

A final adolescent strode into the spotlight and laid hands on the mike, which emitted strangulated whistling sounds. The band gradually subsided. Mendrick glared up at the contestant's feet which protruded over the edge of the stage apron above his head.

"What is that man dressed like? Is he a golfer?"

"What kind of a golfer is that? A singer maybe?"

The singing cashier was distinctively dressed in beige corduroy slacks and crepe-soled sporting shoes, and an expensive woollen sport shirt, open at the neck with long points to its spreading collar, in a mellow pattern of soft narrow red stripes on a grey ground. He wore a pale brown gabardine pork-pie hat with the brim snapped down over his eyes.

"...sing for us tonight?"

"...thought I might take a hack at 'Pennies from Heaven' in B-flat, if Henny and the Gainsboroughs can find the page. Shall we attempt it the way we rehearsed it, men? Here we go, now."

"What is he talking about?"

"A long time ago," said the singer in a voice of surprising depth and roughness, perhaps assumed for the occasion, "a million years BC."

Mendrick executed dazzling runs between the phrases of the verse, which seemed to distract the performer from his purpose. He quickened the pace of his words.

"...and you shouldn't be afraid for..."

The singer drew a long breath, paused, looked into the pit with trepidation, then took the first chorus with a focused vocal tone, in the period style of a thousand competing baritones. "Every time it rains, it rains/PENnies from heaven."

The audience sighed; they knew where they were and could appreciate the performance without perplexity. Soon the opening number ended, and the contestant ran rapidly through a prepared polysyllabic patter—his own description of the continuity.

"Have to fill in a few moments with a segment of prepared polysyllabic patter hot off the tonsils, while the maestro flexes those tired pinkies. Little stiff, Henny? Now for my second once-around in adrenalin time, I propose to give you a taste of a virtuous little number I picked up first in old Spokane."

"How old is this boy?"

"Shut up, Daddy."

"You're speaking to your father, Vincent."

"Sorry."

"He's never been near Spokane."

"Small chart entitled 'In a Little Spanish Town' we used to violate in the company of Mister Skin Young. Nice and easy now, men."

Wasn't that just great, folks? I think we've got a solid contender here for that big winner's certificate. Let's hear your applause for Dom Squatrito from the Mars Grill.

"That's where I've seen that boy! He's a counterman there."

"Daddy!"

The tap dancer came on and charmed the audience as much with her underwear as with her steps, which were vigorous but inexact. She clutched a frilly umbrella, sang in a piping voice such standards as "The Merry-go-round Broke Down" and "Good Ship Lollipop" in a style exceedingly reminiscent of her model, and even of *her* model, a good Toronto girl named Smith.

Mocky Raphael confused everybody with his jokes.

"My uncle Pierre..."

"His uncle Pierre?"

"My uncle Pierre is so unlucky if it was raining borscht he would be caught without a fork. Also he would be missing the potato."

"What? What did he say?"

"He doesn't have the good hands, my uncle Pierre, not like Goody Rosen . . . but seriously, folks, when Goody Rosen was called up to the Dodgers; the Brooklyn Dodgers, that is, when Goody arrived at the ball park the manager said to him, 'What's a nice Jewish boy doing in a place like this?' And Goody said, "Beats Spadina Avenue.""

All right folks, there we are. That's our contest for this Wednesday night, and remember every Wednesday night is Amateur Night at the Rialto. And now for the big moment we've all been waiting for. If the contestants will step out next to me in a row, please, I'll hold the envelope with the Grand Prize of twenty-five dollars in War Savings over their heads and your applause will decide the winner. From left to right as we come across the stage. First the king of the harmonica, Jeff Terpko.

The musician bounded forward, shook himself energetically, produced certain feline squeals on his instrument. The audience clapped listlessly and he retreated.

And here again is Mocky Raphael from the Collegiate.

"Great to be here, folks, you've been a wonderful audience. I love ya."

Ho hum.

And Dom Squatrito, the old groaner from the Grill.

Big chord from Henny Mendrick, ripple of "Where the Blue of the Night" and tumultuous applause.

"He's got good voice, that boy, but he should change his name. Whoever heard of an entertainer called Dom Squatrito?"

"Squatrito, Sinatra, what's to tell?"

"That Sinatra will never amount to anything. And I'm telling you, Squatrito, it's equally nothing, a big fat zero."

And that tiny darling in her frills and tap shoes, little Miss Sherry Church. Let's hear it for Sherry.

More tumultuous applause.

Okay everybody, looks like we've got two winners here. Whaddaya say? I mean whaddaya think? Do we pick a winner between them or do we give them BOTH a twenty-five dollar War Savings Certificate and call it square, courtesy of Premium Theatres and Morty Blum?

"Split it! Split it! Give it to little Sherry! Aaaahhh, give it to the singer. Give it to the little girl. G'wan."

Glares between contestants, fixed smiles. MC into the wings.

Here we are, ladies and gents, right here in this purple envelope, the tie-breaker, another twenty-five dollar Certificate which goes to your local favourite and mine, Dom Squatrito, the crooning cashier and counterman from the Mars Grill, where everything is prepared in the open kitchen in sanitary surroundings before your own eyes. That's our intermission entertainment for tonight, ladies and gentlemen, and now settle back in your seats and enjoy a good cry with Bet Davis and Paul Henreid. House lights down and out and in the wings the contestants find three dollars each in their envelopes. Meal money.

"Mommy. Mommy. I want my money. Where's my twenty-five dollars?"

"Hush, honey, you'll annoy the patrons."

"But I want my War Savings Certificate."

Those old neighbourhood theatres had equipment for stage shows, even dressing rooms with mirrors, and counters for making up. Dom went into the room he'd used before the performance, hung his pork-pie on a nail, loosened the woollen sport shirt, then decided to take it off. He sat at one of the mirrors and began to rub cold cream across his face. As he was wiping the cream and makeup off, the comedian looked around the edge of the door.

"Gee, makeup," he said. "You're a real pro. I guess you really won, eh? I mean the little kid always gets the applause just for being small and cute. I mean you really won. But then, if they give us each three dollars, what difference . . . it was three you got, eh?"

"There's the envelope, you open it."

"That's right, three. Well, I guess we all form part of the show really. They like to have somebody to boo, like that poor bastard with the mouth-organ."

Dom finished wiping his face. He washed his head and shoulders vigorously, feeling like John Payne. He towelled out an ear. Using his deepest speaking voice, he said, "Got to try to stay on the fairway, son. Got to keep that little white pebble rolling for the cup."

Mocky Raphael's face glowed with admiration. "Listen, are you *related*? I think you sound just like . . ."

"I sound like myself."

"You do? I mean, sure you do,"

"If you start off by imitating somebody else's act, you'll always be number two. You have to get your own style, hear? Got to buh buh buh boo in through the middle of the people's hearts."

"If you're going to be in show business, you should change your name."

"Yeah, I've been thinking about that. Any suggestions?"

"Are you Jewish?"

"Italian."

"Don't pick the name 'Sinatra': ha ha ha."

"I was thinking of 'Don Stanley' actually."

They could hear the melancholy, persuasive soundtrack of the movie, all mixed in with what they were talking about. Feeling encouraged, Mocky sidled around the door jamb and into the dressing room. "I love these old neighbourhood theatres," he said. "I wish I could've been in vaudeville."

"You could play clubs."

"How come you know so much about it? You're no older than I am."

"I read the *New Acts* column in *Variety*."

"The what?"

Dom explained himself.

"Where can I get that?" said Mocky excitedly.

"The smoke shops in the big hotels, and for some reason the United Cigar Store at St. Clair and Yonge. What do you think about the name 'Don Stanley'?"

"I like it. Aren't there some other singers called 'Don'?"

"Don Cornell. Don Cherry, the golfing singer. I figure there's room for one more. Come on, let's get out of here. If you want to be my guest, I can arrange a free burger at the Mars."

"So that's the way you talk normally?"

"You can't be on all the time, sweetheart."

When he finished high school and quit his job at the restaurant, Dom Squatrito became Don Stanley permanently. He changed his barber, and the way he combed his hair. As a stopgap, until his career as a singer materialized, he took a full-time job in the Federal Civil Service, beginning as a temporary Clerk Grade One, on the lowest rung of the clerical staff. He was paid seventy dollars a month, and after three years on the job, in the late forties, he took the Civil Service examination for clerical staff up to Clerk Grade Four—an unspecialized, general information, multiple-choice test, in which you blacked-in little boxes with a special pencil, so that the test paper could be scanned by an electronic device. This was an early example of the "mechanical brain" approach to office management.

"Lucked into a high score by staying relaxed," said Don modestly.

He had received the highest score of anybody in the province.

"Gave me a severe case of the whips and jingles when I heard the word."

"Oh, Donald," said Nancy, a young woman with a heart-shaped face and soft brown hair, who pursued him until the fifth reel when he folded her carefully in his arms, almost ad-lib. Just at this time, two years after he took the examination, he got an appointment to the "temporary-permanent" staff of the Treasury Department Bureau in the Unemployment Insurance Commission, as Clerk Grade Three, an unusually senior appointment for a young man of twenty-three. For all practical purposes "temporary-permanent" meant permanent. It wasn't till another six years had gone by—until the age of rock began—that Don finally acquired a permanent appointment with full association benefits and a transfer to Ottawa. That was the year that Presley released "You Ain't Nothin' But a Houn' Dog," and Eddie Fisher disappeared from view like foam in an empty beer glass. Buddy Clark had died a decade earlier. Where was Johnny Johnston?

Johnny Johnston was starring in a movie called *Rock Around the Clock* featuring Bill Haley and the Comets, and the Platters. In Ottawa, Don Stanley's hair was beginning to thin. He considered a toupée, dearly wished to try one, but settled for a collection of hats instead, a yachting cap, a baseball cap, in winter a fur hat of Russian dimensions, very suitable for Ottawa. He was out of the clerical ranks now, with an Administrative Officer grade and a clogged in-tray, long gone from the UIC. In the mid-fifties he took every possible night course, summer course, sometimes even regularly scheduled daytime courses at Carleton and at Ottawa U. He improved his vocabulary until it was of truly impressive proportions. He wasn't fully conscious of what he was doing when he moved in a casual, splay-footed, sauntering golfer's gait, and said things to his superiors like, "Got to keep those workers' gnarled digits digging in the old tax bowl, sahib." He remained an enigma to the mandarins, who grasped nevertheless that Stanley was a comer, a man to be watched, industrious, trustworthy; and above all relaxed. He was known to be studying the French language as a means of self-improvement, perhaps also as an extension of his colourful line of chatter. He wore a beret to the office several times in the late fifties. He took his B.A. in Economics at Carleton after seven arduous years of intermittent course work, and finally married Nancy in 1958. It hadn't been a courtship of the early rock type. Don wasn't a pump jockey, a draftee, an itinerant farm labourer, or in the jailhouse. He was a balding, pipe-smoking, slightly plump, self-made civil servant of thirty with a brand-new diploma and a notion in the back of his mind about getting a master's degree in public finance. He had the great merit of never discussing his special field away from the office. Few were the friends of Don Stanley who suspected what he did at work in an office nearer and nearer that distant region where deputy-ministers revolved.

Unaffected by Elvis, Nancy and Don were wed at the end of their ordinary courtship, thereafter working out the implications of an idyll. Never a public quarrel, though privately Don could be stern, even withdrawn. He toted a putter around the garden, practised his swing continually, never went near tee or green. He carried himself more determinedly erect and springy as the sixties came on. He used to come up the stairs to the conference room at a kind of slow, show-business jog, imitated from the way the acts came on in the clubs. This way of moving and discoursing made Don unique in Ottawa circles, federal government circles. It somehow came to be a special advantage to him, an inimitable aspect of his appearance and behaviour, this possession of indefinable show-business associations. Don used to sing with a band, they would say, Don was a band singer. This was not true. He could have had a show-business career, they said enviously, the Senior Administrators and the Grade Elevens. The only man in government circles who came out of the entertainment world!

"You can't faze Don Stanley."

"He's so relaxed."

"He goes hunting up back of Kaladar. He has a cottage up the Gatineau."

In Canadian life, Don stood out as possessing traits coveted by the Northern soul, never gained: insouciance, charm, glamour. He might rise high on the basis of this exotic bundle of moral gifts. Presleyism never touched him, indeed he repudiated it. He collected big-band records of the thirties, and the 78s of the great vocalists. His collection was sometimes talked about on Ottawa radio as late as the mid-sixties. After that time, of course, a curious decade descended when even Presley, Little Richard, even Fats Domino, seemed voices from before an age of ice, the thirties and forties inconceivably remote. Strange, almost totally unpredictable consequence of Beatlemania: the upwards mobility of Don Stanley stopped. How many cases can there be anywhere of career civil servants whose promotions to senior level were compromised, finally made impossible, by Sergeant Pepper? Don got stuck in the middle grades of the hierarchy for ten years because it was impossible for him to wear sideburns or to let his hair grow long.

Don and Nancy came from that wasted generation too young to serve in the Second World War, too old to enjoy the second half of the century. There is an immense gulf between people born before and after 1945. The postwar babies were the first generation to be weaned on TV; they never knew depression or war or the really great cinema before TV destroyed it. Presley, who seemed the herald of the new dawn, was ten years too old to belong to the new generation, and as he aged he lapsed more and more into the morality of the nice guy, the gift Cadillacs, the style of the crooners. To hear Elvis sing "Blue Hawaii" was to sense the decadence of a great style.

Only a few sensitive barometers like Don Stanley ever recorded all the implications of this evolution. Don had never in all his life hated anybody until he heard Dylan. Then he knew hate, a purifying emotion, purgative, clarifying. There could be no compromise between what he, Don Stanley, and Don Cornell, Don Cherry, Al Martino, Tony Bennett, Eddie Fisher, Buddy Clark, Johnny Johnston, Andy Russell, Johnny Desmond, Dick Todd, Dick Haymes, and the great Perry Como stood for; and the Dylan commotions.

"Motorcycle accidents," Don cursed.

"Drugging. Overalls. *Overalls!* I don't suppose that boy has ever done a stroke of work in his life. Dresses like a ditch digger. Like hell, the times they are a-changin'. The times are staying right where they are. You hear me, Nancy? Right where they are."

"Don, I've never seen you like this."

"We've got to get rid of Bob Dylan! Maybe he's been crippled for life in that accident. Best thing for everybody, really."

"Gosh, Dad, there'd always be the Beatles."

"And the Stones," said a baby voice.

Don swung back his putter and broke a floor lamp. He blamed the breakage on Mick Jagger, and in later years believed that the rock star had actually invaded his living room and smashed the object with his own hands. Don was not entirely balanced on the subject of contemporary popular music; he felt victimized by it, as though he had quite unwillingly descended into hell, or at least the underworld. He wasn't sure that he would ever climb out, and went through a curious, private agony when he found he was beginning to like *Abbey Road*. He tried over a few of the songs in secret, and was simultaneously relieved and horrified to hear Perry Como singing "Something" and, what was worse, singing it damned well in his own style, a derivative style, Don thought.

Was he ever going to get out of middle administration? How? You can't change your whole scheme of conduct in the middle of a life, can you? He was stuck with what he had. Youngsters began to appear in the office, actually in his office, on his staff, with *hair on their chins*, bellbottoms in stripes.

We can't go much lower, he thought.

It wasn't so much the drugs. He didn't mind about drugs. Musicians had been using drugs ever since he could remember. Not Bix, not Louis, but plenty of others. Touring was hard, off the stand at two a.m. and into the bus for the next city, bus all night, maybe two hundred miles through the Alleghenies. A musician might smoke a little something now and then. To hear these kids tell it, they'd invented grass.

It's the clothes. It's the hair. Where are all my hats? He never appeared out of the office without a hat, as though a photographer might snap his bare dome and embarrass him as a matter of public record. I wouldn't mind the music; it's the dirt and the grease in the hair.

Then Dylan began to have trouble with his Sarah, and was no more seen on the road. Rumour abounded. Dylan had been caught up to heaven in a fiery chariot, said the children. He has gone to hell, said Don. Brian Epstein died and McCartney met Linda, litigation over the Apple copyrights ensued. John and Yoko went off by themselves and by 1970 life began to appear tenable again. One more great piece of good fortune and the trapped civil servant might still break out into bliss. He wasn't really old; he was in the early forties and that isn't old. What would happen if he never got out, if his hardly learned French proved inadequate, if he didn't earn his bilingualism bonus? What if the new deputy-minister didn't like him? He was forty-five. Dylan announced a North American tour, and one Sunday morning Don heard a smooth veteran voice lining out "Hey Jude" the way it ought to be sung, and he shuddered, and soon after the Rolling Thunder sounded briefly in the skies, then broke up, was silent.

Why do we hope for the return of vanished heroes, Don wondered, when the best of heroes never goes away? Epstein is dead; Harrison is a plagiarist; Ringo is in the movies; John and Yoko aren't getting along; and Wings are moving, but only at the speed of sound. A promoter offers thirty million for a reunion. What would he give for the Second Coming?

BEATLES REUNITED?
REUNION IMPOSSIBLE: LENNON

Don got a major promotion in 1975, his first move upwards in ten years. Back to Toronto where he'd started out. He knew that this was the end, that he'd been dismissed from the hallways of power, that his smooth cheeks and shiny dome were stigmata, badges of a strange media martyrdom. I will persist, he told himself, and I will return. In the Treasury in Toronto he was at the top, but where the top was not—as far as he could go. Something stirred in his conscience: I should never have gone permanent, he thought. I should have stayed at the Mars Grill. I might own a string of nightclubs by now. He would bend his head over estimates and cost projections, and repress the wish to crumple them into a single globe of waste paper and set them afire.

And August 1977 came around.

KING OF ROCK AND ROLL DEAD
AT FORTY-TWO
ELVIS RESTS AT GRACELAND

Graceland, thought Don, good name, and I hope he does, the poor guy. It's all over now, everything that has done me wrong for twenty years, but I don't care. He watched the tape of the last concert and felt sorrow when the tired singer, sweating alarmingly, very heavy, as he punched his way through the familiar gyrations. The poor guy, he thought, no wonder, and then peace descended. We won, he thought. Dylan is finished. Where are the Beatles? The King is dead. The twenty years are past and spring is on its way and we survived it all, you and me. It's June in January.

On the afternoon of Friday, October 14th, Don Stanley sat calmly in his Toronto office waiting for the word to come back to Ottawa. The move was inevitable. They had to have him. His receptionist tapped quietly on the door, entered the room, her face grave.

"Oh Mr. Stanley," she said.

"What's the matter, Beverly, are you sick?"

"Oh Mr. Stanley. Something very sad."

Every seat in the Rialto was there in his head, every velvet rope, every smoky face, clapping hand, piano key, He stared at her.

"Bing's dead," he said.

"Did you hear?"

"I guessed."

He caught the obit on the eleven o'clock news. "Singer Harry Lillis 'Bing' Crosby died this afternoon on the fairway of a golf course near Madrid, Spain, at the end of a successful round. According to his golfing companions, the world-famed crooner had enjoyed a good round, joking and singing his way around the course. He was returning to the clubhouse when he suddenly stumbled and fell to the ground. There were no last words."

A loud noise which started somewhere in Don's chest suddenly crushed its way through his throat into the air. He was amazed and didn't know what it was. He thought he was sick. The noise forced itself out again and he heard what it was, a long howl of pure grief. He had not cried since before the war.

DARK GLASSES

T
HIS STORY comes from the quality of the light. I don't
know why I went to the party wearing my clip-ons. The
mid-February afternoon had featured strong un-glare
over snow, a hard-edged Northern Lights dazzle and I'd needed
the protection of the smoked lenses or imagined I had, which
amounts to the same thing.

I don't think I had them on during dinner. I don't wear
them around the house. To tell the truth, I feel pretty ambiguous about wearing dark glasses at any time, having read somewhere that hiding behind them is considered by psychiatrists
to be a hostile act which makes the person you're talking to
uneasy and suspicious. Psychiatrists don't say what the content of the situation is when both parties are wearing dark
glasses, but then psychiatrist are full of baloney anyway so
maybe I shouldn't worry about it.

Anyway I was due at the party in the middle of the evening, and somehow or other between dinner and my departure in the car I clipped the dark lenses onto my ordinary
glasses. Thinking back I can remember feeling irritated that I'd
likely spend the whole night taking them off to talk to people
I liked, then putting them back on to conceal my eyes from

other people. These clip-ons are light and cheap, not very good ones, with a thin nose-piece, which I've got in the habit of rolling between the thumb and forefinger of my left hand, flipping the Polaroid eyepiece back and forth, back and forth. My life is full of similar compulsive acts. Madness lies in wait all around.

And desperation. Driving east I rolled through seas of melting slush; the blackness of the night comforted me. I liked seeing the cityscape through manufactured opaqueness. I liked the swimming deception, disguising the way things were, and the impression that I was doing my vision some ghastly harm so that colour-blindness or worse would result. Night darker than night: only a dummy wears sunglasses at night, but I was wearing mine.

I climbed round and round, rising up through the dignities of Westmount to an idle street that ran nowhere, ending after six houses, all big, all bogus: half-timbering and plaster applied over brick, coats of arms carved in shoddy veneer. I parked as close as I could to the last house. Inside was a hall with two suits of armour, one here, one there, making the damn place look like the old Stoodleigh Restaurant under the Toronto *Star* building, something worked up by a decorator much attached to crown and empire. There were more coats of arms, these coloured, on the ceiling of the hall, two storeys above. A timbered staircase mounted grandly, first left, then right, to a gallery running along the south wall at the second-floor level. I don't suppose there really were lances and pennons, stuffed warhorses and arquebuses hanging above the gallery, but that's how I recollect the place and the image establishes the tone. There were two barmen, hired for the night, and two waiters, and a girl checking coats. The house was big but not all *that* big.

I heard somebody saying, "He's a better writer than you" and somebody else saying "You lie in your black throat," and heard an offer of bodily prostitution and the offer rejected, but

I didn't pay too much attention. Later, I thought, later. It was going to be an evening devoted to the public life of politics and affairs and institutional art, to intrigue among persons seeking to have their writing published and avowals of liberal and even radical social ethics on all sides. Men stated their solidarity with the Soledad brothers, ladies analyzed the influence of Marcuse on Miss Davis; nonsense was talked. I had trouble finding a bottle of bitter lemon; people kept offering me champagne. This made me feel guilty of all the hemmed-in, sterile aspects of abstinence.

The big bar lay toward the pantry, where there was a lineup. It was a party to pay off many social debts in a single bound, the best sort of party for all concerned: for the giver because he needn't give another for three years, for the guests because their host's guilt feelings have impelled him to a demonstrative and clearly unnecessary abundance of provision.

All smoked. None smoked anything but tobacco. A party for the over-thirties and forties, with whom I feel the solidarity I cannot extend to the Soledad brothers. If there is such a thing as party spirit, it can validly be shared, I think, only with one's own age-group. It's chronology after all that fixes our allegiances. When I saw Herman Leventhal in the drawing-room, his wife at his elbow as always in a touching show of supportive affection, I felt like a son to him; this is because I'm fifteen years younger than he is, just too many years to feel like a brother though not quite enough in fact to be his son. Where does the generation gap start to show—at fifteen years? There is no generation gap; chronology flows unbroken. What I felt for Herman Leventhal is not the hostility the younger generation is supposed to feel for its elders but admiration and sorrow. Even in this place I might have removed my concealing dark slices of thin plastic for him, if only there hadn't been those others.

I made my way through dense crowds toward Mr. Leventhal until a man stopped me.

"I read a story of yours recently." He gave me the title.

"Oh, yes."

"It's a very sad story, isn't it?"

"All my stories are sad."

"Why is that?"

"How the hell should I know?" I said savagely. "Maybe I can only recognize sad stories. Some people are crippled like that, and can only see disfigurement; we smell out hurt the way a dog traces his quarry. Most days I feel fairly good, but I'm always on the alert for others' misgivings. What else would you like to know?"

"Oh, that'll do." He said this so expressively that I laughed, then he laughed, feeling better. He couldn't see my eyes and I pushed rudely past. I don't often enjoy the luxury of rudeness. To be rude you have to be far far more heavily armoured than I am. This fellow might have punched me, but he was in a crowd and couldn't work his arms free. I felt I could afford to be direct. After I got by him I worked into a clearing in the jungle, a round gap in the mob six feet across. I took a deep breath and looked across the empty space at Herman and Yetta Leventhal, since this last winter more than ever together. She is a stocky woman with smooth grey hair parted on the side and worn with bangs in front. She has the composed face of a person of great capacity, and won't speak to you until she knows something about you, sometimes not then.

I first met Herman Leventhal when I agreed to act as an expert witness in an obscenity trial. That sounds funny. However, I'm not claiming to be an expert in the production of obscenity but only in its detection. I know smut when I see it, and I considered the book on trial as mighty high-class smut, so confoundedly literary as not to stimulate me, which has to be the test, doesn't it? The story of a great big zero. How does a pretentious piece of sentence-making, replete with nineteenth-century descriptions of moons racing through blackened skies, get a reputation as corrupting smut? Feeble, it was, feeble. Nobody was ever stimulated by such a book, or if they were they must have been in perpetual riot of stimulation from panty-hose advertisements and deodorant commercials.

Actually I met Mr. Leventhal some time before the trial began, in his office on top of a downtown office block, so high that I shook with terror the whole time I was up there. The parapet or wall was low and the glass, who knows about it? I remember a horror story about a young executive talking on the phone on the thirtieth floor of such a building; he says to his caller, "Nonsense, the glass wall is perfectly safe," and kicks the panel of glass next to his desk. It falls out, shattering 300 feet below. Contracts, desk-blotter, note-pad, all are sucked through the window. A secretary saves herself by the strength of her grasp on a desk-leg. The young executive pees in his pants. I wasn't crazy about this law office, but in the interests of justice and civil liberty I went to a meeting there with three other smut-smelters. Three of us were allegedly qualified to take the stand on grounds of academic or other appointments or because of work published. The fourth stammered when questioned.

"And of course, sir, as a lawyer, you see, I have no expert knowledge of the field, which is why I've invited you gentlemen today. Everyone knows Mr. A, I think, and Mr. B. Their status is fixed and Mr. C on the faculty of a distinguished institution. You, sir, I must say at once, I don't know. I think we should be frank from the beginning. Can you tell me why I might have been given your name?"

"I've written many of them," said Mr. D.

"Many what?"

"Obscene books."

This declaration was made wholly without shame.

Mr. Leventhal, heir to a sternly legal moral code, and its transmitter to the next generation, was of two minds about this reply.

"Will you clarify that for us?"

So Mr. D furnished a lot of clarification. "I started as a youngster in Paris, when I wrote the famous obscene third part of *Don Quixote* for a publisher whose name was a household word."

"Why was that?"

"Well, he was always on trial, the same thing as here."

"But here it's the bookseller who's been charged. Tell us, Mr. D, what do you think of that, bringing charges against the utterer, so to speak, of smut, if it is smut?"

"Indefensible. Look at Denmark and Sweden!"

Mr. Leventhal didn't undermine this breach of the forms of legal reasoning. All he said was, "What is legal in Scandinavia isn't necessarily legal here. The question is not what ought to be allowed, but what is in fact allowed by our enactments. I must say, Mr. D, that I would consider it an error of tactics to employ you as a defence witness in this proceeding, and I will not do so. But I will rely on you throughout for expert advice. Can you tell me, for example, what the returns are from a reputedly obscene work?"

"It's just like any other literary work," said the author pettishly, "it depends on your publisher and the publicity. A really good dirty book may often be overlooked in favour of one that isn't nearly so good."

"What is the standard?"

"Of merit?"

"First of merit, then of dirt."

Here Mr. D was at a loss. "About merit—if you mean merit as literature—I'm unable to speak. As for how dirty the book is, I think the test must be what it causes you to do." He was about to embroider this view with a wealth of detail when Mr. Leventhal tactfully dismissed him. I note that this is the same view I hold myself and freely advance, though I must state here that I haven't hidden myself behind the initial D. In the recital just concluded, as a matter of fact, I figure unostentatiously as poor Mr. C.

That's how I got to know Herman and Yetta, through attending that meeting and sitting around for days on end outside courtrooms waiting for proceedings, which once under way dragged on interminably, to begin. Like me, justice moves slowly and wears dark glasses.

I learned during those long waits that the Leventhals were famous activists in the vanguard of the civil-liberties movement. In deportation proceedings against socialist seamen, Herman would be valiantly and constantly opposed to the Immigration Department. Trade unionism found in him an ardent counsel. He has fought all his life against all forms of censorship and thought-control: rules against the importation of certain books, harassment of small presses, obscenity proceedings, closings of sexy movies. Such things go on all the time. Book are seized at borders daily. Draft-dodgers, so-called, are illegally detained and bunted into the outstretched arms of their pursuers. This happens. It shouldn't but it does.

Herman and Yetta have hungered and thirsted after justice since the early 1930s. Strikebreaking proceedings against Oshawa auto-workers begun by an infamous government of the most illiberal tendency were their first battleground. Asbestos caused them a second long stand at the barricades. Lady Chatterley leaned on them for deliverance and got it, in the end. They can't be praised enough for courage, for persistence in the face of adversity. Of course I had no way of knowing that when I was sitting, teeth chattering, in that dizzying office hoping that the walls wouldn't fall off—they looked awfully transparent.

If things are to be built of glass, let it be dark glass that confers an illusory solidity. I stood looking across blank space at Herman and Yetta, remembering what I'd heard about them over the winter. Their only son, Chaim, had died suddenly.

I couldn't recall what he had died of; it's a question I never ask when I hear. I keep my horrified questions to myself. What could it have been. Heart? Cancer? Cancer of what? I don't want to know.

Herman said, "We've been wanting to see you." I started to tremble and grow sensitive to the strange modes of light moving in the room. Have you ever been in a dimly lit drawing-room full of rejoicing, drinking artists and writers and their hubbub, and seen what light there was draw in and around the magnified figure of a single person? That's how it was. Herman was wearing a handsome blue suit. If it didn't seem insulting I'd describe him as impeccably tailored. He used to favour dark blue and grey suits that fitted him beautifully; he had stayed thin well into his fifties. His hair is such a smooth, full, close-cropped grey that it's nearly blue, silver-blue. If you were trying to imagine a distinguished civil libertarian who was lean, handsome and aging gracefully, you would imagine Herman Leventhal. Blue and silver and fine chalk pinstripe, neat moustache, penetrating eyes and this absurd halo around him of—I can see I won't get this across—of dark light.

If you ask me how light can be dark, I can't say, but that was exactly how it was. Let me see if I can explain the phenomenon. My smoked lenses may have had something to do with it. You might simply exclaim, "Take them off, stupid, and the effect will go away," but that wouldn't be right, as the event showed. The room was dark enough, and there was a big fire in a fireplace of walk-in dimensions. Firelight in February is apt to induce romantic illusions, as every Canadian knows, but it wasn't simply the firelight or the dark glasses, or the heavy floor lamp over behind Yetta, with its fringe of bobbles. The way they kept looking at me made me feel that I'd risen from the dead without first having died, a dreadful feeling.

"You youngsters never grasp the principles of true socialism, never see how national aspirations may justly be annexed to them; you believe that every time such a program is tried it transforms itself at once into Nazism, but you're wrong. Give national feeling a chance, why won't you?"

I said, "Herman, it's me."

Yetta moved closer to him, taking his right arm and shoulder in a tight grasp. "We learned in a bitter school," she said grimly; "we were in Palestine in '38, you know. You think because you've heard of the Balfour Declaration that you know all about international Zionism and its history. But Herman was invoking the principles of the Hague Convention to free boys on the border of Jordan while you were still dirtying your diapers. You find in textbooks that socialism and the political identity of Israel don't match together very well, and you remember the paradox of National Socialism under Hitler, and you conclude that what we've fought for is self-defeating and self-contradictory. But I say that the impulse to achieve social justice expressible in any post-Marxist analysis of politics or economics, though it may express itself in internationalist terms—the unattainable paradise of the international socialist brotherhood—will root itself in a state, whether Quebec, Israel or the thousand-year Reich."

"Right," said Herman, shaking his arm back and forth in her grip.

I wondered if I was having an hallucination, or if maybe they had jointly taken leave of their senses, so I put my hands slowly to my earpieces, took my glasses off, removed the clip-ons and polished the clear lenses, afterward putting my glasses back on and holding the clip-ons between thumb and forefinger. I started that compulsive flipping, back and forth. Now and then Yetta and Herman glanced first at my hand, then at each other.

With my clarified vision I recognized that the dark light that had so surprised me as it formed around this troubled couple was now if anything intensified. What was it? Where did this alien shadow originate? Herman came close to me, as if about to seize me by the lapel, but I had no lapel, just a sweater. Perhaps my clothes had an unjustifiably youthful air that misled him. I'm forty-three years old and never wear a suit, just sweaters and pants. That must have been it; there was nothing for him to get hold of. He obviously had me mixed up with somebody else.

"I don't know the whole story of socialism or nationalism," I said, "but I'm willing to learn, I really am. Why don't you tell me what you think?" I moved closer to them, working our little group in under a looming shadow, against a corner wall. "How can nationalist feeling work with socialist brotherhood? I can't see how that could happen."

"That's because you don't know anything. Why do you think Marx marked out the Russian proletariat as the inheritors of the traditional Messianic role of the Jewish people? Eh, why?"

"Well, actually, I don't know."

"He admits he doesn't know."

"It's a concession," said Yetta.

Herman said, "Marx was devoted to the suffering and the dying. He wouldn't recognize in the prosperous, bourgeois German Jew a potential saviour. But your Russian proletarian, Jew or Gentile, ah, there was the insulted and injured man, the sufferer who would redeem the world. It was in the tragic history of the weakening Russian regime, not in the German or the American, certainly not in the so-well-satisfied-with-itself British political system, that he discovered the dwelling-place of political man-as-such. Historical movements never begin in the world at large: they must be rooted in a place or they are nothing. The Papacy, with its paradoxical Roman universalism, knew this well enough. You Canadians…"

"You're a Canadian," I said ardently, and Yetta spit at me like a cat. "Look," I said, "I was awfully sorry to hear about Chaim. If I could say…"

"Chaim, Chaim, what is that?" Herman said, making a brushing motion with his left hand. "The error of the activist is to invoke the strike weapon too readily. The strike is like the peace officer's weapon; it must exist but should never be used, and the union leader who pulls men off the job has taken from them something that can never be replaced, a day's productivity. The artist never goes on strike; he can't afford to lose one day, one hour. Let us assume a typical working year of 250 days, multiplied by the 45 years of a working lifetime, this gives your 11,250 days in a man's working life. Every day lost is gone forever, can never be replaced. The union leader may think that an increase in wages or a betterment in working conditions will compensate for time lost, but it never can, it never can. You cannot call back time lost."

I now had the impression that Chaim's ghost was standing in front of me. I seemed to be turning into him. "We have no quarrel with the young" said Yetta her face twisted grotesquely, "we only want to explain certain facts. Let Herman tell you how things really are. He knows."

"I'm ready to be told, I'm listening, say whatever you like."

"No," he said, "no you won't listen, you don't let me tell you. I can't reach you."

I looked at them appalled; they seemed shrunken, huddled together and feeble. I clipped the dark lenses onto my glasses again and put them over my eyes, wishing they would do the same. I wanted their faces covered up. I could not bear the sight of them.

THANKSGIVING:
BETWEEN JUNETOWN
AND CAINTOWN

ERTAINLY those places exist, go look them up! Do you suppose I've imagined this?

So does Blue Mountain. It sticks up on the south shore like a nubbin, a nipple, a giant woman's breast. The skyline runs along, not very high above the water, then there's this—what should I say—this protuberance. I don't like to speak frivolously of my own sex, and our sexual parts. All the same, Blue Mountain is shaped like a tit. I can't explain what I might have been doing, climbing up it like a flea on the breast of a goddess, but there we were. "Three and a half hours going and coming." I don't know where he gets his information. "Who told you that, how do you know, are you sure? I have other things to do. I want to cut some corn stalks and draw them."

"Ron told me."

He has this—this really *pathetic*—dependence on what people tell him.

"Well naturally if Ron told you then it must be true, I mean Ron knows everything."

"He knows the lake; he's lived here all his life."

"Three and a half hours?"

"So he says."

"I've always wanted to go, actually, and the leaves are marvellous this weekend, and we won't be back before spring."

"And there'd be the flies in the spring."

"Got it all figured out, haven't you? Did Ron tell you that?"

"We won't get bitten even once," he said, bouncing joyfully on ahead, incurably hopeful, eager to placate when there is nobody to please, to mollify, no wrong to expiate. He cannot realize that it is exactly his folly that I love; he is so ready to adventure.

We drove along in early afternoon in unbelievable sunshine under skies of unmixed clarity. I don't believe in auguries. Clear skies are mere atmospheric conditions, smog the effect of miscalculation. You will not catch me prancing through meadows, nor does my heart lift at a soft breeze. What I want is an access road to hard reality. I am a dreadful mean woman. I am.

He knew just where to go, up a foul side road with deep pools of muddy water every fifty feet. "Bit of a clip here. Hum hum." We drove due north, and I will allow that the lie of the land was lovely, the way it loped. I thought of snowmobiles and terrified small animals. We left the car on this awful cart track at 1:30.

I said, "Turn it around."

"What?"

"Here's a wide space in the road, we'll be tired and ready to go when we come down, why not turn it around?"

"Good thinking."

He does drive well, and he knows where things are after he asks around. "This fence is the border between Lansdowne and Escott, and the road back there was the fifth concession. Don't you want to hear?"

"No."

"Come on, it's interesting. This here was originally the Austin lot, and over there was all Websters, and they're all still here."

"Dead and buried."

"Darling, we're all dead and buried in the long run."

Hard reality clothed in endearment, perhaps that is the essence of marriage, anyway it was what I got from him on this sunny Sunday on Thanksgiving weekend, and it will have to do me till we finally get somewhere.

I felt the rise in the height of land pulling in my legs, each step forward an infinitesimal lift, the foot in an appreciably higher position than before. A man looking like a scoutmaster swung past us, hurrying along, calling out distances and botanical observations to the four children who followed him—his own children evidently, out for a pleasant afternoon climb. They moved fast, but we kept them in sight. Sometimes one of the children lagged behind his father to give us a lead. Eventually they passed along up ahead.

"We can follow the Hydro line."

"I don't see any Hydro line."

"But there is one. It goes right to the top. I guess they must have run in a power line for the logging; there's a logging road comes up from the lakeshore."

"I don't see it."

"It's good to know it's there."

It wasn't there. It doesn't exist. Nobody ever used electric power on top of Blue Mountain; they chopped down trees the way they did everywhere else, by brute force, using their arm, muscles. And come to that, they never did much logging up there; the brush is uncut first-growth. We passed upward from the fields into this fuzz; then it thickened and the ground rose sharply. I began to pant. I take very small steps and I detest physical exertion. I'm not young. I'm getting fat. We climbed through closer woods over great rocky humps, keeping the sun on our left. My woodsman, my model of crafty lore, he kept hollering cheerfully that the sun was on our left hand, as if he'd invented it. We started to hear cries in the woods from all directions. I noticed that it was hard to tell where they came from; they appeared to move around. A voice might seem to come from up ahead, off to the right, then suddenly move around behind you. This could have been the effect of wind; more likely it was because of these gullies and creek beds we kept crossing. The ground didn't rise gently and gradually, as it had lower down. Voices multiplied. Somewhere nearby there was a crowd, or crowds, hikers, weekenders. We had been climbing for over an hour now and were close to the final rise. It made me think of the ascent of Kanchenjunga or Everest. Base camp at the 27,000-foot level. The final gallant attempt at the summit. Loyal sherpas. Frozen bodies lowered, sewn in canvas sacks and lashed to sleds, from icy immolation on the roof of the world.

Blue Mountain is 700 feet high. A little bit of a hill, what a fuss over nothing. All the same there were things to see. Around three o'clock we came out of thick woods into swamp, an arm of a blocked creek, and the biggest beaver dam you ever saw. Made a little lake over drowned swampland with hundreds of spiny bare unleaved narrow tree trunks standing up dead. A squirrel's nest in every third tree. They must scamper around in the air like circus aerialists on a lace of shivering dead branches. They'd never have to come down to earth; they may live up there.

That dam must be forty feet across, curved, looking like the work of human hands, engineers. We stepped along the rim, making deep soggy footprints along the edge and ruining our shoes. It was hard to get across, but I liked seeing such a place.

After that we were well away, only had to cross another gully, a very deep one, silent, way down in shadow out of the reach of the sun. I could see rays of light striking the tops of trees, and the final hump of rock up ahead, but where we were was dark and still. Many of the trees had shredded lengths of red plastic tied to them, trail markers, used because red plastic doesn't react with anything. When you swallow it, your liver rejects it and it may lodge in your organs permanently. Nothing alters it, not bile, not snow, not sun. When beavers eat it, they die. This is not the material I'd pick for blazing trails. But it lasts forever. When this wilderness has been cut over and destroyed ages in the future, those bits of red plastic will be on the spot, fluttering in an arid wind.

We had to move from right to left and back, casting around for the best place to make our move to the top. Coming right at it, you have to make the difficult ascent up the sheer face. There I go, making like Sir Edmund Hillary, but there really is a sheer face maybe thirty feet high and not sheer in the sense of being at a right angle with the ground. Seventy degrees perhaps, sheer, but not sheerness absolute. At this point we were in sunlight again and had gotten above the tops of the trees. We were beginning to get a view, and what a view! Worth it? I can't answer that; what can you do with a view?

Finally we were balanced on a hump of rock looking up at this 30-foot climb. My man hates heights, so now he let me take the lead. "I made an error," he said, "I looked behind me."

"You shouldn't have done that."

"I ought to have kept my nose flat against the rock. It's the eye focus, you see. It isn't fear of falling exactly. It's something in the eye muscles that frightens me when they move. You don't know what it's like. It's paralyzing."

I looked at the rock. There was a fissure in it eighteen inches wide, enough to jam a foot in for support, then the other, and so up to the top. You had to cuddle in against the face; you couldn't manage where there was overhang.

"I'll go first."

"I wish you would."

"Well I will."

He hung back. He thinks he's a coward. He has no notion what I think. I've seen him overcome various fears and I respect that. A phobia—heights, cats, confined spaces—you're not responsible. A phobia doesn't mean you're a coward. I'm not bothered by heights but I didn't earn the immunity so I don't feel superior, but I can't convince him. Perhaps it's good for him to think that I think he's a coward; it might spur him on.

I started up this fissure and it was easy as long as you didn't mind openness and the long view. I could feel my rear end looming over other climbers and blocking out the sun. I stuck out. I felt awkward. Grace is impossible under pressure of physical laws. I protruded, gritted my teeth, and arrived on top of Blue Mountain and oh, I have to admit, the view!

I called down to where he waited, "Stay there for a few minutes." He smiled. He doesn't sulk. I left him then and crossed the top of the hill and fell over a couple who'd come there to make love. Solitary in the wilderness, concealed from prying eyes by three hard miles of tangle and obscurity, they'd wanted to embrace, to be united, say simply to love, and here I came, fat, clumsy, making excuses, a jolt for passion. "I'm so sorry, I had no idea, do please excuse me, I'll go away, actually I'm looking for a place for my husband to get up. He can't make it." They glared at me, thinking I might be ridiculing them by oblique references to male powerlessness. I passed on, coming finally to a cairn and cleared space facing north.

It was like taking a huge blown-up map of the lake and squinting at it on its edge instead of looking down at it. You saw it all in wide-angle perspective: Ron's place at the creek mouth miles and miles away, the Landing, the Outlet, the five wide reaches lying open like fingers of an almighty hand, Big Water, Deep Water, Running Bay, Webster Bay, Donaldson Bay, thirteen miles across, all lying out there with close unbroken bush falling away in front of me to the shore, no logging road, no power line, primordial.

I became aware of whoopings and rejoicings. Swarms of people appeared behind me carrying cases of Molsons, decks of cards, blankets. I thought of the isolated lovers and wanted to laugh. People crowded around makeshift fireplaces, and soon the smell of charcoal and burnt hot dogs rose up.

"They bused us out to the Junetown four corners."

"Up the eastern trail."

"Trail?"

"Fifty of us. Young Anglicans."

"Is there an easy way to get up from there?"

"Right over there, lady."

"I've got my husband, you see."

"Haven't we all, haw haw haw."

I pushed through the gaping throng—must have been seventy of them. Children. In this mountain fastness. I heard a baby wailing in a papoose pack. A man lurched up and said, "I'm Toby O'Grady. I went to school with your father." He held a beer bottle. How had he managed the climb? Did he perhaps dwell here, the attendant spirit of the mountaintop, an Ontario Jove?

I got back to the edge and looked down and spotted him, the poor thing, sitting by himself. I don't know if he'd heard the merry throng above, hidden from him like the angels. I got his attention.

"Hey, come along to your right, it isn't more than a hundred yards."

"But a hard hundred yards."

"Push through the junipers and be careful where you put your feet." In the end he wandered around in the sunshine to the east end of the spur leading to the top, and came up what was almost a path, surprised by the ease of the ascent, put off by the crowd. He's always hidden back in there, doesn't believe I know how far. So cheerfully withdrawn. "Look at them all."

"Come on up, it won't bother you."

"No, I'm not bothered by a wide open space on flat ground. Look what you can see! I've been wanting to do this for years."

I stood off and watched him and thought about personal incapacity. Things we will not do, things we cannot, spaces, lacks in us. He can't take height. All his actions are worked around this incapacity—driving miles to avoid a high bridge, imposing a special condition upon the possibilities of life, how this must hurt, excise, make impossible, close off ranges of action. And we all do this. I do it. I am aware what I cannot, will not, do. Some things you can't; some you won't; some you neither can nor will, and these terminate, finish, kill, end, oh, oh.

Picnics still going on with laughter.

"Let's go down."

"Sure!"

Already young Anglicans were setting out for Junetown, four miles southeast. They trotted by in clumps, sinking suddenly down into dark on an unfamiliar path, moving quickly. The sun was getting over toward the Outlet and seemed more to the north than when we came up. I guess it was close onto four, maybe five to four, when we started down, and by four o'clock we were alone, the Junetown hikers disappeared, their noises dispersed, now seeming to come from all around, then receding into stillness.

He said softly, "We should be on the other side of that spur."

The sun was at our backs.

"What do you mean?"

"I never came up this way. I came up the other side. We should be on the other side of that spur. I crossed it just about here."

My trouble was that I hadn't been watching when he came up. I'd taken no note.

"It was here. I crossed here."

"All right, so let's go. We'll go back down along the hump, past where you couldn't make it to the big beaver dam and along down!"

"Right."

We went along in silence for five minutes, eight minutes. I knew I'd never seen any of this before. I have no sense of direction. He went on ahead. We came off a ridge and when I looked back I couldn't see the top of the mountain, just a lot of anonymous brush. I trailed him into a swampy tract that suddenly got much too deep, grabbing at our knees.

"Hey, hey!"

"What is it?"

"Do you know where we are? Did you come through this?"

"No."

"Are we lost?"

"Let's go on a bit. The beaver dam should be right over there." He gestured vaguely.

At 4:15 we got down into deep shadow. I thought, it will be dark by six, the second weekend in October. Last night was cold in the cottage. We have to be back at the car before dark. I said, "I don't think we're doing the right thing." It stopped him in his tracks and he turned and looked at me. On his face was an expression I'd never seen and didn't understand.

He said, "Right now we're lost." What struck me was how completely quiet the woods were, not a sound from hikers or lovers, yet they couldn't be more than a mile off. You can be utterly lost in a square mile of heavy cover; you can freeze listening to the sound of motor horns, helicopters, searchers. He began to shout, "Helllooooo," every few seconds. I thought he'd drive me mad. Nobody answered and there was no echo. Time passing. It had taken us two hours to climb up, and it was 4:30. It would be completely dark at 6:30.

I thought: here it is then. I stood on ground I'd never seen in my life, and had no idea in the world how to get back. These gullies ran round and round the side of the hill; you could circle in them and never come down. I thought: don't twist your ankle, don't move too suddenly over rock, you couldn't crawl out. I looked at my husband. I knew he wasn't a coward. I'd always trusted him. We were lost. Good and lost. I, who had never been afraid of anything in my life, thought about dying here. This fear got swiftly worse for fifteen minutes. In a quarter of an hour we got the whole local experience in concentrated form, heady stuff.

"We have to go back to the top and start again."

"I don't think we can find it." I was sorry as soon as I'd said this. I didn't like the way his face went. He cried out again and again, "Helllooooo." I thought of a lost child crying for its mother. I'd have cried out for help myself, but who to?

"Which way is up?"

"Come on," he said, and he led me back through the swamp. "If we keep climbing up toward the sun, we'll be back on top in fifteen minutes. Then we can get our bearings. We know we have to go due south. If we walk straight south for two hours, we'll have it made. We'll be doing just the reverse of what we did coming up." He babbled on. I paid no attention. What could I do? I followed along and thought: building a shelter. How build? We have a penknife. But no food. No matches. No compass. No flashlight. Last night it was cold; we had the stove on, then the heater, then we lit a coal fire. Don't sprain an ankle.

I thought we might last one night if we had to and tomorrow would be Thanksgiving. If the weather was fair, other hikers might come up. If we could go through a night. How do you make a shelter?

"Hey, there it is."

I looked up, and he was right, we'd got back on top, at least there was nowhere higher to climb. It didn't look exactly like where we'd been earlier, but the view was the same. We could spot our neighbour's boat ramp at fifteen miles. My knees shook.

"Look," he said, pulling aside junipers.

"What?"

"Fencing down. A fence."

Late afternoon, sun well down. I was starting to cry. I wouldn't cry in front of him. I would not. I said, "We're three miles up, over bad ground. Can we get down before dark? We'd have to follow the fence hand over hand in the dark."

"It tells us where men have been before. Look, the posts. If somebody planted those posts, we can follow their line and go out. It'll take time."

He kissed me on the forehead. I didn't touch him. "Let's not waste time."

"No."

We had an hour and a half till dark and a line to follow, sometimes interrupted, sometimes lying under heaped-up leaf mold or running through heavy juniper. Once I sat down abruptly from a height of four feet onto a boulder-edge, and bruised a square foot of my hip. When the fence line broke he would turn and say, "Stick right on this spot and watch that I'm keeping in line. If I get out of sight, keep calling out so I can come straight back. I won't go any farther than I know I can retrace." Oh, he was full of ideas. I noticed that he'd stopped calling out and it made me feel better. I began to see that we'd be all right even if we had to spend the hours of darkness here; we could go on walking at daybreak. My hip hurt. My feet were blistered. Here he was, back again.

"I've found the next bit of fence on the other side of this gully. Careful now, stay in line. It ends with this big tree, stay in line till we get to the other side of the break." Full of advice.

"I heard a car horn."

"Yeah, figures. We can't be more than two miles from the road. I wonder if anybody will remember about us, if we don't pick up the car before dark."

"It will be interesting to see." I was puzzled why the sun had moved so far to the north, then terribly frightened again when the fenceline stopped for good. I heard him crashing around in front of me, down a creek bed and up the other side. We kept calling back and forth. "Does it stop for good?" "I can't find it; the line's broken." "What'll we do? Can we keep straight south without it?" "Can you find your way to me, no, wait, don't move, don't leave that end of the fence till we figure this out." "Oh, I heard calling. I heard a train." "Me too, we can't be too far off it now. Hold it, don't move away from the wire. I think I can see some clear space, look off to your left toward the southeast."

"How do you know it's the southeast?"

"I think we've been going southeast without knowing it. And I do see breaks in the trees. So now, watch out, don't lose your line, just come away from the end of the fence and down into the creek. You should see stepping stones in black mud at the low point. Got it?"

Taking directions from him! "Yes, yes, yes, now I see you. I'm coming up. You're right, it is clearing." We stumbled on and in ten minutes, around six o'clock, he slipped in a patch of cow dung. "We're in somebody's back pasture, we're all right now, they'd never let their cattle wander too far away."

It was rocky upland, but cleared, studded with harsh out-croppings, farthest back pasture, welcome sight, with the ruins of a barn and the stones of what had been a cellar set in the middle of the field, with the very faint impression of wagon wheels running away to a chained gate. In the next field were living creatures, cows. Oh happy happy cows, I thought. The light was coming down mighty grey. We came to a road in near-twilight, not the same road we'd started out on.

"We're miles from the car," I said.

"Yeah. We're way over east around the Junetown intersection."

"Oh how do you know."

"I've been up this road once before looking for the mountain."

"When, if you're so smart?"

"Once, once."

We straggled on down this stony track.

"In a while we'll come to a pig farm by a crossroads."

Damn it, he was right. About half past six we came out to this crossroads and sighted a white house, stucco over logs, along a dim grey road in the very last twilight. At the four corners was a stinking square of fenced dirt. Through the gloom I saw an enormous boar glaring at me balefully. He had the biggest testicles I've ever seen, swollen sore-looking grey hemispheres, and made threatening noises, moving toward us.

"This is Junetown."

"*This?* This is nothing."

"There was a settlement here in the old days, and Cain town is along the road. Let's go and beg a lift back to the car."

We went along the Cain town road to the farmhouse drive and so up to the house. In the kitchen four persons were preparing a holiday dinner of roast goose and a lot of wine: a schoolteacher from Lansdowne, a chemistry demonstrator from the city, two bearded musicians, civilization. The chemistry demonstrator drove us five miles in pitch dark west along unmarked back roads to where an oblong dark box lay next to a mudhole, our car. He waved goodbye and drove away to his goose and wine. It was seven p.m.

"I'll drive," he said, "shall I? Will I drive then?"

I had nothing to say. I said nothing.

THE CHESS MATCH

ETTING UP in the morning, Mr. Page Calverly deferred as long as possible his first look in the mirror; that one must shave with the greatest of particular caution was unquestionable, for the sake of decency and dignity. The confrontation of the mirror was inescapable. It could however be put off for some minutes, those first aching minutes of wakefulness after the strange sleep that he nowadays endured.

He had noticed increasingly in the last decade or so that the metaphors for sleep were all young men's metaphors. Macbeth was plainly a young man, certainly not over sixty, if he still considered sleep the balm of hurt minds. As for Keats, thought Mr. Calverly, his notion of sleep was infantile. No poet had dealt truly with the sleep of the very old so unlike the easy drift of the metaphors the comforting warm blanket, the total oblivion.

His own sleep was a horrid parody of wakefulness. He had no dreams. He lay in his expensive bed on the firmest of mattresses, guaranteed against morning backache, and felt aches in his back perpetually, and stiffenings and unstiffenings of his muscle-strings and leaps of his heart, pauses in his respiration, sudden sweats, awful black seconds of unconsciousness which frightened him terribly, though not to death—never to death—nervous tic—he couldn't think and he couldn't forget his situation and the plain fact that his situation couldn't be eased or altered. When you are eighty-six years old, your situation is susceptible of no easement but the last.

He had never been an anti-clerical, despising the attitude as adolescent; but the sight of priests frightened and repelled him these days; they looked like crows or blackbirds.

Waking was merciful; here was another day to get through, an unexpected dividend, something he had no right at his age to expect, and he felt every morning an urge that he'd expected for years to lose the impulse to rise, shake off his fears and the corollaries of his unalterable situation, and go about in this man's world as the equal of anybody. He rolled unsteadily out of bed and stood erect, putting a shaking finger to his eye and flicking out of its corner a ball of dried tears.

It was all still here for another day: the world, the streets, his place in the world, his neat small apartment which he paid for, nobody else, which was cleaned and aired weekly by a woman whom he hired and paid who used his vacuum-cleaner and floor-polisher. He felt a kind of pride, which bothered him—it was almost senile—in his appliances, in the idea that a man born in 1890 should even have heard of such things as floor-polishers. He had visited old folks' homes now and then and the smell of those places had taught him, if nothing else, that floor-wax smelled like perfume when you compared it to some other smells. His neat little place smelled of floor-wax and furniture polish, and his wardrobe smelled like a laundry, all starch and clean linen, paid for by him, and not of old men's urine, spittoons, unaired beds, and lilies.

He had been away from the office now for twenty-one years, as long as a young man's minority. He had been a stock-broker, with seats on the New York and Toronto exchanges and when he had sold out for the last time he had taken enough money with him to last him out a good while. He had never touched his capital, which provided him with a snug income not much affected by the decline in the value of the dollar. The articles he bought hadn't increased that sharply in price so that in 1976 his snug income served him almost as well as it had in 1955. At that time the size of his income had made him definitely well-to-do and there had even been some question of his squiring widows about town. He had tried this once or twice before he was seventy.

These days he was still almost, not quite, to be described as well-to-do. "Comfortable" was nearer the mark. The single advantage that he had discovered in advanced age was the sensible diminution of one's wants. He no longer bought books, couldn't read them with any facility, and anyway he already had books. He bought no more sheet music since his fingers had grown so stiff, the piano was silent. Records mocked his hearing; the best of them sounded like the distorted scratchings he remembered from his young manhood. And yet, he had heard, the new records were extraordinarily lifelike. When he spoke to someone it was apt to be on the subject of the new recordings, which he discussed with easy familiarity although he had never really heard the stereophonic effect as it must sound to those who can hear properly.

What did he do? He kept up his end of the game. He bathed—for of course he daren't attempt a shower—scrubbing himself meticulously. It took him a long time. There are no metaphors for the physical feelings of the aged. A young man says that he feels weak, and he means that his normal strength is somewhat dissipated. Mr. Calverly was weaker all the time than one can describe—there are no standards for comparison. Johnny has a nervous tremor of the hands when he applies for a job. Mr. Calverly was, figuratively speaking, applying for that job every second of the day. His hands shook perpetually, keeping him from extending them in the normal masculine greeting, except when he felt very well indeed which was not often. It was a downright embarrassment to him to have to shake hands.

He was infrequently embarrassed; he made no new friends. When he had bathed, trying to keep out of his mind the disgust he felt as he examined his narrow legs, the legs of some prisoner of the concentration camps, the belly of a starved man, when he had warmed himself with the hot water and scented himself with soap, he let the water drain from the tub, down to the very last drop. Then he mopped out the tub as he sat there determined to avoid a wrenching slip or a fall and, placing his old feet as solidly as he could on the rubber mat in the tub, he climbed laboriously out and as laboriously stood up. He had been a tall man and though he had shrunk a full two inches he was still nearly erect. Each morning after his bath he drew himself as straight as he could, pulled his shoulders back, inflated his chest, slipped his denture into his mouth and gripped shakily at it with his gums. The denture altered the entire aspect of his face, filled it out, changed it from a grotesque to a recognizable caricature. Then he faced the mirror.

What did he see? He only saw what we all see or will see: his face, himself, what else is there to see? It was still the only face of Page Calverly and could have been that of no-one else. The face that had looked back at him since he had used mirrors, how long? It was his own face, the bones were there, the same slight peculiar angle to the cheek bone that had made him attractive to young women at Varsity in the reign of Edward VII. If any of those young women had been alive to tell, they would have put his name to that face at once. There was the plane of the upper lip which belonged also to his father, born in 1861, and his grandfather, born just after the Congress of Vienna, who had talked of Wellington and Peel as the most active of his contemporaries. Mr. Calverly remembered that same long upper lip in a miniature of his grandfather which had been lost, how long ago?

He shaved with every conceivable accuracy though his hands shook almost uncontrollably, and he thanked God as he did every day for the invention of the safety razor. He had long ago determined that there should be no patches of missed bristles hiding in the deep wrinkles that furrowed the skin below his cheek bones. Whatever else happened he meant to keep his person immaculate as long as he could.

As he worked his razor into the folds and corners of his face, he studied the reflection before him, the old face like a shrunken apple, the papery grey skin. He still had much of his hair, grey hair not white, and he combed and arranged it carefully. He had realized—oh, it must be twenty years ago—that one was not obliged to wear the uniform of the aged if one had money. Why do the old wear those club-like sloppy broken shoes and those hideous lavender dresses and rusty suits? He had decided to wear not young men's clothes—he didn't want to appear ridiculous—but clothes that any grown man might wear without seeming to ape the fashions of youth.

The reason why old people wear those awful, unbecoming, dirty and worn clothes is that they have no money. It isn't that they are pleased with them or positively wish to stress the unpleasantness of their condition—but they are trapped, on the shelf pushed into the corner with scarcely money to feed themselves, with none for pretty or handsome clothes, for decent haircuts and hairdressing for laundry, manicuring, extra calories even for razor blades sharp enough to give a decent shave.

Mr. Calverly prided himself on a peculiar discovery of his own; he had decided that he and a few others like him were the first old people in history, excluding the very rich and the aristocracy, to possess means sufficient to dismiss forever the ravages which old age had always previously worked upon the personal appearance.

It wasn't, he had worked out with himself, that one's appearance was the beginning and end of life, even at his age. But those others, the incomprehensible young, wouldn't treat you with their customary contumely if they saw that you were still able to care for your appearance. He meant not to be shelved, not to be put away in the corner; he demanded respect, to be treated like any other human being, old or young, with a private inward life of his own, with interests and affections to sustain him, with money to his credit—with in short his unimpaired human dignity.

He felt like a man playing out the end game of an important chess match, from an inferior position, with few pieces for the defence, against an implacable opponent of great skill and greater patience. He felt himself forced back at every move, at every exhausting calculation, to positions which he had to think out in advance; he had always to prepare some farther inferior place to go. He must be sure that there was a move open. He had to foresee everything over the short run ahead, think about each thing he did, every step down a short flight of stairs, along the smoothest sidewalk. He had to be careful about stepping off the curb and about stepping onto the sidewalk on the other side of the street, and the green light never stayed on long enough for him to get comfortably across. Every move was planned.

He consulted a doctor regularly, not a man he trusted, a man twenty-five years his junior. There were no doctors his own age! All the doctors seemed so young.

He had to wear a white shirt this morning because of the funeral. He preferred striped coloured shirts with button-down collars, soft ones that didn't hurt his neck—his shirt size had grown smaller and smaller. He had seen too many old men who wore stiff collars three sizes too big for them, so that they resembled ventriloquists' dummies. He wore soft collars, size thirteen and a half, which was at that a half-size too large, but the softness of the material and the careful way he knotted his tie and held his head erect on his shoulders minimized the scrawniness of his neck and the twistings of its ropy muscles.

He wouldn't select a black tie, didn't in fact own one. He picked out a wide dark wine-coloured knitted silk, held it against the shirt and decided that it was mournful enough. He slid the knot up to his throat, twisting and securing the material. He inserted a pair of expensive silver cufflinks.

Mostly he wore light or dark grey flannel trousers and one of several good jackets and blazers of which he took anxious care. Today he settled on a pair of very dark flannels and a brown Harris tweed which he'd owned for ten years and which was going to outlast him; he sometimes wondered who would get it. Fastening a black armband—which they had sent him—with great distaste, he eased himself into this jacket, admiring the solid tough fabric, and ran his comb once more through his hair. He felt better, now that he was decently dressed, decided that he didn't look so bad after all, made himself some toast and tea, drank a large defiant glass of fruit juice, and sat down to wait for the limousine.

His nephew Alfred had been sixty-two, he thought, or perhaps sixty-three. Mr. Calverly had no children of his own, and had never been close to his brother's children and grandchildren. They were all, he felt, too palpably wondering what he was holding and to whom it was bequeathed. In fact it was willed to them because, while he didn't very much like them or see much of them, he had no patience with those who leave their money and property to charitable institutions and to their pets. He meant his capital to stay in the family, but he never told anybody this. Either they were acute enough to figure it out and didn't need to be told, or they were fools, in which case he saw no necessity of enlightening them.

He was going to the funeral out of a sense of his social duty, not because he felt any perverse pleasure in the fact that he had outlived his nephew. He knew people in their eighties who were amateurs of funerals, connoisseurs of the various undertakers' establishments, who seemed to feel a friendly dilettante interest in such places, a damned outright comfortable nearness to them. He didn't go to funerals from morbidity; but he wouldn't avoid them either if it was a family matter.

At 10:15 his buzzer rang and the man from the undertakers' spoke to him.

"All ready with the car, Mr. Calverly."

He spoke his acknowledgement, went into the bathroom and carefully relieved himself—there might not be another opportunity. That was another concomitant of his situation, the pestering weakness of the bladder. Then he went carefully downstairs and directed the driver to take him to the funeral home.

"The service will be held at the home, won't it?"

"Yes, sir."

"And from there we go directly to the cemetery?"

"Yes, Mr. Calverly."

He didn't participate in the service at the funeral home, feeling physically incapable of remaining on his knees for any length of time. Instead he went into one of the waiting rooms reserved for members of the family and sat, self-contained and dignified, dryly by himself, watching the other people who from time to time put their heads in the door or came and sat down near him. He turned his head from side to side slowly like an ancient tortoise, his hands folded on the knob of his stick.

Once a young man and a young woman whom he knew, his great-nephew and great-niece, came into the room. The girl, who might have been thirty-five, for she had the unformed features of the young, wept silently. The young man smiled helplessly at Mr. Calverly and then, putting his arm around his sister's shoulders, he looked away.

It was all Greek to Mr. Calverly, so remote was he from the ordinary sequence of human affections. There was nobody left for whom he would weep, certainly not his nephew Alfred who had been in many ways, he thought, a foolish opinionated boy, though his designated heir. He remembered suddenly that he would have to alter his will, and wondered which of Alfred's boys this young man was, Pete possibly, or Eddie. He rather liked the look of the young fellow, who seemed to have some genuine care for his sister's feelings. He watched them get up and go out, making a mental note to find out which of his great-nephews this young man might be.

In a little while the drone of voices from the room where Alfred lay began to diminish, paused, then stopped altogether—the service was over. An attendant came in to tell Mt. Calverly that they would now be leaving for the cemetery and that, in accordance with his express request, he would be alone in the third car in the cortege. The attendant offered Mr. Calverly his arm, meaning to conduct him to the waiting car, but he shook him off impatiently, standing in the doorway as the coffin was borne out. He knew none of the pallbearers.

The surprisingly long cortege—he hadn't expected Alfred's departure to be so impressive—took some time to get out of the centre of the city. Mr. Calverly observed the maneuverings of his driver, as the man tried to stay decorously in line, with a certain impatience. He wished that he'd taken the opportunity to visit the men's room at the funeral home. A long time spent sitting always put more pressure on his lower abdomen than he could comfortably allow. Soon, however, the procession threaded its way out of the downtown area and began to roll northward along Mount Pleasant Road. He adopted as comfortable a position as he could, leaning against the deep upholstery. The car was very quiet and he was almost tempted to snatch a short nap, but remembered where he was and on what errand, thinking that it wouldn't seem decorous, so he stayed awake and thought about Alfred and about himself.

To that young man and his sister, consoling each other in the waiting room, Alfred Calverly must have seemed the representative of the older generation. It made him chuckle maliciously as he thought of it because he, naturally, considered poor Alfred a callow, wet-behind-the-ears youngster whom he'd given his first job; that was forty years ago when he himself had been a middle-aged veteran of the Stock Exchange.

He realized that for almost everybody Alfred *was* the older generation. And he—he couldn't be placed, for he certainly didn't belong with Alfred. He'd simply outlived all the generations and all the usual human desires and wishes. There was no place further for him to go. He had traded away all his pieces but the last, and there weren't very many more squares on the board to which he might move.

The file of his impressions turned back on itself and blurred, becoming inconsecutive. He felt obscurely that his situation set an insoluble problem in translation. His world didn't exist anymore except in history books. Its inhabitants were gone, its manners supplanted. It was as if he were camping out in a totally incomprehensible foreign country where the language was untranslatable because based on absolutely different notions and manners, even the monetary system was different. He still thought of a dollar as a sizeable sum of money out of which one expected change, because it had been so in 1899. It wasn't because he was mean that he hated to leave a paper-money tip. He simply couldn't get used to the new meaning of the old names for money.

The cars stopped on the winding road in Mount Hope Cemetery, and people began to stream along the narrow spaces between the graves to the open excavation in the Calverly plot. Mr. Calverly scrambled out of the limousine, and made his tortoise-like way along behind the throng, taking his time; he had seen all this before.

When he reached the graveside the short burial prayer had been concluded and the cemetery workmen were already lowering the coffin into the ground. People began to chatter amongst themselves and to disperse, some going back, doubtless, to their offices or to lunch, members of the family returning to their altered home. He stood aside and let the crowd flow around him; people jostled him and this made him angry and tired. It had been a long morning. He craned his thin neck and stared down into the grave. Already it was partially filled up. So. There was an end to Alfred. He turned and began to move slowly away to the waiting car, almost the last to go. As he picked his way along, some foolish movement of sorrow and family feeling led him to take his eyes off the uneven footing and stare a last time behind him at the grave. As he did so he stumbled over a fat lump or tussock of grass and mud and, to his horror and fright, fell full-length on the damp ground.

The lump of grass and mud pressed heavily into the pit of his stomach, nauseating him, and half-supporting him off the grass. He found to his intense shame and discomfort that he was too weak and tired to stand up by himself. He lay there with his arms and legs moving feebly, like a great impaled spider. Once he called out and nobody seemed to hear, and all at once he felt very frightened. He didn't see how to get up.

Then to his relief he felt a hand under his right arm, and 395 another one under his left and against his ribs. A young man's voice said clearly, "You're all right, Uncle Page." He felt himself lifted up, got his feet under him, straightened and looked with gratitude at his saviour. It was the young man whom he'd noticed at the funeral home.

"It is Uncle Page, isn't it?" asked the young man coolly, almost, it seemed to him, with amusement, and he nodded his old head, staring at the young man. And as he stared into the young man's cool eyes, he saw and recognized the stare of the other chess-player. He saw what he'd expected and feared to see for so long, pity in the cool eyes, pity. And behind that, at the back of the remote familiar eyes, contempt.

EVOLVING BUD

THE LANDING. What a grand place it was for the youngsters back in 1975 or 1976 when there was something for
them to do over there, a place to go where they could enjoy
themselves and stay out of grief. Around the clock from May
to September you could hear the sound of outboard motors,
seventy-five horse, ninety, a hundred-and-fifteen, speeding
up the long reach from Wide Water or Bonteen Bay, racing for
the three docks at the landing: the public dock which in those
days was sinking lower and lower in the water; the gas pump
beside the big store; then, to port the smaller wharves for the
other grocery stores and marine suppliers with competing
Esso, Texaco, and Fina gas pumps and services. Each dock had
its own clientele. The smallest dock, Minto's Marina, handled
Fina products, fishing equipment, groceries, Coleman stoves
and lanterns for the old-timers, folks with island cottage who
only came in once a week to buy supplies; they came from
really remote parts of the lake where there were no Hydro
lines and a summer place might look exactly as it did in 1875.
You saw a certain number of codgers around Minto's—Billie and the boys never went there—who still hung on as professional guides for Americans at the hotel, half-submerged

flotsam from the era of the balky Evinrude two-and-a-half with lures and flies stuck in their hatbands and crazed looks acquired during epic trolling for a legendary thirty-three-pound pike in the cold isolate reaches: Rummer's Reach, Slick's Bay, Palmyra Cove where, they said, the lake might be five hundred feet deep.

The middle store, Hanlon's Groceries and Variety, was where the comfortable middle-aged cottagers went for the papers, gas and oil mixed in the correct proportions for their big engines, paperbacks, and memberships in the Cottagers' Protective Association.

The largest store at the public dock was the trading-post for the summer children and their local rivals in love. The summer children seemed to be mostly girls like Billie, fourteen, fifteen, with a talent for water-skiing and huge insatiable engines you don't see anymore. It seems so long ago and it's only a decade; those sunburnt girls are all married; they have sailboats and conserve energy; they have one child with another on the way. Their brothers work for data-processing suppliers or are doing graduate degrees at some business school. Or they write speeches for some middle-level politician.

At that time the rivalry between the seasonal boys and the descendants of the codgers was an engaging thing to see. For a mile up and down Landing Road lean, heavily tanned lads with cutoff jeans bleached to the faintest cottony-blue trailed the girls from the large runabouts and tried to get an arm around them: these boys had the local names; Minto, Slick, Shuckerly. They went over to Athens by Landing Road to the high school through the fall and winter; their fathers worked in construction or farmed or sold each other real estate or did all of those things. These old families had been taking their living one way or another from the lake and the summer people for a century. The hotel still bore traces of the elegance of the nineties. There were faded striped awnings over the verandas from June through Labour Day; you could buy your fishing license at the desk beneath wall plaques of stuffed muskies and pickerel and try to read the fading print on notices about the Ontario Fish and Game Regulations thumbtacked to the wall in the thirties.

The year Billie was fifteen some fugitive movie producer used the hotel all summer for interiors. The sagging upstairs corridors with sudden surprising changes of direction, the doors which swung shut unpropelled, the enormous photographs of long-dead picnic parties gave the finished film a persuasiveness offered by few of its other aspects. The colour stock wasn't bad.

Americans still came to the hotel and discussed the places to look for the big fellows in measured, ignorant speculation. There was a wonderful slow-to-serve, ill-lit dining room next to a bar already showing signs of rowdiness to come. There was a superb anonymous cook. Once or twice a summer a cottaging family might take the twelve-mile drive around the shore on the twisting rocky roads to the Landing to eat fish or steak and justify a vacation. Summers were distinguished by planked pickerel or char-broiled filet.

"That was the year they were making those rhubarb pies. Gollies, but they were laxative in effect!"

"But they sure were tasty!"

"And then the next year everybody was selling blueberries and there were no desserts that didn't turn blue on sight. Blueberry flan. Blueberry shortcake with whipped cream, oh my."

"The fruit cups!"

Billie used to leave the table to stroll down Landing Road to the dock and socialize with the locals while her elders lingered over coffee. She was in her jujube phase at the time, keeping complex statistics on the occurrence of green, yellow, orange, red, and black in sackfuls of chewy delights. She would come home long after the rest of the family had driven back to the other side of the lake, squired across Wide Water by some knave in a fibreglass runabout with a hundred horses at his command, a tale of jujube frequencies on her lips, giggling, unworried, our girl.

"Why are the red ones invariably the most frequent?"

"Ah child, these are the romantic secrets that only great age or great wisdom can illuminate."

"And then there are always far fewer green ones than anything else ... I think the black ones come in second in order of frequency."

"The other mystery, jujubewise, is their shapes. What are they supposed to be?"

"Little black babies," she would gurgle.

"Look, these are lanterns."

"No, silly, they're barrels."

"What's this orange one?"

"Isn't it a peeled orange in sections?"

"So it is; and this is a little bunch of grapes, I think; and this is a banana."

Ah, summer.

Billie would seek her silken couch. The water-skier who had brought her home would nod in embarrassment and withdraw, filling the scented night with the roar of immense power which would gradually fade. Tales of eager teenagers who smashed open the stoutest fibreglass whizzing through Stone Fence Gap in the dark circulated at that time at the Landing like a *chanson de geste*, often built around the distressful image of some overbold youth turning over and over high in the air like a thrown football, flung out of his boat as though from catapult by the shocking abrupt stop. One boy died in this way and a summer or two later a revolving red light was placed in the gap by the authorities. This accomplished little. Spectacular accidents continued. Good old times.

Billie has never been eager to bust her noggin on some spur of limestone issuing from the depths; she would go in slower boats or on the pillions of dirt bikes, never on street bikes without a helmet, one prudent girl. She'd have been sixteen by now and was never really impressed with the high-speed operators, though she would accept a boat-ride home from the Landing, a ride on an XL-170 around the Barn or somebody's free games on a Commander America pinball machine. At that time the Barn was in full efflorescence; it had just forsaken heavy metal for disco.

It really was an old barn and not some weatherboard fantasy standing at the top of the hill, up Landing Road for a long long time. Whoever owned it did a smart thing in 1976: they added a lean-to at the north end with a counter and stools and burgers and fries, lined the barn walls with pinball games, and installed an enormous coin-operated record player with thunderous amplification; they went from Chicago to Donna Summer in the course of six weeks during the first season of operation. There was a rudimentary stage platform which might, once upon a time, have formed some part of a feed-loft. The planking of the walls showed starlight through a hundred chinks and knotholes but the roof was sound and the hard rain never came on down; the flooring was laid on level ground which would not give or vibrate under press of rock or disco. When you got in there with the speakers giving tongue, the bells of the pinball machines ringing and clanging, the shuffle of kids' feet whispering along the polished pine and the sound of dirt bikes whining around and around out back, it was stereophonic, man.

Billie loved the big bad Barn. They all did, the summer girls and boys and the natives. Families could leave a couple of daughters there at ten p.m. on a Friday or Saturday, secure in the conviction that someone or other would bring the girls safely home in big boats. The whole scene was memorable for the sound of motors—bikes, hundred-horse muscle-outboards— and for voices, that long rippling giggling gurgling and growling blend of girlish laughter and boyish persuasion. Harmless, immemorial, shot with luck, defined by pleasure craft of wondrous variety.

A certain red punt began to incur upon the scene, an undistinguished little boatling of ancient conception and design: flat-bottomed, slab-sided, homemade, handpainted with a five-horse Johnson suspended from a transom deeply marked with roundels punched into the yielding wood by the retaining screws. Probably forty years old and leaked like a son-of-a-bitch; had that peculiarly smelly tang of the wooden skiff left long in stagnant berthing. Late at night on big weekends, after the fibreglass runabouts had holed up for the party, you might hear this low-key pop-pop-popping and it would be the red punt, solitary boatman astern easing the thing along in the dark, heading around Bessborough Point towards an unidentifiable destination up the creek mouth. There were six or eight ancient cottages back in there (which more recent arrivals seldom saw), the property of aborigines who had built up the cottaging tradition early in the century. Their names were visible on hand-lettered signs tacked to trees, arrows pointing up shore roads or across limestone ridges on which no city-dwelling weekender dared risk his muffler. *Gavin and Markell, Leeder, Alguire, Bairstowe, Charland.* Pick-ups and graders drove up in there.

Very late one Sunday night when the Barn was closed, Billie came home in the red punt, sitting in the bow to trim the graceless hull which had about an inch of freeboard. Well, say six inches. The boat came creeping along the shore without any running lights and drew in under the circle of clarity provided by a Japanese lantern hung on a pine and meant to serve as a leading-light for late visitors. The lantern was orange-coloured and it gave the otherwise ordinary cement platform an air of imaginative chic. Billie hopped out, thanked her escort, and came tripping up the stairs waving a paper parasol which somebody had bought for her at the Landing.

"Good night, Bob," she hooted into the shadows at dockside. There were grunts in reply; then the creaking hull disappeared, blocky form in the stern hunched over the motor, one of those antique devices with an exposed flywheel and a hook-on rope. It might have qualified as some sort of marine-museum piece. The boy had likely inherited it from his father, one of the Leeders, Bairstowes, Charlands of longtime local affiliation. The underpowered little motor and the ugly old boat—and the boy—seemed strangely like the creations of an earlier time.

The midnight boatman began to come around to the dock by day; they all did, everybody who ever brought her home. There was this one hockey player, almost a household word, who owned a whole island down Rummer's Reach. He used to take her water-skiing on Wide Water for hours at a time. The hockey player taught Billie to operate his huge boat then did all sorts of acrobatics astern: stood on his head on one ski; criss-crossed the wake; showoff stuff; one great athlete. He was killed two years later in a hang-gliding incident on another lake. There were dozens of American kids (who thought Billie was a Northern princess), costive Montreal anglos with choked accents, and the sons of professional men from the river cities twenty miles away. And the locals who never had much of a look-in. And this Bob or whatever, a hard person to know.

Never had much to say for himself and looked like an otter. Might have been fifteen, perhaps a year younger than Billie, not exactly shy, more watchful than anything. He would dive from the rocks into five or six feet of water in a neat flat racing leap. No stomach at all and even at fifteen those ropy knotted muscles hard physical labour confers on certain forms not in themselves beautiful. He swam in a choppy, exceedingly speedy style and would jump off any of the fifty-foot cliffs along the shoreline, always testing the depth of the water first.

There was some confusion about his identity. "Bob? Bob? What Bob?"

"How should I know?"

"What's he doing on our beach then?"

"Swimming, silly, can't anyone?"

"It's a private beach."

"Oh, it is not!"

"It is if you pay attention to politeness. We don't go over and swim at the Mellanbys' without being asked."

"That damn Jean Mellanby. What's she got to be so stuck up about?"

"Several million dollars."

"Money means nothing to me," Billie would declare and that was true; it didn't. She never was one to pick and choose among her boyfriends on the basis of their prospects or their parents' investments. And just look at who she finally hooked up with!

Anyway, Bob. Yes. She got this Bob to stay for dinner one evening and nobody could get a word out of him. He sat at a corner of the table with his place-setting sandwiched between Billie and her mother looking up slantwise from under a heavy forehead.

"Is your cottage around here, Bob? Have you always come here for your summers?"

"Did your dad build that boat for you, Bob?" It looked like rough carpenter's work. "Did he teach you how to make them; are there any others like it on the lake?"

The kid could eat, no question about it. Not like a glutton but steadily, with plenty of wristy follow-through. He had the appetite of a grown man accustomed to physical output. When he'd finished a plateful of Fudgee-Os and Oreos he finally straightened out his neck and held his head up and said to the table at large, "Actually, my name is Bud."

"Bud?"

"Yup."

Billie was flustered. "Bud?"

"He just said so."

"Well, anybody can make a mistake."

After that his name got worked into every sentence. "I think it might rain overnight, isn't that right, Bud?" (This in the accent of the summer visitor consulting local sage.) "Sounds like the wind's getting up a bit, eh, Bud?"

"What about that boat of yours, Bud? Is she going to be okay in these waves?"

"We'll bring her onshore, Bud. No need to let her swamp. Maybe have to dive for your motor, eh, Bud?"

"How about it, Bud?"

"Are you going to be all right, Bud? Do you want us to take you home in our boat? You could come over for yours tomorrow, Bud. What do you say?"

He got his boat home just fine. Probably sidled along the shore and around into the creek mouth without any trouble, probably heard foolish echoes of his name sounding like confused birdcalls in the trees. "Bud Bob Bud Bob Bud Bob."

Everybody felt mighty silly.

He was just one of the Charlands, that's all, a notable local family that used to hold all the land on the east side of the lake from the village down to the highway, eight or nine miles of shoreline and a big stand of back-country brush and abandoned nineteenth-century roads, wonderful cross-country trails and snowmobile runs. About the time Bud Charland came upon the scene, the provincial department of natural resources began buying up much of this land for reforestation. None of the purchases was made by expropriation; in every case a high price was paid. All land that might be useable for recreational purposes was left in the Charlands' hands. From being a poverty-stricken band of back-concession failed farmers, they began to metamorphose into an understated sort of local aristocracy, an old family, people with a century-and-a-half of township affiliations behind them. Billie had no notion of this; neither did anybody else. All the same, Bud Charland's name and his appearances at the Barn, during the short time left to that institution's career, began to have special undertones.

"He's somebody important," Billie said a little suspiciously. She knew nothing about township history. Billie is a city girl.

She still has that paper parasol and now claims that Bud Charland gave it to her. Nobody knows for sure if that's true but she enjoys teasing her husband about it. He never gave her a parasol; but he has interesting holdings of his own in Mississauga.

In the second or third summer of its operations, say 1977, the Barn began to be affected by changes in the locality just as the Charlands and the Bairstowes were on the other side of the lake. A special kind of money began to circulate around the Landing, loose money, beer-drinking, dirt-biking money, snowmobiling money. Two snowmobile dealerships opened on Landing Road, Arctic Cat and John Deere. People began to spend a little wildly at the same time that unemployment and inflation were in flood, confusing issues. How could prices and unemployment be high at the same time? That didn't make sense. Everybody was buying porn mags at $2.50, then $3.95 a copy. Times were hard but exhilarating in an odd way.

When Bud Charland entered the Barn that last summer all the girls wanted to dance with him; after all, if the Charlands had been able to hang around the lake for 150 years, they might be good for a few—maybe many—more.

Bud had nothing to say, naturally, but looked older and even stronger. Swam off Billie's end of the dock at her personal invitation, needing no introduction.

The Landing was less fun than it had been because the recreation money had moved into the hotel and the dining-room clientele was changing; the chef left. They had a sex show on Friday nights and a country-and-western concert on Saturdays which often blurred into Sunday morning. People started to come from as far away as Elgin. Sectional rivalries, forgotten for a century, now surfaced; there were fist-fights outside the hotel every weekend in the early hours of Saturday and Sunday morning. The rough crowd started to turn up in the Barn around nine p.m. to kill time until the strip shows came on.

It killed the Barn as a place for kids. Some of them sneaked into the hotel bar but most of them simply stopped strolling up Landing Road from the docks: they concentrated more and more on their boats. The government reconstructed the dock and improved the moorings. The price of gas continued to rise.

That year you would see burly OPP types lounging around the lunch counter in the grocery store. It seemed a very short time since the presence of a policeman at the Landing caused surprised comment. Now they were there frequently, collecting evidence, waiting for something serious to happen. Finally one Friday night towards the end of the summer of 1979 some wise guy burned a stripper on the leg with the tip of his cigar. In the fight which followed, a death occurred. Nobody was ever charged with anything. No arrest was ever made. But the hotel closed soon after. The Barn had shut down the summer before. Outboard motors were shrinking. Dirt bikes were out of vogue. Snowmobiling continued a popular winter sport and cross-country skiing boomed. You supplied your own energy and grew healthy.

The Charland property on the other side of the lake slowly increased in value. As long as the provincial government was determined to buy up scrub bush and reforest it, just so long would lake-country property rise in price. A painful banality.

In the winter of 1979, about the time Bud was getting into his twenties and Billie was receiving her first proposals, the Charland family opened up an old farmhouse back in the woods which had been built, then speedily abandoned, in the late nineteenth century. They didn't paint the exterior although they did put in acceptable heating and some rough furniture and called the finished results Charlands' SnowTrail Clubhouse. They sold memberships and rented skis and marked trails for cross-country and snowmobiling.

The big store at the Landing laid in a stock of snowmobile suits which looked from a distance like mummification, peculiar polyester sarcophagi, garments worn by mediaeval knights on their tombs, completely wraparound, bulky, puffy with heraldic colours and stripes, zig-zags and checkers.

Billie lost all her beauty of form in a snowmobile suit, but gained in the exchange a subtle mystery. She always detested snowmobiling, too darn cold, but would risk a trail-run in pursuit of fashion and dominance. She got out to Charlands' SnowTrail Clubhouse—with immense difficulty—the week after Christmas with her boyfriend two years ago. The holiday developed into one of those comic fiascos that go down so well as half-hour sitcom segments on television.

On the first night they found their reservation was only for a single room. Then Bud Charland stepped into the picture, all taciturn chivalry, the authentic outdoorsman, to arrange another room for the boyfriend.

"Do we really need favours from this Daniel Boone?"

"Angel, he's just trying to be nice and we can't sleep in the same room."

"Who says we can't?"

"Not me." Business of crossing arms and looking demure.

"Who then?"

"I wouldn't want to embarrass the Charlands."

"Bugger the Charlands!"

"You'll feel better after a run up the creek, invigorated." She laughed at the boyfriend, then—as she tells the story—kissed him in a sisterly manner. It was at this moment that Bud appeared in the room to remove some of the excess baggage.

"I'll just carry these down the hall if your *friend*..." (Heavy work with lowered forehead and twitching eyebrows.) "... if your *friend* will follow me."

"Bud, I'd like you to meet my future husband. Arnold, this is Bud Charland. You know, the Charlands own everything around here for miles, timber rights, the paving company. I don't know what-all."

Your basic townmouse-countrymouse confrontation.

There was a heavy silence which Billie broke by exclaiming, "Bud Charland, that was a chaste, sisterly kiss. I won't have you making a federal case out of it."

She plunked herself down on a brass bed of somewhat studied antiquity and began to cry with a pretty air of distraction. Bud and Arnold grinned at each other like travellers who, upon meeting and going some way together in a desert, eventually recognize a familiar oasis.

They ignored her manoeuvres for the remainder of the week. They went on long snowmobile runs together. From the veranda of the lodge, Billie suffered the indignity of watching the two men zipping round and round on the vast spread of ice in the creek mouth.

On the next-to-last day they made her come ice-fishing. The three of them sat for hours in a tiny, smelly shack on a single bench next to a round hole in the ice taking turns dangling a thin filament through the aperture. They had a fire in a cutoff oil drum. A Coleman lantern hung from the roof. There were no windows in the shack, only an ill-fitting door through which hyperborean blasts shrilled. Billie sat clad in her snowmobile suit looking, she says, like a brass rubbing of Princess Mathilde of Anjou, only the exquisite oval of her face showing, the rest armoured by plastic fabric. And Arnold ... Arnold ... Arnold all at once hooked the legendary thirty-three pound pike through the hole in the ice. He will never let her forget it!

There are new methods of mounting fish now, which keep them from getting that greyish-greenish look of painted plaster characteristic of displays in the old summer hotels. Maybe they freeze them instantly and cement up the guts. Who knows?

Arnold got that fish out of the back country and up to the city the same day. It was hard. They had to pack their clothes in half-an-hour and carry everything back to the access road in three snowmobile trips over progressively darker trails. The woods were dark and deep but unlovely, Billie said later, fraught with visions of collisions. Their car was parked next to the abandoned grocery store of McIntosh Mills; their retreat occupied hours. It was early-winter dark when they finally laid the huge fish on the back seat of Arnold's gas-guzzler and set off for civilization.

"I won't let the soft flesh of my fish be scarred by decomposition," swore Arnold, moved erratically towards poetry by intensity of emotion. Billie thought that he had stronger feelings about his big fish than about anything they had done together. Her recollections ran back in half-sleep (she was exhausted) to the perfectly round hole in the ice, about the size of a manhole-cover, under the glare of the Coleman radiating the glitter of polished snow crystal and foot-thick ice, shining grey streaked with veins of dead white, underneath the ice floor the living water and the blind fish. She imagined herself as such a fish with blood that would never warm, circulating in super-cooled dark in a medium that flowed with her, swam along her fins. Down through the exact circle of pale yellow like the sun at the frozen end of the world, into her depths dangled a filament so thin as to disappear in the cold swimming dark, traces of living oil (bacon fat?) signalling out along the chilled current to the organs of fish, drawing them to the three-pronged hook. She bit.

"Hey, wake up, baby, hey! Throw newspaper around my pike."

Arnold got his fish to his Mississauga freezer and then to a Toronto taxidermist on the following Monday. The mounted pike, laminated in almost-transparent plastic—just the faintest hint of ocean blue in the laminate—is permanently fastened to the wall of the poolside changing rooms at the place near Brampton where he and Billie live. Three miles away are acres of Arnold's condos.

The family misses Billie but kids grow up and away; if they don't actually inhabit new towns and condominiums they change themselves so that you can hardly tell them for what they used to be. Driving along the hazardous road around the east side of the lake, early this spring, just after the runoff, the family found they had to pick their way carefully over erosion ruts where trickles from the high ground had been powerfully freshened by torrential rains. Not snow, rain. There hasn't been any snow to speak of in the 1980s and it rains hard in late February.

At one point they were obliged to stop the car, get out, and lay some small logs in a particularly deep gully. The Charlands don't permit any blacktopping.

When they got back in the car and inched gingerly across the insubstantial surface they heard a tremendous noise developing near them from back in the bush. It swelled to a roar. Everybody trembled.

From the recesses of Bairstowe/Leeder/Charland territory there burst a muscle-car, a 1973 Dodge Charger hardtop with double-reinforced shocks on the rear wheels tilting the car upwards with peculiar insolence to expose immensely fat dragster tires. Rubber spun and grabbed and dug at the road surface, threw up fine gravel and old clotted crankcase oil in a wide spray. Visions of a flaming chariot.

Bud Charland sat erect behind the wheel sporting enormous sideburns, a long cigar clamped in a corner of his jaw. He waggled the cigar once as the Charger, cherry-coloured with black rally stripes, threw improvised fill behind him. Logs, branches, big stones. An unknown girl sat immediately on his right, no visible daylight between them. Small and dark, she gazed up at him adoringly, rocking sidewise on the seat. The huge tires bit deep, the hardtop lunged away around the next bend and headed for town. Nobody could decide whether the cigar, the girl, the tires, the shocks, or the sideburns pissed them off most.

THE VILLAGE INSIDE

F ROM SAINTE-ANNE-DE-BELLEVUE to Pointe-aux-
Trembles is thirty-five miles—which sounds like the refrain
to a folk song:

In summer on this island
God's sweet sun smiles.
From Sainte-Anne to the Point
'Tis thirty-five miles.

And from the port to the back river, at the widest span, is
fifteen miles. These distances may not be precise to the foot, but
it's a big island, a lot bigger than, say, Manhattan and therefore
with plenty of open space between the dozens of municipali-
ties dotting the countryside: Sainte-Anne de-Bellevue, Pointe-
Claire, Dorval, Pierrefonds, Dollard-des-Ormeaux, Saraguay,
Ville Saint-Laurent. These place-names are like musical notes
in a rich orchestration, each with a history and mythology and
traditions.

In summer I do a lot of bicycling, the best way to explore
the outer reaches of the island, because of the fair weather and
the distances involved. In an afternoon or evening's ride, you

can get over twenty miles out and twenty back. Starting from the centre of town where I live you can't quite get off the island, east or west, and back again, between lunchtime and dinner, or between dinner and the eleven o'clock news—that's a bit too far, unless you were foolhardy enough to bicycle along one of the main highways, the Metropolitan or Number Two, or Côte-de-Liesse, which would be courting instant death.

Sticking to back roads and the main streets of suburbs, twenty miles out and back is plenty, and will take you almost anywhere you might wish to go to investigate and see how the city has remorselessly enveloped the identity of one village after another, often without the formality of political union, an oversight which now causes endless trouble in the management of essential services, the smaller towns retaining their formal independence with great jealousy. Sooner or later we'll probably come to some sort of borough government. Already the towns on Ile Jésus, to the north, have agglomerated, and the provincial authorities and the city council are urging further steps in the process.

Cries of "They'll never take us alive!" from Westmount, Outremont, the Town of Mount Royal, and other places.

And at that they have a point, especially the more distant communities, because it isn't long since most of them existed quite independently of the city, and naturally they have local institutions and customs, and powers, that they mean to safeguard. In the thirties, before the Metropolitan and the Trans-Canada were built, a small town ten miles from the centre of the city—even though in full view of the dome of the Oratory—might enjoy a somnolent nineteenth-century style of life, without excessive gasoline fumes and traffic, without shopping centres and intimidating prairies of blacktop, without every modern inconvenience, because such a place could only be reached with some difficulty on narrow local roads.

Just this side of Terrebonne, east along the back river, there used to be, and perhaps still is, a bridge so narrow and frail that automobile traffic was only permitted one way at a time; there was an ingenious traffic light at either end which allowed cars to proceed south for a short time, then reversed itself and let people come the other way. Not too many people took that route to Terrebonne without good reason. Now that this rickety anachronism has been superseded by a four-lane concrete structure a few miles west (a genuine advance, I'm not knocking it for a minute), Terrebonne is bigger, noisier, richer, and fully into the twentieth century.

Sometimes the overlay of city on remote village can be traced, building by building, along an old main street. In August, ranging wider and wider on my bike in the evenings, trying to crowd in all the sunshine coming to me before autumn, I discovered rue Sainte-Croix out in Saint-Laurent, not really remote, simply the continuation of Lucerne after it passes under the elevated highway. True enough, it's no more than five miles from the centre of town, but you can detect the ancient village inside the suburban growth, like an attenuated ghost, traceable by houses spotted along the street as you ride north, interrupted by modern installations of a qualified beauty and utility.

Coming north from the Metropolitan, you ride first of all along a characterless strip of land—to your right a modern burial park without any headstones. I once went to a funeral there, stepped out of a limousine onto a flat recessed plaque of debased design, and remarked to the widow without thinking that it was the kind of place where you didn't know who you might be walking on. I really didn't mean to upset her.

On the left are various industrial buildings rimming the highway service roads, and then, between these and the memorial park, the traffic is funnelled towards a highly inconvenient railway crossing, always jammed with heavy trucks. Once across the tracks, you see on your right the first of a long chain of enormous ecclesiastical and collegiate buildings, the oldest dating perhaps from the late eighties, all belonging in one way or another to the administration of the Collège de SaintLaurent, the principal educational institution in the town. There are various classroom and residence buildings and a great church, and off behind the campus the Saint-Laurent arena with attached sports facilities, a shooting gallery, gymnasium, and so on, apparently run by the college.

Juste en face on the left side of Sainte-Croix going north, there begins to appear the ghostly presence of the old town, which must have dozed peacefully in the August sun, remote from all urban troublings of the heart, at least until the mid-forties, to judge by the age of the buildings. Between rue du Collège and rue de l'Eglise, facing the expanse of institutional lawns and flower-beds, are five or six small wooden buildings of unexampled beauty, two of them abandoned or to let, the others perverted from their original purposes to rather mean uses, as coalsheds or small offices for industrial storage lots. One of these buildings must have been a group of three dwellings, row houses, a storey and a half in height, with low mansard roof. A sagging verandah stretches the short length of the row, and the entries (two of them boarded over) are of great delicacy.

Further up the street there's a superb stone farmhouse of the kind you still see all over the richer farmland of western Québec, two storeys and an attic, of immensely solid irregular stones, maybe a hundred and twenty years old and now the offices of a small local construction company. Further along there's a Victorian mansion with a tower surrounded by balconies, red brick with a pattern of darker, almost bluish, stone let into the wall. Who can have lived there? An early mayor, the richest man in the village? Houses like these, about ten of them set among gas stations and gravel yards, suggest the tidal-wave movement of an enormous city's advance in every direction, like debris surfacing from a sunken wreck.

Sainte-Croix isn't the main street of Ville Saint-Laurent any more; west a few blocks we find the northern stretches of Decarie, and west again from that the truly modern street,

Boulevard Laurentien, a four-lane divided highway running north off the island. Here are the offices of Canadair and the eastern border of Cartierville airport, haven for light planes and local airways. On the other side of the local airport, five or six miles west and south, is Dorval International, one of the busiest airports on the continent, jets coming onto the east-west runways almost every minute round the clock.

It's an eerie sight, standing on rue Sainte-Croix, in front of the evident ghost of a nineteenth-century Québec village, to see overhead jet after jet slanting down and in towards the Dorval runways, almost without intervals between arrivals. You have the impression of one time superimposed on another, with both visibly present, something quite rare.

Boulevard Laurentien is all tremendous breadth and modernity and speed, with light planes of every size parked in dense ranks on the west side, and vast infinities of blacktop— a Dali horizon—on the east, supermarkets and shopping centres shrunk into distant insignificance by the grandeur of the black space around them, with its beautiful and complex pattern of yellow parking marking. Off to the north and east are housing developments, their tone just opposite to that of rue SainteCroix. And nevertheless, oddity of oddities, these opposed patterns merge at one special point, in an extraordinarily graphic way.

There must have been outlying farms stippled around the village a few hundred yards apart. On one amazing corner, now, this year, you come past a mile of blacktop—the shopping centre can scarcely be seen in the distance because of the glare—and suddenly you see a hundred-and-forty-year-old wooden farmhouse standing on a fifty-by-fifty plot of land, on the extreme corner of the titanic parking lot, ready to fall off the edge into history. It's a magnificent house. It seems incomparably more lonely in its present situation, under the perpetual jets, than it could have in 1867 when the night lights of other farms could scarcely be distinguished.

The front door faces south, away from the prevailing winds; there is no garage nor any room to park a car on the property, no TV aerial. A pump stands at the back of the house, black-green, unused perhaps for fifty years. I know there's electricity because one room—never more than one—is lit at night.

I often bicycled past this place in the early August evenings, drawn to the site to admire the way the soft grained sheen of the walls took the light just after sunset. Once, I recall, there was a sensational display of sunset colour of the kind that entices bad painters, a whole western skyful of grey and rose tones that you might perhaps see in nature once in ten years, but which you'd be crazy to put in a painting—nobody would believe it. As I stood across the street from the farmhouse, the colours reflected on its western wall began to deepen; night was coming on and overhead immense airplane after airplane drew down over me roaring, landing-gear already out, lights at wingtips. There was a stiff breeze blowing from the north down the highway. Rose tones darkened and were merged in deep blue; all at once it was night. In the house the single light came on, downstairs in what was probably the living room. For some reason my curiosity about the people in the house became intense and, spotting a hamburger shack two blocks south, I went and had a coffee, and made the inquiries which elicited this story.

Victor Latourelle, a farmer born in the nineties, had always lived in the house. When he was born, this was full, deep countryside, no highways, no cars, for all practical purposes no city, no Oratory, no university tower, at nights nothing in the sky but the moon and stars. On the back river, serious and unpolluted fishing and hunting. The Latourelle family owned seventy acres, blissfully ignorant of the potential value of the land; they got their living from it, that was all. They had always done so, or so it must have seemed because at that time the house was already close to seventy years old.

Victor Latourelle must have crept across stubbly fields to dirt tracks into the village, so as to attend parish school for a few years, with here and there a barn lifting on his horizon, and in the village the raw new collegiate buildings, ambitious and outsized, which we find there still. At twenty he was left untouched by the *crise de conscription*; he didn't recognize its existence. He helped work the farm and lived as he'd always done, and nobody bothered him.

Perhaps in the 1920s, when automobiles made their way more regularly along those outlying country roads, the accelerating pace of social change may now and then have impressed him faintly. Some crazy biplane, alone in the sky, may have impelled him to point it out and laugh. Here an occasional rudimentary gasoline pump, there (very distant) a minor industrial installation. His children began to grow up; there were only three of them (to rebut the myth of the large French-Canadian family), a daughter and two sons, all born in the decade between 1915 and 1925. The daughter, Victorine, the youngest, was always his favourite, and after modern life began to touch the Latourelle farm, to some degree his cross.

After the second war, the signs of the impending destruction of the traditional Latourelle family life were evident, pressing, impossible to ignore. The boys had never lived on the farm, the first generation in the family to live and work in the city. But Victorine married a local boy who came to live on the place, ostensibly to assist in its operation. Their wedding took place in 1947, and in a year or two they began to agitate for the sale of the land, as was perhaps only natural in their position. In the next twenty years, the property regularly appreciated in value, enough by 1965 to enrich the family, and more particularly Victorine and her husband, André Savard.

Consider M. Latourelle's position. He had never lived anywhere else, and didn't want to. He was into his late fifties and might very comfortably live out his time where he'd been born, leaving the farm to be disposed of after his death however the children might decide. He had no false romantic ideas about the place, no semi-mystical commitment to the land such as we read about in novels. He just hoped to stay put. He knew that the boys, and his grandchildren, had abandoned his kind of life forever, that sooner or later his home would be swallowed up. He simply didn't want to be the one to take the final step.

Now a seventy-acre farm is just barely viable, if that, in today's market. Victor could see that as soon as the first little slice was taken off his land, the rest would inevitably follow. He fought very hard against family pressure, especially from M. and Mme Savard, right there in the house with him; but after nearly ten years of constant cajolery from Victorine, whom he loved, he sold off a ten-acre strip at the east of his place to some real-estate developers (perfectly honest and fair-dealing men, as it happened) who ran a road along it, threw up something they called Airview Park, and made a pile of dough from what was actually a pretty small project. Ten years after that, which brings us up almost to yesterday, that ten acres is assessed at a figure which bears no relation whatsoever to what M. Latourelle got for it, to his daughter's abundant justification. When the sale question recurred, she always needled her father about his failure to get what he should have from the first sale. She would walk over to the edge of Airview Park, in the late 1950s, and stand there sadly for an hour, wondering what the development was worth in the aggregate, at present prices. After sadness came anger and reproach.

"Next time, *pépère*, at least let us do the bargaining. It's always the same story with you, letting people take advantage of you. You could have got three times as much for that land. More. Let André handle it next time."

Her father said mildly, "Perhaps there won't be another time."

"Of course, there will. There are real-estate men buzzing around here like flies. André was talking to one this morning. Crooked? He'd take the place from you for nothing if he could."

"Then I won't sell. Time for that afterwards." He meant after he was dead, which was not lost on Victorine; she didn't want to wait that long. She hoped to ride the booming real-estate market right to the top of the wave, and then hop off to the enrichment of the whole family. There was never any intention in her mind of cheating her brothers, or doing her father an injustice; she was in effect the voice of progress. She thought they ought to wait a certain length of time, but not till her father died, that would be too long. He was in excellent health and came of a long-lived stock; by then she'd be too old to enjoy herself. She was thirty-five, she remembered, and she put more and more pressure on her father.

"Don't sell yet, but soon, soon." This was in the early six- ties, at the top of the market, when every other stretch of land in town had been dealt off years before, when in fact the municipal council was eager to complete the development of all former farms, pushing through new streets, laying sewers and completing power circuits. Nobody in town wanted the sixty-acre Latourelle farm to remain undeveloped much longer, neither the real-estate men, nor council, nor the family.

In 1962, accordingly, M. Latourelle had to take another step in his strategic retreat, selling off an L-shaped thirty acres on the north and east sides of the farm for a very handsome figure, but not quite what Victorine would have asked. She consulted her husband at length, and her brothers' families, and they vowed that the next and last deal would be handled by the younger generation, no longer quite so young. She was bored with the old house now, especially when she shopped the new places going up all around: shower doors that rolled silently back and forth, with frosted glass and designs of fish and other marine subjects, chic bathroom wallpapers in floral or heraldic motifs, bathtubs in unusual, Pompeian shapes, diamonds or circles, his-and-hers washbasins. And the kitchens, and the closet space, and the two-car garages. She and André wanted to buy further north, towards the back river and certain new shopping and entertainment facilities. Their share of the final sale would set them up permanently in such a home.

Here the affair turned nasty, as it sometimes does. When her father decided to hang on to the last of the property till he died, she began to insinuate that he'd lost his mental competence, and that he shouldn't be allowed to stand in the way of progress. She took this argument to the council first of all. Her father was incompetent to handle his affairs and ought to be compelled to surrender his authority to his children.

"Can't you take legal action against him? Can't you expropriate or rezone the district?"

"Madame, we might rezone to allow industrial development, or apartment construction. We don't rezone to exclude or disallow a single-family dwelling on twenty-five acres. Your father is within his rights and can hold out as long as he likes."

"Aren't you interested in the future of the town?"

"Certainly, Madame, but we can't force a property owner to sell disadvantageously. We have the legal right to insist on installing necessary services, and your father has never tried to stop us. When we put in the sewers and power lines, he was glad to have it done. He said it would make the property more valuable for you. Aren't you being a little unjust?"

"But think how it looks, that big square of stubble in the middle of the city. It looks ridiculous and ugly. He isn't farming it any more, and he's let the outbuildings fall to pieces. It's an eyesore, and you should do something about it." She felt frantic that even the government wouldn't back her up. "It's your duty to expropriate."

"On the contrary, it's our duty to preserve an open real-estate market, so that your father—and you—can get the best price for your holdings. If the owner doesn't want to sell, for whatever reasons, it would be quite wrong for us to force him, unless for a major public work, and we have nothing planned for that district."

"What about the shopping centre? Don't you want it?"

Here Mme Savard approached spongy ground. Certainly the council wanted the shopping centre, *in abstractio*, so to speak, *sub specie aeternitatis*, in the same way that every North American, English, French, Spanish, Eskimo seems to be convinced that a new shopping centre, preferably of the largest conceivable scope, given local topography, is an inevitable harbinger of economic épanouissement. But a shopping centre, or plaza, to use the more modish term, is a commercial venture for private profit, and municipal officials everywhere, while normally ready to abet their construction, are chary of being identified with the interest of private developers, for the obvious legal and ethical reasons. Nobody in council was going to twist Victor Latourelle's arm to make him sell to a commercial developer. That sort of move can make you look very bad at an election, or in front of a board of inquiry from the Department of Municipal Affairs.

Mme Savard then took the more extreme step of trying to have her father certified as incompetent by a psychiatrist, with the aim of committing him to an institution for the aged. Here again she failed because her father, though by now seventy years old, was plainly excessively sane, if that's possible, so much so that not even the most unscrupulous practitioner would commit him for fear of detection by some meddlesome public authority.

After Victorine started to invite psychiatrists to the house, poor M. Latourelle caved in emotionally. "Have I deserved this?"

"What, Papa?"

"I'm saner than you, Victorine."

"Then sell!"

He broke down at her insistence, and an arrangement was quickly made which gave the remainder of the property, except for the fifty-foot square the house actually stood on, to the development corporation. They were not entirely happy to have the southwest corner of the parking lot encumbered by a decrepit vestige of the past. But M. Latourelle was past seventy, obviously failing, so the house would surely be available for demolition within a reasonable time.

That's how matters rest. Victorine and André took their share of the money and bought a split-level ranch with copper plumbing, up near Boulevard Gouin. Victor Latourelle lives alone, leaves his home only to buy food or visit the bank, lights a lamp in whichever room he sits alone in through the oncoming dark. Sometimes he looks out of his windows at the asphalt seas surrounding him and sees cattle grazing, his father working in their thick green truck garden, his uncle Antoine bent in a distant cornfield. Hallucinatory no doubt, but you can't really blame him.

GOD HAS
MANIFESTED
HIMSELF UNTO US
AS CANADIAN TIRE

W EDNESDAY the eight-page supplement is in the *Stars*.
Interior acrylic satin-latex in nine carefree finishes
and up to four hundred and thirty-two beautiful tones.
Baby Car Seat by Travl-Gard conforming to all government
safety needs. We'll never need one of those. Tossabout robes
for car or boat, that's more like it. The supplement is printed
in black and white and red, with drawings of hunters in the
snow, decoy ducks, faithful plumy-tailed dogs on point. Canadian Industries 402, the natural shotgun, light, beautifully
balanced, sling swivels and handsomely grained wood stock.
Kills at any reasonable distance. The Winchester 94 lever-
action carbine rooted in the traditions of the Old West also
available in the .44 magnum. Blow a hole in you the size of
a volleyball. Smiling homemakers among their Teflon-Ware
in the gay Spice-O-Life pattern. Good deals on scenic-backed
bicycles.

After supper Dreamy comes and snuggles up beside me
on the arm of our Naugahyde recliner.

"I want the eight-ply steel-belted Polyester Radials," she
whispers, "with the added protection of Hiway-Biway Winter Big Paws." She leans closer, blows in my ear as I turn the

supplement inside out. There's a terrific buy on STP in the centrefold.

"We smoke up? We get a little potted, baby?"

"What have we got?"

"There's this little baggie of Tucumcara Gold, smell it, sweetie." She rolls over on top of me and I think: beachballs.

I can smell her toiletries. Hairspray, underarm spray, vagina spray, and at the other end Desenex Foot Powder. Dreamy is covered, I think, triple-armour-proofed from head to toe, my Breck girl, my One-a-Day girl, made of necessary iron supplements. As Dreamy grows older—being a woman—she needs more iron than you'd ever guess and of course she provides her family the same healthy defenses. I'm her One-a-Day boy. We lie in our Naugahyde and smoke and turn the pages.

"If I had a hydraulic lift jack I could fly you to the moon."

"Don't wanna go to the moon." Snuggle tickle snuggle.

"I could lift one-and-a-quarter tons."

"That's my big old buddy; turn the page. What else is there; will we go to the store tomorrow night? What will we buy?"

"I want a T-shirt with YAMAHA on it."

"I want one with the friendly bugs."

Dreamy draws double the minimum wage, hundreds a week to spend. We live on my money; it feeds us; we don't eat that much any more. Who needs food anyway, says Dreamy, food is yechhy, you can't grab a high on Hungry-Man dinners.

"The peas keep rolling into the dessert."

"Yechhy. Turn the page."

"MotoMaster Turbo-Fire. Motormaster Superoyl."

Dreamy in a car is my blue heaven; she has this little Hornet with the optional 360 blown and re-bored, a WowWow, a WowWow, a Vrooooommmm Vrooommm WowWow. "There goes Dreamy, man, looka her go."

Sometimes I call her my MotoMama. I met her at the Alexis Nihon Plaza: coming out of RETURN OF BILLY JACK at Cinema One. I was going up the escalator when she was coming down wearing terylene dimple boucle and LycraSpandex high separation bra. I couldn't see the girl for the goods. I thought, "Look at all that Fortrel," and wanted her bad, but I was already in the parking garage at the top of the Plaza. I could hardly wait for the escalator. I ran round and round the levels down the stairs and round and round along the down escalators, going down fast. I could see her at the bottom wandering into Miracle Mart and from the last escalator I spotted her away off in front of a stack of Sesame Streets by Fisher-Price in the familiar blue, yellow, and red cartons, marked down as a pre-Christmas loss leader. I could tell what they were by the colour spinning and striping blue red yellow as I ran around the escalators. Above the piles of coloured cardboard I saw painted plywood cutouts of kids' drawings stuck on the wall for a display, little red houses, little creamy moons. I tell Dreamy she's the greatest miracle ever came out of Miracle Mart.

"Aw, no, A.O. You're putting me on."

I followed her into RETURN OF BILLY JACK and sat behind her breathing popcorn down her back; after that we witnessed MACON COUNTRY LINE, SUGARLAND EXPRESS, WALKING TALL, and WALKING TALL TWO together.

"A.O.," she says, "you remind me of Buford Pusser."

"How in the world could I remind you of Buford Pusser? Why he's a hero, Dreamy, and I'm just an alert consumer like the man in that frog song:

Je suis je suis suis suis
Un consommateur averti
J'attend la revolution mais mais mais
Franchement j'aimerais
Mieux devenir motard acheter un bel HONDA
Une belle KAWASAKI MOBYLETTE
Bongo bongo bingo.

They've got it too, the itch to buy.
LE CAMPING CHEZ COLEMAN STOVE.
TONDEUSES A MOTEUR.
DIEU SE MANIFESTE DEVANT NOUS SOUS
     L'APPARENCE DE CANADIAN TIRE.

It's the biggest force for unity in the whole world. Miracle Mart, Steinberg. DE CHEZ EATON. We never go near Eaton, Dreamy and me. It's a snob store, not for us, for the others, the ones that like good taste.

"Don't you dare talk to me about good taste, A.O. It's yec-chhy. If I want to wear purple and green and orange and puce I'll do it. I'll wear flares at dinner and see-through blouses in church and I'll have six-inch platforms. I want bobbles round my windshield and a bronzined statue of the Blessed Virgin standing on my Hornet dash. I want to beautify my bathroom with twin-door vanity and johnny pole, well-hung wall cabinets, his-and-hers dual over-the-tank toiletry starers for my Desenex, Breck, Ban, Norforms."

"Dreamy, do you ever think of us getting married?"

"What makes you talk like that, A.O.?"

"Sweetie, we've got the his-and-hers dual cabinet with twin-door vanity. Shouldn't we maybe sanctify our union?"

"A.O., don't I let you use my blower-styler? We couldn't be any closer if we were married and we'd be tied down. You wouldn't like me if I was tied down. I wouldn't be your Moto-Mama."

"It's true."

"Don't tie your MotoMama down, A.O. I should make up a song about that, like Bonnie Parker."

Don't tie your MotoMama down
Don't Xood her up with vapour locks
Your old brake shoes
Just born to lose

Are begging begging begging
For a new set of shocks
Give me some Turbo-Fire plugs and points
Rotor, condenser, and cap
Don't make your MotoMama misfire
Don't give me none of that crap.

"A.O., you want a homemaker or you want me?"

"I want you, terylene queen. I want instant everything from Swansons and McCains: you're the primadonna of the convenience foods. Don't you ever soil your little fingers with can-openers, lady, order out for Chinese, for triple-anchovy all-dressed, for St. Hubert Bar-B-Q." Our apartment is always under attack by squads of little cars with signs on the roofs CHAMPION EAST-END RAVIOLI, LE ROI DE SMOKED MEAT, MARTIAL ARTS SUKIYAKI, bringing cardboard cartons of cookery convenience. Dreamy hurries to the door and back, flings them into the Proctor-Silex ToasterOven-Deluxe, takes two frozen dinners at once, operating on Easi-Read controls. Never burns, never overcooks, never interrupts your train of thought. "Sweetie, sweetie, sweetie..."

"Ummmmhh?"

"Is it good?"

"What?"

"What you're eating, silly."

I have to think it over. "You tell me what it is, and I'll tell you if it's good."

"It's bean-curd soufflé, A.O. New from the Peking Pizzeria."

"It's good then. If it was chocolate custard it would be bad; it wouldn't taste like it was supposed to. I tell you, Dreamy, I don't really know what a bean-curd soufflé tastes like. I can't really taste anything any more, since I found you."

"You're my sweetie, A.O., and one of these nights I'm going to surprise you. I'm going to stay home from work and get you a whole meal all by myself."

"Could you do that?"

"I really could, loveboat. I could look them all up in the Yellow Pages just like any old Mrs. Breakfast Nook. You just follow the letters along in the alpha ... alfalfa ... what is that word?"

"Alphabetical?"

"What you said. In that order. In alpha-whatsis order. I would just let my pinkies do the walking till I came to the order-out and then I would buy stuff. It all tastes pretty much the same."

"Right on."

"Well then, let's finish eating and go. Where'll we go tonight? It's Thursday, where'll we go, Azlex, Place Ville-Marie, les Galeries d'Anjou, Côte-des-Neiges Plaza?"

"Couldn't we just go to Canadian Tire? There's everything we need right there under one roof, two major shopping floors with watchful attendants glad to be of service."

"I shouldn't even have asked, A.O., just you wait while I get my credit cards."

Dreamy has BankAmericard, Chargex, American Express, Diners' Club, MasterCharge. I told her she should have MistressCharge. She's the darling of the credit companies, always pays a whole lot, always owes more and never closes an account. I guess they know they'll never collect it all but Dreamy goes right on paying. She's all right as long as she lives. She's got them all in a clear plastic accordion and in the big stores she just runs along trailing her credit cards behind her. Leave them alone and they'll come home.

"Nothing to worry about as long as we give them something from the Unemployment Insurance."

"Going to quit your job, Dreamy?"

"I been on it long enough for the insurance, now I'll relax for a while. I've got a lot of shopping to do anyway." Here she comes with her credit-accordion. "We'll take both cars, we'll have things to carry."

The store is all different colours, so many colours it's the end, the best, everything you could ever want except for food God Has Manifested Himself and bed linen. Everything else is handy, right there, leisure equipment and every automotive need. And Mandrels, Routers, Conduits, Snips, Toggles, Goggles, Flexible Shafts, Sabre Rasps, Butt Chisels, Sterasyl Purifiers. I think sometimes there is so much in the store I'll never take it all in, all those wonderful things, and in a minute after we get there I'm all by myself. Dreamy can't stay put; she has to move; has to cover everything in case she might miss something she needs to buy. She never exchanges the goods; she hangs right on to them all, you bet your life. The apartment is filling up with appliances and power-tools and all descriptions of goods. Somebody once tried to tell me that it was all too much, this SOCIAL WORKER for God's sake. 431

"Freud wouldn't approve. Marx wouldn't hold still for it."

"Who gives a shit?"

"Don't you see, A.O.? It isn't good for you to want all those things. It isn't good for your wife. She'll have unfulfilled expectations."

I had to laugh. I said, "She's not my wife. She's just staying here. And any expectations she's got, she fulfills as soon as she can get off work."

"So that's how you want to live, is it?"

"Doesn't everybody?"

"Marx wouldn't have bought it."

"What's he want us to do, sit around and suffer?"

Dreamy knows, oh yes, she knows.

Sometimes watching her run through the store I think back to when I was young in the sixties and all I did was trade up or trade down. I almost always traded up; trading down is for losers. By the end of the sixties I had it all or almost all. Pro football season tickets, the major appliances, the minor appliances, skis, golf clubs. My place was jammed but I knew all the time there was something missing, and that something was love, which I first knew when I met Dreamy in the mid-seventies.

"Now the very first thing we have to do with you, A.O., is get rid of all this terrible old shit you've collected. Look, what is that awful thing?"

"That's my typewriter."

"Your whaaaat? Look at it, it doesn't plug in. It isn't even molded styrene. Get rid of it."

"I write my letters on it, Dreamy."

"Baby, you won't have to write letters because I'll always be here."

She dropped it out the window and it fell five floors to an awning above the sidewalk. It didn't break. It lay in the awning in the rain for years, rusting and turning colour. Finally it fell apart and sifted off as red dust, and then Dreamy bought me something to replace it.

"I'm sorry, baby. I didn't think you cared about any old machine like that. I've got you something new to play with, a CompuMatic, calculates in ten digits, accepts logs . . . logs . . . whatever. It accepts them. You can do anything with it, and for adding in the sales tax you can't beat it; fits in your trousers."

I've got so I keep it in my pocket all the time. I can figure out the price without even looking at the buttons, just press, press, and then I hear the whirring and clicking in my pants, calculating and computing on two "D" batteries, fully transistorized at only $39.95, and only last year you couldn't touch one for under a hundred, or say $89.95. It's the turnover that cuts the price; enough turnover and your price per unit has to come down.

If it weren't for Dreamy and me, who'd take care of the cost of living?

When the store closes Thursday night we carry our things out to the car, in heavy cardboard containers. Tonight we've got a Coffee Magic superactivated dripolator, a convectortype baseboard heater to get a little extra warmth into the bedroom, which is cold all the time, and a drum-type humidifier, all things we've been wanting and never thought of buying. You'd think if you really wanted it enough you'd remember to buy it, but sometimes it doesn't work that way and you make an impulse purchase instead. There's a spending gap between wanting and remembering but we never let it bother us. We know we'll get it sooner or later. We've needed a drum-type humidifier for years. We've got the wick-type but it doesn't really wet the air down. The bedroom has been like a desert. If we can get the baseboard heater and the humidifier just balanced off, we'll be back in business.

We stick one carton in my trunk and the other two in hers, and race each other home to see who can be first to plug something in. Fuses. Right away I'll insert thirty-amp fuses into all the circuits instead of fifteen, so we can carry the extra load. Then we'll turn the TV on and lie in bed together switching channels and zooming in and out on our manual controls. We've got so we can catch all our favourite commercials by having the colour set and the old black-and-white beside each other and switching around. We never watch the programs, just the commercials. We have our favourites and they change around a lot. We have to keep phoning Channel Eleven and Channel Thirteen to make our viewer preferences known, so they'll rerun the great old classics: the original Right Guard characters, Sidney and Ethel, the man who ate the whole thing, all our friends. It's terrible what you have to sit through to see something that's really worth watching. Two or three periods of some dumb hockey game just to catch Albert for Laurentide talking to Anita. "You may not know anything about art, Anita, but you know what you like." Then she wipes her lips with her thumb and looks at you something like my MotoMama.

"Don't look at her, A.O., look at me."

"Shhhh, honey, don't talk for a minute. It's Ralph in the Heinz commercial, you know, where he asks for a bottle of the best and they bring him catsup under a lid."

"And his old lady tells him he's so sophisticated?"

"That's it, that's it."

I don't know why I like that commercial so much. I like it when the other guy says, "I am the maitre d'." And Ralph says, "Yeah? Well that's okay." Nobody impresses him a bit. My favourite commercial characters are all like that, impossible to ignore. There's that one guy who gets washed up on a beach without even any clothes. All he has is his American Express Card. Before you know it he's dancing under the stars in a rented tuxedo and a cummerbund. You should see how he crushes this fag desk-clerk. A real rub-out, turns him into a nothing.

They're best of all around Christmas. I could watch all night through the middle of December when they revive all the old-time holiday favourites. It's getting more and more like a festival devoted to the great commercials of yesteryear. The sexy brunette with the French accent who gets into bed and says, "Eeeet's 'ow a woman should smell." I've tried to get Dreamy to say that, "Eeeet's 'ow a woman should smell," or to buy the product, but she says a woman shouldn't use artificial scents like perfume or cologne, only the simple, natural smell of Right Guard or Ban.

We lie together arguing about the Christmas commercials, the ones she likes best, the ones I like best. Her favourites are the girls with bouncy hair that lasts around the clock, or the Wonder Bra ads because of all the terrific places they take you to. She also kind of goes for the man and lady in that Volvo commercial where they have a big dinner in this great hotel. They talk to Charles the waiter as if he was an old friend or a servant. She often tells me that commercial like it was a bedtime story.

"Good evening, Mr. and Mrs. Such-and-Such." I never can catch the name but Dreamy knows.

"Good evening, Charles." This is very classy. "It's good to see you again." They treat him like he was their own servant;

it's great. When it comes time to pick out their food, they just tell him to look after it, and then you see the lady saying, "Oooohh, I'll have all of that." You can bet she doesn't have any stomach disorders or gastro-intestinal upset. No way. You can see she's thinking about bed from how they look at each other. That must be where they go when they get home in their Volvo in the rain. Dreamy could be the lady, easy. She can do anything, or anyway almost anything, the one thing we never get around to anymore is actually ... well ... screw. There doesn't seem to be any point to it. It's more fun to watch what's on the commercials. You never hear a dirty word, nobody ever gets tired or hungry. We don't really have any need to make love now. It's all right there in front of us, so we just lie in each other's arms and listen to the big voice saying:

NEW FROM K-TEL. TWENTY AMAZING HITS AVAILABLE AT WOOLWORTH, WOOLCO, ROSSY'S, ZELLERS, BAD BOY, GIANT TIGER, BONIMART, KRESGES, OGILVY'S AND THE BAY. ALSO AT EATON'S, SIMPSONS, AND DUPUIS WHERE PHONE ORDERS ARE ACCEPTED.

Amazing LiquiPour. Twenty Daffy Dances. Canadian Gold. Eddy Arnold. Paul Anka. Gladys Knight and the Pips.
Good taste is dead.
Marx is dead.
The sixties are over.
Freud is dead.
Keep on truckin'.